Gift of the Grenadier

A Novel

Pat Wray

Gift of the Grenadier

Copyright 2017 by Pat Wray

Published by Outdoor Insights

All rights reserved. No part of this book may be reproduced in any form or by any electronic or mechanical means, including information storage and retrieval systems, without permission in writing from the publisher, except by a reviewer who may quote brief passages in a review. Scanning, uploading and electronic distribution of this book or the facilitation of such without the permission of the publisher is prohibited. Please purchase only authorized electronic editions, and do not participate in or encourage electronic piracy of copyrighted materials. Your support of the author's rights is appreciated. Any member of educational institutions wishing to photocopy part or all of the work for classroom use, or anthology, should send inquiries to Outdoor Insights, P.O. Box 513, Corvallis, Oregon 97339 or to patwray@comcast.net.

This is a work of fiction. Names, characters, organizations, universities, businesses, places, events and incidents are either the products of the author's imagination or used in a fictitious manner. Although the novel as a whole is meant to be as realistic as possible, I've taken creative liberties in several areas, including bank, university, military, criminal gang and law enforcement operations. Any resemblance to actual persons, living or dead, or to actual events is purely coincidental.

ISBN 978-0-9742923-5-9

Dedication

This novel is dedicated to my wife, Debbie, whose love and support have been the linchpins of my life since I was seventeen years old and have made everything I've accomplished possible.

PAT WRAY

Chapter 1

You don't need a reason to be afraid of the dark. Darkness is reason enough. The black of night sucks courage from the strongest man and Jared McCauley knew he was no longer strong. He'd been afraid plenty during daylight hours, but at least then he could see the threats. The darkness was different; it hinted at dangers that might be there... they could be there.

It's not enough to be absolutely certain nothing dangerous threatens you. Certainty is an intellectual exercise. Fear is visceral. It doesn't have to make sense. Jared had walked and ridden this trail many times. He knew where he was going and what to expect. Hell, he even had a battery-powered headlamp that showed him the way. But the headlamp lit only a small part of the night.

As if on cue, a large animal spooked from the trees a few yards away, crashing through the brush as it ran. Jared jumped involuntarily, shook his head and smiled as the sound faded. *You are pathetic, McCauley. There's nothing up here to be afraid of, if you don't count bears or mountain lions.*

Jared didn't consider black bears a threat and although he knew mountain lions could occasionally be a problem, he also knew a lion would never make that much noise. No. It had been a moose or elk. Both lived up here in the Frank Church River of No Return Wilderness, elk much more so than moose. That's what he was doing now, hunting elk, after so many years away from it. Who would have believed it after all this time?

Jared continued walking up the trail. The moon had risen early and was long since gone. The sky was clear and full of stars but little of their light found its way through the canopy of pine and spruce. The temperature was in the mid-20s and the fog of his breath froze on Jared's scruffy red mustache. Even with his headlamp, it was hard to pick out rocks and roots protruding from the trail and Jared stumbled several times.

Every so often the soft light at the edges of his headlamp reflected on two blazes on trees along the trail. The main trail, which Jared had left two miles back, was marked by three blazes. In this country, they were the same as road signs, though a little harder to see than the highway signs he'd become used to in the past 15 years. This trail, which headed generally east, would skirt high country surrounded by the Salmon River, then gradually turn south and join a half-dozen other trails that crossed the Chamberlain Basin.

The long-underwear shirt Jared wore began feeling clammy, so he slowed his pace slightly to avoid getting chilled. He could afford the delay—the sky was still dark and there was not far to go.

Even poking along slowly, Jared almost missed the turnoff in the uneven light. He turned left and headed up a small rise. It was only 60 feet above the main trail, but it was steep and years of horse traffic had chipped away most of the dirt around tree roots. As the loosened dirt had been washed away, only the roots remained and they formed interlocking stair steps. It was essentially possible for a man to walk the steepest part of the trail without ever touching the earth. Horses could not, however. They needed to step carefully and slowly, finding space for their hooves between the roots. Experienced mountain horses and mules went through with no trouble but more than one rodeo had occurred when someone tried to come through too fast or with green horses.

Horse hooves had also removed dark bark from the roots, and the remaining cream-colored tendrils formed a surrealistic cobweb pattern that shimmered in the combination of headlamp and soft dawn filtering through the trees. Jared was thinking about how beautiful the pattern was when he stepped a little shorter than he should have. The sole of his hunting boot, a stiff, aggressive pattern designed for traction on dirt and rock, had absolutely no affinity for the frost-covered root wood and slipped off just after he'd transferred his weight to it. His foot shot downward in a short but violent arc, coming to an equally violent stop when his shin rammed onto the upraised knob of a root. The knob, which had been clipped often by hooves, had a sharp edge that helped it slice through Jared's pants leg and skin, en route to his shin bone.

The pain was instantaneous and overwhelming. Jared felt the blood rush to his head even before he pitched forward onto his face, his pack and slung rifle propelling him even harder into the dirt.

"Shitshitshitshit!" The whispered words came out like a hiss.

Pain splintered his mind, blocking every thought and leaving only the force of a habit he thought he'd left behind years before. Jared unslung his rifle and slammed the stock to his shoulder, searching uphill for the enemy. *Wait.* The sight picture was wrong. *Where was his platoon?* The sudden knowledge he'd lost himself somewhere between the past and present unhinged him, mentally and physically. He felt lightheaded and nauseous, as though he'd been spun around too fast and for too long. He scrabbled sideways off the trail, taking shelter behind the stump of a lightning-struck tree and vomited into the dirt.

It took a while for Jared to put his world back on track, but it couldn't have been too long because it was not yet full daylight when he remembered he wasn't in Vietnam, he was elk hunting in the mountains of Idaho. He hadn't been shot; he'd slipped on a damn root. His recovered self-awareness didn't help the pain, which was still excruciating. Hell, he hadn't puked even when he actually had been shot. Jared's left hand strayed unconsciously toward his shoulder, toward the little hole just under his collarbone. Of course, that one hadn't hit bone and, in fact, he hadn't even known he was hit until after the fight, when he was trying to get the platoon formed up again. The other time had been shrapnel and it hadn't hit bone either, though the damage had been much, much worse. The wound that kept on giving.

He felt immediate guilt at his self-pity. *Jeez, what about the guys who came home without legs or arms or faces burned off? Or didn't come home at all. Here you are, McCauley. Hiking all over the mountains. You got it good, pretty good, anyway.* His thoughts of the past forced Jared's present pain into the background. He finally began to feel like he could move.

Jared got to one knee, leaving the hurt leg extended. He twisted around to lean back against the hillside. He brushed dirt and leaves from his face and a little vomit from his chin. At least he hadn't caught the sharp roots with his face. Small favors.

With some effort, Jared reached down and pulled his pant leg up, revealing a short cut traversing across the shinbone two inches below the kneecap. There was little blood but when he raised the flap of skin he was looking directly at the bone. By now the pain had weakened to a dull throb. It took a couple minutes to rinse the cut with water from his canteen, pack some Neosporin into it, cover it with a gauze pad and tape it in place.

That pretty well shot his wad of medical supplies. All he had now were Band-Aids. Shane had made fun of him for the weight of his pack but Jared was adamant. Space blanket, meat sacks, first aid gear, water, food, knife, twine, ammunition, surveyor's tape to mark blood trails. It added up but Jared knew from experience just how rarely things went according to plan. A 20-pound pack was pretty cheap insurance.

He stood up and put some weight on the leg. It throbbed from the knee down but the pain was manageable. He hoisted his pack, shouldered his rifle and hobbled up the hill. By the time he reached the top Jared was striding more easily, the pain receding farther with each step.

The land smoothed out once he reached the top. This was Long Ridge. It ran for the better part of a mile to the east and was a proven elk spot. Elk came up out of the canyons at night and fed on scattered bunch grass on the flat. Jared planned to hunt along the northern edge, where several fingers and canyons reached down toward the river. If he wasn't lucky enough to ambush a bull elk up here, Jared figured he could poke around the tops of the draws, maybe entice one up into range with his diaphragm call. The elk were in the rut and if he could simulate the spiraling, screaming bugle made by a rutting bull, he had a chance of bringing a competitor within rifle range. Or if he couldn't get one to come, an answering bugle would at least tell him where to find a bull.

Jared moved slowly, stopping only behind trees and brush. He placed his feet carefully, feeling through the needles and leaves for branches that might snap and give him away before putting his full weight down. Up here on the flat, there was a slight westerly breeze that gusted occasionally. Jared used the wind to cover his noise, timing his movement so he could take several steps while the wind was loudest.

A loud crack from the left startled Jared; he took two quick steps forward, pulled his rifle to his shoulder and rested it against a tree. It might have been a branch breaking naturally, but Jared didn't think so. It had sounded more like antler against wood. He waited, looking out over the scope, trying to see as much as he could without moving his head. The sudden sound of a heavy animal moving behind him shocked Jared and he almost spun around but caught himself in time. *Not good. Don't give yourself away with movement.* The breeze was blowing directly through Jared and to the noisemaker behind him.

Two bulls, Jared thought. *I walked right in between two bulls sparking each other, getting ready for a fight. No chance at the one behind me. He's going to whiff me any second now.* As if in answer, there was a sudden flurry of sound from behind him and the thunder of hooves as the animal fled directly away. Jared still didn't look in that direction. *No good shooting at a running animal. I didn't come back after all these years to gut-shoot some poor bull. Besides, I've still got a bull in front of me.*

Jared stood without sound for another five minutes, then, leaving the rifle braced on the tree between his shoulder and left hand, he slowly took a diaphragm call from his left shirt pocket and placed it in his mouth. He reached down and pulled the grunt tube that hung from his shoulder to his lips. Shifting carefully so the end of the tube pointed away from the elk, Jared produced a high-pitched scream that was oddly without depth. The lack of resonance was indicative of a young bull. A mature bull's bugle typically sounds like it emanates from inside a 50-gallon drum. Jared wasn't interested in sounding like a big bull. He wanted to sound like a spike bull that's likely to get his ass kicked. He produced another spike squeal, while continuing to point the end of the tube to his rear, hoping to make it seem like the sound was originating from a position behind him. Jared knew just how accurately a bull elk can pinpoint another's bugle.

After two squeals Jared waited. With the rifle braced on his wrist and his hand grasping the lodgepole sapling, he could wait for a long time without moving. So he did. The breeze stayed steady. There was a chance the second bull would take off as well but Jared didn't think it would. The elk was more likely to circle downwind, to make sure what he was dealing with. If the bull's circle was so wide he remained out of sight, Jared would be sunk.

This is the critical time, Jared thought. This is the time when mistakes are made. When you lose faith in your plan and your spine gets wobbly. When all of a sudden you jump into a completely different, usually ill-considered course of action that turns sour. I'm not doing that. I'm staying.

He stayed. A woodpecker landed in a tree six feet away and pecked its way around the circumference. Snow began to fall lightly, carried directly into his face by the breeze. Not a good time to wear glasses, as the light specks landed on his lenses and turned quickly into droplets.

Suddenly the bull bugled from just below the crest of the hill, 50 yards away. There are bugles and there are BUGLES, and Jared reflected that this was definitely one of the latter. The sound seemed to reach down into his soul and squeeze. His breath began coming in short, choppy sips. Within seconds Jared saw movement just down the hill. It was antler tines quartering toward him and coming up the hill. The bull was trying to circle around him but his circle was going to be small. He probably thought he was going to pass well out of sight of his rival. Big mistake.

Jared watched the bull approach tine by antler tine. At first, only two tips could be seen, one on each side. Then, as the bull came higher onto the hill, more tines became visible. Two, four, six…whoa! Big bull! The animal crossed at 30 yards. Jared was ready to shoot but the timber was thick and Jared wasn't sure he could poke a bullet between the trees to hit the spot he wanted behind the shoulder. As the bull came level with him Jared gave a cow call without the tube, which by now was hanging again from his shoulder. At the sound the bull turned instantly to face Jared and froze in a thick stand of timber only 25 yards away. Jared was looking through his scope for a shot but couldn't get one he liked. He was totally motionless and knew staying that way was the only chance he had. If the bull spooked he would wheel and disappear so fast a good shot would be impossible.

Jared was shooting a 300 Weatherby Magnum, a powerful, flat-shooting caliber, but if the bullet clipped a branch on the way it might be deflected off its target. Not much, inside 25 yards, Jared knew, but he wasn't willing to take the chance. He would make a good shot or none at all.

Jared prepared to make another cow call. With the diaphragm in his mouth and using no tube, he could make the call without movement. He settled his scope on the bull's chest and waited. If the bull took one step forward, he would pull the trigger. At the call the bull leaned forward and Jared's finger tightened, but the bull stopped again. Suddenly the animal wheeled and retreated into the brush another 15 feet, still visible but leaving Jared with no shot at all. Jared relaxed and breathed deeply for the first time in minutes. He was ready. He'd finally been able to separate killing big game from killing men, though it had taken a while. This felt right. This seemed like the days before Vietnam. Back then he'd always felt closer to nature, to the earth and to God when hunting.

"It's a connection to our heritage," he'd tried to explain to a young woman in college, "a connection to our primitive selves that we've lost in almost every other way." She hadn't bought it, he remembered, but it didn't matter. She still shared his bed that night and showed him a thing or two about being primitive. What he hadn't told her, what he'd never been able to put into words, was the feeling of excitement, of being alive, that came from trying to make something else dead. He couldn't even explain it to himself without sounding like some sort of blood-crazed maniac. *It's our collective guilt,* he thought. *We can't experience the joy of the hunt like our ancestors, like the Indians, like African tribes, like primitive people all over the world. It was the Puritan's gift to us all, the concept that anything fun, anything exciting must be bad.*

The bull bugled, a primal challenge that shattered Jared's reverie and started an internal quiver again. It was so loud Jared imagined he could feel the blast of air from the animal's lungs. The elk began to thrash the brush and trees around him with his antlers. Branches fell and were thrown 10 feet, small saplings snapped like pencils in a strong man's hand. Forest duff and rocks were scattered as the bull tossed his head from side to side. Then the bull stopped, stiffened and sent a gushing stream of urine across his belly and chest. A steamy cloud enveloped the elk and wafted up and through the falling snow. The effect was surrealistic. The bull bugled again, louder this time, with his mouth pointed directly at Jared, who sniffed involuntarily, to see if he could smell the animal's breath. He could not.

The bull was almost beside himself now. He would step forward very soon. Jared hesitated a moment. *You dumb son-of-a-bitch. Look at what you've gotten yourself into, following your dick around like that. Not so much different than a young man on Friday nights, I guess. Not so much different from me, from the way I used to be, anyway. If I'd known that goddamn grenade was going to hit a tree and fall so close behind me I would have tried to get under cover. If I'd even had my legs together I would have been all right, but no, I had them opened up, giving me stability, helping me get down as low as I could…proving without question that spread legs cause problems for men and women alike. One piece of shrapnel. One. Hell, I'd never even heard the word scrotum before.*

Jared closed his mind to the thought. After all these years, he could do so nearly at will. He gave another cow call. The bull sprinted forward but skidded to a halt in almost his former exact position, covered by trees and branches. Another cow call, the elk leaned forward, leaned further, raised his nose to the wind and took that last, little step. Jared squeezed the trigger.

Elk, especially bull elk, have big bones and big muscles, but a 180-grain slug, moving at more than 3100 feet per second, doesn't care. Jared's slug hit low in the center of the bull's chest and mushroomed as it powered through the top of the sternum and through the lungs, clipping one of the arteries along the way. It ran out of energy and came to rest just shy of the abdomen. Because most of the bullet's energy was expended going through bone, the effect was to lift the bull over on his back. Jared lost sight of the animal during the rifle's recoil but got reoriented in time to see the bull fall. He was shocked to see the bull get back up again and run downhill. Jared hurriedly chambered another round, aimed at the animal's neck, and gave it a little lead. He was squeezing the trigger again when the bull suddenly nosed forward and skidded on its belly in the light skiff of snow, coming to rest just 35 yards away. Jared felt the bull's impact on the ground through his boots. He walked up behind the animal, watched its dying breath and its eyes glaze. He knelt beside the animal's head and stroked the hair on its head and neck.

"Sorry," he said. "Thank you."

It had been a long time since Jared field dressed an elk and he was out of practice. He first rigged up a system of parachute cord to hold the animal's legs apart so he could remove the penis and open the abdominal cavity. "See," he whispered as he pulled the offal out and away from the carcass, "I told you, bad things happen when you spread your legs."

Jared used snow to wash his hands, then replaced the long underwear shirt he'd removed while working in the animal's chest cavity. He cut down a small sapling and lashed it horizontally between two trees at head height. He removed the loins, placed them in a small bag with the heart and hung them from the pole. *Mmmm. Heart and loins tonight, maybe some fried potatoes and onions, too.*

Jared skinned out and removed the hindquarters, placed them in mesh meat bags and hung them up. He stripped backstraps from the sides of the vertebrae and each one went into a bag with a forequarter.

Then it was time for future hamburger. Jared removed meat from the neck, flanks and between the ribs. The resulting pile of meat was also split between the two forequarter bags. Now the four bags were nearly equal in weight. It would make loading the mules a much easier task. He draped his emergency space blanket over the pole and tied the corners down to protect the meat from rain and snow. He put the heart and loins into a plastic bag and put them in his backpack.

Jared washed his hands again in snow and packed up his gear. He and Shane would bring the mules back tomorrow to pack the meat and antlers back to camp. He looked down at what remained of the carcass; head, neck, backbone, ribs and forelegs were laid out on the skin; stomach, intestines and organs off to the side. And all of it being hidden now by a thickening layer of snow. Jared looked up at the sky and was suddenly aware of the failing light. His work on the elk had taken far too long. He was out of practice and out of shape. But he had a nice bull elk and that was a great start. Jared smiled, tightened the straps on his pack, adjusted his rifle on his shoulder and reached down to touch the animal's antlers as he walked past.

Chapter 2

By the time Jared reached camp there were two inches of snow on the ground and it was too near dark for a lonely hunter to feel comfortable, especially one without his space blanket. He'd almost missed the turnoff from the three-blaze trail to camp, but he'd guessed right and the sight of Shane's big yellow wall tent, glowing golden with the light of the lantern inside and smoke coming out gave him a warm, safe feeling. Jared unloaded his rifle, leaned it up under the rain flap and stepped in. You didn't want to keep taking your rifle in and out of a warm tent from the cold. It would sweat and rust. Better to leave it outside once it was out and just cover it from precipitation.

Shane Larrimer was mixing two drinks.

"How'd you know I was coming?" Jared asked, reaching for a drink.

"I didn't but it's almost full dark and I figured if you weren't back shortly I'd drink a second one in your memory."

Jared took a long swallow. "It might have been an uncomfortable night because I left my space blanket draped over the meat."

"You've spent uncomfortable nights before."

"Yes, I have. As I recall, we spent several together. You must have gotten an elk early and close to be back in camp, cleaned up and drinking already."

"By golly, I did. Nice little six-point threw himself in my lap about a half-mile from here, before I even got to my honey hole. How about you?"

"You and your nice little six point. There is no such thing as a little six-point bull. They are all massive. Mine, of course, is even more massive or is it massiver?"

"Not so fast, cowboy. My bull is massivest." He noticed Jared setting down his empty cup. "By the way, would you like a drink?"

"Didn't I already have one?" Jared began to strip his clothes. He kept his back toward Shane and left his underwear on.

"Yes, you did but you didn't do it well and you need practice. Jesus! Nice job on your leg. You shoot yourself first to see what it was like?"

"No, I slipped on a root. I've already done graduate work on being shot."

Shane's heart sprang into his throat with the realization of his gaffe but he plowed ahead, trying to make the best of it. "Ah, yes. Shot and blown up, too, as I recall." He made himself meet his friend's eyes. "I'm sorry Jared. I didn't mean to…"

"It's OK, Shane. Really."

"Sure. I've got some water heated so you can shower and then we'll eat."

Jared poured hot water into the plastic shower bag and carefully mixed cold water into it to achieve the right temperature. He left it pretty hot. They'd rigged a cover from the tree where they hung the shower to keep out the rain but there were no sides. The snow would ride the wind in on him, and really hot water helped to overcome the intense discomfort of the cold. He grabbed the plastic shower bag, threw his towel over his shoulder and walked out of the tent.

Shane stuck his head out of the tent and read the thermometer tacked to a tree. He called, "It's still a good solid 36 degrees so you should be perfectly comfortable." He mixed another drink for his friend as Jared washed. People didn't spend a lot of time showering in sub-40 degree temperatures, no matter how warm the water was. It would probably be in the mid- 20s by morning. He laughed at the sound of Jared's howls and groans in the biting cold. He thought they mixed nicely with the noises of the string of pack animals tethered outside the tent. He would have liked to have taped those sounds and played them back for Lacy and the kids. It would be fun to have tapes of various times of elk camp. We could have one of shower noises, one of trying to get up and start the fire when it's 20 degrees in the tent, maybe one of trying to saddle the stock with frozen tack. Mostly they would consist of cussing, Shane figured. Cussing with a few burps and farts thrown in. He wasn't so sure how much Lacy would appreciate it but it would sure be fun to play when the guys got together.

He laughed to think about just how cold Jared must be out there with the wind blowing all that snow in on him. It had been uncomfortable enough for him and he'd taken his shower while the sun was still up. It takes a while to get all the blood off after field dressing and quartering a bull elk.

Damn! He wished he hadn't made that crack about being shot. He knew how sensitive Jared was about his wound. Jared had essentially dropped from sight after he'd come back from Vietnam in 1970. The rumors had swirled around their town when Jared had returned. Shane flared to think of the joking and sneers he'd heard from Smokey Stover and his three ne'er-do-well friends after Jared had returned. Those ignorant assholes!

Jared had come home and disappeared with his wife Misty into his folks' house. He'd stayed in there for several months while recuperating. The whole town had reached out to Jared during that time. They cared about him. His family had been there for 35 years and Jared had been a popular student and athlete all through high school. The problem was, Jared never reached back. He didn't take visitors and he didn't go outside. His wife and mother greeted visitors in the living room but Jared never appeared. He even avoided Shane, his best friend since kindergarten. That took some doing. Shane had made himself difficult to avoid, showing up at the house at all hours, calling whenever he felt like it, once even sneaking around back to catch Jared sunning himself on the porch. That hadn't worked out well at all.

"Hi, Jared," he'd said with a self-conscious smile as he came through the gate.

Jared had looked up through watery eyes, but his voice had been clear, if flat. "What are you doing here, Shane?" Jared had responded.

"I came to see you, Jared. We're friends." *Pleading*, Shane thought to himself. *You sound like you are begging.*

"A friend would let me spend some time by myself when I needed to," Jared said. And with that, Jared stood up and hobbled slowly toward the sliding door. It was the last time Shane had seen him for sixteen years. Jared and Misty had left not long after that ill-advised meeting and headed east. They settled in Bowie, Maryland. Shane could never understand why people like Jared and Misty, born and raised in the mountains of Idaho, would move back where states were small and there were no elk. He suspected it was an attempt on Jared's part to get away from the prying eyes and flapping lips of his hometown. And it had been successful. Jared and Misty had essentially disappeared from sight and over the years, even dropped from the gossip radar in Grangeville. People found other things to talk about.

Misty's parents had moved to Florida shortly after her father retired, so the only real sources of information available about Jared were his parents, who were decidedly close-mouthed about their son. Shane and the rest of the town had been given only snippets of information. Jared wasn't working yet. He'd been given enough of a disability that he didn't have to work until he wanted to. Misty had gone right back into nursing. She'd had no trouble finding work back there and the pay was much better than in Idaho. Now Jared was feeling better. He'd gone to work as a real estate agent. Misty had moved up the ladder into management. Yes, they were still in Bowie.

To the occasional insensitive question about grandchildren, Sarah McCauley was unfailingly polite, but equally vague. "No, still no grandchildren yet," she'd say. "Young people now are waiting much longer than we did to have children. There's still time." During these encounters, her husband Simon would knead his heavy forearms. Simon's tendency was to be upfront about Jared's situation but he'd had a horrible row with his wife about that shortly after Jared had come back.

"Jesus Christ, Sarah!" he said after some well-meaning visitors had left. "Why don't you just tell people the truth? Most of them know or suspect it anyway. Jared can't have children because of his injuries. It's a terrible tragedy but it's nothing to be ashamed of. If you keep lying you'll just have to tell them the same lie next time."

"He might get better!" she'd hissed angrily. "He could still get better."

Her anger and his own deep-seated sense of loss sent him into a rage. "He was castrated, Sarah, castrated! You know what that means, don't you? The doctors had to remove what little was left after the shrapnel hit him. What he needs to make babies just isn't there, anymore. He's not going to get better, ever. He won't. He's had a terrible time but Jared's making his own peace with that. You have to do the same."

With each word Sarah seemed to shrink, until at the end of his tirade she was slumped into the corner of her flowered couch, her shoulders heaving with each sob. Simon's anger broke, then, and he found himself huddled protectively over her, hugging her, holding her. "It's OK, Sarah. Jared will be OK and so will we."

They stayed there on the couch silently for a long time, until getting up and going about their business. They never spoke about it again. A few weeks later someone else asked about possible grandchildren and Sarah answered the same old way, there were no grandchildren yet but young people waited longer to have babies nowadays. There was still time. Simon was only mildly surprised. He didn't say anything then or afterward.

Shane hadn't tried to see Jared again for several years but he always found a way to get in touch three or four times a year. He always sent a Christmas card. It was the only card he sent. He would occasionally call unexpectedly and wish them a happy birthday. Misty was always glad to hear from him but Jared wouldn't get on the phone.

Until two years ago. Two years ago, Jared had actually called him. Called him! Shane sat up so quickly he almost fell off his chair.

"Shane, it's Jared."

"Jared who?"

There was a pause. "I've got problems enough, Shane. I don't need my best friend yanking my chain."

Shane struggled with his next response. What he really wanted to say was, "I don't have a best friend. I used to but he hasn't even talked to me in a couple decades." But what he said was "I know. How are you, pardner?"

"Doing a lot better now. I think I'm going to be OK."

"Hell, you were never OK before. That seems like way too lofty a goal."

Chuckle. "Yeah, I'm probably setting my sights too high but Misty says I might reach it and Josh seems to think so, too."

"It's nice having your wife and son believe in you."

"It is."

"A bunch of people have believed in you for a long time now, Jared."

"I know. I guess I wasn't ready."

That's OK. You're back now."

"More or less. Better than I have been in the past."

"Just a hop and a skip, now. When are you coming back here to live?"

"That could take a while," Jared answered. "We've kind of settled here. But I might be ready to come back for some visits. Maybe you'd like to go elk hunting together?"

Shane's smile creased his face. "You're damn right! Can you take 10 days or so to pack up into the Frank next September?"

He and Jared had hunted the Frank Church River of No Return Wilderness many times as young men and it was in the Frank where Shane conducted much of his outfitting business. It was nearly December. They'd have to put their applications in by January. Shane was rarely involved in guiding anymore so that wouldn't be a distraction. He'd gradually stepped away from the day-to-day operation over the years, concentrating on law enforcement and leaving the outfitting business almost completely to Chester Wewa.

A Nez Perce Indian who'd come to work for Shane after an abrupt and painful end to a rodeo cowboy career, Chester had started as a wrangler 14 years earlier and gradually grown into a minority partner. Chester certainly didn't need his help for the hunting season.

Shane and Jared could use his family's saddle horses and there were enough spare mules to get them up the mountain. He had plenty of extra camping and cooking gear. Of course, he'd have to cancel out on elk hunting with Todd Reckert. Shane and Todd had hunted together for several years now but Jared would probably want some privacy and Todd would certainly understand. Hot damn! Jared really is snapping out of it.

"I think so. I'll have to check with Misty. She'll just need to set up someone to watch Josh after kindergarten. But yeah, I don't think it would be a problem." He hesitated. "Shane, I never thanked you for taking care of Smokey Stover and his crew. I understand that was a little dicey."

"Dicey? Oh, hell. That wasn't dicey. Those boys were all hot air. Besides, that was 16 years ago. Back then I could take care of those assholes without breaking a sweat." He laughed. "Of course, taking care of them got me into a kind of trouble that I haven't been able to shake even after all these years."

Smokey Stover was a Grade A jackass who'd been in trouble from the day he could walk. His mother Rita was a town drunk and part-time hooker who left Smokey with anyone who would watch him whenever she'd hit the bottle, which was often. Sometimes she forgot to leave him with anyone. More than once she had sobered up to find the infant Smokey dehydrated and near death from two days of neglect. The young Stover was not named Smokey until he was 6 months old. In fact, he had not yet been named at all, his mother being of the opinion that names should reflect an event or condition and not just be an arbitrary label. One of her many male friends allowed as how she should call her son Starvation Stover, reflecting his typical condition but it just didn't take, probably because that particular friendship was even shorter in duration than most of the others.

What finally got Smokey his nickname was a house fire, started by his mother's cigarette falling from her unconscious hand. The neighbor who rescued Smokey had tried to bring Rita out too but was beaten back by the smoke and heat. Deputy Sheriff Cutter was next on the scene and he succeeded in bringing the unconscious woman out, but at a terrible cost. His hands were burned so badly he lost a great deal of movement in three fingers. Several of the doctors who examined him recommended a disability retirement but Cutter refused and Sheriff Kowalski wouldn't force him. Cutter returned to full duty long before anyone in the Sheriff's Department thought he should. For months after he returned, Cutter received private evaluations from the Sheriff. Kowalski would give Cutter his shooting tests alone, during closed hours at the range. Each time, he graded Cutter expert.

When one of the office wags made a crack about Cutter's getting a good deal, Kowalski offered to cover any bets and gave five to one odds that Cutter could outscore any other officer at their next day on the range. The wag, a good shot in his own right, bet $50. When the day came at the range, Cutter beat him by 20 points, pulling the trigger with the little finger on his left hand, "because that's one of the few that works." Kowalski used his winnings to fund a Department picnic.

Rita survived and went right back to her old life of prostitution, drinking and drugs. The six-month old baby coughed for weeks after the fire from smoke inhalation, at which point she decided he deserved the name Smokey, which she entered at the hospital and county courthouse as his official name. Rita lived only five more years, finally freezing to death in the alley behind a seedy bar, where she'd passed out after an even seedier sexual liaison.

Smokey, then almost six, was placed in the foster care system and bounced from one foster family to the next. It didn't help that his mother never taught him to speak. Smokey could not complete an intelligible sentence until he was eight, by which time he'd amassed a lifetime's worth of rage, at the people who made fun of him, at people who tried to help him, at people in general. He never got rid of a pronounced lisp, comments about which kept him in fights for decades. He was small and stringy, with dirty blonde hair and clear blue eyes that seemed unhinged in the strange, darting way they viewed the world. He was mean and absolutely fearless. In fights he was a dervish, coming at his opponent without stopping, hitting, kicking, scratching, clawing and biting. He lost several fights, but only because he was small and only after being knocked senseless. Even then, the fight was not over until Smokey decided it was. Often, Smokey waited months for an opportunity to fight again, then came at a former opponent without warning. The only reason Stover never hurt anyone badly was because he never used weapons.

"He eschews weaponry," Sheriff Kowalski said to Cutter one day. He was hoping for a rise out of Cutter but he was disappointed. Cutter had learned that word in school and even if he hadn't he wasn't going to give Kowalski the pleasure of lording it over him. Cutter had perfected the art of acting as though Kowalski's big words were nothing new to him. He could usually figure them out by the context. Kowalski countered by starting to use big words in the wrong places, so if Cutter *didn't* say something, he could point out Cutter's error of omission. Cutter had no idea why Kowalski got so much enjoyment out of throwing big words around but he didn't mind. Kowalski could be brutal on some of the younger deputies but he never, ever embarrassed Cutter in public.

Kowalski was of the opinion that Smokey was a murder waiting to happen so he went out of his way to keep the young delinquent off the streets as much as possible. Smokey cooperated by taking part in a continuous string of misdemeanors and minor felonies that sent him twice to the reform school. But to Kowalski's chagrin, he kept coming back.

Smokey disliked lots of people, but he retained a special loathing for those he considered 'cool.' In a town of 2,500 people based almost equally on logging, agriculture and ranching, there were not a lot of fashion plates and fops, but Smokey's vision of cool guys had little to do with fashion. He was enraged by people who got along, who did well in class and took part in athletics. He particularly detested Jared and Shane, who represented everything he hated. Both were good looking and capable athletes. Jared was the football quarterback, basketball point guard and the school's resident goof-off. Shane played fullback and linebacker, was an all-conference wrestler and a gifted pitcher with a 400-plus batting average. Although both boys were mild troublemakers, they were as popular with their teachers as they were with girls. They made Smokey sick. In fairness, they made plenty of other boys sick, too, but few besides Smokey would have considered acting on their feelings.

Smokey had considered Jared and Shane his enemies since elementary school. Jared and Shane rarely considered him at all. One day, during a school recess, Smokey overheard Jared talking to Shane, laughing as he referred to someone as 'dumber than dirt.' They both looked his way as the words were said and Smokey knew, *he knew*, they were talking about him. He'd snapped, attacking Jared without warning and knocked the larger boy onto his back. Smokey sat astride Jared's chest, pounding him mercilessly, until at some point, something fundamental changed. Jared, who had been trying ineffectually to block Smokey's blows, began not only to block them, but to return a few that hurt, even from his supine position. At the same time, Jared began to roar, a primal cry of pain and rage that did not sound at all like someone who was being badly beaten. Shortly after, Jared reached up to grab Smokey's hair and yank it backwards hard. With Smokey's throat exposed, Jared punched it hard twice, taking "the fight right out of the little shit," as Shane later described.

Unfortunately for Smokey, the fight was not nearly out of Jared, and he proceeded to punch Smokey's face with both fists until Shane and one of the teachers pulled him off. He was able to kick Smokey's face twice before he was pulled out of range.

Smokey must have considered that fight over because he never challenged Jared again, although Jared never turned his back on him either. Jared later described Smokey to Shane as "the scariest 5-foot, 7-inch son of a bitch I've ever seen."

After high school Smokey seemed to get over his problem with Jared and Shane; he spent most of his energies in various illegal activities that Kowalski was only occasionally able to pin on him. It wasn't until Jared had come back with his terrible injury that Smokey began taking notice of him again. By this time, Smokey had attracted a small group of hangers-on, the type who gravitate toward someone with great physical courage and disdain for authority.

Suddenly Smokey was all over town, laughing and joking loudly about Jared's wounds. *Jared's dick had been bitten off by a Vietnamese hooker. He wanted to join the Vienna Boys Choir. He was headed south to be a buckaroo, since he'd get along so much better with steers than normal men.*

One night in the Riverside Bar and Grill, Shane had gotten tired of their bullshit. Four of them, Smokey and three of his hyenas, laughing and joking about Jared as though any one of them was good enough to carry his bags. Shane told them to shut up but he hadn't been as careful as he should have been. He'd let one get behind him and when the dust had cleared they'd thumped him pretty good. They'd broken his nose and cracked a rib and tore one of his ears half an inch from his skull. His hand went to the ear, which didn't lie quite smooth on his skull and gave his face a slightly off-centered look.

He'd been conscious the whole time and though he didn't remember all the punches and kicks, he remembered the things Smokey had said. "Where's your master now, Shane? How's it feel to be Jared's pet squirrel, Shane?"

Pet squirrel. He might have just gone home and nursed his wounds if it hadn't been for that. Instead he went home and prepared.

He and Jared had been friends since forever and for as long as he could remember, Jared had been first among equals. Shane never even questioned their relationship and it wasn't until the boys were in high school and had gotten into trouble for joyriding that Shane's mother threw it in his face.

"You've been following that McCauley boy your whole life, Shane. When are you going to start to think for yourself?" Shane couldn't come up with an explanation, in part because he didn't want to admit to his mother that taking the car had been his idea and Jared hadn't wanted to. Just then he received some help from an unexpected source.

"The person in front isn't always the leader, Mother, and the person behind isn't always following." Ben Larrimer said. He winked at Shane and patted his wife's ample bottom. "Most people probably think I'm the one who calls the shots in our marriage, too."

Shane appreciated his father's support but the truth was that Shane never questioned his relationship with Jared. Jared was his brother in every way but blood; in fact, they had become blood brothers several times over the years, when the idea came up and one of them had a sharp knife. Jared was the most honest, straight-up guy Shane had ever known and if he followed Jared it was because Jared deserved it. As comfortable as he was with that notion, Shane still didn't like other people assuming he was some unthinking follower. Pet squirrel for Christ's sake!

So, for the next several weeks, while his nose, ribs and ear recovered, Shane worked a little in the shop behind the Mountain Outfitters headquarters. He put a few wraps of tape around a spare maul handle. He'd wanted to use one of his old baseball bats but decided the chance for serious injury was too high. So he drilled a quarter-inch hole through two-thirds of the length of a framing hammer handle and stuffed it with lead from the rolls he used in steelhead rigs. It added about a third of a pound to the handle, just enough for a little heft, Shane figured. Not enough to do any real damage. He wrapped the striking surface of both with thin leather.

Shane was waiting in his pickup in the Riverhouse parking lot at 12:30 Friday night when Smokey and two of his bottom-feeding friends came out to drink beer and be more obnoxious than allowed inside. He waited a few minutes for them to get comfortable on the tailgates of their pickups and then he got a break. One of them moved out into the darkness to relieve himself, leaving Smokey and another on the tailgate. Shane walked carelessly up behind the one urinating, the crunch of his boots on the gravel loud but unthreatening. The target assumed another of his friends was coming.

"How's it hang…?" he tried to say, before the maul handle hit him behind the ear. He dropped like a sack of potatoes, hand still on a leaking dick. The sight made Shane smile. "You've just been popped by the most valuable player on the 1965 Grangeville baseball team, 12 homers, .413 average."

He walked to the truck from the front and hit the closest drinker in exactly the same spot with the same result. *A consistent swing is the key to good hitting*, Shane thought. Smokey was sitting on the other side of the tailgate and he had time to jump down before Shane could get to him. Smokey blocked the first blow with his left arm. There was a sharp snap. Shane checked quickly to confirm that it wasn't the maul handle that had broken. It wasn't. He jabbed the handle into Stover's stomach, bayonet style, and Smokey doubled over hard. Shane tried to pull the handle out to give him a roundhouse but the asshole had a death grip on the maul handle with his right hand and wouldn't let go, even as he retched and cried.

"Pretty strong for a one-armed guy," Shane said. He let Stover have the maul handle, pulled the weighted hammer handle from his belt and popped Stover in the back of the head. Smokey went down hard onto his face.

Shane looked quickly around to be sure he wasn't watched. No problem. All the normal people were inside having fun. He grabbed up both weapons and started for his truck.

He threw the handles into his pickup and drove to the river. He stripped the tape off the maul handle, wadded it up and threw it in the river. He then wiped both handles with an oil soaked rag and threw them in the river. The maul handle floated down with the current. The weighted hammer handle sank, but probably not to the bottom. Shane figured it would also drift down the river for miles before it hung up. Besides, he doubted that anyone would search the river for handles. He drove back home and smiled for two hours until the adrenaline wore off and he drifted into a peaceful sleep.

Two deputies came by the next day, asking questions, but Shane simply pleaded ignorance. Stover had muttered something about Shane when they'd first found him but his blood alcohol content had been .16 at the hospital, and by the next morning he'd forgotten everything. The others had seen nothing and though they were fairly certain Shane had been their assailant, they were hesitant to finger him, because doing so would uncover their own beating of him earlier.

In the end, nothing was done. Shane kept busy at the outfitting shop for a few days, figuring there was no real reason to parade his face around town until things quieted down. Just as he was starting to feel comfortable, Shane received a visit from Sheriff Kowalski and Undersheriff Cutter.

Kowalski was pushing 60 and had been on the force for 32 years, since leaving the Phoenix police force as a young man under conditions that were cloudy but involved excessive use of force. He was a good fit in this small Idaho town. He was soft-spoken and easy going but frightening in his response to violence. Townspeople liked the way truculent loggers and miners got wide-eyed and easy to handle when they were told Deputy Kowalski was on his way. After 10 years on the force Kowalski was appointed to complete the tenure of Sheriff Higgins, who'd died on the job. He was then elected in a close election over a well-liked, lifelong resident and long-term deputy named Daryl Cutter. Upon losing the election, Cutter quit the department in bitter disappointment and went into business for himself doing concrete work. Two years later, practically destitute, he came back and asked for a job. Kowalski greeted him like a savior instead of a supplicant and hired him as his Undersheriff. The two men had been fast friends ever since. They'd solved five major cases in that time, quickly and efficiently and quietly, just the way people liked them. So close had the two men become in the last 20 years that their names had merged in the collective consciousness into KowalsCutter. On those rare occasions when anyone even tried to run against Kowalski, the two men printed up signs saying "Re-elect KowalsCutter…Two for the Price of One." Of course, both men still got salaries so it wasn't really two for the price of one but everyone knew what was meant and no one minded. The signs confused the hell out of state election officials and many others, but every voter in Idaho County understood and Kowalski figured that was all that mattered.

Shane knew he was busted when both men got out of the car. The men just sat down in his office and waited until one of Shane's clients finished booking a trip and left.

"Lock the door," Kowalski said. It was not a question.

Shane locked the door and put up a Gone to Lunch sign. He turned and waited. Cutter waved him to a chair. Shane thought it strange he was being invited to sit in his own business but he sat anyway and said nothing.

Kowalski spoke. "Smokey Stover doesn't have insurance for his broken arm and the bill was $700, even after explaining to the doctor how important it was to keep the price down."

Shane raised his hands and shook his head, preparing one of several lies, but Cutter just waved him off…again. Kowalski continued. "All of them needed x-rays. The total bill is going to be in the $1,400 range, which we have offered to pay out of the Police Benevolent Association Fund."

Shane opened his mouth but Kowalski continued without stopping. "Why, you ask? One, because all three of the jerkoffs, including Smokey Stover, have agreed to leave town if they can get out from under their hospital bills. This is a good thing.

"And two, because if we can't make the case go away we'll have to do some actual police work and there's no telling what we might learn about who did it.

"The problem, of course, is the Police Officers Benevolent Association Fund is designed to aid officers in need."

Shane thought he was beginning to understand. "Perhaps I could make a generous donation to the Police Officers, ahhh, Fund… of $1,400 or so?" Even as he made the offer Shane realized that if Kowalski wouldn't take payments, he was screwed.

Kowalski seemed to consider this new idea and then shook his head. "That would be a good idea in the future, when I expect you to be a dedicated donor, but it wouldn't look good right now. Right now, the only way out of this problem is for you to join the fraternity." Cutter nodded thoughtfully as he stared at his ruined hands, looking for all the world as if his boss had just proposed a new theory on reversing the aging process.

"Fraternity? Uhhh." Shane was beginning to have a bad feeling.

"The law enforcement fraternity, Shane."

"I…but I…I already have a job; I have employees." Shane motioned with both hands to the office around him, to the two men working on rafts out in the warehouse.

"This is a good part-time job, Shane. It's probably something you could run on the side while you did your real job."

"My real job?"

"Sure, Deputy Sheriff. We need one. Someone with local roots. Someone with a physical presence who's not afraid to stand up for what's right. To stand up for his friends. You're him. We actually were going to approach you about applying but now we don't really need to ask, do we?"

Shane couldn't quite understand what was happening. He shook his head, trying to explain. He was happy as an outfitter, things were looking up. He was doing well, actually. Kowalski pursed his lips and sighed resignedly. He glanced at Cutter with sadness. Cutter nodded and leaned forward, pulling his handcuffs from behind his belt. Suddenly Shane realized he was being given a choice, a not too difficult choice at that.

"When do I start?"

"A month or so. Soon as Smokey leaves town. That'll give you time enough to set up your business so someone else can run it."

"Am I working full time?" Surely they didn't expect him to work 40 hours a week. Kowalski was through talking. He got up and looked out the window.

Cutter took up the slack. "Yup."

Jesus, 40 hours! When am I supposed to hunt and fish and play? "But for how long?"

Kowalski turned back from the window. "Cutter, what's the penalty for assault with a deadly weapon?"

Cutter puzzled over the question for a moment. "Mmm, first offense…he might get out in five, six years."

Jesus! Five or six years! I could have been a pilot in the military and been back in that time. But, hey! I was ineligible for the draft because of my feet. Maybe I can use that!

"Sheriff! I wouldn't mind doing it, I mean, it's an honor to be considered, but I have six toes on each foot and…"

"Larrimer, I don't care how many fingers and toes you have. This ain't the military and I recall you moving around pretty well on a football field. Now, I'm getting tired of talking to you. Are we done here?"

It's a sad day, Shane reflected, when the only words you can think of are "Yes, sir." But there he was, roped, tied and branded. And he'd stayed that way for the last 16 years. As he looked back now, Shane realized that it probably couldn't have worked out any better.

They'd fitted him for uniforms and put him to work right away. Surprisingly to Shane, if not to the brothers KowalsCutter, he took to the job from the beginning. He was widely known around the county and people responded well to his easy, laid-back style. In those rare instances when he was forced to act aggressively, he was willing and able to do so. He was surprised as well at the difference in the way people treated him when he wore the uniform. At first, he enjoyed the feeling of power that went with looking like a cop. But after a few months he began to resent it. He felt like people were looking at the uniform and not seeing him as a human being.

Once he'd confided to Cutter how he felt. Cutter had nodded and thought for a while. Finally, he raked his crumpled fingers through wispy blonde hair and said. "The uniform's just a fact of life. You can't get away from it, and you don't want to. There are times when it gives you an edge you need. The rest of the time it's just clothes. The way people truly relate to you will depend on how you relate to them."

After a while Shane stopped thinking about the uniform. The Department sent him to the police academy and five years later, after ascertaining that "he'd be sticking around," they sent him to the FBI Academy, the first county officer ever to go. After that, things just seemed to go well for him. His college degree and experience with the FBI put him in position to help the Sheriff's Department transition from a small town, backwater outfit to an efficient law enforcement organization. He had made friends with officers and agents from around the country while at the Academy and over the years those contacts came in handy. He learned how to search out and apply for various federal and private grants available to small community law enforcement agencies and money began to trickle in. Some of the grants he got were small, and so tied up with restrictions they were almost useless but others were large and flexible enough to make even the Brothers KowalsCutter smile.

When Shane scored a $100,000 research grant to "explore the impact of modern transportation on the effectiveness of a small-town police force," the city council gave him a standing ovation and award suitable for framing. Grangeville received three new, state-of-the-art, high-powered cars. Shane was chagrined to learn that $30,000 of the grant was allotted to pay for a researcher but he got over it after meeting the young lady doing the research. Lacy Thomas was a 26-year-old Boise native who was doing her graduate work at Stanford, where the grant was administered. She was tall and tomboyish with green, sparkling eyes, freckles and long, reddish-blonde hair she almost always wore up or in a ponytail. She regularly wore baggy jeans and flannel shirts in an attempt to disguise an athletic and very attractive body. Neither Shane nor any of the other men in the department were fooled.

The first time Shane met her was when she walked into his cubicle to introduce herself. Shane stood up quickly and tried to say "Hi" but managed only a squeak. He was about to say more but she smiled and that put an end to any chance of actually speaking. He struggled for a moment, then turned on his heel, walked outside and stood on the steps of a side porch in a raging snowstorm.

Kowalski and Cutter were sitting in their shared office space when Shane stumbled outdoors not far from their window.

"It's 20 degrees out there," Kowalski said.

"I thought he had more sense than that," Cutter offered.

"It's that woman."

"I wouldn't be surprised if she ends up more trouble than three cars are worth."

Kowalski thought about that for a moment. "That particular woman is worth a good, solid 10 police cars."

"Not to mention three shotguns, four pistols, five Kevlar vests…"

"And a whole bunch of handcuffs."

In a sudden motion that would have shocked anyone but Kowalski, Cutter stood up, wiggled his pelvis, thrust his arms to the ceiling and howled loud enough to be heard throughout the building, "Arrrggghhhooooo!!!!"

Two of the younger deputies leaped to their feet; one actually drew his sidearm. Both were calmed but confused by the addition of Chief Kowalski's booming voice, also in a piercing howl. The entire Sheriff's office stood transfixed as they listened to their two leaders laugh until they choked and then laugh some more.

Only Eva, the office manager for 30 years, seemed unfazed. She kept working but muttered to herself. "They should be ashamed. Neither one of them a day below 60 and acting like this is the first time a young girl comes in."

The howling, though uncharacteristic, barely dented Shane's consciousness. He was no more affected by it than by the cold, which seemed oddly separate from him. He'd had plenty of girlfriends, several pretty serious, but suddenly he was overwhelmed by a feeling of connection, of rightness, of perfection, of …

"What the hell is wrong with me?" he said out loud.

"You're freezing to death," said a voice, THE voice, behind him. "You're experiencing hallucinations and delirium, which is common when you're freezing to death, although we prefer to call it hypothermia, now. Have you noticed that nobody freezes to death anymore? They die of hypothermia."

Shane had turned at her first words and now stood looking up at the puffs of steam coming from her mouth, at the way her lips slid across her teeth and her freckles crinkled across her cheeks and nose and her chest rose with her breath. The snow was landing on her hair but it didn't melt. He didn't hear a word she said.

"Are you all right? ARE YOU ALL RIGHT?" she asked.

Shane was embarrassed. He realized all at once what an idiot he seemed but just as quickly he realized that he didn't care. Only one thing mattered now.

"You are the most beautiful woman I've ever seen."

Lacy had been moving forward to look more closely at him but reversed and backed up three steps. She was used to come-ons, some of them remarkably original, but the sheer intensity in Shane's eyes almost frightened her. This was Shane Larrimer, the deputy who'd put the grant together, the man everyone talked about. Even when she'd questioned Sheriff Kowalski about some aspects of the research, he'd put her off, "We'll have to see what Shane thinks about that."

Shane was the originator of her grant and now he stood before her, bareheaded and coatless in a blizzard, acting like a 13-year-old boy at his first dance. His mouth was moving but no sound came out. It was actually kind of cute, Lacy decided.

"Thanks. I got dressed up special," she said, motioning un-self-consciously to her jeans and flannel shirt. Shane thought it was the most graceful movement he'd ever seen.

"Dinner?" he croaked.

Lacy smiled. She could enjoy this. "It's not even lunchtime, yet."

Shane's eyes became tortured. "Tonight?"

She smiled again, which Shane decided was an unfair advantage.

"Together, you and me?" she said, almost laughing now.

Shane was beginning to get hold of himself now, or maybe it was the shivering that helped. At any rate, he smiled and said, "Together, you and me, side by each, all in a bunch."

"If I say yes, will you come inside?"

Shane liked the sound of that. He nodded and in they went.

And that had been that. Shane and Lacy had been a perfect fit from their first date and they were married a year later, shortly after her research was completed. The Brothers KowalsCutter were pleased with the union because it removed a potentially divisive problem from the force. Luckily Lacy had never shown the slightest romantic interest in anyone else but Kowalski worried because the possibility was always there. Then, too, Shane's marriage and Lacy's subsequent pregnancies (they had four children now) lent an aspect of maturity and stability to the young man that had previously been missing.

From then on, life had gone smoothly for Shane. Promotions had come regularly. His proven track record in enforcement and in administration put him in line for patrol sergeant, the third ranking position on the force, where he quickly established himself as a leader who inspired confidence and loyalty among his men.

His outfitting business prospered and as time went on, required less and less input from him. Chester Wewa was a fine guide and competent foreman. His relationship with clients was even better than Shane's. Hunters who went with Chester invariably asked to be paired with him again, even when they'd gone home empty-handed. Chester now had eight guides and packers working for him during hunting season and twice that many guides and support people during the fishing and rafting season. Chester ran the day-to-day operation, did the hiring and firing, did the client contact, kept the books and oversaw the advertising.

In general, as Chester explained to Shane during a meeting, "I do everything that needs to be done in this business and then I tell you about it afterwards." This explanation came just a few sentences before Chester demanded a full 50-50 partnership in the company and creation of an executive vice president position for himself. "You'll still have the final say, Shane," he said.

Shane had expected a request for a raise but he was more than a little surprised about Chester's demand for a full partnership. His initial inclination was to turn it down outright. After all, he had started the company and nursed it through the early years. Many of the clients were still people he had attracted the first few years of the business. After a moment's reflection, Shane began to waffle a little. The business had really taken off only after he'd started work with the Sheriff's Department and turned over regular operations to Chester. Lacy had mentioned several times her belief that Chester was worth more than Shane was paying him. Besides, Shane was actually taking home more income from Mountain Outfitters than he was making as a law officer. He could afford to be generous and Chester deserved to have his earnings tied in with performance. Shane thought about it without speaking for almost two minutes.

Meanwhile Chester's legs were about to give out on him. He'd felt bad even asking for 50-50 but negotiations had to start somewhere. He'd hoped for a raise, dreamed of a small percentage partnership but hadn't held out any real hope. Shane was a good man and a fair boss but Chester knew from long experience how tightfisted Shane could be. But the big man was actually thinking about it. This could turn out better than he imagined. After 10 years with Mountain Outfitters, Chester knew it was time to make a change. He had two kids of his own. He didn't want to work for wages the rest of his life. He didn't want to move on to something else but Shane would have to make it easy for him to stay.

Shane did exactly that, and more. Abruptly, he snorted, rubbed his face and declared, "You're a partner, as of today. You'll receive 25 percent of our profits, starting next month. Providing the company continues to meet or exceed our previous year's gross, your percentage of the profits will increase 5 percent every five years until you reach an absolute cap of 40 percent. You can be the executive vice president or the shit hot poobah or whatever else you want to call yourself but I retain the controlling interest and the final say on any decision about the operations of this company. What do you think, partner?"

Their handshake had sealed the deal between the two men. Chester was on his 20th year with the company and he would not reach the 40 percent level of partnership for another five years. Even though Shane had given up a portion of his yearly take to Chester, his overall income from the business had continued to climb, owing primarily to Chester's business creativity. He'd now expanded their activities into photographic pack trips and high lakes fishing trips. He'd even begun scheduling pack trip weddings each summer, in which the participants rode horseback into the high country with an adventurous pastor and married on a rocky promontory overlooking the Salmon River.

About the only major problem to surface in his sideline business was the 1982 reappearance of Smokey Stover. Smokey had walked in to the Sheriff's Department office one summer morning and asked for Shane. Upon seeing him, Shane was struck by his appearance. Smokey was now lithe and strongly built. His rail thin body had given way to hard, ropy muscles that seemed to extend into his face. The thin, scraggly hair was cut short and Smokey had grown a neatly trimmed mustache that actually looked good on him.

Shane looked at him for a while and finally blurted, "Who are you and what have you done to Smokey Stover?"

"It's me, Shane." Like his physical appearance, Smokey's voice was similar, but different from his youth. It took Shane a moment to recognize the difference. It no longer dripped with embarrassment. The lisp was almost non-existent. Smokey seemed to have shed the self-consciousness that had poisoned his outlook and his relationship with other people. His eyes were clear, and he stood there looking calmly at Shane, his feet planted firmly on the ground.

"What in the world are you doing here, Smokey?" Shane asked. He was more than a little aware of Smokey's predilection for violence. He'd notified a couple of the other deputies to be available when the secretary had called to tell him Smokey Stover was waiting to see him and he knew they were waiting just down the hall if they were needed.

"I came to ask you for a job."

Shane could not have been more surprised if Stover had flapped his arms fast enough to hover.

"Me."

"Yes."

"You want me to give you a job."

"Yes." Smokey made no attempt to follow up. Shane was slightly unnerved. This could not be Smokey Stover.

"Smokey, you and I have quite a bit of history, all of it bad. Why in the world would you want to work for me?"

Smokey hesitated, for the first time seeming to be uncertain, but his eyes never left Shane's. "You stood up for your friend. When you got thumped you came back and took it to us." He stopped for a moment and took a deep breath. "You're the only one I know to trust."

Now there's a sad statement if I ever heard one, Shane thought. He said "I haven't even seen you in what, ten-twelve years?"

"I haven't met too many trustworthy people in that time."

"You've been in prison." It was not a question. The kind of muscles Smokey wore came from a prison gym.

"Four years in California. Armed robbery. Me and two other guys. I got caught less than a year after I left here. I've been out and straight for the last eight years."

"How'd you get off so light with your priors?"

Smokey sighed and leaned against the door jamb. He'd expected the question.

"During the robbery, one of the guys I was with went nuts and started beating the kid behind the counter with his gun. He was berserk. He was going to kill him. I popped him with the barrel of my pistol and knocked him out. I stayed and tried to take care of the kid."

"You didn't run?"

How could he explain? What words could he use to connect with Shane Larrimer, the Golden Boy of Grangeville? How could someone who'd grown up loved, admired and emulated ever understand the toxic waste that had been his own life, the rage and frustration and self-hatred? How would he describe the one shining moment, and to this day he still thought of it as a shining moment, when he'd made the first good and honorable choice of his life? He had hated and envied Shane Larrimer his entire life, but it didn't really matter what Shane or anybody else thought. I was proud, I am proud of that moment and it will carry me forward whether I get this job or not. I'm a different man than I was, a better man.

"Nah, watching the beating that kid got took everything out of me. I just didn't want to be a part of that stuff any longer."

"So for the last eight years you've been...?"

"Fishing in Alaska, recently. Before that I fought fires, set chokers, planted trees, worked on ranches. I've done pretty well. I just want to settle down now and make a real life. I've got letters of reference. Chester said you were looking for a good man."

Damn, Shane thought. *He's already talked to Chester. Why would Chester send him to me? Hiring and firing are his decisions. He wouldn't have known Smokey's history at all…unless Smokey volunteered it. Surely Smokey wouldn't have volunteered something like that. Well, he probably would, knowing I'd learn about him soon, anyway.*

Shane didn't know why he'd even bothered to listen this long to Smokey's story. Just pure curiosity, because he sure wasn't going to hire Smokey Stover, no matter how much he'd changed. Shane didn't have a lot of faith in the ability of ex-cons to make something good of themselves. But Smokey stood there, with his crazy blue eyes looking straight at him, completely calm and at ease.

I don't care what kind of act you're putting on now, Stover, but you don't have a chance of getting a job with me.

"OK, Smokey. Leave your letters of reference here. I'll talk to Chester and if we're interested, we'll make a few calls. Check back with me tomorrow."

Smokey turned to go. As he reached the door, Shane spoke up.

"Smokey!" Stover stopped and turned. "What made you change your life like that?"

Stover hesitated, thinking. "Part of it was shock at the way that kid was beaten. I'd never seen anything like it. But mostly I just didn't want to be that kind of person any more. Being an asshole takes so much energy." He turned and left.

Shane waited until lunch to run down to Mountain Outfitters. When he did, the first words out of Chester's mouth were, "Well, what do you think?"

"What do you mean, what do I think? The guy was a first-class asshole, he's been in trouble his entire life; he's done hard time in California. Give me a break, what do I think. Jesus."

"Yeah, so?"

"Chester, you can't seriously want to hire the guy."

"What he was, he was. I don't think that's what he is now."

"He's smart enough to have faked a few letters of reference."

"He didn't fake them. I've already made the calls. All his references would take him back in a minute. I talked with his old probation officer, too. Did you know he tried to stop a robbery he was taking part in?"

"Yeah, he told me. Knocked a guy out who was beating a kid. He shouldn't have been there in the first place. Not exactly earth shaking as far as I'm concerned."

"You didn't ask about the third bad guy?"

"No, I didn't really care."

"No. I didn't ask either but the probation officer volunteered it. He said the third guy got pretty excited after Smokey coldcocked the other one and started throwing rounds. Smokey covered the checkout kid with his body and shot back a couple of times."

"Jesus, a gunfight between the bad guys?"

"Yeah! And Smokey won."

"He didn't say shit about that."

"Yeah, well they found the bad guy dead less than 100 feet away."

Shane leaned back and looked at the ceiling as if it held the answers to all his questions. "Damn," he said. "I'll be gotohell."

Smokey Stover started the next day as a wrangler and camp boy. He was good with horses right from the first, which surprised Shane a little. "He just connects with them," Chester said. "Not many white men can do that."

Smokey seemed to get along with people, as well, which surprised Shane a great deal. He decided to relax and wait for Smokey to screw up, a virtual certainty in his mind. *One strike, you're out, Stover.*

But Smokey didn't screw up. He started out strong and kept getting better. After a year, Chester made him into a river guide, where he slowly developed a talent for maneuvering rafts through heavy water and rocks. He had the knack of squeezing the maximum amount of excitement out of any rapids, without actually putting the clients in jeopardy. "He's pretty good at making things look more dangerous than they are without taking any chances," Chester told Shane during one of their many discussions about Smokey.

A year after that he started helping experienced hunting guides. During Smokey's fourth year Chester scheduled him as the lead guide on a hunting expedition with four first-time clients. Shane came within a hair of vetoing the idea; only his loyalty to Chester kept him from doing so. The hunt was a complete success. Four happy clients took three bull elk, and each of the clients rebooked for the following year, specifically asking for Smokey as their guide. Shane just shook his head when Chester told him.

The following season, a state senator, famous for his prickly disposition, booked an elk hunt with several of his high roller friends. When Shane and Chester got together to plan the season, Chester made the comment that they needed to be sure to schedule one of their best hands for that trip. Then he waited, silent. Shane hesitated. The look on Chester's face wasn't quite a smirk.

"I suppose you could take them," he said.

Chester shook his head. We'll have five hunting camps out during that season. No way I can tie myself down to one hunt."

"Well, then, it's got to be Cole and Billy."

"Cole's wife is expecting right during that season. She lost her last baby. He already told me he won't leave that late in the pregnancy. Billy's a good wrangler but he's not a lead guide."

Shane felt like he was sliding down a slippery slope…with Chester's hand on his shoulder, guiding him.

"Maybe we could schedule Carl and Jamie for that one."

"Carl's a little rough around the edges. He's not the guide for an obnoxious character like the senator."

Shane looked quickly to see if Chester was actually smirking. Nope. He wondered for just a moment if it was possible to fire a partner.

"Well, what do you want to do?"

"Not my call."

"Not your call. Shit. Not your call. You make all the calls. Now you've got me stuck here and you're telling me a decision you always make is not your call. You are twisting the knife, you Indian asshole."

At that Chester smiled broadly. "Tomahawk. I am twisting the tomahawk. We've got to choose our best man. Who do you think it ought to be, Boss?"

"I've never liked you, Chester and now I remember why." Shane leaned back in his chair and raised his hands in defeat. "OK, Smokey Stover it is. Will we send Billy with him?" Chester nodded, still smiling.

"Good choice."

"Yeah, like it was my choice." Shane got up to leave. "Jesus H. Christ.

Smokey Stover, taking Mountain Outfitters' most important clients. Proof positive the world has turned upside down."

Chapter 3

In the camp tent, Shane was hesitant to tell his friend about Smokey, wondering if mention of the man would be a sharp reminder of that terrible time in Jared's life. To his amazement, Jared only laughed and slapped his hand on his leg.

"Smokey Stover! Working for you? I'll be damned!"

"I was a little worried it would bother you," Shane said.

"No. Hell no. Smokey had his own set of problems and you and I probably contributed to them. Everybody deserves a little happiness. His came late but I'm glad he found it."

"Happiness? I remember a conversation back in college when you said happiness was an overrated commodity."

"Did I, really?"

"Yes, it was one of those nights at the lake when we were drinking beer and being philosophical."

"Well, that shows you how stupid we were. We should have just drunk beer and been happy instead of practicing feeling pain we didn't even know anything about yet."

Shane nodded. "We had it pretty good as kids."

Jared nodded. "Maybe too good. We weren't…at least, I wasn't, prepared for the real world."

"Jared. Vietnam wasn't the real world. It was a mistake, a tragedy."

"Yep. That's what makes it the real world. This, up here, what you have in Grangeville? It's a dream world. It's wonderful but it's not the real world. At least, it's not my world. Not anymore."

"Why not? You've got a wife who's stuck with you for twenty-some years, a great five-year-old son you got the Koreans to let you adopt. What more do you really need?"

Jared turned on him. "Balls would be nice," he snarled. "A little testosterone, maybe. Look at me, Shane." Jared stood up from his chair, swaying slightly. His long underwear accentuated the flare of his hips and the rounding of his breasts. "Does this look like me? Is this who I am? Christ, Shane, even my voice has changed. It's higher now. Tell me you haven't noticed."

"I noticed," Shane said, looking at his boots.

"And as for the wife. Misty is wonderful and she always has been. God knows what she's been through with me but what can her life be like without a man, without a real man?"

"Shit, Jared. Even I know there's a lot more to love and sex than just a stiff dick."

"Sure there is. There's a lot more to hunting than just shooting an animal, too. But once in a while you really just have to let the air out of something, you know? Otherwise, you're just taking walks in the woods."

He looked for a long time at the wood stove. "Once in a while Misty would like to get laid. And for a change, I'd like to be the one who did it."

Shane was silent. Their days together in the mountains had peeled away some of the bark that had grown between them but not that much. Not enough to even begin to respond to that statement. He'd wondered about Jared's situation many times. What would it be like for a young healthy woman to be married to a man without any equipment? He had a pretty good idea what it would be like for a man. Whenever he went away for more than three days he started thinking about sex even more than food. Kowalski referred to that randiness as a 'high white count.' "Better go home and lower your white count," he was fond of telling his deputies when they'd been on duty for an extended period. Shane assumed that Kowalski's white count referred to the sperm count, but he wasn't sure. Jared, he thought painfully, didn't even have a white count.

"I'm sorry," he said finally.

"Oh, it's OK, Shane. I don't hold it against her. She is never indiscreet. And as far as I know, she's never been emotionally involved. I think she just gets laid occasionally. I'm as sure as I can be about something I don't know for sure. I'm sort of past worrying about it. I have Josh, now. We have Josh. Helluva a name for a Korean kid, don't you think? With him, somehow, everything is OK. You know what I mean?"

"Absolutely," Shane said. "You take the most important things and hang onto them. They'll keep you afloat when the flood hits."

Jared laughed bitterly. "Yes, the flood. Nice analogy. I held onto Misty for all those years until she started to drown along with me. She had to save herself. But luckily Josh came drifting by and now I hold onto him."

"Bullshit!" Shane exploded. "You were always the one everyone else held on to. Including me. And it didn't change when you went to Vietnam. Three of the guys from your unit came through town hoping to see you. They talked about what a fine leader you were, how they could depend on you when things got shitty. Two of them stayed in town for a couple days, telling stories about you down at the Riverhouse. What would they think to see you pissing in your own shoe like this?"

"One of the best things about getting your balls blown off, Shane, is you lose the hormone that makes you care what other people think."

Despite himself, Shane found himself smiling. Then chuckling. Then laughing loudly and completely. To his surprise, Jared was laughing too, silently, his sides heaving. Jared couldn't get his breath and almost fell into the wood stove, a move both men found hilarious.

"Well, that seems rather extreme, but…..I suppose it might be worth it."

"Oh, I recommend it. I really do."

"Jared. I'd have given anything to have gone with you."

"Shit, I'd have given a lot to have you go in my place. Oh, hell, Shane. I know you wanted to go. I know how hard you tried to go. But there's just no way the United States Marine Corps could accept some kind of web-footed amphibian. Six toes! Six toes! When I think of how many scams people were using to get out of the military and there you were trying to get in but you couldn't because you've got webbed feet!"

"My feet are not webbed. I have the normal amount of skin between my toes. I just have too many toes."

"Is it hereditary? Do your kids have the normal number of toes or are they like you? How are your kids, by the way? I know you've got Marshal at 12, Craig at 10, Julie at 7 and Jessica at 5."

"You've got the girls backwards."

"Huh?"

Jessica is 7, Julie is 5."

"Oh."

"They're fine. Marshal is a tough guy and a bit of a trouble-maker. Reminds me of you. Craig has learned how to stay out of trouble by watching him. Jessica seems smart and Julie is in charge of everyone. None of them, unfortunately, have extra toes. Still, that's pretty impressive. How do you know all that? And why in the world would you care, when you wouldn't even talk to me for the last 16 years?"

"You talked to Misty. She talked to me. It wasn't that I didn't care about you. I just didn't want to talk to you. I think I just was so caught up in my problems I didn't have the energy to deal with anyone else."

"Well, what happened? Have your problems changed?"

"No, my big problem hasn't changed and it never will. I think Josh happened. When we adopted Josh he helped me put things in perspective. Maybe my problem isn't the most important thing in the world now."

Shane thought back a few years to one of the conversations he'd had with Misty during one of their infrequent visits back to Grangeville. He'd asked after Jared and been saddened when Misty told him Jared was still struggling. He'd said something positive, and referred to Jared's lifelong reputation for toughness and tenacity, but Misty had just murmured, "No. Not any more, Shane," she said. "That man didn't come back. A nice man came back. A dependable husband came back but the old Jared stayed in Vietnam."

Misty's vitality and friendly, sparkling eyes had always been her most engaging feature but now there was an underlying quality of sadness. For the first time he could remember, Shane realized that Misty was not particularly pretty. He'd always thought she was prettiest girl in town. Her warm smile and bubbling good humor drew admirers from all around. Her uneven teeth simply highlighted her refreshing charm. And if you weren't hooked already, she was just so smart and well, friendly. If it hadn't been Jared dating her, Shane knew, he would have been in the hunt as well.

Shane wondered how a young woman like Misty adapted to life with a man to whom sex was a memory. It has to be tough, he thought. He had a vague idea that women didn't have the same urges as men but they must have some, he reasoned, otherwise we men would never get anywhere at all. Everything considered, his sympathy lay with Jared. What must it be like to want so badly to plunge into a woman, have her legs wrapped around you, but not be able to? Maybe that's the trick, he thought. Maybe Jared's injuries prevented him from wanting women, so he didn't think about what he was missing. He'd asked his father one day not long after Jared had come home from Vietnam.

"I doubt that Jared has lost the urge," Ben Larrimer said when Shane brought it up. "I've cut horses before and you've got to do it young. If you wait until they are all nutted up then castration won't do any good. They still think they're studs and they act like it, too. That's the way it is with Jared. He may not be siring any kids but he still has the mind and the heart of a stallion."

Now it seemed that Josh had saved Jared from the depression that gripped him for years. There's nothing wrong with that. Shane knew from experience how children place a hold on you nothing else could match. Children live only because their parents create them and survive only because parents keep them safe, saving them from injury and death multiple times every day. There's nothing wrong with people helping each other. He'd seen old people who'd given up any desire to live suddenly become animated and strong, simply because they'd been given a kitten or a puppy. Seemed like a child would be even better. *And now here he is, back out hunting with me. This story's going to have a happy ending after all.*

Jared put another two logs into the wood stove and leaned back in his camp chair. His face tingled slightly from the drinks he'd consumed but he didn't feel drunk. Of course, a few minutes earlier he'd almost toppled into the wood stove, so he couldn't trust his feelings. But he could trust Shane. Of all the men he'd ever known, even those good men he'd led in the Marine Corps, Shane was the most loyal, most dependable of them all. Even up here in the mountains, after all these years, Shane had settled into his place as the rock on which Jared was built. After almost two weeks in a tent together, the two men had settled into the same easy, collaborative relationship they'd held all their lives. Jared was amazed. He'd never felt so peaceful. It wasn't so much the talking to Shane that had released him, though it had helped far more than the endless hours he'd spent talking with therapists, it was just being with him here, in the mountains.

Killing the elk had helped too. In some elemental way, the death of the big bull helped to re-establish him, even if just in his own mind, as a competent, confident man. The kind of man who could stand up for himself, make his way in the world, protect his family. Had I lost so much? Jared wondered. Had I pulled so far into myself that I'd completely lost my sense of self-worth? My God! How could I have sunk so far? How could I have forgotten who and what I was? Every day, Shane has been talking about the old days, about the things we did in school, in athletics, in our beer bashes. In each one of those memories, I play an important role. I know Shane is picking the stories that play into his agenda, but they are real, I remember them, too. I must have just been repressing them.

Chapter 4

Misty dropped Josh off at the kindergarten and headed back across town to the hospital. Thank God for kindergarten. With Jared out of town, she would have had to pay for full-time day care without it. Josh still went from school to day care for an hour or so each day but that certainly wasn't bad, considering what other families had to do. The Patuxent River Day Care was one of the best around and Josh loved going there. Thank God for day care and kindergarten. As much as she loved Josh, she needed a break from the energetic five-year-old. That's why she appreciated work even more now than ever before. She'd had to revert back from administration to being a floor nurse in order to get the half-time position that usually allowed her to be home in the afternoons, but that was ok, too. Even days like today, when she had to work 3-11 p.m., were not too difficult since she was only working 20 hours each week.

She'd missed the interaction with patients and the feeling of accomplishment that went along with nursing during the past five years, while she'd been a supervisor. But she'd liked being a supervisor, too. Her promotion to administration seemed to verify all the talk about her potential years before. No matter how good a nurse she'd become, she was still only a nurse, and for some people, including her parents, it was not nearly enough.

Her mother was always careful to introduce her as a "nursing supervisor," and she'd continued to do so now, even though, technically, Misty was no longer a supervisor. Misty didn't feel slighted. She knew how important her job was each time she looked in the eyes of one of her patients or their families and saw the gratitude.

Traffic on the Beltway was bad; it was going to take longer than normal to get to the hospital. Misty slid her little sedan into the passing lane and tried to speed up a little. After all these years in Bowie, she knew she should be used to the traffic but many times she found herself remembering when a traffic jam was a herd of cattle was being moved down the two-lane road near Grangeville. It was funny, she had never been able to shake the idea that she and Jared were just temporarily displaced Idahoans. In her heart, she'd always expected to return to Grangeville and raise their kids there.

Of course, that dream was predicated on their ability to have kids, a plan that had died 16 years ago, when Jared came back from Vietnam with the shrapnel wound that destroyed his manhood, shattered his confidence, and changed their lives beyond imagining. Misty did imagine, though. Even now, when she had a few moments alone, she found herself wondering how things might have been if Jared had returned from the war unharmed.

Their lives would have been perfect or close to it. Of that she was certain. Jared would have been an immediate success in anything he had undertaken. He had always been that way, in high school, in college and in the Marine Corps. And she would have been happy in her nursing career. Of course, she would only have kept nursing for a few years and then quit working to have the five children she and Jared had planned on. They'd even picked out names. Misty would have happily given up work. She probably would have home-schooled the kids, although that would have occasioned an argument with Jared. He would have wanted to recreate his own high school experience for their children, so they would love their teenage years as much as he had.

Of course, that imaginary argument could only have taken place with the old Jared. The new Jared didn't argue. He simply agreed with anything Misty wanted. Easy to get along with, Misty knew, but she often wished for the old Jared, the one with strong opinions. That Jared, while slow to anger, had a terrible, raging temper once he ignited.

Misty had seen examples of his temper several times and it was enough to make her pull away from him, even when he'd acted in her defense.

On one occasion, during Jared's senior year, two drunken elk hunters had come into the grocery store where she worked as a cashier to buy last-minute items before they headed into the mountains. They were loud but not particularly obnoxious, the kind of customers who don't really require action but whose departure will make everyone take a deep breath. One of them became too full of himself and came on to Misty as she rang up their sales. She ignored him, but as she was giving him change he gripped her hand and pulled her toward him for "just a friendly little kiss," as he afterwards explained it. In the process her sweater was accidentally pulled and her breast pinched. The hunter's partner was as startled as Misty and practically ran out the front door. Undersheriff Daryl Cutter, off duty and in civilian clothes, moved quickly from an adjacent line, grabbed the hunter by his collar and pulled him back through the line and away from Misty.

His backward momentum was probably all that saved the hunter from a cracked skull because as soon as Misty recovered from her shock she began swinging one of the belt separators. Because the cash register was between them Misty had trouble landing a solid blow. But the cash register was no hindrance at all to Jared, who had just entered the store to buy a sandwich and was coming up to say hi to Misty when he saw the commotion. Jared was more confused than anything else until Misty began screaming and trying to hit the man. At that point, as he later described it, "I stopped thinking."

Jared came up the checkout aisle at full speed and hit the elk hunter in the face with the top of his head, driving him back over Cutter. Jared leaped up and began pummeling the man, who was crying and scrabbling with both hands at his bloody mouth, trying to find his two front teeth. Deputy Cutter removed himself from the melee and walked calmly over to Misty. "Are you all right?" he asked. When she ignored him and moved toward the fighting, he took her face between his hands, looked into her eyes and asked again with exaggerated slowness. "Are…you…all…right?"

"Yes, but Jared…"

Cutter smiled and said. "I believe Jared's just fine. You won't be needing this now, will you?" He removed the metal separator from her grasp and put it back on the conveyor belt. He led Misty back around to her position behind the register, shook her shoulders slightly and said, "You stay here, now. Got it? Stay here."

Cutter's calm demeanor and quiet competence helped to settle Misty but did nothing for Jared, who had tired of swinging punches and started kicking the hunter, now in a fetal position. Cutter watched for a moment more, then sauntered over to a nearby broom display and picked one up. He examined the brush and felt the heft of the handle, then walked over and stuck the brush into Jared's face. The first time or two Jared didn't notice, he flicked the broom away like it was a fly. The third time the broom scraped his face Jared stared past the broom at Cutter. He blinked continually, trying to focus through the blood pouring down from the cut on top of his head where the hunter's teeth had connected on the first collision.

"That's enough," Cutter said. "He deserves a beating. He doesn't deserve to die."

Jared knocked the broom away and charged, roaring. Cutter reversed the broom and jabbed the handle hard into Jared's mid-section. Jared dropped to his knees and began vomiting. Cutter replaced the broom back in the display and patted Jared on the head. "I don't think it's too bad, head cuts look worse than they really are. But by golly, I think one of his teeth is still stuck in your hair." He reached back onto his belt, pulled out his Leatherman tool. Using the pliers he extracted the tooth. Jared was still vomiting and didn't notice. Cutter unbuttoned the hunter's shirt pocket and dropped the tooth in.

He replaced the Leatherman and turned to Misty, saying, "I'm sorry, Misty. If I'd read the situation a little better I might have stopped this idiot before he got out of control. He's probably better off dealing with Jared anyway. I imagine you would have brained him, for sure."

He took a $20 bill from his pocket and laid it on the belt. "You and Jared go out to dinner on me." You both deserve it. He reached down and lifted the hunter to his feet, then half-carried and half-dragged him toward the door. "You, on the other hand, deserve exactly what you got. Let's go find your friend. Maybe he'll take you to a dentist."

That event had been a watershed in their relationship, Misty remembered. It had shown her just how much Jared cared for her. Until then, she thought they were dating casually. It also, she smiled to recall, put a sudden and complete end to calls and invitations from any of the other boys in Grangeville. From that point on, everyone, including her and Jared, assumed they were an item.

The fight in the supermarket also forever changed her feelings about Jared. Even as she grew to love him, she never completely forgot how easily he rolled into violence. She'd been mad, herself, and had been ribbed for years afterward about her dangerous wielding of the grocery separator bar, but what she'd seen in Jared's eyes had been something far beyond anger. She'd heard about his fight with Smokey Stover, of course, and one or two other events that had dimmed with years, but she knew he wanted to kill the elk hunter and would have accomplished it had Undersheriff Cutter not been good with a broom.

Later, Misty talked with her father about the incident. He smiled in that quirky way he had when he was going to hide something smart in a foolish response. "Most men are just dogs, Misty."

"I know, Dad. That's what Aunt Cheryl says."

He laughed. "I mean it a little differently than she does. Some men are Pekinese. They want to be held on a lap and petted. They'll bark and bite but it's all for show. Some men are Labrador retrievers. They are loyal and strong and will always do what they're told. Some men are coyotes. They are sneaky and mean but they'll never stand up for anything. Some men are German shepherds. Just as loyal as Labs but quite a bit more capable of fighting and doing damage if it is necessary. If I were going to guess, I'd say Jared is a shepherd."

He looked at her for a long time, as though uncertain. Finally, he began to speak again, this time much more seriously. "Misty, I'm your father. The most important thing in the world to me is that you are safe and happy. I know the fight at the supermarket scared you and with good reason. That sort of thing is not pleasant. But just because a man has that sort of ability doesn't mean he will ever use it. Before you chose a man, you'll have to know in your heart that he will never hurt you, that he will always protect you."

Her father smiled again and she knew what was coming before he said it. "Besides, any man you marry would have to worry a little bit about what you might do when you got your hands on one of those grocery dividers."

Misty laughed and hugged her father and they sat together quietly on the front porch for a long time.

She had taken her father's advice, of course, and followed her heart right into Jared's arms. Not that there'd been much doubt about it, Misty thought as she passed a silver Cadillac with a song playing so loudly it was painful to her ears. She suspected she'd have ended up with Jared even without her father's gentle coaxing.

She'd never regretted her decision, though there'd been many times after he'd come back from Vietnam when she wondered how she could go on. When she sank to those depths, she tried to remember Jared as he'd been in high school. He was good looking, with his curly red hair and freckled face, but not particularly so; smart but not one of those quick, clever comedians. He was a good athlete, as well, but not the best. He was just magnetic. She remembered being jealous of the attention he received beginning their freshmen year. At that point she was still skinny and gap-toothed and pretty much ignored by everyone, but Jared couldn't go anywhere without a crowd following him. He wasn't a showoff or a real talker, he just had an absolute self-confidence that people found irresistible.

In their sophomore year, however, she and Jared had been paired together in biology lab and they began spending a lot of time together. By that time, she had developed into what her father liked to describe as a 'smart mouth' and she used it to great advantage on Jared in a never-ending effort to keep him off balance. "Is that the best you could do, McCauley?" she was fond of asking about almost everything he tried, athletic or physical, academic or social. She was fond of it because it never failed to shake, if only for a moment, Jared's otherwise unshakable self-confidence. She was always amazed at the way that simple question seemed to rattle him.

Much later, Misty realized the reason her question shook Jared was because he was never absolutely sure he'd done the best he could—not the very, very best. In Jared's mind, there was absolutely nothing he couldn't accomplish if he tried hard enough, so anything less than complete success made him question himself. But the temporary confusion she caused didn't really shake Jared's self confidence, it simply made him re-examine his thoughts and actions. As Misty would learn, no one was more honest with himself, or harder on himself, than Jared.

Her sophomore year was when Misty began dating. Her body had only just begun to fill out but her eyes and sparkling personality, according to the yearbook, had begun attracting boys on a fairly regular basis. Jared, who seemed to stop by to talk at least once a day, would always make fun of the boys she dated. He never seemed jealous, but he always knew who she was dating and more often than not, he knew what they had done on their last date. And he always made fun. Misty didn't take offense; she wasn't quite sure why.

During that period she'd actually been attracted to Shane more than Jared. Shane was big, bigger than most of the other boys and his body had matured and hardened while Jared and the other boys were still developing Adams apples. For all his size and strength, Shane didn't seem to fill a room the way Jared did. He was quiet while Jared was talkative, still and calm while Jared was full of nervous energy. And he was always smiling like he knew a secret no one else even dreamed of. Even now, driving down the Beltway, Misty could see Shane's smile as though he was right in front of her. They'd never gotten together but not because she hadn't tried. Shane simply seemed to arrange things so the possibility of them dating just never came up. Once, Misty got downright aggressive but Shane gave one excuse or another and slipped away. Over time, she'd given up trying to get romantic with Shane and their relationship had then grown into one of true friendship. They'd shared secrets and dreams unabashedly throughout their upper-class years and through college. Jared had never shown the slightest bit of concern about her friendship with Shane. "Why should I worry?" Jared had asked her when she'd asked him if he was jealous about her friendship with Shane. "I trust you almost as much as I trust him." That shut her up. She'd never tried to dig at him about Shane again.

Years later, she and Shane got together for a Coke just after Jared left for Vietnam. She asked him straight out.

"Why didn't you ever take an interest in me? I was practically falling all over you."

"You were Jared's," he'd said simply.

"I was not! He and I weren't even dating back then."

"Didn't matter. You were always the one."

"He told you that?" she'd asked.

"Didn't have to. Everybody knew, except maybe you. Personally, I think you knew, too. You were just pretending you didn't know to make him wiggle on the hook."

"So, you were protecting Jared. You didn't want to hurt him?"

"I was protecting myself from Jared. You know how he is when he's mad." He smiled broadly and poked her nose. "Even you wouldn't have been worth that fight."

By the middle of their junior year, Misty had become a bigger part of Jared's day, although not quite like he'd wanted. She refused to be a part of his retinue. Whenever the herd of people who followed him showed up, Misty simply left. Because it was almost impossible for Jared to rid himself of the herd, he found it difficult to spend time with her. He began to chafe at the constant attention he couldn't escape.

"Why don't you just tell those people to leave you alone for a while, Jared? Tell them you want to spend time with Misty," Shane asked at one point.

Jared looked at him like he'd grown tusks. "You must be kidding."

"No," Shane said. "I'm not kidding."

"It doesn't work like that, Shane."

"Of course it does. They are your friends, Jared. They'd be happy to leave you alone for a while."

"Why can't Misty just hang around with the rest of us? Why can't she be part of the group? Why is she such a pain?"

"I don't think Misty wants to be just part of your group."

"Yeah, well, there are plenty of girls who do."

And that's the way it had stayed throughout their junior year. Jared continued to go about his business with a happy trail of followers in tow. Misty continued to date a series of boys. By that year, Jared's natural athleticism had erupted. He'd taken over as the starting quarterback on the high school football team and then as the basketball point guard. At 6'1" and 180 pounds Jared was stronger and faster than many of the people who played against him. But his true strength lay in his indomitable personality. The same certainty in his own plans and abilities that drew people to him in school gave his teammates faith in him.

"Jared doesn't think he can be beaten," Shane told Misty in one of their frequent chat sessions. "So he always plays with the attitude that the next play he runs is the one that will win it for him. The guys feed off of that. It gives you a lift, you know?"

In one game, after Shane had been stopped for no gain on the first two downs, Jared had called for a delayed quarterback sneak. Cliff Martin, the center, had actually complained in the huddle. "Jared, it's 3rd and nine, for crying out loud. Don't you think we ought to pass?"

Jared's eyes had burned then and when he spoke his voice shook with intensity. "No, Cliff. I don't THINK anything. I KNOW you can seal off their middle guard and I KNOW Shane can pancake their asshole middle linebacker and I KNOW I can run for a first down, if everyone else does their job. On two. Ready, break!"

It had worked just as he'd described. Jared had faked a handoff to Shane, who flattened the middle linebacker. Cliff turned their middle guard and drove him five yards down the line where both men collided with the outside linebacker and fell in a pile. Jared took a short drop and looked downfield as though to pass, then took off through the hole Cliff and Shane had created. Once past the line he found himself in a backfield that had been spread out to protect against the anticipated pass. His speed and natural agility carried him past three would-be tacklers and into the end zone, a run of 47 yards.

It became a standing joke on the team for the remainder of the time Jared was in school. "Third and nine, Jared. Let's run a sneak." But that joke masked the real confidence his teammates had in Jared. Even Shane, who knew Jared better than anyone else, suspected that Jared might possess some kind of supernatural power. The rest of Jared's teammates were convinced of it.

That sort of hero worship made it even more difficult for Jared and Misty to spend time alone together but Misty didn't mind. She was having fun dating and being on the cheerleading squad. When spring came around she was the top runner on the cross-country team. Misty had developed into an outgoing, vivacious and self-assured young woman, popular with both girls and boys. She was not, as she came to admit, a beautiful woman. Her nose was a little too big, her teeth were gapped and her forehead too broad.

"It's the whole package that counts, Misty," her father told her. "Anyone who judges a person by one or two characteristics just isn't smart enough to count for much." Misty's mother was upset by his implicit acceptance of Misty's homeliness and tried unsuccessfully to make him assure her that she was beautiful.

"Everyone's beautiful in their own way, Babe," he said. "Misty knows she doesn't have a model's looks. If I told her she did, she'd know I was lying." He turned back to Misty. "You are wonderful, though, Princess. Your mother knows it and I know it. And so does that pile of boys who are always falling all over each other trying to go out with you." He smiled and put his arm around her. "But the most important thing is that you know it. I think you do."

Initially, Misty had been as shocked as her mother. But she learned to appreciate her father's honesty and she learned as well to adopt his straightforward approach to life and her own limitations. That conversation marked the end of her tendency to downgrade her looks to others in hopes of a denial. It wasn't that fulfilling an experience if the other person didn't deny it.

She'd never discussed her appearance with anyone again until near the end of her senior year, after she and Jared had declared their love for each other and begun plans for a family.

"I wonder what our children will look like, Jared. I hope they don't get my nose or my gapped teeth."

Without hesitation, Jared had looked her in the eye and said, "Well, Misty, I think you are beautiful. I'd love for our kids to look just like you."

Misty smiled to think of that day. That simple statement, with such obvious honesty behind it, had sealed her love for Jared as nothing else really had.

Their senior year began much like the others. Jared was an established sports star, excelling in football, basketball and track. He did equally well in the classroom, though he had to work at it more than he would ever admit. Shane got less local adulation but was actively pursued by colleges both for his football and baseball prowess. At 6'4" and 220 pounds, Shane was considered an excellent linebacker prospect for smaller colleges. He was a step too slow for the bigger schools.

"It's the extra weight from that sixth toe," Jared was quick to tell him. "That and the webbing between your toes. It wrecks your aerodynamic fluidity. It keeps you from being fleet, like me."

"I don't have webs between my toes and if I did, it wouldn't affect my aerodynamics while I was wearing shoes. I'll admit the sixth toe probably slows me down, but it also makes me 4F, as opposed to 1A, like you and all your toe-challenged friends. While you are slogging through the humid jungles of Vietnam, dodging bullets and catching diseases, I will be back home with my six toes, watching over the womenfolk and making my way through the ranks of professional baseball, where they couldn't care less how many toes you have, as long as you can chew tobacco."

"Yeah, well, considering that you puked your guts out the last time you tried to chew tobacco, you probably don't have much chance in baseball."

"I'm pretty sure they have classes on chewing in the minor leagues."

"While you're taking those classes, think of me. I'll be over there defending your freedom."

"Bullshit! You'll be in class in some college."

"Well, I'll be daydreaming about Vietnam while I'm in class. I'll just get a quick Bachelor's degree and be on my way as an officer of Marines, a leader of the world's finest fighting men."

"With a little luck, we'll be out of Vietnam by the time you graduate."

"Jesus! I hope not. I'd hate to miss the fun. Maybe I can go to summer schools and graduate in three years."

"You sure won't be able to do that and play football, too, Jared."

Jared sighed. "No, but I don't think I'll be playing college football. I don't have a good enough arm to play quarterback and they say I'm not really quick enough to play defensive back. The only colleges showing any interest are real small schools that don't offer much of a scholarship. I can do better than that with an NROTC scholarship. Then I can join the Marine Corps and get on with my life." He took a deep breath and faced his friend.

"No, Shane. You are the only one of us with the skills to go higher in athletics."

And Shane had gone on. He'd been drafted in the fourth round by the Oakland Athletics and had reported to their single-A team in Stockton, California the summer after graduation. Although he'd been a fine hitter in high school, the A's drafted him for his 90-mile-per hour fastball and wicked curve. After only one year in single-A he was promoted to Oakland's AA team in Midland, Texas where he quickly established himself as an up-and-coming talent. Pepper Grimes, his pitching coach with the Rockhounds in Midland, was high on Shane, both for his talent and his workmanlike approach to the job. Shane was always prepared, always warmed up, always in shape. He took good care of himself. "You are a good changeup away from The Show, Shane," Pepper told him.

Shane worked on the changeup and continued to work on his fastball, too. It is axiomatic in baseball that pitchers learn to throw fast by throwing hard. Shane had worked his fastball up to 92 miles per hour and was doing long toss during practice one day when his shoulder came apart. It was a near complete rotator cuff tear and although the team stuck with him long enough to let him complete his rehab, it soon became obvious that his speed and control were never going to be the same. The Athletics let him go and Shane went home.

He'd been careful with his money and still had most of his signing bonus left. It was enough to buy a raft, a trailer and a new pickup with enough left over to pay for his first year of college at Boise State. On weekends he would take friends on white water raft trips. As he became better known, he began taking his professors and their families. Soon, he found himself in demand and realized he could make it into a business.

By the end of his freshman year, Shane had saved enough money to pay for his sophomore year. By the end of his sophomore year, he'd bought a drift boat and branched out into fishing. By midway through his senior year, Shane was employing three part-time river guides. He had little time for schoolwork and his grades showed it.

As he approached the end of his final quarter, Shane's grade average was so close to 2.0 that he couldn't afford anything less than a C in any course and he needed every credit to fulfill the minimum number for graduation.

"I am in a serious jam," he told Jared by phone. Jared had finished Officer's Candidate School in Quantico, Virginia and was close to finishing The Basic School, an advanced infantry officer's school. He had already received his orders to the 1st Marine Division in Vietnam.

"Bullshit," Jared said forcefully. "Let me tell you what I've learned here. You already meet the minimum standards. If the minimums weren't good enough, they wouldn't be the minimums. You just need to talk with your professors and make sure they know you need a C in their courses. Hell, you're running a business. They've got to be impressed. They'll help you out."

So Shane went so see the professor in the course he was most concerned about. He was in borderline D territory in English Grammar, which was taught by Professor Rick Welliver, a renowned grump.

"I really need to get a C in this class, Professor."

"I don't know what to tell you, Mr. Larrimer. You'll get the grade you earned."

"Well, while I was earning that grade, I was also earning a living as a guide. It wasn't easy doing both."

"It never is. I worked graveyard shift for three years in a foundry while I was going to college."

"That must have been tough. Did you walk through the snow to school, too?"

"Don't be a wiseass, Mr. Larrimer. You're here to beg for a favor, remember?"

"Did I tell you I played baseball in the Oakland A's farm system, Professor?"

"No. And I appreciate it."

"Sometimes people are impressed."

"I'm sure some people are. I'm sorry you won't get a C in this course, Mr. Larrimer. I am particularly sorry if it causes you trouble with the Draft Board."

"Oh, I don't have to worry about that. I'm 4F for toes."

"What?"

"I've got six toes on each foot. The military worries they'll be a problem in marching."

"You have six toes?"

"Yes."

"On each foot?"

"Yes."

"Let's see them."

"Are you serious?"

He was. As it turned out, Professor Welliver also had six toes, though only on his right foot, a fact that made Shane feel just slightly superior, though he was careful not to show it. Welliver, though, was absolutely webbed. He actually had webbing between each toe. He seemed extremely proud of this, though Shane couldn't figure out why. He'd always vehemently denied any webbing. Welliver seemed ecstatic to find a connection of some sort. He'd taken Shane out for a beer right then and he'd talked for hours about the noble history of six-toed people. He'd actually given Shane a B instead of a C and had also booked a fishing trip with him for the summer. He had booked a trip each year since then as well and each year he and Shane drank a toast to Shane's college degree and to six-toed people.

Shane graduated number 1004 out of a class of 1006 with a Grade Point Average of 2.00134. On the day of his graduation he owned three pickup trucks, four trailers, two drift boats, three white water rafts, two wall tents and camping equipment for 12 people. Within days of graduation, he incorporated his business as Mountain Outfitters.

Chapter 5

By the time Shane graduated, Misty and Jared were married and spending his 30 days of annual leave together in anticipation of his departure for Vietnam. Now, as she approached the parking lot of the hospital so many years later, Misty yearned for those days again. They'd driven all over the Northeast, camping and exploring and loving each other as though each day would be their last. In a way, she knew, they had been.

Jared had been amazing in those days. He had been transformed by Marine training. Always confident, it was now impossible to look at him without realizing his willingness to confront a problem, any problem, and take care of it.

Many times, lying in their zipped-together sleeping bags she and Jared had talked about his coming departure. She was consumed by fear of what might happen. He was as confident as he'd been before any high school football game.

"Isn't there any way you could put it off for a while?" she'd asked, lying in a tent in the Adirondacks.

"Why would I do that? I've been looking forward to going for years. Besides, I'm trained for it now. I'm ready." He held her close and looked into her eyes. "I'm good at this, and I'm going to get better. Nothing's going to happen to me. I'm going to come back in 13 months and we are going to start having babies, lots of them."

In that moment, Misty had believed him totally. Had believed that he could come back from Vietnam unscratched by force of will alone. From that day forward, Misty had believed in his invulnerability. When the call came, she'd almost gone into shock. How could Jared—invincible, indomitable Jared—have been so badly wounded? But after she recovered from that initial feeling, she became enraged. Not at the Vietnamese who'd done it, or at the United States Government, who put him in position to be hurt. Misty had been angry beyond all explanation with Jared. He had joined the Marine Corps, virtually guaranteeing a visit to Vietnam. What was wrong with the Navy, the Air Force, the Coast Guard? He'd become an infantryman, a grunt, and had volunteered for immediate duty overseas. He'd made no attempt to delay his departure. He'd made noises about wanting a family but he'd refused to let her get pregnant before he left.

"How could I let you go through an entire pregnancy without me?" he'd said. As though he'd cared. He hadn't cared.

If he'd cared he would have chosen me over the goddamned Marine Corps! If he'd cared we could have gone to Canada. It would have been better than this! Anything would have been better than this!

The information she received over the phone and by mail was so clinical and so frightening it was impossible to absorb. Even her training as a nurse didn't help. She couldn't come to grips with what this meant. "Loss of both gonads. Penis badly damaged and surgically repaired." Surgically repaired. Oh, Jesus. What did that mean?

After she'd gotten over her anger at Jared, she'd decided to learn as much as she could about the challenges he was likely to face. She didn't have a lot of time.

For the next few days, she immersed herself in the literature. There was no good news. Loss of his gonads meant loss of sperm. No future chance for children. It also meant the loss of the body's ability to manufacture testosterone. And that, she thought to herself, is what makes Jared who he is. Gonads, she read, are occasionally surgically removed from men with prostate cancer. The elimination of testosterone drastically reduces the chances of relapse. Men who have experienced the operation commonly develop heavier breasts and higher voices. They can experience wide mood swings and extensive bouts of depression.

They had medevacked Jared to a hospital in Hawaii but he only stayed there for a few days before they moved him to Balboa Naval Hospital in San Diego. She and his parents met him there. Shane called and asked to accompany them but she said no. There would be time enough for the two old friends to get together, she told him. For now, the important thing was letting Jared get stabilized. That was 16 years ago, she thought to herself, and we still haven't gotten Jared stabilized.

When she first saw him at Balboa, Misty was amazed at how good he looked and how upbeat he seemed. Lying there in the hospital, Jared was friendly, funny and outgoing. He introduced his visitors to the men in the room with him, all of whom had more debilitating, or at least more visible wounds than his own. During the two hours they stayed during their first visit, Jared was as much a Master of Ceremonies as he was a patient. With jokes, quips and stories he kept the audience spellbound, especially because his stories were invariably about others. He reveled in the opportunity to get one of the young enlisted men to tell about themselves. Jared was clearly a celebrity in his ward, and Misty could tell the young men all looked up to him.

All three of them were excited about Jared's appearance and obvious positive attitude, but a visit with the doctor later that afternoon dampened their enthusiasm.

"You folks need to realize that Jared is facing a long, uphill struggle," he said. "He is dealing with one of the worst injuries a man can face. Physically and mentally, he's really up against it."

He was not impressed when Jared's mother told him about her son's high-spirited activities on the ward earlier that day.

"We see that a lot, Mrs. McCauley, especially among the officers and NCOs. They won't admit fear or pain or depression in front of junior troopers. And he'd be even less likely to show weakness in front of his parents and his wife—not now, not when he's more vulnerable than he's ever been before. Later on he will. He'll have to, and once his defenses are down, then your difficulties will begin in earnest.

"This injury more than any other," he looked directly at Misty as he spoke, "wounds other people as well as the man who was hurt. His lack of future sexual function, his inability to father children, will be a burden for both of you in the coming years."

"But Jared is strong and tough…" Misty began.

The doctor interrupted. "And it's exactly those qualities that will make him most vulnerable. He, and probably you as well, will need counseling for the foreseeable future. There's no reason the two of you can't get through this. After all, good sex doesn't necessarily involve an erect penis…" Jared's mother gasped but the doctor ignored her. "You will need to be sexually creative and understanding, but you'll need to be demanding as well. Men with injuries like this frequently become despondent and reclusive underachievers. You'll need to be ready to push him when he needs it."

Simon McCauley had flinched imperceptibly when the doctor first referred to Jared's sexual function, but he'd covered it quickly. He would deal with this new unpleasant reality. His left hand gripped his wife's elbow, transmitting his own force of will to her. He now spoke for the first time. "Jared could never be like that. You've seen him. You know what he's like."

"I know what he's like right now, Mr. McCauley, propped up by the young men around him and the presence of his family. Don't get me wrong, his inner strength is obvious; a lot of men would have gone to pieces already. But you need to understand that Jared will also be dealing with hormonal imbalances in the future that we don't completely understand. Nor do we have the ability to replace them with any degree of exactitude. Hormones, especially testosterone, affect men in many different ways. It's impossible to predict all of the impacts, but I'm sure there will be many."

Misty often wished she could have spoken more with that doctor during the intervening years. His frank, open explanations and warnings, brutal as they had seemed at the time, had done more to prepare her for the future than anything else. But even he wasn't enough, she thought bemusedly, as she turned into the hospital parking lot. Even he couldn't have told her all they would face.

She flashed her identity card and the automatic gate opened into the hospital's new multi-story parking lot. Misty found the monolithic gray, concrete structure forbidding and ugly but she was also quick to remind herself how much better it was than the old, unlighted lot she'd used for years before its construction. Now, in the relative safety and comfort of the Big Ugly, she felt free to let her mind wander back to Jared's time in the Balboa Naval Hospital.

During the days that followed her initial reuniting with Jared, the doctor's cautions receded from her conscious thoughts as Jared continued to show his old strength and fire. His mother was overjoyed and Misty felt like a terrible burden had been lifted from her shoulders. She'd not yet really begun to contemplate what Jared's injury meant to her, as a person, a woman, a wife. *First things first*, she told herself. *I need to make sure Jared's OK. Then I can deal with the rest.*

And all indications were that Jared was, indeed, OK. He seemed pleased to see them and he kept up a steady, happy, positive chatter, while they were with him. Only once did his solidity seem to falter, when a Marine Lieutenant Colonel Ames came by the ward to present him with a Purple Heart. He was erect and formal in his dress green uniform. Five rows of medals established, Jared later told her, his own bona fides. He'd been where the action was.

"It's nothing big, Mom," Jared said when his mother began to sniff. "I know plenty of guys who got these for hangnails and insect bites."

"Maybe so, Lieutenant," Lt.Col Ames interrupted. "But yours was awarded for wounds as a result of enemy action. You have a right to be proud of your sacrifice for your country."

Jared looked shocked, then amused and ultimately, simply exhausted. He lowered his voice so his family couldn't hear.

"Please forgive me, Colonel, if I find it hard to be proud of sacrificing my nuts."

"I understand, son," Ames said, in a softer tone, a voice that carried with it the sadness of too many wounds and deaths seen, too many medals delivered. "But I've heard you've been recommended for the Navy Cross, as well, for your heroism on the day before you were wounded." He turned to Jared's parents and Misty. "The Navy Cross is our nation's second-highest award." He looked for several seconds at Simon, reading the signs. He nodded, as though to himself. "Where did you serve, sir?"

Simon hesitated for a moment, then said, "Iwo, the Canal."

"You know what a Navy Cross means, then?"

"Yes, I know, Colonel." Then, "But you know what? We were plenty proud of him before."

A month later, Jared flew into Boise to begin his recuperation at his parents' home. Although Misty would have preferred to have been alone with Jared, they had no place of their own. She'd stayed with her folks while Jared was in Vietnam.

Jared's wounds were still painful but he was up and around enough to take care of himself. Physically, he was getting stronger and more capable each day. Mentally and emotionally, he was going backwards fast. He refused, from his first day home, to see anyone at all, even Shane. This was a decision Shane didn't take lightly. He called once every day or two, asking to speak to Jared, asking permission to visit.

"Just tell him to stop calling, Misty!" Jared had exploded after the fifth or sixth time Misty told him of Shane's requests. Tell him I'll call him when I'm ready to talk. And tell your friends the same thing, Mom. I'm not ready to see anyone yet."

And he didn't. Jared retreated into his shell as soon as he'd returned home and it was months before he made any real attempt to communicate with anyone. To Misty's intense disappointment, it was not to her he reached out, but to his father.

Simon McCauley had seen many wounds. He himself still carried shrapnel in his buttock, scars from a bullet wound in his shoulder and a bayonet wound in his back. He knew the doctor was right about Jared's future difficulties. He was also a realist, and quickly forced himself to come to grips with what the future held. A son who had been permanently and terribly damaged, no possibility of grandchildren—ever. Jared was their only son. The McCauley name would stop. The thought made him cringe with pain, but more than anything else, with guilt. With all he knew, with all he had done, how could he have let his son go to war, especially a pissant little war like Vietnam?

Simon had seen so much death on the Pacific Islands. The blood had drowned out all his young man's beliefs, all his patriotism, all his idealism, his enthusiasm, his ambition. He'd come back a broken husk of a man who needed all his strength just to get out of bed in the morning. He'd drifted up to Grangeville in the months following the war and lucked into a job at the saw mill. There, in the noise and commotion of the mill, he was able to forget, at least while he was working, the fear-crazed nightmare of war in the Pacific Islands.

He rarely talked about his wartime experiences. Even when Jared became interested in the Marines and began asking detailed questions, Simon had avoided specific answers. He'd been afraid to make his experience sound exciting. When it became obvious Jared was preparing to sign up, Simon was torn between pride and fear.

Once, he'd come close to telling Jared what war is really like, the hopeless panic when the enemy artillery finds you, ears ringing, pissing your pants as you try to dig in under what is left of Joey Drakas, using his poor, pathetic carcass to protect you, careless of his blood and leaking bowels in the hope he will shield you from the shrapnel. Then the artillery ends and the Japs come screaming and you kill first with your rifle and then with your bayonet and when it sticks in a Japanese backbone and the rifle is torn from your grasp you pick up weapons from your dead friends and kill with them. And it all is a blur except for the one Jap who isn't quite dead. And never really dies, because he keeps coming back to you in dreams and you have to kill him over and over again. When the battle is over you are so tired you can hardly breathe but every breath you do take is drenched with blood and piss and shit.

That's what he should have told his son, Simon thought, the truth about war is the smell of blood, piss and shit, yours and everyone else's. But he hadn't and now his son knew a different but equally valid truth… the truth of a wound that will never end, and will be in his thoughts every day for the rest of his life. Each time he sees a small child, each time he notices a good-looking woman he will be reminded of his loss.

After he arrived in Grangeville after the war, Simon worked for two years at the mill, pulling green chain. During that time, he never went out at night, never got together with his co-workers. On his days off Simon tried to get overtime, or if it was unavailable, he'd offer to take someone else's shift. When he was working, when his mind was occupied, the Japanese soldier could be held at bay. When there was no work to be had he would sit in his room. But gradually, the noise of the trucks, forklifts, the chain, the lumber slamming through the line took the place of artillery and machine guns and screams. And the smell of fir and pine and cedar and diesel gradually supplanted the visceral smells of war. Simon woke up one Sunday and realized he'd slept through the night, something he hadn't done since the Island campaign. He wasn't sure, but he thought he might be getting better. He almost smiled when he saw the sunshine.

As a celebration, Simon decided to see a movie. The only movie theater in Grangeville was showing Red River. Simon didn't like the movie and he didn't like sitting in a dark room with a lot of noisy, smelly people. He probably would have spent the rest of his life working had he not been hit by a car while walking back to the boarding house—and had the car's driver not been a beautiful red-headed wisp of a girl named Sarah O'Leary.

He never lost consciousness; he was aware of every crack, bump, crunch and slide and he was talking as soon as the weeping driver got to him.

"Oh, my God!" Sarah wailed. "I'm so sorry. I didn't see you. Oh, my God! Oh, please forgive me."

"Not your fault," he whispered through the pain. "Not your fault."

One of Simon's most vivid post-war memories was of Sarah's tear-stained face looking down on him as he lay on the road, her guilt and agony overwhelming even his own physical pain. He used his right arm, the one that still worked, to pat her shoulder gently.

"It's OK," he whispered. "It's all right." Then Simon's world faded softly into a gray haze, in which he was only aware of the soft hand squeezing his own.

When he woke in a hospital bed, Sarah was sitting by his side. And she stayed there, with minor absences, for the rest of Simon's time in the hospital. After a couple more efforts to ease her mind, Simon stopped trying to make Sarah feel better, realizing the best thing he could do for her was to get healthy. This took a little doing, as his injuries were severe. His left leg was broken, as were his left arm and several ribs on his left side. There was some internal bruising but after a few days of pissing blood that seemed to clear up. He made an effort each day to tell her how much better he was and the way her smile brightened had him lying to her on a regular basis.

The most damaging injuries, as far as Simon was concerned, were the ugly scrapes and cuts on his face received as he skidded across the street. The raw, bloody flesh reminded him of things he'd worked hard to forget. Even worse, when they changed his bandages, the wounds made him look grotesque, ugly. The look shocked him, almost as much as the realization he cared about his appearance. He hadn't thought about his own looks for several years.

"Can't we leave the bandages on for awhile?" he'd asked, when, three days after the accident, the doctor told the nurse to remove them for good.

"No, son. We need to get those scrapes exposed to the air and scabbed up. Chances are you won't have any scarring at all."

"But Doc, the girl…"

"You think those scrapes will scare her off…is that it?"

Simon nodded silently.

"Well, young man, evidently you don't know Sarah O'Leary very well. She doesn't scare. None of the O'Leary's scare. Her father runs a logging business and half the time Sarah sets chokers for him. She's seen plenty of people banged up in the woods and chances are she wouldn't have blinked at your injuries if she hadn't been the one to cause them. Her father, Dan, is my hunting partner and good friend. He and Sarah are downstairs right now making arrangements to pay your bill and move you to their house for your rehab."

"They can't do that! I don't want to…" Simon's words trailed off as he considered his situation.

"Good," the doctor chuckled. "I like a man who considers all his options." He treated Simon's scrapes and cuts, then gave him a few, last-minute directions.

"Stay off the leg completely for a few more days. After that, use only crutches whenever you move around. Don't worry much about your ribs. If you're taking care of the leg, your ribs will be fine. Besides, they'll tell you when they don't like what you're doing."

A few minutes later Sarah walked in, followed by a man she introduced as her father, Dan O'Leary. O'Leary was not tall, maybe 5 feet 8 inches with graying hair, a receding hairline and a slight paunch. It would have been easy to overlook him in a crowd…until he spoke. O'Leary's voice sounded like it was reverberating from inside a bass drum.

"Well," he rumbled, "We always knew Sarah would be breaking young men's hearts. We just hadn't planned on her breaking bones as well. You look a little rocky, young Simon."

Sarah pursed her lips and shook her head, shot her father a look he blissfully ignored. Simon laughed for the first time, he suddenly realized, in many months.

"Thank you, Sir. I feel pretty good, too."

"I bet," Dan said. "Well, we've come to take you home with us. Now, no argument and no complaining. We pay our debts."

And so Simon had gone with them. He'd been welcomed into the family and absorbed into the culture. Sarah sat with him whenever she could. Now that he was obviously mending, Sarah stopped the guilt-ridden apologies and began to return to her natural personality, which was a lot less uncertain and a lot feistier. Simon found he liked the real Sarah more than the apologetic Sarah and their friendship grew rapidly. His face scabbed and healed with little scarring, and gradually he felt less and less self-conscious.

Meanwhile, there was simply no time to feel sorry for himself. No time even to think of the Japanese soldier. When he wasn't spending time with Sarah, her mother gave him jobs to do. Snapping beans, peeling potatoes. As he became more mobile, Simon began sharpening saws and mending leather chaps and doing other light maintenance work for Dan's business. Simon, who had grown up with a sullen, itinerant farmhand father, was initially ill at ease in Sarah's big, loud, raucous family, but gradually he became more comfortable and began taking part in the good-natured bickering which was as natural and constant to the O'Leary's as the breeze across their mountain home. It was obvious to Simon that Dan was the architect of this banter and though his tongue could be sharp as well as funny, Simon grew to like the family patriarch more and more as time went on. For his part, Dan O'Leary thought

Simon McCauley was the best thing that could have happened to his family. Quiet and almost withdrawn when he came, Simon still possessed an inner strength that drew people to him. Sarah was obviously falling in love with him and the rest of the family treated him like a long-lost brother already. Only one thing bothered him, and in typical O'Leary fashion, Dan confronted it head on.

Dan arranged to take Simon in for a final doctor's appointment. This was a little more difficult than he'd anticipated because Sarah wanted to go, but he asked his wife to request Sarah's help at home. After the appointment he'd taken Simon to the tavern for a beer.

"I'd like you to come to work for me," he said after the beers arrived.

Simon looked at him. "I'm not sure that would be a good idea. I may have designs on your daughter."

O'Leary's gray eyes twinkled and his voice boomed even louder than normal. "By God, I should hope so because Sarah certainly has designs on you." He became serious and lowered his voice.

"Simon, I missed both wars. I don't know what you've gone through or what you still carry with you. But I've known people like you who've had a lot of trouble when they came back. I don't want to pry, but before I give you a job or my daughter, I'd like to know more about you. What can you tell me?"

Simon knew he owed it to the man to tell him something but he was determined to keep it to the basics. So he began to talk, at first about his childhood, hazy memories of his long-dead mother, following the harvest with his father from southern California to Washington. But then, when he started talking about his time in the service he seemed unable to stop. With O'Leary's cool gray eyes showing compassion but no pity, nodding occasionally without comment, Simon found himself telling more than he wanted. He shared the fear, the rage, the panic, the hatred, even the sense of emptiness and loss. Finally, when he thought it was over, Simon even blurted out the story of the Japanese soldier and the ugly, venal way he'd died. He was talking fast now, trying to get it out. When he was done, Simon was sobbing quietly. The bartender was staying on the other side of the big room, pointedly staying out of hearing. Dan motioned to the bartender for two more beers, then sat quietly until their order arrived and the bartender departed.

"Son, nobody could blame you for what you did over there."

Simon looked up with bloodshot eyes. "I don't care what other people think," he said quietly. "It's me that did it. It's me that's got to live with it."

Dan sat quietly for several minutes more. "Are you ashamed of what you did?" he asked.

Simon took a long drink and stared for several seconds into his beer.

"Damn straight. Shame is the focal point of my entire life," he said. "I don't care about all the rest of them. It was war and we were all trying to kill each other, but that one soldier ... he cut me and what with the pain and all the killing I went after him in a way I never did before. I hurt him and I took pleasure in it and I kept hurting him until he died."

Simon looked up and his eyes were dripping with need. "What kind of man would do such a thing?"

Dan shook his head. "I don't know what to tell you, Simon. I suspect that any man would do something like that if the fear and danger and pain are all bad enough. I can tell you this, though I'm not sure if it's what you are asking. I think you are a good man. I think you'd be good for my Sarah."

Simon was silent.

O'Leary looked away and then back again. "What you need is a mint, young Simon."

Simon looked at him quizzically.

"Yup. You need a mint. A mint will put your troubles in perspective. A mint will help you forgive yourself." He pulled a roll of multi-colored mint candies from his shirt pocket, loosened one from the top and held it out to Simon.

"So, this will help, huh?" asked Simon, smiling. "They seem like awful little pills to take care of a big problem."

"Don't you believe it. My mother used to give me one whenever I'd done something I regretted, which was pretty often. I have a bit of a temper, you see."

Simon smiled. Dan's modus operandi was best described by his wife as *Ready-Fire-Aim*.

Simon put the mint in his mouth. "It's good. What are they called?"

"That one you have is the best flavor. It's called a tone mint."

"A tone mint, huh? Clever. Atonement. Isn't that something God has to grant you? Don't I have to do something to make up for the wrong I've done? I'm not religious. I don't think it will take."

"We're not religious, either, my family and me. Well, maybe we are but we don't take our religion through the church any more. Here's what I think: God will forgive you if you forgive yourself. In fact, they are probably the same thing. If you can forgive yourself, it means God has already forgiven you. Eat the mint, son. Don't worry about the bad things you've done. Think about all the good things you can do for the rest of your life. Eat the mint."

Simon turned a corner after that day in the bar with Dan O'Leary and he got better as time passed. When he recovered from the collision, Simon went to work full time for O'Leary. He became a gifted and dependable timber faller but long before that day he married Sarah. Their first child was stillborn and the second miscarried. Two years later, Jared Michael McCauley was born, a boy who absorbed all the love, hopes and dreams of the O'Leary's and the McCauley families and then carried them on his strong shoulders until a poorly thrown grenade clipped a tree branch.

Jared had been home from the hospital for a month when he first approached his father. He came into the shop where Simon sat resizing cartridge cases for his .257 Roberts. Simon was overjoyed to see his son enter the room but he showed no reaction as Jared took a seat in the chair where he'd spent hundreds of happy hours helping his father load rifle, pistol and shotgun rounds. Neither man said anything at first. After a couple of minutes Jared began to wipe lubricant from the cases. A few minutes later Simon broke the silence.

"How you feeling?"

"Fine. A little sore, but I can move around easier than before."

"The doctor said you'd get better fast once you start walking around."

"Yeah. I'm getting better."

Both men felt the tension straining between them like a tightly drawn barbed-wire fence. No communication was possible across that fence. Simon could feel another opportunity slipping away. Finally, in desperation, he simply began talking about his own experiences in World War II. For the second time in his life he told the story of his enlistment, training and time on the troop ships and his island landings. The story he told his son was the same as he'd told to Dan O'Leary 30 years before but this time it was just a story and not a cathartic explosion of emotional pus. He told it as objectively as he could, he talked of the fear and of the friends he'd lost. He didn't talk about the Japanese soldier he'd tortured. Simon talked for almost an hour and when he was done Jared knew more about his father's military experience than ever before. For the first time since he'd left the hospital Jared felt as though he was in the presence of someone who could understand some of what he was going through.

"Why didn't you ever tell me any of this before?" Jared asked.

Simon hesitated. He fiddled idly with the shells they'd loaded. "I didn't want you to think war was something glorious. Little boys always want to know how many people you killed and how it happened and I didn't want to go through that with you. The other thing is…and I've never told this to anyone else in the world except your Grampa O'Leary…I did something during the war I'm very ashamed of. And I just couldn't keep thinking about it." He inspected the last cartridge carefully—and then inspected it again. Jared remained silent. Simon didn't want to go any further. He didn't want to talk about himself at all. I should be talking about Jared, about his troubles, not mine. But he knew, without understanding how, that helping Jared meant being able to talk with him and somehow, this conversation was the key to being able to do so. He sighed deeply and rolled the .257 cartridge between his thumb and fingers. He looked up at his son, who sat patiently.

"I killed a lot of people over there, Jared. Not that I was particularly good at it, there were just so many of them and they were so close. At one point on Guadalcanal, my company was attacked by a Jap battalion. We chopped them up—they just kept screaming and running into our guns. But after a while they got through our lines and then it was hand to hand. We were almost out of ammunition and we couldn't take time to reload anyway. After everything was over, one of the not-quite dead ones reached up and stabbed me in the back. I don't know how to explain it, but that bayonet hurt! I'd already been shot once and had a couple dings from the artillery barrage that came before the attack, so it's not like I hadn't already experienced some pain. Maybe it was because I'd let down my guard, or maybe because he stabbed me from behind. I don't know. At any rate, I went berserk and took the bayonet away from him and killed him with it but I did it in a way that he stayed alive a long time and went through a lot of unnecessary pain. I was cruel, Jared. I was cruel as a man can be. It's been more than 40 years and it took me most of that time to make my peace with what I did. Just talking about the war made me think about my shame, so I didn't want to talk about it much, especially with my son. Sorry."

Simon looked into his son's eyes and saw sympathy. "I understand, Dad. I've seen people do similar things, and with less provocation."

"What did you do about it? Did you do anything?"

"Yes, I stopped them."

"How? I don't think anyone could have stopped me in the rage I was in."

"I killed the man they were working on. Put him out of his misery."

Simon nodded. "Yes, that was good." He shook his head. "War does things to us—makes us do things. We can never be the same." He took a roll of mints from his pocket, took two from the top and offered one to his son.

"Here, have a tone mint."

"No thanks, I…ha! A tone mint, huh? I've never heard that name before and you've been eating those things for as long as I can remember. Funny you never told me about them before."

"I kind of hoped you'd never need to know."

"Well, you were right, at least so far. I've never done anything I felt I needed to atone for. Just a few things I wish I could have done differently. I sure wish I could have been just a few feet one side or the other from that grenade."

"God! Me too. Jared, I'm so sorry for what's happened to you. I truly am. I'd give anything to make it not be so."

"I know, Dad. It's all right."

No, it's not all right and I won't pretend it is. "It's the end of a dream, son. Not the first and not the last. But it's not the end of your life. You can still accomplish great things. You can still leave a wonderful legacy. As bad as your injury is, I'd rather you be hurt that way than do what I did and have your life stained with shame."

Jared stiffened. His face became red and his jaw grew tight.

"You would, would you? You'd rather me get my nuts cut off and my dick severed than have me deal with a few regrets? Well, I've got news for you. I'd rather have the regrets. Give me your regrets! Give me your guilt! I can take the damn guilt! Shit! If it would make me whole again I'd cut those fucking dinks into thin strips with a goddamn butter knife! Jesus Fucking Christ, Dad! How can you say that? How can you even think that? Don't you have any idea what this injury means? What I'm going through? What I'll never have? Give me the guilt! Jesus Christ, Dad!"

Jared got to his feet and walked out the workshop door without so much as a look at his father.

Simon's shoulders sagged. He put his face in his hands. Jared didn't set foot in the workshop again in the six remaining months he and Misty stayed with his parents. Nor did he have another meaningful conversation with his father.

Chapter 6

Misty went through the hospital doors, waved to the receptionist and headed for the elevator. For some reason, just going through the doors gave Misty a feeling of well-being, of belonging. She'd wanted to be a nurse since high school and she'd always been glad of her decision. She'd watched the nurses work in St. Luke's Hospital in Boise when her father had gone there for back surgery and she'd known right away she wanted to be one of them. They were friendly and efficient, helpful and just plain competent. Misty remembered wondering if she could ever be as sure of herself as those nurses were. She knew she was smart but her good grades came from good study habits and slow, careful reflection. She was not a quick thinker and she knew it.

Jared and Shane had laughed at her uncertainty during a conversation shortly after they'd graduated from high school. Jared was worse, of course. "You must be kidding, Misty. You'll be a great nurse. Your biggest problem's going to be the guys trying to grab you. I think you'll need to be one of those nurses who only work with women. Women patients, women doctors. Then I won't worry."

"You won't have to worry anyway, Jared," Shane laughed. "Just make sure Misty carries her grocery separator. No one will stand a chance."

"You both should be glad I don't have one right now," Misty growled. "This is serious. I'm not good at making split-second decisions. And nurses have to."

Shane looked thoughtful. "You do fine when you're driving, don't you?"

Misty blinked. "Well, yes, if you don't count that time I backed into the power pole in the Safeway parking lot."

"Oh, that doesn't count," Shane said. "I'm talking about the kind of split-second decisions you have to make every minute or two when you are driving at 40 or 50 or 60 miles per hour. It seems to me that driving a car is a pretty good example of what you can do with proper training. You wouldn't be able to make those decisions if you hadn't had driver's ed and time behind the wheel. So, once you get through nursing school and have a little experience, you'll be as good a nurse as you are a driver."

It made sense to Misty, and for the first time she began to feel reasonably confident of her professional future. Then Jared waded in to put things in his own unique perspective.

"That's good, Shane. And here's another way of looking at it, Misty. You might consider it a mathematic proof. There are lots of other people who have become nurses, Misty. You are at least as smart and capable as they are. Therefore, you can be a nurse, too. How's that?"

Misty laughed, but between Shane's thoughtful analysis and Jared's simplistic view of the world, she now had two real reasons to think she could, in fact, become a nurse.

As she thought back to that day, Misty was struck yet again by Jared's absolute confidence in himself, and by extension, in her. Of course, all that had changed after he'd been wounded. He'd stayed in bed for weeks after he returned home to Grangeville and even after he'd begun walking around, Jared was tentative and slow. He lost muscle tone and began putting on weight. He generally spurned conversations, especially after the disastrous talk with his father, and when he did talk, his voice was slow, and unsteady, his thoughts distracted.

As time went on, Jared's body seemed to mend but his confidence did not. Even now, so many years after he'd been hurt, Jared seemed to Misty to be unsure about things that would never have caused a moment's hesitation in the past. He was still a charismatic, likeable man, Misty knew, perhaps even more likeable than when he'd had such overarching confidence, but Misty missed the power that seemed to emanate from him in those days. Jared had quietly become a successful real estate agent. People who worked with him once trusted him, and recommended him to others. In addition, a couple of the men Jared had served with in Vietnam had become well known businessmen near the Beltway. They made it a point to push business his way.

Misty signed in and headed up to the recovery ward. She spent 10 minutes reviewing the charts and then began her rounds. It was a slow day, with only four patients in the rooms surrounding their central desk. With three nurses on board, the workload promised to be light. The three friends decided to split the patients between two of them and let the third work on restocking equipment and supplies. Misty took the two patients on the east side of the counter. The first was Marvin Milligrew, a 52-year-old widower recovering from gall bladder surgery. Marvin was in good spirits and doing well. He expected to be discharged the next day. He and his kids were laughing and joking when Misty came in and had her laughing by the time she left.

Her next patient was a 38-year-old man, Tony Corrarino. He'd come in two days earlier with a high fever and intense pain in his side. His problem had been diagnosed as a ruptured appendix and he'd been sent for surgery. The surgery had been successful, but poisons released by the ruptured appendix had caused a serious infection. He'd been battling it with the help of massive doses of antibiotics until this morning, when he'd been released from the Intensive Care Unit to recover in Misty's ward.

"Hi, Mr. Corrarino. My name's Misty. I'm going to be taking care of you tonight. How are you feeling?"

Corrarino turned his head and opened his eyes. Obviously Italian, Misty noted, and he looked flushed and feverish. She took his temperature. It was 102 degrees.

"Feel pretty warm, Mr. Corrarino? She smiled at his answering nod, then excused herself. "I'll be right back."

She went out to the nurse's station and paged Dr. Warner, Corrarino's physician. When he came on the line, Misty asked if perhaps Corrarino should be kept in the ICU until his fever was a little more under control.

ICU was overwhelmed, Warner explained, and Corrarino's fever was on the way down. "Just give him a little extra attention, Misty," Warner said. "His fever should drop by morning and he'll be out of here in a couple-three days."

The first few hours went by quickly. Misty brought all the paperwork up to date and had no trouble keeping up with the patients. Mr. Milligrew went to sleep at 8:30, just after the end of visiting hours, and slept clear through to the end of her shift. He barely woke up when she checked his temperature and blood pressure and gave him his aspirin.

Corrarino was a different situation entirely. Although the antibiotics seemed to be slowly working on the infection, the fever hung on tenaciously. His sleep was fitful and restless. When he did wake up, he was groggy and a little confused. When Misty went in to check on him about 9 p.m., Corrarino was still tossing and turning, obviously uncomfortable. Misty checked his temp and pressure, adjusted his IV and leaned over to wake him for his pills. For the first time, she noticed a large discolored area on the back of his neck. Looking closer, she realized it was a terrible burned area that extended down from his hairline along his neck. The burn was alternately pink and brown with spots of black speckled into it. It looked to Misty as though someone had sprinkled dirt into it while the wound was still raw and then allowed it to heal. Surely this burn was not treated by medical people.

Corrarino turned his head in his sleep, obscuring her view of his neck.

"Mr. Corrarino? It's time for your p…"

Corrarino's eyes came wide open at the same time he grabbed both her upper arms, hard, pinning them to her sides.

"I'm sorry," he hissed. "I'm so sorry. "I didn't want to!"

"Mr. Corrarino—Tony! Let me go!" She tried to twist away but Corrarino was pulling her forward, pulling her off balance, and she couldn't develop the leverage to pull away. Misty was frightened and nearly screamed for help but the more she looked at Corrarino the less worried she became. He seemed delirious but not truly dangerous. His eyes, wide and red-rimmed, were infinitely sad, but without anger. Misty stood still and stopped trying to escape.

"It's all right," she said softly.

"I would have died," he said. "I had no choice. I…" He began to cry, softly at first—a gentle blubbering—but it soon progressed to deep racking sobs that shook his entire body and Misty's as well.

"It's all right," Misty said. "I understand." She didn't, of course. Nowhere close, but it didn't seem important. She stood there for several minutes, bending her right arm at the elbow just under his hands, to stroke his head, trying to get him to relax. It was a long time before she realized his hands had fallen away and he no longer held her arms. When he'd finally lain back on the bed, Misty called the attending physician. The doctor prescribed a sedative and Corrarino soon went into a deep sleep.

Shortly afterwards, Misty had been reassigned to help out with the neo-natal unit, so it wasn't until she was on her way home that night that Misty had a chance to reflect on the evening's events. Like most nurses, she'd been around many patients who were distraught and even hysterical, but this was the first time a patient had ever laid hands on her. She'd been scared but she'd settled down and gotten through it pretty well. She felt good about her response. After an initial rush of fear, she had evaluated the situation and defused it. She'd come a long way from the teenager who'd attacked the obnoxious elk hunter with a food divider. Wouldn't Jared and Shane get a chuckle out of this one? No, she realized. They probably wouldn't, at least Jared wouldn't. But she didn't want to talk to Jared about Tony Corrarino. She wasn't sure why, but she suspected it had something to do with Corrarino's deep brown eyes. Sorrowful, pain-filled eyes aching for forgiveness. But forgiveness for what? A dozen different scenarios went through her mind about Corrarino. He was a mafia killer forced by the Godfather to kill someone or be killed himself. He was an innocent man caught by accident in a gang war and forced to protect himself. He was a raving, paranoid lunatic who talked to ghosts. Misty smiled as she thought of the way she'd allowed her imagination to run wild. Had she known how close to the truth her guesses were, it's safe to say Misty would not have smiled at all.

Chapter 7

Tony Corrarino was, in fact, a member of a crime family, though by blood and not choice. His father, Salvatore Corrarino, a respected and ambitious mob lieutenant in New York while Tony was growing up, had progressed to become the boss. Sal was a second-generation Sicilian who had broken the hearts of his own immigrant parents when he'd gravitated toward the band of hoodlums whose greatest goal was to be accepted into the Family. He'd begun by doing odd jobs, running numbers, then picking up receipts for the regular shakedown routines, graduating in time to enforcement. Slight, good looking and well spoken, Sal Corrarino was not the typical gangster thug and his bosses worried at first if he had the ability to instill the necessary fear into people… and if he could, if necessary, follow up his threats with violence.

"Here's what I want to know, Sal," said Angelo Carmelo, his boss in those early days. "I want to know can you make their livers quiver?" He grinned savagely. "And if you need to, can you cut their livers out?"

Sal stared straight at Angelo and gave the response that would make him a legend in the New York City underworld.

"I can do both, Angelo. And if they piss me off I'll feed them their own livers while they're still breathing."

Years later a cynical old New York City cop described Sal's early career in this way. "It wasn't so much that Sal said it, though it certainly got people's attention. What scared everyone was when he actually started doing it."

During Sal's four years as an enforcer three people were found dead with gory evidence that parts of the livers had been forced into their mouths as they died. All three had fallen afoul of the Family in some fashion. One had infringed on Family territory with his drug sales, one was found to be a police informant and one had stolen part of the Family collections on his pickup rounds. The informant was a former classmate and friend of Salvatore Corrarino.

Very soon, collections ran more smoothly in the section of the city where Sal worked and his efficiency was noticed.

"You done good so far, kid," Angelo told him. "You got people's attention in a big way but it's time to take it easy. You lean as hard as you need to lean but no harder. If someone needs to get whacked you do it professional. No more of this cuttin' and pastin'. Got it?"

"I got it," Sal told him and two people were relieved. Sal because, although he liked the challenge and the excitement of killing, he disliked the knife work. He'd only done it because he'd recognized the need to stand out from the pretenders. He had big plans and he knew you didn't move up in this business without first making your bones in ways that people would remember.

"Friends are the second most important thing," he would occasionally say in his later years. "The first most important is fear. Fear is like grease. Just a little bit makes everything go smoother and faster." The recipients of this homily would invariably smile, nod and agree, worried that if they did not, good old Sal might well have them killed as they slept that night in their beds.

Angelo was relieved because he was terrified of Sal. An experienced killer in his own right, Angelo had never been so frightened of anyone as he was of the slender, 5-foot, 10-inch Corrarino, and with good reason. Sal intended to learn everything he could from the older man, then find a way to kill him and make his death look like an accident. Salvatore Corrarino was NOT waiting around for old timers to retire. As it turned out, Angelo didn't make it to retirement; he died of a massive heart attack, brought on in no little part by the extreme stress of working closely with Sal, of knowing he was in the younger man's sights.

Sal moved steadily up the Mafia ladder. As effective as he was at frightening (or killing) people when he wanted to, Sal was also personable and outgoing by nature. Women found him charming and he moved easily in polite society.

Over the years, Sal's reputation had become burnished with time. Most people knew he could be a hard man, but the liver incidents had passed into myth and few people still believed them. All the same, within the Family, an invitation to visit Salvatore Corrarino still made strong men shake and occasionally wet themselves.

His effect could be the same on his own biological family. His two sons responded, as children often do, in exactly opposite ways. Tony, his older son, struggled against his father's domination, and in his struggle, learned to distrust the things his father tried to teach him and hate the things his father believed in. Charley, a year younger than Tony, idolized his father, and believed in him implicitly. He absorbed his father's teachings and lived by them.

By the time the boys were in high school, Charley had already supplanted Tony as his father's favorite. Even more than Tony's continual rebellion, which Sal Corrarino could almost understand from his own youth, Sal hated the boy's obvious disgust for his own life's work, the Family. In Sal's mind, the Mafia was his business, a lifelong commitment he wanted to pass on to his sons. Tony would have none of it.

By the time the boys entered middle school, Sal had not been personally involved in violence for a number of years. He was by then a highly-regarded lieutenant in the organization. He'd been instrumental in the diversification of Family interests into legal businesses. Only occasionally did Sal actually come in contact with the seedy, criminal aspects of life that were the primary source of the Family's wealth. Prostitution, gambling, protection and drugs were hard to paint with a legitimate brush but once their proceeds had been run through the Family's car washes, restaurants, construction companies and garbage-hauling concerns, Sal felt like a pillar of the community.

Tony never saw it that way. He was ashamed of his father and made no real effort to hide it. Sal didn't know where Tony got the idea that his father was involved in a shameful business, and if he ever found out he planned to get back in the liver removal business.

"This is why I pay to send the boys to St. Mary's Catholic School, so they won't be subjected to that sort of crap," Sal complained to his wife on a regular basis. "How can he come home thinking his father is some sort of criminal?" At that point Sal had been indicted three times but never convicted.

Once they reached middle school, Sal began giving the boys little insights into his world. He often took them into the back room of Panetta's Restaurant that served as his office. He intended for this to be a reward, an exciting opportunity for the boys to see the way business was conducted in his world. He wanted them to see the way people deferred to him, asked his opinion, waited for him to sit down before they did, laughed when he laughed. He wanted the boys to understand he was a man of power, of respect. And he was successful in this endeavor, at least partially.

Tony was not surprised to see the way people treated his father at his office. He was just disgusted. Disgusted at the way they kissed his ass. Disgusted at the way they all wore the same kinds of clothes. Tony couldn't remember when he'd started hating the Mafia or the people in it. Maybe it was a television show or movie, maybe it was a chance remark from one of his teachers, though Tony doubted any of them would have been so stupid.

Who knows how we develop our feelings and beliefs? Tony Corrarino grew up in a loving, supportive family. He was well educated and trained from an early age to step into his father's business. And yet he wanted no part of it, was embarrassed by it and refused to be involved at all. Sal was heartsick at the widening chasm between himself and his oldest son, but he was powerless to do anything about it. And he was far too proud to make overtures he considered undignified.

"Don't try to force him, it will just push him away," his wife Maria said and Sal took her advice, backing off and allowing Tony his freedom. Occasionally, in those rare introspective moments when Sal came closest to being honest with himself, he wondered if Tony's rebellion was God's way of evening the score. He, Sal, had left an honest, hardworking family to join the Mafia. Now his own son had repudiated his father's criminal activity and was returning to the straight life. If he hadn't been so embarrassed and disappointed, Sal might have been proud of the boy.

Meanwhile, Charley stepped in to fill the vacuum left by his older brother's departure from his father's affections. Sal's invitations to Tony became less frequent, while Charley became more of a regular fixture at his father's office.

By his junior year in high school, Tony had created a life separate from his family, or to be more accurate, from his father. Maria stayed connected with Tony by attending parent-teacher conferences, school functions, athletic events. When Tony won the district cross country meet, his mother was the only family member in attendance. It was his mother who came to the school play to watch Tony say his seven lines. And it was Maria who took the call from an apologetic police sergeant who explained that Tony had been caught drunk at a party of underage high school students. When the sergeant offered to drive Tony home himself, Maria knew without being told that the man was on Sal's payroll. She told him no. Please put Tony in the drunk tank. She would be there in the morning. As Tony occasionally said later in his life, "I was raised by a single parent, just not the same one who raised my little brother."

Chapter 8

———⟨●⟩———

It was a strange arrangement, to be sure. Tony could have used a father's guidance but he wanted no part of his father, and his father gradually became resigned to their disconnection. Charley was desperately in need of a mother's touch and love, but was being absorbed into his father's world. Although she would never have confessed it to anyone and tried hard not to let it show, Maria didn't like her second son. During her introspective moments, which were far more frequent and honest than her husband's, Maria often admitted to herself that she was instinctively afraid of Charley. As a result, Charley was left drifting without the anchor a mother typically provides and drifted completely to his father's side.

Charley was a single year behind his brother but could not have been more different. Where Tony had his father's slight build on a taller frame, with a distinct grace in his movements, Charley was short and muscular. He tended to carry his head ahead of his shoulders, giving the impression of moving forward aggressively. While Tony was breezing through advanced classes in a pre-college curriculum, Charley was having trouble passing classes at a vocational level.

"Charley's smart, Mr. Corrarino, or maybe clever is a better word, but he shows absolutely no interest in his studies." This statement, consistently delivered by each of his teachers, was a terrible disappointment to Sal. He knew much of his own success resulted from his ability to speak intelligently with politicians, businessmen, intellectuals and artists.

He explained this to Charley time and again. The boy was invariably contrite and promised to do better in the future but when the future came around, it was the same old thing, poor grades.

On one occasion, during Charley's junior year, Sal lost his temper, an uncommon occurrence in their family.

"GODDAMMIT!" he bellowed. "You need an education. You think it's easy to get where I've gotten? It's not. You need to learn, you need to be smart."

"I am smart, Pop. I am. And I'm learning stuff, too. I'm learning at your office every day. I'm a big help down there. I'm learning the things I need to know to run your business."

"Hey, Smart Guy! You're not going to get a chance to run my business if you don't learn some things in school. I work with important people, people who make things happen. People like that don't sit down with a punk who can't even make it through high school. You have to have some education just to understand all the numbers and things they throw at you. You've got to speak their language if you want to be able to convince them to do what you want. You get what I'm saying? You get it?"

Charley bowed his head. "I got it, Pop. I'll do better. I promise."

But when he walked out of his father's office, Charley muttered to himself, "Convince them to do what I want, my ass. I can make them afraid NOT to do what I want."

Nonetheless, Sal's message hit home. Charley began to work harder on his studies. The vocational curriculum demanded little effort and he was soon caught up in classwork and on his way to graduating on time. As soon as he caught up on his high school work, Charley began taking night classes in business and attended every seminar he could find on entrepreneurship and intelligent investing.

One evening when Charley got back from class, Sal was still up, sitting in his black leather chair and drinking port.

"So, Charley. Where you going with these classes?" he asked.

"Don't know for sure, Dad" was the answer. "But like you told me before, making money is only one-half your problem. The other half is making your money seem legit and making it work for you. I think these classes will teach me how to make the money work without putting us at risk. They are giving me some ideas about new businesses and new ways of moving money around. Just fine tuning some of the things you started years ago."

Sal was impressed and pleased. Nothing either boy had ever done touched Sal so deeply. He responded by bringing Charley further into his confidence. By Charley's senior year in high school he was a trusted part of Sal's operation and the boy was ecstatic. In the comfortable surroundings of his father's office, Charley began to develop the kind of financial insight that would make him invaluable to the Family. He also began his first forays into extracurricular activities that would make him a pariah.

Charley was mesmerized by power. As a child, he had considered his father a God. Later on, in middle and high school, Charley realized Sal could do anything he wanted and nobody would say a word. Sal didn't talk about details of his work but gradually, Charley began to absorb the essence of his father's aggressive character and make it his own. The problem was, Charley didn't also absorb Sal's sophistication and self-control.

Where Sal was polished, intelligent and well-spoken, Charley was smart, a smart-ass, and mean. Sal was a savvy street fighter who became an energetic, if reluctant killer, maximizing the impact of his deeds for their business effect. Charley was hypnotized by power in all its manifestations, and loved using it. While Sal used his power as a means to an end, for Charley power was the end. By the time he was 16, Charley had developed into a full-fledged and dangerous bully, whose favorite pastime was using his rock-hard body and aggressive instincts to impose his will on those around him. He was generally successful in these efforts because those young men who might have been a match for Charley physically were always aware of his family connections. No one with a lick of sense wanted to mess with Sal Corrarino's kid. It was a bitter pill for them to swallow, because the price Charley demanded was total subservience. No one in Charley's circle was an equal. All were toadies. As a result, those young men with a positive self-image avoided Charley completely.

As the tales of Charley's exploits became more and more common knowledge, Sal struggled with how to handle his younger son. Charley was picking fights on a regular basis, and only allowing his targets to escape when they apologized for imagined slights and acknowledged his superiority. In essence, Charley was never happier than when he could make someone cry and beg for mercy.

When he was 18, a chance encounter with a young man from North Carolina changed Charley's approach to life forever. LeRoy Jaynes was 22 years old, black and fresh out of four years in the Navy. Jaynes was short and slim and "just about the happiest person in the world" according to his supervisor in the engineering spaces of the USS Dubuque, where Jaynes had spent the previous two years. Jaynes was also, as his supervisor would often vouch, "about the meanest son-of-a-bitch in the world when he gets pissed."

Jaynes, whose mannerisms were mildly effeminate, was one of those rare people who seem to move faster than everyone else. His reflexes, especially when he was excited, were nothing short of remarkable. He'd demonstrated those reflexes numerous times during shipboard boxing smokers and even with absolutely no training, Jaynes nearly secured a place on the Navy Boxing Team. He'd only barely withstood a furious recruiting effort by his commanding officer and others to re-up for another four years. "You could go to the Olympics, Seaman Jaynes," the Captain had told him. But Jaynes wasn't interested in the Olympics or the Navy. He wanted to be a singer and dancer and New York was the place to do both. He'd had a promising audition that afternoon and LeRoy was celebrating with a few drinks and a night out.

He was leaving Giapetto's when he accidentally bumped into Charley at the door. LeRoy apologized and attempted to walk past. Charley would have none of it and quickly became belligerent and abusive. LeRoy continued to smile and apologize until Charley called him a "dumb, fucking nigger ballerina." At that point LeRoy stopped smiling and made the abrupt transition his friends in the Navy had described. The result was a fight in a nearby alley that haunted Charley for the rest of his life.

Charley was several inches shorter than LeRoy but he had long since stopped worrying about size. He was used to beating people much larger than he and his greatest weapon was his fearless, attacking style and his powerful upper body. With Charley's pal Gino guarding the alleyway entrance, the fight began as Charley charged. His initial charge ended two seconds later when he stopped abruptly and staggered backward, his nose crushed across his face. And from Charley's point of view, things went downhill from there.

LeRoy didn't give Charley a chance to recover, he waded in with fists so fast and accurate that Charley never actually blocked one punch. Within 30 seconds Charley was out on his feet, arms hanging at his sides, held up only by the punches still snapping his head against the brick wall behind him. Finally, LeRoy allowed Charley to collapse slowly to his knees, where he stayed, hunched over, spewing blood, snot, spit and two teeth. Things had happened so fast that Gino had not had time to react. Now, as he moved in to help, LeRoy held up one hand, motioning him to stop.

"You just stay there, big man. I have a little more business to discuss with your friend here and there's no need for you to be hurt, too."

Gino considered this. He saw no reason to be hurt, either, but fear was not what made him want to abandon his friend. What did was the deep-seated and carefully hidden disgust he had for Charley. Having borne much of Charley's cruelty for several years, Gino was overjoyed to see Charley soundly beaten. However, Gino knew he could not allow this to happen without trying to help. His own life would be forfeit. Gino lowered his head and charged.

LeRoy sidestepped gracefully and pulled Gino through hard as he went by, adding a few more miles per hour to the velocity with which Gino's head collided with the brick wall. Gino collapsed to the ground and didn't twitch. LeRoy took a step back and looked around carefully to make sure no one was watching, and then proceeded to administer the lesson to Charley Corrarino he suspected Charley had in mind for him.

Charley was conscious, and though he was unable to protect himself, he was alert enough to feel pain. Within three minutes Charley Corrarino was reduced to a shuddering bag of fear and self-pity. Charley was not a coward, but his own pathological focus on the domination of others left him no defenses when the tables were turned. He could anticipate each kick and punch, because those were the things he would have done. But anticipation of the coming blows magnified their impact, made them even worse. Charley could deal with the pain but his own utter helplessness broke him completely. He began to beg and plead for mercy, blubbering uncontrollably, but LeRoy Jaynes was not a merciful man and Charley's agony continued until he lost consciousness.

By the next afternoon, when Sal's people had pieced together the events of the previous night, LeRoy had also learned who Charley, and more importantly, who Sal Corrarino was. He was on the next bus back to Naval Station Norfolk, Virginia. The USS Dubuque was still in port there. His plans for a singing and dancing career were going to have to wait.

Charley spent six days in the hospital where he was treated for a broken nose and jaw, a fractured orbital bone in his eye socket, a ruptured spleen and bruised kidney, three broken ribs and a torn anterior cruciate ligament in his right knee. By the time he recovered from those injuries, Charley was a changed man. Having experienced total domination from the wrong side, Charley's aggressive self-confidence disappeared. Having been beaten and totally dominated by a slightly built 'ballerina' shook Charley to the depths of his being. If someone like that could beat him, anyone could. For the rest of his life Charley Corrarino would be afraid. As a result, he never attempted to bully another man. He concentrated on women and children instead.

Chapter 9

While Charley was making his way up and into his father's criminal enterprise, Tony was moving farther and farther away, physically and emotionally. Tony knew that even if he were not involved in the criminal activities, his last name would brand him. Both parents supported his desire to get a college degree and they were delighted to learn he'd applied to Villanova and La Salle, because both were located in Philadelphia. Distant as he might be, Sal Corrarino still held out a father's hope that someday his son would return to the fold. Tony harbored no such hopes and secretly applied to several West Coast schools, as well.

He was accepted at all the east coast schools, as well as Stanford and the universities of Oregon and Washington. His father hit the roof upon learning about his desire to go west, however, and only his mother's intervention averted an ugly showdown. She convinced Sal to 'have a sit down' with his oldest son.

"What's wrong with the East Coast schools? You could be away from home and still be close enough to see your mother occasionally."

"Nothing's wrong with those schools, Dad. I just don't want to go there."

"Tony, you and I haven't gotten along as well as we should and I understand you don't want to be in the family business…"

"It's not a business, Dad," Tony interrupted. "It's…"

"Watch your mouth, boy!" Sal's voice became dangerously flat, and behind the door, Maria Corrarino gasped and prepared to come in to protect her son.

"Listen, Tony." Sal was controlling his temper. Maria could hear the strain in his voice. "Let's try to stick to the subject and not make each other mad. Like I started to say, you've made it clear you don't want any part of what I do. I can live with that. But you don't have to go across the country to get an education. Stay on the east coast, at least. Don't go to California. That's a crazy place."

"Dad, I've got to get away from the places where everyone knows you. I want to be my own person. I can't do that around here. Anyone who hears my last name will associate me with you... or ask if we're related. I've got to get away from that. I've got to build my own life."

"I won't have you acting ashamed of me, goddammit! I built us a good life. You've never wanted for anything. Your father is a leader, a boss! Your father is treated with respect by everyone, everyone! You should be proud of me. Not ashamed!"

And in that statement Tony heard something he'd never heard before, an uncertainty, a self-doubt in his father's voice. It shook him to the core. His father had never once shown any regret or ambiguity about his work, but here he was, obviously insecure. Shocked as he was, Tony recognized the opportunity. He said something that surprised him even as it left his lips.

"I'm not ashamed of you, Dad. I love you. I just don't want to be... in your line of work."

It surprised him not so much because he said it, though he would have bet money those words would never have crossed his lips, but because they didn't feel like a lie.

"Shit," Sal said and turned away to look out the window.

Tony stood silently, amazed beyond words. Right then he knew, he KNEW, he could do whatever he wanted. Suddenly he was ashamed of trying to manipulate his father's uncharacteristic sentimentality. But not so ashamed he didn't do it.

"Well, Dad, I sort of had my heart set on Stanford, but... maybe I could go to the University of Oregon instead."

His father turned to look at him. "Bullshit! You're just trying to get as far away as possible."

To Tony's absolute amazement, his father was actually smiling. Sal continued, "You think I'll be so happy to keep you away from California I will actually agree to let you go to Oregon, right?"

So much for manipulation, Tony thought. "Well, yeah. I guess so."

"It's not a bad plan," Sal said. "I hate California, hate the people, hate the stupid way they act. You're not going there, no matter what."

Tony bristled. "Dad, I'm going to be my own man, no matter what you say. I can go to California if I want." He half expected Sal to knock him across the room and evidently so did his mother, because there was a distinct click in the door knob.

His father yelled without taking his eyes off Tony, "Goddammit, Maria! If you're going to listen at the door, try to be quiet while you do it. Get in here! You might as well hear all of it."

Tony's mother walked in with her head held high. No one would have guessed she'd just been caught eavesdropping. Sal shook his head and smiled.

"Your mother thinks she has to protect you from me. But she doesn't. I would never hurt you. But I won't let you leave this family either. You can go to school wherever you want..." Tony and Maria both drew deep breaths... "as long as it's not in California. But you finish college and settle somewhere near here. Be a dentist, a shyster lawyer. Be a damn skydiver," Maria tightened her lips, "but do it somewhere close enough we can see you occasionally."

He glanced at his wife, who smiled and nodded so slightly only a husband could know. He looked for a long time at his son.

"Sound like a deal?"

They shook hands and in that moment of deciding to leave, Tony felt closer to his father than ever before. A few months later, Tony was on his way to the University of Oregon.

If Sal Corrarino had known what the University of Oregon was like, he might have been more supportive of Tony going to Stanford. U of O was an extremely liberal campus smack in the middle of an even more liberal town. When Maria came west to get her son enrolled for his freshman year, she was appalled at the hippie culture evident throughout the campus. It was everything Tony could do to keep her from calling his father and pulling him out of school.

"You're going to have to trust me, Mom. I'm not going to turn into a druggie. I'm going to study and get a good education. I'll settle down near you."

In the end, she was convinced and Tony was left to begin what he later described as "the finest years of my young life." Freed for the first time from what he considered a stifling family life, Tony quickly became acquainted with the college party scene. During the fall quarter of his freshman year, Tony studied occasionally and received passing grades in his class work but his real effort was in off-campus activities. Personable and outgoing, Tony quickly made friends and within weeks after arriving in Eugene he was "dialed in to the party scene." Recreational drug use was rampant on the U of O campus but after an unpleasant experience with LSD, Tony confined his party tools to alcohol and occasionally, marijuana. He dated regularly and to the chagrin of several of his co-ed friends, consistently avoided long-term entanglements. He was determined to get the most out of his college experience, including maximum exposure to members of the opposite sex. All through the fall and winter, Tony studied enough to get by and partied hard enough to excel.

He even walked on with the track team, a short-lived and unsatisfying experience. The University of Oregon track team, under legendary coach Bill Bowerman, consistently fielded Olympic caliber distance runners and it was not long before Tony realized he had no real chance of ever being able to compete for the University. His last day with the team was the day he ran intervals with a fellow freshman named Steve Prefontaine. Already an Oregon legend from his Herculean high school performances, Prefontaine would go on to an incredibly successful college career and run in the Olympics. Tony knew of Prefontaine, but as he described to Dean Taylor, his roommate, later that night, "Knowing how good he is still doesn't prepare you for watching him run away from you. I always thought I could beat anyone if I tried hard enough. But I can never run with Pre. Never. That must be what they call a hard lesson."

Dean, a youngster from the Alsea Valley of coastal Oregon, listened silently to Tony's story. Over the first two quarters, he and Tony had become close friends and both valued their late-night bullshit sessions. When Tony had finished his story, Dean shook his head and smiled.

"No, having Pre run away from you in intervals is not a hard lesson, you whiny little New York wop. A hard lesson is having Pre lap you in the mile run on your home track in front of 4,000 people, including your parents and your girlfriend."

"Four thousand people?"

"Well, a good solid 400."

"He lapped you?"

"One full lap. In front of God and everybody."

"When?"

"Last year. The wound has still not healed."

"Jesus. You weren't very good, were you?"

"I guess not, although it was never quite so obvious as it was that day."

"So, what did you learn?"

"Learn?"

"From your hard lesson."

"Oh. Not the same as you. I already knew there were some things I couldn't do. I learned that just being there on the same track made me special. My father says Pre is going to be one of the world's greatest runners and I will be glad to have run against him."

"So, are you glad?"

"No, not yet. Now I still hate him."

"Yeah. Me too. By the way, don't call me a wop."

"Well, don't call me a hick."

"I didn't call you a hick."

"You were thinking of it."

"No, I wasn't. I was thinking of yokel."

"I knew it. Let's go get a beer."

Without hesitation, both young men began walking to the door.

"Or maybe redneck."

"Now, that's original. You're buying… for lack of originality in name calling."

"What? Did you make wop up?"
"Be careful, asshole, or I'll wop up the floor with you."
And out the door they went.

Chapter 10

—•—《(●)》—•—

Tony's relationship with Dean opened up a whole new world to him. City born and bred, Tony had absolutely no connection to or knowledge of the outdoors. Beginning in the spring of his freshman year that changed rapidly. Dean was the seventh of nine children of a fourth-generation Oregon logger and farming family, to whom the outdoors was a vitally important source of food.

"We all buy fishing and hunting licenses," Dean explained. "And we stick pretty much to the limits, except for deer, but only five or six of us hunt regularly. We just fill the tags for everyone else."

"What do you mean, except for deer?" Tony had asked.

"Well, deer are all over our farm. We take as many as we need. They cause a lot of damage to our fruit trees and our garden and even the rose bushes and flowers my mother likes to grow. Deer are pretty much our primary source of meat, them and elk, but we have to work a little harder for elk, so we generally only kill three or four of them each year."

Fish, too, were important to the Taylor family, and Dean was an excellent fisherman. In the evenings or when they didn't have class, the boys would drive up the McKenzie River, which flowed very near the U of O campus. They would fish for trout from the bank and do well but after the first week Dean got tired of it.

"Bank fishing is for people who don't know any better," he said. "Or can't do any better."

A few days later he disappeared overnight. When he came back he was towing a small boat behind his pickup. Tony was amazed.

"It goes up on both ends," he said.

"It's a McKenzie River drift boat," Dean said. "It was designed for this river right here, but boats like it are used all over the Pacific Northwest, wherever there's fast water and rocks."

With a lot of help from Dean, Tony soon learned the reason for the drift boat's strange, banana-like design. With both ends out of the current, the oarsman could maneuver the boat against and across current, making it easy for a fisherman to deliver his lure or fly into hard-to-reach spots.

Dean was an experienced oarsman and Tony was amazed at his ability to bring the boat through heavy water and rocks. At times he rowed against the current, slowing the boat enough to let Tony cast into promising water. At other times he would drop the anchor hanging from the stern, holding them in one place so both young men could fish. After four or five boat trips, Tony asked if he could row.

"I thought you'd never ask," said Dean, and Tony's outdoor education began a new phase.

There were several hard bumps and a few near-sinkings but Tony learned fast. He soon mastered the technique of rowing upstream and maneuvering the boat across the river. Gradually, use of the oars became second nature; he no longer had to think about the effect his various actions would have. His hands and arms worked almost of their own accord and the boat responded. Even so, Tony would occasionally get into trouble because he couldn't muscle the boat away from holes and rocks.

After enduring one particularly painful episode of what Dean described as "Tony's Big Bang Theory of River Boating," Dean offered some rare guidance. "It's a lot like splitting wood, you can wear yourself out hitting a piece of oak with a maul as hard as you can, or you can pick the right spots and the wood just falls apart for you. Same way on the river. You can fight it for hours or you can see what the water wants to do and let it help you. Of course, sometimes the oak is so cross-grained it just won't split… and sometimes the river just wants to kill you. So, you have to be ready to fight, but recognize when it's not necessary."

"Oh, Swami," wheezed Tony, "I am overwhelmed by your pusillanimous pulchritude."

"Is that another way of saying bullshit?" Dean asked.

"I don't think so, but I'm not sure. The problem is that I don't know what either word means, much less if they go together." Tony answered. "They sound good, though. For what it's worth, I have never in my life split even one piece of wood."

Dean snorted. "OK, Grasshopper. I tried to help you." And he turned to concentrate on casting a Hare's Ear nymph under some overhanging branches.

Meanwhile, Tony, who recognized the accuracy and importance of what his friend had said, despite the unfortunate metaphors, made a concerted effort to work with the river rather than against it. Dean noticed the difference.

"Ah, I see you have taken some of my wisdom for your own, Grasshopper."

"Yes, thank you Master," he replied, and then pulled a short oar to soak Dean with the cold mountain water.

Over the next couple of months, Tony learned to make up in anticipation and finesse for what he lacked in power. He learned to read the river accurately and respond early and fast. He felt like he'd fallen in love. He spent as much time as he could on the water, often taking the boat for a few hours in the afternoon by himself when Dean was still in class.

One evening, after Tony had returned late with the boat, Dean looked up from his desk and posed a question.

"So, what are you going to do this summer?"

Tony considered the question. "Guess I'll just go back to New York. Haven't thought about it much. Why?"

"Well, you could stay here and work. We could fight wildfires. Make some serious money."

"Don't you have to work with your uncle this summer? I thought you crewed on one of his boats."

"I generally do, but he's just got two boats and there are more than enough of us kids and cousins to crew them. My father told me to go make enough money to pay for next year's school. I could crew on someone else's boat but I'm sort of tired of fishing and if it's a dry year, I can make more money fighting fires than I can fishing for salmon.

"They're hiring crews right now, so you have to make up your mind pretty quick." Dean hesitated. "Listen, you can stay here and fight wildfires in some of the world's most beautiful land and make a shitpotfull of money, or you can go hang around New York for the whole summer. It doesn't seem like a hard decision."

Tony grinned. He'd fostered Dean's mistaken impression that he needed to make money during the summers to pay for school, when he could have all the money he wanted just by asking. Nonetheless, the idea of fighting fires for the summer intrigued him. The more time he spent outdoors the better he liked it.

He nodded twice. "Sure, let's go fight some fires." And the deal was struck. Tony found it easier to get a job on a fire crew than it was explaining to his parents why he wasn't coming home for the summer. In typical fashion, Sal had one of his people research firefighting and the company that had hired Tony. What he learned convinced Sal to let his son stay out West.

"Listen, Maria. This firefighting is big stuff out there. They have wildfires every year and lots of college kids make enough money in the summer to pay for the whole year of college."

"He doesn't need money. We have plenty of money. Why can't he come home and spend the summer with us?" Maria sobbed.

"He's getting to be a man, now, Maria. As long as he's doing something useful and not getting in trouble, we should go along with it."

"Since when did you become Mr. Go-Along-with-Everything? Why can't you just tell him to come home?"

"Well, for two reasons. One, he might just disobey me and then we'd have a major standoff I would be forced to win. And two, if he did come home, what would he do? He wants to get out from under my shadow. How could he do that here?"

In the end, Maria acquiesced, with the understanding that Tony would come home for a couple weeks before school.

That summer changed Tony's life. It was a long, dry fire season and Tony's crew fought fire almost constantly from the middle of June through the middle of September. They were on fires in Oregon, Idaho, Alaska and California. Living in tent camps and working 12 or 14 hours each day in steep, difficult terrain gave Tony a whole new perspective on life and on people. The rough and tumble men and women who fought wildfires were like no one else Tony had ever been around before. They were loud and boisterous, just as quick to laugh as to fight, but they were also solid, dependable and fearless. None, Tony realized after a few days, gave the impression of incipient danger he was used to in his father and the men like him. None of them seemed *deadly*. Tony warmed to them and they to him. In the space of a few short weeks, the young people on Tony's fire crew were as close as heat, danger and cramped, difficult conditions could make them, which is very close indeed.

The end of the fire season was one of the saddest days of Tony's life. He would have cheerfully continued fighting fires for the rest of his life, if only the weather had cooperated, and he hated the thought of losing track of his new friends. Many, like Tony and Dean, were headed back to college. A few others were headed off to Alaska, where opportunities for work were seemingly unlimited and a few were going into the military. One, a friendly, laughing Washington boy named Lonnie, was headed into the Army Warrant Officer Program, which would prepare him to fly helicopters.

"Don't you need a degree?" Dean had asked him during their last night's beer bash.

"Nope," Lonnie explained. "Just a high school diploma and good scores on some tests. You need a degree to fly for the Air Force and Navy and Marine Corps, but they make you commissioned officers, like lieutenants and captains. Warrant officers are not commissioned. They are like a set of ranks between enlisted and commissioned."

"I sure wouldn't mind learning to fly," Dean said.

"Well, there are all sorts of opportunities in Vietnam," Tony said, laughing. But he noticed neither Lonnie nor Dean laughed with him.

Chapter 11

With only 10 days left before classes picked up again, Tony made a quick trip back to New York. His visit was pleasant in many ways but equally disturbing in others. His mother, grandmother, cousins and aunts all had endless big dinners in his honor. He was amazed at how much he'd missed good, home-cooked Italian food and how glad he was to see his family.

Even his father was almost exuberant, and missed no opportunity to praise his schoolwork and his work as a firefighter. Over and over again, Sal asked Tony to tell stories of his time on the fire line to groups of family and friends. He had obviously made peace with the idea of Tony moving off into his own and was taking pride in his accomplishments. For the first time in his life, Tony experienced a feeling around his family that was completely foreign to him. It was comfort. Tony was comfortable. Gone was the ever-present tension and fear of being second-guessed. Instead of anticipating condemnation, Tony began to anticipate acceptance and support. It was weird. He realized that this was how Dean felt every day of his life, and for the two-millionth time, Tony found himself envying his Oregon friend.

But not every member of his family was glad to see him. His brother Charley was cool, even antagonistic. Though they'd never been close, neither had they been actively hostile, and hostility is what Tony was feeling whenever he was in the same room as his brother. He tried to talk to Charley but was rebuffed without explanation. Finally, he asked his mother about it.

"It's not your fault, Tony. Charley is having problems with everyone now. Ever since he was beaten so badly he's been bitter and unhappy. He doesn't have friends anymore. We don't know what to do."

Actually, Charley had never had real friends, only hangers-on who hoped to use him as a stepping stone into the mob, or goons like Gino, who had no place else to go. And Charley didn't miss them now. His problem didn't have anything to do with Tony either, though he didn't appreciate the way his father fawned over his older brother. Charley's rage was far less focused than that. He was literally and figuratively, angry at the world. Since his beating at the hands of LeRoy Jaynes, Charley had lost his own sense of self-worth, which had been based, in his own tormented way, on his ability to frighten and dominate people. He wasn't sure how he was different, or why, just that he was. He still had the same urges to smash, to hurt, to make people cry and ask for mercy. But whenever those urges rose, Charley was beset by his own fear. *Maybe that guy is a lot tougher than he looks. Maybe he knows karate or another one of those weird religions.*

Charley could not escape the terror he felt at the possibility, no matter how remote, that he might be physically beaten again. Three weeks in the hospital. Six months of physical therapy. His knee was never going to be full strength again. And on top of all of those things was the recurring nightmare of a merciless, grinning black dervish beating him, kicking him, stomping him. Charley broke into cold sweats whenever the memories of that night forced their way into his consciousness.

Charley's father had underestimated the impact of the fight on his son. He'd tried to approach it as another of life's lessons.

"You just lost a fight, Charley," Sal had told him. "It's no big deal, though I admit that nigger damaged you worse than he had to." Upon learning the identity of LeRoy Jaynes, Sal had dispatched two men to 'break him up worse than he beat my boy.' But by the time they'd picked up his trail, Jaynes was safely ensconced in the Navy Base at Norfolk, Virginia, and had reenlisted with orders to join the USS Kitty Hawk in Japan. He was way too smart to leave the safety of the base.

"But you learn something and you move on, Charley. Nobody wins all their fights. I've been beaten several times."

Any chance he may have believed Sal evaporated in that instant, because Charley knew, he KNEW that no one could possibly have ever beaten his father. Their conversation tailed off, with Sal thinking that Charley would recover fully and Charley wondering why his father had lied to him.

As time went on, Charley learned to hide his ever-present misery and fear, at least from people who didn't know him well. With family members, he became distant and unapproachable and at odd, unpredictable moments, rude. His work within the mob didn't seem to suffer, though. He became more and more a part of Sal's operation, particularly when it came to the integration of criminal proceeds into their legitimate business fronts. As his teachers had noticed, Charley was clever. He learned to invest in businesses far from the normal mob scene, and to manipulate them in small, subtle ways so the various law enforcement agencies would not notice his involvement. He also found ways to disguise the Family involvement in the historic cash cows like prostitution, the construction industry, garbage collection and legal gambling so they brought in more money with fewer legal problems.

At the age of 21, Charley was an accepted member of one of New York's major crime families, a creative entrepreneur in an organization not normally known for creativity. He was accepted professionally, but disliked personally. Both men and women tended to recognize his inner turmoil and though he was careful never to lose his temper, his ever-present rage at the world soured every possible relationship. He was so unsuccessful with women, Charley began to spend his leisure hours either alone or in the company of hookers. Because he was paying for their time, Charley felt free to indulge his baser instincts of cruelty and sadism. In the beginning, he satisfied himself with simply slapping them around, or handling them so roughly they whimpered and cried. He liked it when they cried, and gradually, his own sexual release became more and more dependent on his partners' pain or fear. The more fear he saw in their eyes, the more they whined and screamed, the more excited Charley became, and the better he liked it.

Over time, his dealings with prostitutes became increasingly violent and crazy. Even the most hardened hookers wouldn't go with Charley a second time and his reputation on the street filtered up to his father. Sal tried to ignore it but after the third time one of his underlings reported having to bribe the cops to keep them from coming after Charley, Sal had had enough. He called his son to the office and told the rest of his people to go outside.

"You've been beating up on women," he said, without preamble.

Charley looked around. He'd never been in the back room of Panetta's alone with his father and he was uneasy. Not fearful, just uneasy.

"Just hookers," he answered, grinning uncertainly. "I didn't mean to put them out of commission but we've got to expect a little wear and tear on the merchandise."

Sal was out of his seat like a cat and Charley took two steps backward without thinking, but not fast enough. Sal was in his face.

"They are not merchandise," he growled. "They are women and men don't beat up on women, hookers or not. For damn sure my sons don't do it."

"Dad," Charley's voice was an octave higher than he wanted it, "Dad, they are not like regular women."

Sal grabbed him by the tie and shook. "I'm not asking you!" he roared. "This is not a goddamn discussion. You don't beat up on women, I don't care how they make their living. Got it? Got it?"

Charley nodded silently but evidently not contritely enough, because Sal slapped him hard in the face, then slapped him again. Charley was appalled and ashamed. He knew the wise guys outside could hear the conversation, and the blows. How could his reputation recover from this? But that was a problem for the future. Right now, he had to get his father to calm down. He'd never seen him so mad and for a brief moment Charley began to wonder if he was in real danger, if this was the last sight Sal's enemies saw before they died.

"OK, Dad, OK. I'm sorry."

Sal didn't slow down; he was still so angry he was shaking. "If you got to beat somebody up you go take your chances with another man, goddammit. Maybe you can handle one of them if you get a second chance. Just stay away from the fucking fairy niggers. But if you beat up another woman, you are out! You understand me? Out!"

Charley nodded and fled. He practically ran out through the main dining area, keeping his head down, not meeting anyone's eyes. He went directly to his apartment and stayed there for two days, wondering almost incessantly what his father had actually meant by "You are out." On the third day he resurfaced, and went again to Panetta's, where his father welcomed him as though nothing had ever happened. None of Sal's minions ever said a word or gave any indication they knew anything had occurred between Charley and his father. If his shame were not so deeply ingrained in his soul, Charley might have believed the whole thing was a bad dream. But it wasn't a dream. He knew it, and he knew a direct threat from Salvatore Corrarino was the only way the entire thing could have been hushed up. No story was so good it was worth being fed your own liver.

Charley appreciated the silence. It let him get on with his business and his life. In a strange way, the absolute silence surrounding his humiliation strengthened Charley's hero worship of his father. No one else in the world could have put a cork in the story. No one else could have stopped the sneers and wise cracks that would have certainly followed. Charley was not about to go against his father's wishes; he didn't want to disappoint him again. He completely stopped abusing women. He took his sexual proclivities and moved carefully into the shadowy and super-secret world of children.

By the time Tony came back home that summer, Charley had recovered from his run-in with his father, and was feeling pretty comfortable at work, if not at home. He knew his mother didn't like him; he'd known it for years, but she didn't really bother him. His father was the one who mattered. As for Tony, Charley wouldn't have cared less about the skinny little asshole, except for the way Sal made such a big deal about him. For Christ's sake, Tony was just some college boy who happened to fight fires. Big fucking deal. He, Charley, was single-handedly changing the way his father's organization was doing business, as well as the perception of the way the organization did business. And perception, at least on the part of the cops and feds, was what mattered. If they didn't *perceive* a crime, by God, a crime hadn't taken place.

Charley had never cared about Tony's ability in school, or distance running ability or his natural charm. He didn't care a flying fuck about those things, because he had always known he was tougher and stronger and meaner than Tony. He'd always known that Tony would go off somewhere into the twilight and he would take over from his father. He would run their section of New York and people would bow and scrape to him like they did whenever his father walked by. Charley understood that no matter how many friends his father had, no matter how many city councilmen and senators and bankers sat at his father's table, they were not there because of friendship, but because of money and fear. And Charley had once thought he could instill fear into people as well as his father had. But everything had changed since his beating by LeRoy Jaynes. Now he no longer had the confidence that had derived from his physical skill and courage. All he had left was the internal rage and bitterness.

Chapter 12

On those occasions that summer when he could not avoid the family get-togethers, or ignore Tony completely, Charley was simply unpleasant and rude. Tony soon took the hint and kept a discrete distance from his brother, spending time among the other relatives and friends.

Tony enjoyed his family more than ever during those ten days. A caravan of uncles, aunts and cousins came to an endless number of lunches and dinners. He smiled and laughed so much his face hurt.

The day before Tony was to leave, his father turned to him and asked, "Would you like to come down to the office with me today, Tony, and see some of the boys? I'd like to show you off to them a little bit."

Tony had known the question would come, and for the first time in his life he was tempted. He'd gotten along so well with his father that he wanted to go, but he knew that if he went, the visit would be more than a simple reconnect with the 'boys.'

Sal would be pulled into discussions and decisions and Tony would be pulled in right alongside him. Charley stood silently behind Sal, waiting for Tony's answer but inside he was seething. It was everything he could do to keep from saying "We don't need him, Dad." But he kept his mouth shut and waited.

Tony said, "No thanks, Dad. I'll see you when you get back." Sal and Charley went out the door.

Soon afterward, Tony headed back to school. His departure made Charley as happy as he'd been for years.

Tony and Dean roomed together in school again their sophomore year. Tony wanted to move off campus but Dean was chronically short of money and couldn't swing the extra rent.

"I've got some money in the bank from last summer," he told Tony, "but not enough for an apartment. My older sister is in med school now and my folks still have two kids behind me. I don't want to ask them for help. I'll understand if you want to go off campus, but I'll have to stay here."

"Oh, nice guilt trip, Shithead. You know I won't leave you here alone. You'll never become sophisticated without me."

"No, sophistication is too lofty a goal. But I'm already suave and debonair." He pronounced them 'swayve and de-boner' and both young men howled with laughter.

Tony and Dean would look back on their sophomore year as one of the, if not *the* best in their lives. Dean, hitherto a marginal student, finally figured out college life and began getting Bs and As.

"I've discovered something magical," he once told Tony. "If you do your homework as soon as you get out of class, you get good grades."

"What a concept!" Tony said. "You should write a book."

"Don't be a wiseass," Dean said. "You don't have the right. You do homework about once a month."

"I generally get my homework done during class," he grinned.

"Being a showoff is even worse than a wiseass."

Having a handle on his schoolwork made Dean much more available for extracurricular pursuits than he had been the year before and he and Tony made the most of it. They used the extra time almost exclusively on outdoor pursuits. They fished for trout and steelhead until October, when Dean indoctrinated Tony in the finer points of deer hunting.

Using a borrowed Model 94 Winchester lever action 30-30, Tony followed Dean through Oregon's coast range mountains. The entire idea of hunting was alien to Tony, and it took him several days to get a feel for the way his friend moved through the forest. Even after Tony became relatively proficient at walking quietly, he still had trouble seeing game animals.

During their third visit to the woods, Dean suddenly froze. After a short time, he motioned Tony to his side. Tony moved up quietly.

Dean whispered, "Up ahead, about 40 yards. Go ahead and shoot it."

Tony could see nothing. "Can't find it."

"Don't look for the whole deer. Look for the antlers or an ear."

Tony looked until his eyes ached. Nothing. He shook his head imperceptibly.

Dean cursed silently and raised his own rifle. At the blast, Tony saw a buck materialize from nothing, leap into the air, take two faltering steps forward, and collapse on its nose. Even before the animal fell, Dean chambered another round.

"Jesus Christ! What a shot! Holy Shit, Dean! You got him!"

"Tony, he was 40 yards away, standing broadside. I hope to Christ I got him. Stop jumping up and down. I'm starting to worry about you. Well, did you learn anything?"

"You bet your ass! I learned not to stand close when you shoot. My ears are ringing so loud it hurts!"

They moved in slowly. Dean kept Tony away as he slowly touched the barrel to the animal's open eye, his finger curled around the trigger.

"Sometimes dead critters come alive," he said, "And they can do some real damage. You touch their eye with the muzzle. If they don't blink, they're dead. If they do, you pull the trigger."

"OK, yeah. I got it."

Dean cleared the chamber of his rifle and leaned it up against a nearby tree. He shucked his pack and pulled his sheath knife from his belt. He handed it to Tony.

"OK, Bubba. You'd better roll up your sleeves. Time for you to learn something."

That fall, when Tony wasn't in class, he was with Dean, hunting deer or elk. He killed his first deer a few days after Dean got his, an accomplishment that made him as proud as anything he'd ever done. And a month later he killed a bull elk. The bull ran almost a quarter mile before it died and Dean needed every bit of tracking skill he had to find it. He was moving slowly through the brush when he stopped and pointed.

"There's your bull," he whispered.

"Is he dead?"

"Why don't you go find out?"

Tony moved slowly, his rifle high and ready. The bull was lying on its side, its eyes already filmy and its tongue lolling out of its mouth. The sight of the massive animal affected Tony more completely than either of their deer had done. It was dead, bereft of its natural beauty and dignity: body steaming, blood streaming from an exit wound behind the shoulder, feces dropping from its anus, plop, plop, plop, as muscular control relaxed. Tony sat on the ground, hard. He could not speak. He was devastated and could only think that he would never, ever do this again. Never take the life of any animal. This was wrong.

And then Dean came charging up.

"Yow! Wow! Yeeeehaaaaa!!! He danced through the thick brush as though it weren't there at all, rifle held above his head. "You are a big bull killer!!! Eeehah!! This may be the biggest elk of all time."

"Are you kidding?" Tony asked, suddenly interested.

"Hell, yes. I mean, no. This is a big bull. This is the kind of animal people pay thousands of dollars to hunt. Now you are a man, my friend. Don't ever kid yourself about your first sexual encounter, if, in fact, you've had one. It was, or will be, nothing compared to this. You can't be a real man until you've killed a bull elk. And now you have. Wait 'til my family hears about this. Hell, wait till they see your bull. Holy shiterooteee! You are a man among men!"

Tony found himself smiling under Dean's onslaught of happiness. Dean was truly, honestly happy for Tony and despite the remains of his revulsion about killing the animal, Tony found himself becoming excited over his success. Dean seemed to read his mind. He sat down.

"Remember this, Hiawatha. All life springs from death. Every living thing feeds, in one way or another, on something else. This elk will help feed my family through the winter, and it's a big family. This is a good thing. And it is even better because you arranged to have the elk run all this way and fall so close to the road. We won't have to haul it out by quarters." He clapped Tony hard enough on the shoulders to cross his eyes. My God, you are a helluva man!"

A few days later, Tony accompanied Dean when Dean got his own bull, which dwarfed the animal Tony had killed. It turned out Tony's bull, contrary to what Dean had said, was a puny specimen, commonly described as a raghorn five-point. But neither Dean nor his family ever gave Tony any indication his bull was anything but a massive trophy. Even when he pointed out that his bull's antlers fit inside the antlers taken from Dean's bull, Dean's father simply shrugged and said. "Well, Dean's bull was an exceptional animal, no question about it."

Such a gift, Tony thought. *Such a gift the Taylors are to me.*

By late November, the boys had shifted their focus to waterfowl and rare were the mornings they didn't spend out on farmers' fields or on one of the many backwaters and sloughs of the Willamette River, calling in ducks and geese. It was a golden existence. Each week or two, they would pack up the frozen ducks and geese they kept at a local freezer and drive up to Dean's family farm to make a delivery. Dean's grades, which had begun to slip under the pressure of deer and elk season, began to rebound during the relative ease of morning waterfowl hunts. They even had enough time and energy left over to party occasionally.

Waterfowl season ended in late January and the boys were left with nothing to hunt. Their grades made an even more impressive jump and at one point in March, Dean came bursting into the dorm room to announce that his student advisor had declared him free of academic probation, a description that had been a near constant since early in his freshman year.

"Be careful son," the old man had said. "You might end up being a college student after all." When Dean asked what the man thought he'd been for the last two years the advisor had said, "Up to now, you've just been a dorm room renter." Dean wanted to argue, he explained, but couldn't quite mount an attack.

"Unlike you," he said to Tony, "I can't argue passionately about something just for the fun of the debate. I need to believe in my argument and that old son of a bitch had me dead to rights. I simply cannot lie. I wasn't a serious college student before. But now I have seen the error of my ways. I want to excel here in the academic environment. I want to make a difference and help lead misguided students such as I was to success. I've decided to pursue a graduate degree and become a college professor. In short, I was lost, but now I'm found."

Tony interrupted loudly, laughing in spite of himself. "Jesus fucking Christ, Joanie Baez! You are so full of shit! What was that about not being able to lie? You couldn't care less about school work. You just want to get out of here with a degree, same as me."

Dean was undeterred. "Aw contrary, bonhommy. I am committed. I am dedicated. I am…" At that point Dean was hit by two quick pillows and a package of Twinkies, followed soon after by Tony's entire body. He protected himself as best he could but he was laughing so hard he couldn't cover all the places Tony was hitting. After a minute or so, both boys collapsed on their sides, laughing.

When he got his breath, Dean gasped, "OK, so I don't really want to be a college professor, but today was the first day I ever felt like I might actually get a degree. You know, I've been on academic probation since my first quarter here. This feels pretty good."

"Good enough to buy the beer?"

"Well, good enough to buy the first two. After that, it's every man for himself."

Chapter 13

They were halfway through the spring quarter, a quarter in which Dean was publicly explaining to anyone who would listen that he was going to make the Dean's List.

"Dean on the Dean, that's me this quarter."

Tony gave his friend a hard time but the truth was Dean had a pretty tough schedule, and he was still doing well. Tony, too, was doing well in classes; he couldn't very well let Dean best him, but Tony said little about it, preferring to let Dean bask in the glory of his own adulation.

In fact, Dean had begun to use it as a pickup line, with uneven success.

"Here's the problem," he explained to Tony one evening after a few beers at their favorite off-campus beer joint. "I don't seem to get much impact from subtlety. You know, like being subtle."

Tony leaned back in his chair and spoke through a mouthful of peanuts. "Ahh, so that's what subtlety is, being subtle."

"Yes, you start out by asking women how their courses are going and then maneuver the conversation to you. Then you say something like, 'Yeah, I know what you mean. I've got the same problem, except this quarter I'm going to be on the Dean's List.' The smart ones aren't impressed and the dumb ones think I'm bragging."

"Which of course, you are not."

"Absolutely not. I am simply stating an understated fact."

"You are understating a fact."

"That's what I said." Dean's eyes were beginning to narrow.

"You are making a statement about understatement."

Dean sighed wearily and took another drink. "Not so much about understatement, but about me being on the Dean's List, which is not technically an understatement but, an, er, accomplishment."

"You are making a statement about your understated accomplishment."

"If you say one more word about understatement or about whatever in hell it was we were talking about I am going to kill you."

"That is not subtle," Tony was dangerously close to inhaling his peanuts.

"No."

"And it worked. I am desperately afraid you will kill me if I mention understatement, or almost anything else."

"Good. You should be afraid."

"I am. I am also wondering if a lack of subtlety will help you with women as well."

"A lack of subtlety. You mean like straight talk?

"Yes I do. Let them know right up front who they are dealing with."

"Good idea. I think I will." Dean stood on his chair and then stepped up on their table, steadied himself and cleared his throat loudly. "I am soon going to be on the Dean's List and I'm available for a night of revelry and risqué behavior. And comfort. I'm also available for comfort. I can either provide or receive comfort." It was at that point he leaned slightly, the table leaned slightly more, and Dean clattered to the floor, bringing a sudden quiet to the room, except for the crunching sound of peanut shells collapsing beneath Dean's writhing body.

It was a bad fall and Tony was initially worried, but within seconds, two nice looking young women had descended upon Dean and begun to minister to him. Tony watched in absolute amazement as the two dabbed at his friend's bruises, asked him questions about his well-being, and then one held his head in her lap as they gently poured more beer down his throat. Dean was moaning repeatedly but became better whenever one of them rubbed his forehead.

"I think I need to lie down," Dean said, weakly.

"Where do you live?" one of the beauties asked.

"It's too far," Dean said.

"Maybe we could let him crash at our place," the smaller one said.

"I guess so, he seems harmless…which would be too bad." Dean had a minor convulsion at that point and Tony exhaled a few pieces of peanut. In minutes Dean was gone and Tony was almost overcome with a desire to stand on the table and scream out, "I'm going to get a four point this quarter!"

Chapter 14

The next day was Saturday and though the boys had tentatively planned a steelhead trip on the Rogue River, Tony figured it would be cancelled. Given the situation Dean had fallen into the night before, Tony wasn't at all sure he'd see Dean again until Monday. He'd stayed at the bar until midnight, then grew tired of the animal acts and went home. The phone woke him at 9:30. Expecting Dean, Tony was surprised to hear Dean's mother on the phone. She was obviously crying but doing her best to hide it.

"Tony? Can I speak to Dean, please?"

"He's not here right now, Mrs. Taylor. Can I have him call you back?"

"It's kind of important, Tony. Do you know when he'll be back or where I can find him?"

Jeez, if I knew where those two babes lived I'd be over there now trying to talk my way into their good graces. Really good graces. "No ma'am, I don't. It shouldn't be too long now, though. Mrs. Taylor, is…something wrong?"

"Yes, Tony. But I need to be the one to tell Dean. Would you please ask him to call as soon as you can?"

"Yes, ma'am. I'm sorry. I hope everything's going to be all right."

"Thanks, Tony. But I don't think anything is ever going… I have to go. Please ask Dean to call."

"I will. Goodbye, Mrs.…." But the line had gone dead.

Tony threw on some clothes and ran out the door. He didn't know what sort of tragedy could make Dean's mother so sorrowful but it had to be bad. She was a farm wife. She'd raised nine children. She killed, cleaned and cooked her own chickens, pigs and cattle. She'd ministered to a family of loggers and fishermen for 30 years. She was imperturbable. As he ran across campus, Tony was so afraid he was cold.

He found Dean eating breakfast with his two lady friends outside one of the many Eugene eateries that bordered the campus. From their laughter and close physical contact, it was obvious that things had gone well the night before, and Tony briefly considered waiting until breakfast was over before interrupting them. But Mrs. Taylor's concern had been palpable and drove him forward.

Dean's eyes were bloodshot but he knew there was trouble before Tony got within 10 feet of their table.

"What's the matter?"

"I don't know. You need to call your mother. I've got a credit card you can use to call from here."

But Dean heard nothing after 'mother.' Shaking off the hands of the two girls who'd reached up to console him, Dean kicked back his chair and took off at a run toward campus.

Tony looked at the girls. Their concern was real. "I'm sure he'll call you soon." Then he went running after his friend. After a hundred yards, Tony slowed to a walk. It wouldn't help to be in the room while Dean was on the phone with his mother. He needed to give his friend time to finish his conversation. He walked slowly, noticing the spring flowers, the slow, early morning pace of the campus. It took an almost superhuman effort to walk slowly back to the room. He was almost too late. As he turned toward the dorm he could see a figure running for the parking lot. It was Dean, no question. Tony broke into a run, as well, yelling for Dean to stop. "Dean, wait up! Dean, hold on!"

Dean didn't wait, though, and he was backing his pickup out of the parking spot when Tony arrived at his window. He reached in to grab the steering wheel. "Dean, wait! Jesus! Tell me what's going on."

Dean stopped his pickup and stared at the steering wheel. Tony had never seen such sadness. "My dad died this morning. Died in the crummy on the way to the logging show. Just tipped over in the seat. Heart attack."

"I'm sorry, Dean. Jesus. Jesus. Let me go with you. You're in no shape to drive. Your hands are shaking. Let me go too."

For the first time, Dean looked directly at his friend. He nodded and almost smiled through eyes wet with tears. "You're a good friend, Tony, and we'll want you to come out to the house soon. But not now. I'm OK. I'm going to block everything out but driving. I'll be fine. Now let me go. My mom needs me." He squeezed Tony's hand and drove away.

Badly shaken by the news, Tony was left to watch the pickup disappear. A powerful man who'd spent his life in the woods, Gage Taylor had seemed indestructible. If somebody's father was going to die, it shouldn't have been Mr. Taylor. It could have been any of the fat, sloppy fathers he saw visiting their kids on campus. Even the death of his own father would have been easier to understand than Dean's. Sal Corrarino wouldn't die from health issues, though. He was much more likely to die in a hail of gunfire from a rival gang. And Tony was sure the mourners at Mr. Taylor's funeral, though undoubtedly less numerous than those likely to attend his own father's, would honestly care for the man.

Most of the people who would attend Sal Corrarino's funeral would simply be there in order to solidify connections, to lobby for promotions in the new order, whatever that was. What would the new order be? Tony wondered. He knew how much Charley wanted to step in after his father, but Tony doubted if Charley had what it took. He had a feeling, with little to back it up, that the mob guys had little respect for Charley. He'd noticed small things, body language, a tendency not to include Charley in conversations, or if he was already there, not to ask his opinion. Nothing meaningful, if considered by itself, but taken together, it all seemed to point toward a decline in Charley's standing, and Tony knew that in the world Charley and Sal frequented, standing was everything.

If Charley didn't take over for his father, would there still be a place for him in the Family? And what would his mother do? He was sure his folks had plenty of money, and all the relatives were there in New York, so she'd probably be fine. Only his own future would be uncertain, but no more uncertain than it was right now. He'd long since broken from his father's life; all that remained was for him to make his own life.

Tony suddenly realized he was still standing in the parking lot, thinking about his own family, when it was Dean's that was so badly shaken. What sort of selfish shit would get caught up in his own problems, which were largely theoretical, when his best friend's family had just been devastated? He forced himself to focus on the Taylors.

They lived in an old farm house, the original size and shape of which had long since been hidden in a series of renovations, additions and improvements. It was paid for, Tony knew, because Dean was proud of the fact and mentioned it regularly. Each member of the Taylor family old enough to work had contributed a portion of his or her paycheck regularly to the house fund, and the loan had been paid off while Dean was still in high school. "We went to church," Dean had said. "And we contributed there, but we tithed to the house fund." As long as they had the house, Tony figured, Mrs. Taylor and the kids would be fine.

The next few days blurred by. Tony went around campus first thing on Monday morning to talk to Dean's professors. They were understanding. He attended his own classes but with little interest. He felt like he was drifting, disembodied, as though Dean were his root system to the University and his roots had been pulled up.

Dean called on Monday evening and told him the funeral was scheduled for Saturday. He asked if Tony could come on Thursday and stay through the weekend. Tony said "Sure" and never even considered his own classes. He was honored that Dean wanted and needed his help. It helped make his own devastation understandable. He wasn't the only one who thought of himself as part of Dean's family; the Taylors did, too.

Tony had never seen anything like the Taylor household during the preparations for the funeral. Two dozen people were already there by the time he arrived on Thursday afternoon, camped in tents and trailers across the farm and along the river; there were three big recreational vehicles parked alongside the road. A steady stream of neighbors came to the door; all carried a large dish of some sort. An enormous mobile barbecue pit came rolling in behind a pickup truck and was set up in the small meadow by the river. This was to be the center of the festivities, and though Tony didn't like thinking of the funeral in those terms, he couldn't help it. He was about to take part in a back-country celebration of life and in the manner of people who appreciate life and accept death, there was none of the overt grief and sadness he'd seen at so many New York Italian funerals.

Tony began pitching in to help wherever he was needed. It was more than two hours later when he finally ran into Dean, who was using the farm tractor to drag firewood logs to the meadow. Dean shut the tractor down and came over. They shook hands and then hugged.

Tony turned and spread his arms, encompassing the mass of humanity surging around the farmhouse, his eyes registering wonder.

Dean laughed, "Yeah, well, my six older brothers and sisters are married and all but one of those has at least two kids. They are all here with their in-laws. We've been here for four generations so we're either related or friends with most everybody from Alsea to Waldport and Deadwood to Siletz. Most of them will come, and so will a bunch of folks from Corvallis, where several of us Taylors went to college, and Newport, where my uncle runs his boats. We had to borrow a spare refrigerator and freezer from my aunt and uncle to put all the food people are bringing, but most of it will be eaten on Saturday." He smiled. "What? Isn't this how you do funerals in New York?"

"Probably got the same number of relatives, but it's pretty tough to do them like this, since no one has a damn yard, much less a zillion-acre farm."

"One hundred and sixty."

"Huh?"

"Only 160 acres. A quarter section. Not a zillion."

"Right. Sorry. Well, how are you doing?"

"Better. Not great. But better. My mom is sort of being real business-like about the whole thing and I think it's helping keep everyone together. Dad was the real deal, you know? We all sort of hung on him. No bullshit. Just a straight-up guy." Dean blinked twice and looked away.

"So are you, Dean. A straight-up guy. Your dad raised a whole pile of kids just like him."

"Yeah, thanks. I think he did. Well, I've got to finish with the firewood."

Tony would always look back on the celebration for Gage Taylor with a sense of wonder. After a full day and a half of preparations, the actual funeral took place in a small, riverside meadow in a corner of the Taylor place. Dean said the church pastor wanted to have the ceremony in his church but Mrs. Taylor said no; she and her husband had decided long ago that any 'doins' would take place in the meadow…for both of them. Besides, it was obvious there would be far too many people for the small church. When the pastor pressed the issue, Dean's oldest brother Brian had stepped in.

"Did you want to do the service, Padre, or should we look for someone else?"

Letting someone else conduct the ceremony for one of the Valley's most prominent families was not high on the pastor's list of choices and so he agreed. The meadow it was. And everyone afterward agreed that he'd done a masterful job. He knew Gage well and summarized his life accurately. He told a story of a young mountain boy who'd been something of a hell raiser in his youth who'd settled down with a good woman and raised a wonderful family.

Sounds a lot like Dean, Tony thought to himself. That's exactly what Dean is going to be like; …he'll have a great wife and a great family. Who knows? Maybe I will, too. I'd like to settle down out here, be near Dean and the Taylors. I could make my life here. My father wouldn't like it but I could go back to visit a couple times a year. It could work.

The pastor was finishing his reflections as Tony finished his daydream. Mrs. Taylor moved to the podium.

"Thank you all for coming," she said in a strong voice. "And thanks to Pastor Reelaw for a beautiful service. "And now we're going to…" she hesitated, as if uncertain. "We're going to…" She looked around her, confused, and Dean's older brother Brian stepped up from behind her. Tony could see Dean and a couple of his siblings begin to edge through the crowd toward their mother. Brian took her arm and spoke forcefully to the crowd.

"The pig is done, the beer is cold, the music is just about ready to start. We all hope you'll join us in celebrating our dad's life. We've all grieved for him and that's not going to stop. But now we're going to have a party for him." He looked slowly around the crowd. "And that's not going to stop, either. At least not until tomorrow!"

The crowd erupted with laughter and began moving towards the kegs and the barbecue. Soon, the only people left in the meadow were Taylors. Tony watched as three dozen or more of the Taylor clan moved slowly toward the spot where Mrs. Taylor and Brian stood, as if drawn by magnetism. As they arrived, each person reached in and touched Mrs. Taylor, on the arm, the shoulder, the hand. At each touch, she turned to see the person and smiled warmly. Sometimes she squeezed their hands, sometimes she hugged them, but each person was greeted personally. After paying their respects, the members of the Taylor clan moved slightly off to the side but made no effort to leave the meadow for the food and drinks. Some of the neighbors and friends initially made to join the group, but soon realized it was all family, and continued on to the picnic area. Tony stood off to the side and watched, mesmerized, as the clan came together. He expected Brian or someone to say something, but near as he could figure, they seemed to derive strength by their mere closeness. They stood together for three or four minutes, then, almost as one, they began to break up, to dribble in twos, threes and fours back to the picnic tables, where they joined with the dozens of guests to eat and drink at a prodigious rate.

Stories. And more stories. The speakers were usually men, though several of the women had wonderful stories of their own. In the beginning, most of the tales dealt with Gage, but as time went on the accounts became less and less specific; all they shared was a desire to poke good-natured fun at someone else. Most of the stories dealt with loggers and fishermen, mistakes they'd made and close calls they'd had. The underlying theme, Tony began to realize, was danger, and for the first time he began to appreciate just how chancy logging and commercial fishing are. With that realization, Tony began to pay closer attention to the speakers. He was struck by their size. Even the short men seemed to be massively proportioned with heavy shoulders and substantial forearms; many had malformed or missing fingers. In contrast, Tony, while lithe and strong, seemed like a waif.

"What the hell do you people eat around here?" Tony asked Dean the next time he passed by.

"What do you mean? Not enough pig for you?"

"I don't mean that. I mean, look around at these people. They are all linebackers. You are practically a midget and you outweigh me by 20 pounds."

"They eat the same as you and me, but they are running chainsaws or pulling nets eight hours a day, not sitting in class. Even the bubble-butted log truck drivers started out setting chokers. Like that guy over there with the suspenders and the big belly? He drives truck. But he's also the strongest man in this part of the country. If he puts his hands to something, it moves—including people." Dean laughed and punched Tony in the arm. "Besides, that extra 20 pounds I'm carrying is the only reason Prefontaine was able to beat me in the mile."

"Pre didn't beat you. He lapped you. He destroyed you."

Dean laughed again. It was a good sound, a clean, healthy sound. "Shhh. I'm hoping people around here forget that episode."

"What? Forget about the time that stud Steve Prefontaine crushed you in the mile race? We pretty much all ate our dinners waiting for you to get to the finish line." The speaker was a tall, dark-haired girl with almost unnaturally white skin. Her complexion was perfect, unblemished. She had clear, blue eyes and she stared unselfconsciously at Tony, even as she spoke to Dean.

"I should have known it would be you, Raven." Dean said with a smile as he put his arm around her shoulders and hugged. "Tony, this is my cousin, Raven. She is part of the rebel Taylor clan that moved out of God's country a few years ago and down to Roseburg. She's going to school at Southern Oregon College in Ashland. Raven, this is my roommate, Tony Corrarino. He's Italian."

"So I gathered, Dean, but thanks."

"You're welcome. Listen, I'd better go check on my mom and stuff. I hate to leave you alone here with her, Tony. Watch out, she's trouble." And Dean ambled off to the crowd.

Tony looked appraisingly at the stunning girl in front of him. "Trouble?" he said.

"Ugly rumors," she laughed, and took his arm. "Come on, I'll show you around the place."

"I've actually been here many times," Tony said.

She relaxed her grip on his arm. "Well, we certainly don't have to go if you don't want to." Tony realized that her lips made the perfect pout about the same time he realized he was on the verge of a terrible mistake. He pulled her in close to his arm, covering her hand with his. "Whoa, don't give up on me. I'd like to see anything you want to show me. Let's go."

And so they did. And she showed him a great deal and kept showing him until early the next morning, when she left to join her family in their trailer.

Tony slept in his tent for a while after she left, and then awoke to a hazy dawn, with the sun filtering through a thin fog hanging low over the valley. He used one of the portable toilets, washed his face and brushed his teeth with help from a garden hose and then began to pick up trash around the homestead. Gradually, more people appeared from tents, trailers, barns and pickups. All moved slowly and quietly. A large pot of coffee came out from the house. Then another. After a while people began to talk. There was even a little laughter, though it sounded querulous. Gradually, people began to work together, carrying picnic tables, heavy cans of trash, empty kegs of beer. Tony stood for a few moments and watched the scene before him. The creeping sunrise washed through the fog and onto the Taylor homestead, creating a surrealistic scene of slow, plodding people surrounded by a hazy glow. The fog attenuated sound as well, lending the scene an otherworldly flavor. From Tony's location, he could see movement but could hear nothing. He smiled to himself.

"Looks like the morning of the living dead," said a familiar voice behind him. Tony jumped in spite of himself and turned to see Raven, smiling at him, holding two cups of coffee. She offered one.

"Thanks," Tony said, as he took it. "You look even better this morning than you did last night."

"You're either a liar or you put your contact lenses in backwards, but thanks anyway. How'd you sleep?"

Tony glanced sideways at her. "Very well for an hour or two after you left. Before that, I wasn't interested in sleep."

She laughed. "Me too…and me either. But in case anyone asks, we drove out to Waldport and walked on the beach, OK? It will be tough to explain why no one could find us unless we were gone."

"Are you worried about your folks?" Tony hoped he hadn't created trouble for Dean's family on a day that should have been devoted to grieving for his father.

She laughed and tousled his hair. "No, not really. More likely your best friend, bosom buddy, blood brother Dean would have come looking for you."

"I imagine he had more important things to worry about than me."

"Yes, I suppose he did, but everybody in the family knows how much he thinks of you. The big joke last night was that you're like the seventh son they never had."

Tony chuckled, pleased beyond measure.

"I can see why," Raven bumped him gently, hip to hip. "You're a pretty neat guy." She turned to look him square in the face. "Do they know you are part of a New York crime family?"

Tony was struck speechless. Almost two years in Eugene and no one had ever made the connection between him and his father; at least no one had ever said anything—until now. For his first several months in Eugene, he'd had a story ready in case it was necessary. No, he was not from that branch of the Corrarino's. The families may share some similar roots in the old country but the only family business his father was in the stock market. A different kind of crime. Ha, ha, ha! But his cover story had been unnecessary until now, and now it was way too rusty to use. He stared at her for several seconds, watching her eyes widen.

"I'll be damned," she breathed.

"You didn't know; did you?" he said.

"Not until now, but you're not much good at keeping a secret."

He snorted disgustedly. "No, I'm sure not. Damn!" He took a deep breath. Raven stood quietly. "Yeah. Sal Corrarino is my father, I'm part of his family, but I'm not part of his business. I didn't want to be, that's why I came to school out here. How did you know?" She shrugged. "OK, why did you guess?"

She smiled, put a hand on his shoulder. Left it there. "Don't worry. I'm not going to say anything…to anyone. I'm taking a class this quarter called Crime in America and your father's name came up when we were discussing the Mafia. He was just a name mentioned, but it's a really unique name and I thought it would be fun to ask. As it turned out, it wasn't that much fun. Sorry."

"It's all right." Tony sat down heavily on a nearby chair. Raven grabbed another one, pulled it over next to him and sat down. "But I'd appreciate it if you didn't let the Taylors know, at least until things settle out from Mr. Taylor's death."

"I told you. I'm not telling anyone anything, although I'm sure someone will make the connection someday."

"Yeah, I'll tell Dean when he gets back to school."

The conversation lagged; both Tony and Raven were unwilling to talk about the future. Each was uncertain of the other's intentions and didn't want to weaken themselves by asking. Finally, Raven stood up. "Well, my folks are going to head back early this morning so I'd better go."

Tony was suddenly uneasy; he realized how much he didn't want his relationship with Raven to end. He took her hand. "Well, maybe we could…" he stopped, uncertain how to continue.

Raven turned and looked at him, a slight smile on her face.

"I was thinking we could get together again…sometime…maybe."

"Yeah, maybe. That would be nice." Raven smiled and kissed him lightly on the lips. "Give me a call sometime." And she walked toward her family's motorhome.

The rest of the morning passed quickly. Family members and guests worked together to make short work of the mess and by ten o'clock the place looked as good as new. Mrs. Taylor, with help from her clan, brought out bowl after bowl of leftovers from the night before, and Brian scrambled several dozen eggs, creating one of the more memorable brunches Tony had ever seen.

Afterward, Dean came over to Tony. "Well, how was breakfast?"

"It was great. I don't think we missed too many food groups, all of which were made better with barbecued pork."

"Yeah, well, there's still plenty left. We probably didn't need two 200 pounders." He looked at Tony from under his brow. "So, how'd you like Raven?"

"Oh, she was OK." Tony smiled. "Shit, she was great. I really liked her. I'm going to see her again. Is she really related to you?"

Dean laughed. "Yep. And she's one of our favorites, too, so be careful how you behave."

Tony raised his hands in mock alarm. "Hey, we drove to Waldport last night and walked on the beach."

"Oh, please! Do you know how many times I've used the old, 'we went to Waldport and walked on the beach routine? Save it in case her father comes looking for you. Jesus! Raven should know better." He laughed, and then laughed harder when he saw that Tony was taking him seriously. "Look, fool! Raven is a big girl, and she can handle herself." He grew serious. "But I do want you to be nice to her."

Tony started to respond, but Dean waved him off.

"Not to worry. You are the last person in the world I would worry about with my cousin."

"Hey! I resent that! I'm a worrisome son of a bitch!"

Dean laughed even more. "I know. I know."

"Besides," Tony came closer. "I really like her a lot."

"Yeah, well, get in line. Every guy who sees her feels the same way, though I have to admit, you seemed to do better than most. Anyway," Dean dismissed the subject with another wave, "this thing is over and it's time for you to get back to school."

Tony felt his heart sink with the words. "What do you mean me? I mean, I know I have to get back but so do you. You're coming, right? The quarter is almost over and you already missed a week." He was conscious of the pleading tone in his voice but it was done. He couldn't take it back or make it sound any better. He stood there.

Dean sighed, one hand kneading the other. "I'm coming back, Tony, but I'm going to wait until tonight, so I can make sure Mom's going to be all right. Then I'll come back and finish the year with you, OK?"

Tony nodded, unconvinced, but he had no other arguments, so he nodded again, shook hands with Dean, and after an extended farewell with the rest of the Taylor clan, he headed out. As he always did before leaving the Taylor place, Tony took a moment to look around. The fog had long since burnt off; the sun was high in the sky and illuminated their whole farm, an event that, though not rare, was certainly uncommon enough to be appreciated. The old farmhouse was bounded on one side by an orchard of apples, cherries and pear trees. A large garden swept toward the hay fields on the other side of the house. The Alsea River bordered the Taylor land 200 yards from the house. Hay fields ran west between the highway and the river. A large barn stood next to the highway, 300 yards from the house. Tony smiled. Despite their recent tragedy, he would always associate the Taylor farm with happiness, and carry especially fond memories of the barn and Raven. Those memories would help sustain him in the years to come.

Chapter 15

As promised, Dean showed up at their dorm room that night. He seemed a little subdued perhaps, but generally normal. Better than Tony had expected. Dean got right to work at his desk, saying "I put a lot of work into these classes… I'm not going to let them go down the tubes at the last minute."

As it turned out, the timing of Gage Taylor's death was fortuitous, at least in respect to their school schedule. Dean had missed the week before Dead Week and although two of his professors had given quizzes or assigned papers during that period, both agreed to let him drop those assignments from his final grade. Now, with Dead Week ahead of him, Dean put every effort into catching up and preparing for his final exams. He worked constantly, begging off from the occasional beer attack they'd always shared. Even the possibility of hooking up with his two co-ed friends from the night before his dad's death didn't seem to attract him. That's when Tony knew something was wrong. But Dean wasn't talking much, and that's the way they went through Dead Week and their exams.

Dean's last exam was on Thursday. He packed Thursday night while Tony was studying, then headed for town on Friday morning, as Tony left for his last exams. "I've got a few things to take care of before I head out for the summer," Dean told him.

Tony was packing his own stuff that afternoon when Dean walked in.

"How'd the exam go?" he asked.

"No sweat," Tony answered. "I nailed it. Haven't had much chance to talk this week, how'd you do on yours?"

"OK, I guess. Hard for me to care much, one way or another."

"Yeah, I know."

"Yeah. Well, it's not just because of my dad. I'm done with school for a while."

Tony stood silent, uncertain what to ask, what to say. Finally, he tried. "What do you mean? What are you going to do?"

Dean pursed his lips, looked out the window in the direction of the Cascades. "I signed up for Army Aviation this morning. Took the test and everything. I already took the physical before. I'm headed out in two weeks." He turned to Tony and smiled ruefully.

"But Dean, why? You've been doing so well. You said yourself you broke the code on this school stuff."

"Don't know, exactly. All I know is, I don't want to go to school anymore. I want to do something meaningful, move forward, be somebody."

Jesus Christ, Dean! You go in the Army you've got a 60-70 percent chance of going to Vietnam. Fly helicopters and it's probably closer to 100 percent. Then you can be somebody, but you'll be somebody dead. Shit! You got a death wish?"

Dean shook his head slowly. "No, I don't. I just want to do something different."

"Fuck different! Go do something different then. Be a ski bum. Go in the Peace Corps. Just stay out of the goddamned Army!"

"Anything other than the military, you *know* they'd draft me in an instant... and then I'd go right to the grunts—no chance for aviation. This way I have a little control over my destiny. Look, Tony, I know you don't like the war and you don't like the military. But I'm not the same as you. My father was in the Marines. All my uncles and grandfathers served. My brother Gary is in Vietnam right now..." he held up his hand as Tony started to speak. "I know, I know. I wouldn't go over while he was still there. He comes back next month and it will be almost a year before I go. My mom will have plenty of kids looking after her."

Tony started to speak but Dean interrupted, holding up his hand once again. "One other thing, Tony. I know this doesn't mean much to you, but I believe in this country. I want to do my part. Other guys are over there fighting for their country. You remember Lonnie from the fire crew? He's headed over in less than a month. I want to pay my dues."

Tony stood silent. The concept of paying dues was a near constant with Dean. He'd told Tony he'd be a good oarsman after he'd paid his dues, he'd be a good fisherman after he'd paid his dues, he'd be a good hunter after… in Dean's mind the dues paying never ended. Tony had to admit that Dean's approach made more sense of Vietnam than any other argument he'd heard. Nothing about the war itself, or the reasons for it, seemed logical but now, seeing the earnest look in Dean's eyes, Tony suddenly understood why he wanted to go to Vietnam. It was one more till in which to place his dues. It was a yardstick on which a man could be measured. It didn't matter whether the Vietnam War was really a worthwhile war or not. Their leaders said it was. Good enough. When the call went out, men like the Taylors and countless thousands more like them answered… and paid their dues.

This was a totally alien concept for Tony. The only real loyalty Tony had ever felt was for his family and his friends. His father and brother, he knew, were loyal to the Mafia, an extended family in their case. But none of them were dedicated to the country; they weren't patriotic, not like Dean. None of the people Tony knew from his days in New York ever went into the military. New York boys with mob connections simply didn't get drafted.

Tony's introspection ended when Dean coughed and held out his hand. Tony could sense his friend's uncertainty but Dean's strong grip and steady gaze covered well.

"Well, be careful on the fire crew," he said.

"I will. You be careful in helicopters. Come back safe."

Dean turned toward the door and then stopped. "Be nice to my cousin," he grinned.

Tony laughed. "I'll be as nice as I can."

"Yeah, see you later."

Chapter 16

—·‹(●)›·—

Trey Cannon shifted his weight slightly from his right elbow to his left and pursed his lips to blow air straight upward at the mosquito sitting on his nose. The mosquito flew, but Trey was sure he'd be back again soon. He wished he was well enough hidden to use his hand to squish the obnoxious creature, but no matter how complete his camouflage, Trey would never jeopardize his mission with rapid hand movements. Success, and his survival, depended on his staying still.

Trey was lying prone on a brushy hillside above a beautiful southern California villa. He was about 200 yards from the backyard pool. He hated the inactivity and boredom of a setup like this and that was probably why he was so good at it. He'd learned long ago that his kind of hunting required long periods of being still, and being still is not simply an act of will. It is an act of being comfortable. No matter how dedicated you are, your muscles will betray you if you aren't comfortable.

Trey had prepped his site in the darkness the night before. He'd spent an hour clearing rocks and brush and smoothing the dirt where he would lie. Then he added sprigs of freshly cut sagebrush to the puny bush just in front of his face. Enough to break up his outline and that of his rifle but not enough to limit his sight. He dug the bipod legs deeply into the hillside to stabilize them and to establish the necessary downhill trajectory. He placed two small beanbags under the stock. Now, all he had to do was cradle the rifle with as little movement as possible and he would be very close to on target. Finally, he threw a few handfuls of dirt and brush up and over his back and legs and relaxed. Three more hours to daylight and he had the equivalent of a rifle range bench setup. He lowered his face slowly to the ground, then raised it smoothly until his eye looked directly into the 2.5-10 power Zeiss scope. The crosshairs were still centered on the large red pool chair. He flipped the scope covers into place.

Trey lowered his face once again to the dirt and relaxed his entire body. The camouflage face net protected his face from the dirt. He didn't like face nets; he would have preferred camouflaged face paint, but paint was difficult to remove in a hurry and he would be leaving in a hurry for sure. He was as comfortable as it was possible to be; the temperature was mild; the air was still. He was well camouflaged, had a good, dependable rifle and a bird's eye view of his target's back yard. He had good intelligence about the target and most importantly, he had a carefully considered plan of escape. It was a perfect sniper's morning. He smiled at the thought.

The target took early morning swims nearly every day and with a little luck would do it again this morning. If he didn't, Trey would be in for a long, uncomfortable day. In that event, he would have to stay hidden until well after dark tomorrow so he could leave undetected. "Let's hear it for strong habit patterns," Trey said soundlessly.

If there was a weak spot in Trey's plan it was the bodyguards. Any bodyguard worth a nickel would check out this hillside before he let his boss come out to the pool. At the least Trey's setup would have to make it through intense visual inspection with high magnification optics. But the truth was, no one truly concerned with security would live in a house so vulnerable to attack from a nearby hillside. This made Trey think the bodyguards were just for show, somebody to keep the paparazzi away. He hoped so. He didn't relish having an eagle-eyed bodyguard glassing the hillside meter by meter. Reflexively, he raised his head to make sure the scope cover was on. He didn't need reflected light giving him away. Trey knew the first indication he would have of discovery would be a high-powered rifle shot he never heard. "It's what you might call incentive to do it right," one of Trey's instructors had told him years before.

The target was a big money guy, a real estate developer who'd branched out into everything from Hollywood to Las Vegas. The man had ridden roughshod into societies and economies that were not at all what they seemed. Even without a full-blown dossier, Trey could take a pretty good guess at the situation. Unsatisfied with being incredibly rich, the target had wanted power as well. He'd begun to acquire properties and businesses in an attempt to become one of the real west coast movers and shakers. Even if the true ownership of those building blocks was obvious, which was highly unlikely, the real leverage and power within and behind the companies were always carefully hidden. The target had undoubtedly received one or more warnings, but the warnings were probably subtle and he may not have recognized their serious nature. Perhaps he thought he'd get a second chance, a more serious sign, like a severed horse head in his bed. Sorry, pal, this ain't the movies. In this game, two strikes and you're out.

The target had almost certainly run afoul of someone with mob connections in New York or Las Vegas, someone with connections to the people who hired Trey Cannon. But the people or the reasons why didn't matter and Trey didn't really care. Someone in a position of power, real power, had designated the rich guy a target. His violent death was a foreordained conclusion and the instrument of his death was Trey Cannon. It would be today, or tomorrow, or the next day. However long it took was how long it took. Trey planned his hits as though they would take up to a year. That sort of long-range planning was a gift from Carlo Benuscio, his late friend and mentor. It was because of Carlo that Trey was in this business, a gift for which he was not always grateful, but it was also because of Carlo that Trey would someday be able to leave the business, a rare and valuable gift indeed.

Trey smiled into the dirt as he remembered meeting Carlo for the first time. He'd come into the Appean Way after finishing his shift on the ambulance. The Appean wasn't his regular hangout, but he'd heard good things about it from one of the firemen in his house. The restaurant was considered one of the best Italian places in Long Beach and the bar was a popular late-night destination, with good live music and excellent, if expensive, drinks.

Trey sat at the bar and turned to watch the band and dancers. Three bartenders were working hard and fast; one of them slowed down as she passed and said, "Be with you in a second, sir."

But 10 minutes later, Trey still hadn't given his order. Suddenly, a short, fat man sitting two stools away exhaled in a disgusted snort and hopped off his seat. In remarkably quick movements, he stepped behind the bar, moving purposefully toward Trey. Surprisingly, none of the bartenders confronted him; they simply moved out of his way. One, the woman who'd spoken to Trey, bent down as she passed the fat man and whispered, "Sorry. Joey called in sick. We're having trouble keeping up." The fat man ticked his head slightly in acknowledgement and came to a stop in front of Trey.

"Good evening?" he said, looking Trey full in the eyes.

Was it a question? Trey wondered, and though he'd prepared to ask for a beer he decided to answer it.

"Not bad," he said. "Long shift, but plenty to do, so it went fast."

"Whatcha do?" The fat man had not yet taken his eyes away from Trey.

"EMT. This your place?"

The fat man smiled. "Yeah. Pain in the ass, sometimes. Drink?"

Trey was beginning to like the fat man, even though his truncated way of speaking was disconcerting at first. "Yeah."

The fat man smiled even more broadly. "Care what it is?"

"No." Trey wondered what to expect.

"Good." And he poured a full glass of Makers Mark bourbon over two ice cubes and handed it across.

Trey slid a $20 across the bar. The fat man slid it back. "On me."

"Thanks. Are you familiar with the concept of complete sentences?"

The fat man laughed out loud. "Yeah. Don't like 'em. Carlo." He stuck out a thick, short-fingered hand.

Trey laughed as well, and took the hand. "Trey."

And that was the beginning of many things, Trey thought to himself. The closest friendship of his life, a profession that had made him rich by almost any standards and a long-time taste for Maker's Mark bourbon. Carlo and he quickly became close friends. Carlo, a transplanted New

Yorker, was in his early 50s. Short and fat, he was also deceptively fast and remarkably strong. He had almost nothing in common with Trey, six feet tall with long blonde hair and a surfer's body, tanned and muscular. But, as he explained in later years to his bosses, Carlo had recognized in Trey a kindred spirit, a quick mind and a sharp tongue. "Knew him quick. Straight up hardcase. No bullshit. Good guy."

They sat and talked for two hours after the bar closed that night. Trey laughed most of the time. Carlo was hilarious, with his one-and two-word statements and total irreverence about essentially everything. Trey realized in short order that Carlo was the most cynical human being he'd ever met, but unlike many cynics, Carlo didn't seem to harbor any bitterness. He simply recognized human foibles and laughed about them. On the rare occasions where there were no foibles in evidence, Carlo manufactured them, "and his synthetic foibles," as Trey explained one night to his sister, "were always as good as the real thing."

Carlo was also a gifted listener and it wasn't many months before he knew much more about Trey than Trey had intended to tell him.

"So, you're an EMT."

"Sort of. A paramedic."

"Ahh, a smart EMT."

"Yeah."

"Like me."

"Like you, how? You own the restaurant."

"Just a smart waiter," and Carlo rocked with laughter.

Trey had told Carlo most of it in dabs and dribbles during late-night bullshit sessions, while Carlo watched over the bar or served a few select customers. About half of Carlo's sentences, Trey realized, began with the word, "So." It was his way of continuing a conversation that had been broken for one reason or another. If he had been talking, Carlo would simply roll back into his story with "So there I was, doing...." and off he'd go. If Trey had been talking, Carlo would begin for him with "So, you were..." and wait expectantly. It was a wonderful way to lead the conversation, Trey realized, shortly after he realized how much he'd been talking.

"So, before you were a paramedic you..."

"The Navy." And Trey gave him the basics. Joined the Navy at 17, became a Corpsman. Attached to a Marine rifle company in Vietnam. Spent a little more time in the Navy, then tired of it and got out. He'd been a paramedic ever since.

"So, d'you like being a corpsman?"

Trey had loved it. He'd been appreciated by the Marines for his medical skill and fearlessness. They called him Doc, as they call all Navy corpsmen, and later, after things had gotten hairy a time or two, they'd recognized his fighting skills as well. Nothing strikes a Marine's fancy like a corpsman who can fight, unless it is a corpsman who wants to. After the first time, when his Lieutenant had given him an M-16 and put him into the ambush line, Trey's legend began to grow. After word got out that Trey was getting into the combat end of things, Master Chief Blackmon tried to get him reassigned to the battalion staff. But the Lieutenant said bullshit, and got the Colonel to step on the Chief and that was the end of that. Until the Lieutenant got blown up, and then Blackmon got his revenge. Trey was assigned to battalion, doing sick bay for the sick, lame and lazy for the last month of his tour.

He went in to talk to the chief about staying in country for another tour, but the chief told him he'd have to spend his second year in the hospital in DaNang.

"Let me see if I understand this, Master Chief. You are going to punish me by keeping me out of combat?"

"Keep up your wiseass shit with me, Cannon, and you'll be disinfecting shitters for the rest of your time in the Navy, got it?"

"Yes, Master Chief."

"It's not good to stay down in the boonies with the grunts for too long, Cannon. After a while you go native, and from what I hear, you're most of the way there already."

So, Trey had gone back to the states, stationed at the dispensary at Coronado. He'd been there for almost a month when a Navy lieutenant had shown up wanting to talk with him. The Lieutenant, a muscular black man, sat down with Trey in a vacant office and said he'd heard good things about Trey from a couple of his friends. Wondered if he might be interested in trying out for the SEALS.

"Why in the world would I want to do that, Sir?" Trey had asked him, but he was already quivering with anticipation.

"To see if you're good enough, Corpsman." He wrote some information down on a prescription chit. "Call me if you're interested." He turned to walk out the door.

Trey didn't have it in him to delay, even a bit.

"Sir?" The lieutenant turned. "One question, how did you happen to get my name?"

"Master Chief Blackmon is an old friend of my C.O. I understand he made a phone call on your behalf. Something to the effect that you might be oriented toward our line of work."

"I'll be damned," Trey mused. "I thought he hated me."

The lieutenant laughed. "He probably does and this is the best way he has of punishing you. If you take this opportunity there will be plenty of times you'll wish you hadn't… if you don't wish you were dead. And of course, you'll have to reenlist to be eligible for the school."

Trey did some quick calculations. He was almost 21, with absolutely no plans for the future. "I'm interested."

The lieutenant looked at him for a long time, his eyes suddenly flinty. "Good. I think we can get you into the next class. You look like you're in pretty good shape but I advise you to begin some heavy workouts. Our dropout rate is high."

"Aye, Sir," Trey had answered, and had begun his workout regimen that afternoon. And if Master Chief Blackmon had intended to make Trey's life miserable, he'd certainly failed. Trey had loved everything about the SEALS. The physical challenges had been intense, but Trey excelled in those and in the academics as well. He was the honor graduate of his class. He'd gone on to advanced training in demolitions, hand-to-hand combat, parachute operations, wilderness survival, long-range shooting, SCUBA and even more medical, although, after a year as a combat corpsman, Trey was well ahead in that regard. In general, as Trey noticed, his SEAL training prepared him for any kind of military operation, with an emphasis on killing people in a variety of ways. Predictably, the Navy found a number of situations to put his skills to use and again, Trey excelled. Trey loved the SEALS, loved the challenge, the camaraderie and loved the fighting—the opportunity to kill an enemy. Intellectually, Trey took no pleasure in the taking of life. But in the moment, when his blood was up, when he was afraid for his own life, when the success of the mission rested on his shoulders and on his cold-blooded willingness to kill, when the lives of his team members depended on his 'brutishness,' Trey experienced a 'rush' unlike anything he'd ever known. At that point he was capable of killing, efficiently and well. In every case, he prepared himself by thinking of the slope-shouldered man. Each time Trey killed, he was killing that man.

Had it not been for a tangled parachute cord, Trey might well have been a career Navy man. A training jump, for Christ's sake, he thought. An annual requalification jump had turned bad when his primary chute had become tangled above him. After several frantic seconds spent trying to free it, Trey had cut the primary away and deployed his belly-mounted backup. Something had gone wrong there, too, and one of the cords had somehow wrapped around his left arm. When the chute deployed it pulled his arm out of the socket and tore the rotator cuff almost completely. With his ruined arm stretched above him, Trey had been unable to prepare for a hard landing. The resulting impact had broken both legs below the knees and cracked two vertebrae.

Three days later, the same black Navy officer who'd recruited him to the SEALS walked into his room at the Balboa Naval Hospital. Now a Lieutenant Commander, Richard Cottoner had become a friend and mentor to Trey over the last four years. In his typical, no prelude style, Cottoner dropped a sheaf of papers on the table next to Trey's bed. "Time to re-up, Sailor," he said.

Trey was foggy from painkillers, but he'd had several visits from doctors, including the doctors who tended to SEALS. Their message had been frank. At the least he was out of the operational end of the business.

"I can't see it, Commander. Re-upping to ride a desk for the rest of my career?"

"*I* ride a desk, Petty Officer Cannon." Cottoner's eyes went hard for a moment, then softened. "Listen, Trey, even the healthy ones have to pull out of ops in their 30s. This is a young man's game. You just got old before your time. You can still do great work, even if it is from behind a desk."

"It's not for me, Sir." Trey shook his head.

"OK," Cottoner put his hand on Trey's shoulder. "That's what I thought you'd say. Here's the backup plan. Our doctors said your injuries are bad enough to warrant a medical retirement. Your legs should heal fine but your back and shoulder are likely to dog you for the rest of your life. A medical retirement will give you a good part of your pay plus health care from now on, and you can go on to whatever you want to do with the rest of your life."

Trey smiled lopsidedly. "I suppose being a baseball pitcher is out of the question."

"I don't know," Cottoner said as he sat down next to Trey's bed. "Even as bad as your arm is you might still be able to make it in the Padres' system."

Three months later, Trey had been mustered out of the Navy on a medical discharge. He'd returned to Long Beach, to his parents' home, where his mother and remaining sister still lived. He'd moved in with them while he continued his rehabilitation. As LtCmdr Cottoner had predicted, the legs healed well. His back was not a problem as long as he stretched each morning. The shoulder was a different matter. Even two months after his retirement, Trey couldn't throw a ball or scratch his back. He went back to the VA hospital for rotator cuff surgery. After extensive physical therapy and almost a year's recovery, Trey had full range of motion and could do 50 pushups and 20 pull-ups. A year after leaving the Navy, Trey became a paramedic in the Long Beach Fire Department. They were glad to get him; Trey had more extensive experience than anyone else in the department and he quickly became a popular addition.

****

A light came on in the house below. Probably the bodyguard. Trey shifted his body slightly. Tensed, then relaxed various muscle groups. Took a series of deep breaths. Stretched his back. Flipped the forward scope cover up. The sky to his left was brightening. The kitchen light came on and a shadow moved behind the shade. The sliding glass door to the swimming pool opened and a man stepped out. Broad and muscular, the man walked slowly around the pool. The bodyguard was careful. He checked out the pool area completely, then turned his attention to the hillside where Trey was hidden. He wasn't using binoculars. Good. There was no way he could see Trey with the naked eye. The bodyguard went back in the house. Two minutes later he came back out followed by a smaller man.

Was he the target? Trey moved his eye to the scope, shifted the rifle slightly so he could look directly at the smaller man's face. No. Not the target. A second bodyguard. Not good. There would be a period of 10 seconds or so when Trey would be visible as he ran for cover and if he was visible he could be shot. He could kill the target and one of the bodyguards easily, but the second bodyguard could be trouble and he didn't have the time or the inclination for a long, drawn-out gun fight. He seriously considered giving up on the hit for today, setting up for another time when he might find the target alone or with just one guard. No. The risk was acceptable. He settled imperceptibly into the rifle.

The bodyguards took positions on either side of the pool and waited. A moment later the door opened and his target walked out.

****

Trey didn't tell Carlo about the SEALS at first. Too much of an ooh-ahh factor and though Carlo was not easily impressed, Trey just didn't want to answer the questions that always followed the word SEALS. For a long time, they'd just talked about family stuff.

Carlo was divorced. His ex-wife and two grown daughters lived in New York. He'd moved west, away from the pain.

"Daughters got kids, families, you know?" he'd explained.

"You didn't want to stay near them? See the grandkids?"

"They come out once a year. It's plenty. Girls got shitheads for husbands."

"Ahh, that probably takes the fun out of your visits." And the two men laughed until people stared.

"What did you do back in New York?" Trey had asked.

"Oh, this and that. Owned a store, another restaurant. Did some consulting."

An interesting and unfulfilling answer, Trey thought, but before he could follow up, Carlo asked about his family once, and then again. Trey had not really intended to talk about his family, but as usual, Carlo weaseled it out of him, without seeming to. Pulling rocks out of the way until the dam burst and Trey began talking and couldn't stop.

He was born one of three triplets, the other two, girls. His parents had named them Trip, Trey and Tri.

"Trip, Trey and Tri, no shit?" So, you got two sisters named Trip and Tri?"

Trey nodded, smiling. "Yeah, doesn't everybody?"

Carlo laughed deeply. Everybody I know, for sure. Whereabouts?"

"Not far from here. My father was a musician and my mother was a psychic."

"No shit?" Carlo had asked again. "A musician and a psychic? What was that like?"

Trey hesitated, but only momentarily. He was telling things he'd never told anyone before and somehow it felt good; it felt good to share his history with Carlo.

"It was great. For a while. My parents were happy, fun-loving people. We had a great time. We did a lot of surfing, all three of us swam competitively and were in gymnastics. We played music and sang at night when my father didn't have a gig somewhere. My sisters were gifted musicians and they inherited my mother's psychic talent, too. Sometimes the three of them were scary, the way they could communicate without speaking, the way they knew things they shouldn't have known. My father would laugh and tell me our family was a tough one to keep secrets in."

Trey smiled at the memory and took another drink. His hand stayed on the glass, his fingers growing white.

"How 'bout you? D'you have talents?" Carlo asked.

"Not like the others. I could play the piano a little. I could carry a tune. But I'm not psychic. Sometimes, I get feelings about a situation… maybe it's tense, maybe something bad is going to happen. I usually know if someone means me harm. It's almost like being sensitive instead of psychic, like just being attuned to the things around you."

"Sounds like a good thing."

Trey's fingers tightened around the glass again. He began to rotate the bottom of the glass in a circular motion on the bar, tracing a thin line of moisture in its wake.

"It can be." But only if you pay attention to it. Only if you take action right away.

"When we were 12 years old a man broke into our house and killed my father, raped my mother and kidnapped one of my sisters."

There. He'd said it. Clinical. He could do this. "My mother sort of lost her mind and my other sister withdrew deep into a shell."

"Ahhh, shit."

"Yeah. Shit."

"So, did you know it was coming?"

"I think so, looking back. I was lying there in my bed. I had a bad feeling about something, but it was the first time I'd ever really experienced it and I didn't know how to interpret the sensation. Then I heard a scream and realized we were in trouble, but it was too late.

"Actually, it might not have been too late, if I'd taken the right action. If I'd just called the police, if I'd run to a neighbor's, but I didn't. I ran to my parents' room and into a bloodbath. My father was lying on the floor with his throat cut, my mother on the bed flapping her arms at the man tearing her nightgown off. My sisters were tied into chairs with their mouths covered with duct tape."

Trey had not even slowed down as he entered the room, had hit the attacker at full speed from the side, knocking him off his mother and onto the floor, but then the man recovered, and had beaten Trey so badly the girls thought their brother was dead. The intruder then took his time on Trey's mother, in full view of Trip and Tri. And then it got worse. The man said he was going to take one of them with him and made a real production out of the process of choosing which one. The girls were torn between the terror of being kidnapped and a desire to protect their sibling. Finally, he'd taken Trip, but not before terrorizing Tri with a threat to cut Trip's head off if Tri helped the police find him.

"You were 12," Carlo said. "Wadn't your fault."

"Yeah. I know. Thanks."

"D'you ever find him?"

An interesting question to ask, Trey thought. Most people would have phrased the question differently. They would ask whether *they'd* ever found his kidnapped sister, in reference to the police or the authorities. Not Carlo. He recognized the personal aspect of the crime and the punishment. He wanted to know if Trey, 12 years old at the time, had found the kidnapper personally. And for the first time, Trey realized, he was sitting across from someone who could see directly into his heart.

"Not yet."

Carlo nodded.

Trey had started preparing to find his father's killer as soon as he got out of the hospital following the attack. Over the objections of his mother's sister, who'd moved in to help take care of things, Trey gave up swimming, gymnastics and surfing and signed up for self-defense courses. He went to martial arts class three evenings a week for several years. He had no use for what he described as the 'soft' styles, like judo; he wanted to learn and perfect ways to subdue and kill people. Martial arts were not about discipline or self-control for Trey. They were about doing damage. Every punch he threw, every move he made was aimed at the slope-shouldered man he'd seen mounting his mother. Time after time he relived that terrible night in his dreams and each dream ended with him attacking and killing the intruder. It wasn't until late in his Vietnam tour that he stopped dreaming of the attack on a regular basis—by then he had newer, if not more horrific nightmares to relive.

Trey never stayed with a specific style of martial art for long. Sometimes he grew bored, twice he was thrown out of classes for not pulling punches, but by the time Trey was a senior in high school he was highly proficient in hand-to-hand combat, using a broad repertoire of moves and attacks. He wanted to join the Marines as soon as he graduated, but he was still 17 and his aunt wouldn't sign the permission slip. Only if he were going as a corpsman would she give him permission. And so, rather than wait two months for his 18th birthday, Trey joined the Navy and became a corpsman, attached to the Marines.

He felt bad about leaving for boot camp. His mother was barely functional and his sister still spent most of her time in her room. But they had plenty of money, both from his father's estate and life insurance, and his mother's sister had adjusted her own life to move in with them permanently.

****

Trey slid his eye behind the scope, slipped the safety off and rested his finger on the trigger. He was hoping to kill the man before he got into the pool but the target never stopped after walking through the door. He tossed a towel to the nearest bodyguard and dove into the water.

"Shit," Trey breathed. He kept the crosshairs on the target as he swam laps. Trey didn't like to shoot at moving targets and would wait for days until he had a stationary shot. He relaxed slightly and put his finger outside the trigger guard. He could wait.

****

Trey's mother and sister had done all right while he was away. His mother walked around with a vacant stare most of the time and babbled occasionally. Luckily, she could feed and care for herself enough so that her sister, who'd met and fallen in love with a man she'd met at the grocery store, felt comfortable about moving in with him. Tri had recovered almost completely. Under her aunt's guidance she'd finished school with home tutors and she now took care of the house, including the paperwork associated with bills. She'd learned to drive and regularly went to the store, although those trips were the extent of her activities outside the home.

His mother became ill shortly after Trey returned home from the Navy and she was now in the final stages of terminal ovarian cancer. Tri and Trey were caring for her at home with the help of Hospice nurses.

The conversations with Carlo continued several nights a week for almost three years. Trey grew to depend on Carlo's cynical honesty, wit and genuine support. For the first time in his life, Trey shared his past, present and dreams for the future with someone else. He trusted Carlo absolutely. For his part, Carlo came to look at Trey as his own son. He now knew in reasonable detail of Trey's experience in Vietnam, both as a medic and a SEAL and the knowledge increased his affection for the young paramedic. Trey had been in more than his share of difficult scrapes while with the Marines, but the missions that had had the most effect on him were the small team assassinations. Although he'd been careful not to give up specific details ("We promised…for national security, you know?") Trey had discussed killing men at 1,000 yards, setting bombs in cars and garroting.

"Didn't bother you?" Carlo had asked once.

Trey had thought for a long time before answering. "Sometimes. A little. Especially when it's up close. Messy. But the folks I killed were enemies of my country, you know? The ones in Vietnam were obvious, and those in a couple other countries were obviously working against us. They were dangerous."

"Yeah, better that way."

Trey waited for some more explanation, but Carlo just looked down at his drink and remained silent, thinking.

You're lucky you got out before you learned better. Sooner or later you'd have learned that in the end all killings are personal, not business.

Carlo couldn't help but be impressed, primarily because Trey was so obviously honest and aboveboard about his experiences. Trey had made his bones several times and in Carlo's mind no one could be a true man until he had done so.

****

Although he never said anything to Trey, Carlo had initiated a search for Trey's sister and the man who'd kidnapped her. The chances of success were poor, he knew, but the people looking at his behest would look in completely different places and in different ways than the police had. You just never knew, Carlo thought. He couldn't expect the same all-out effort he'd once been able to demand, but loss of influence was part of the price of his ostracism from New York. Loss of influence, Carlo had decided, was an acceptable price to pay in order to go on living.

He was still connected, after a manner of speaking. The Appean Way was a Family venture, after all, and he took care of Family-related business out here. "You be a liaison," Sal Corrarino had told him on the day of his dismissal. "You'll be sort of a deep cover for us. You make the restaurant run well. That's your living. That's *all* of your living." And Carlo understood then the completeness of his removal. He found it hard to believe Sal was going to allow him to live. He'd skimmed money from the receipts, after all, a lot of money.

Sal read his mind. "You are family, Carlo. The husband of my sister, father of my nieces, so you don't have to worry about them. They'll be well taken care of."

Carlo had almost gone for him, then; almost taken his chances with the two tough guys who stood on either side of him, but Carlo knew he had no chance against them and for that matter, he wasn't sure he could take Sal. If he didn't, and if he didn't die in the attempt, Carlo had no doubt that Sal would feed him his own liver. The thought paralyzed Carlo in his chair, as it had many men before and he nodded, even though he knew he was giving up his wife and daughters for the rest of his life. His wife was a shrew and had been for 10 years, no big loss. But his daughters were the loves of his life. How could he leave them? He looked at the pitiless ferocity in Sal's eyes and he quailed. He felt his love for his daughters shrivel and retreat to some small hidden place inside of him and he learned to keep it there.

Carlo had moved to California that day. He never even had a chance to say goodbye. He'd taken over the restaurant and run it well. He made a good living and once a year he sent a good portion of his take to each of his daughters; cash in an unmarked envelope with no return address. For the most part he was completely disconnected from the New York mob, but occasionally they wanted him to set up some Family venture. He would deliver messages to people, facilitate meetings, arrange for long-range punishment for someone living or hiding in the western states. Nothing major involved and certainly nothing that involved large amounts of money. His time with big money was gone, although he washed a little Family money through the restaurant. Sal sent accountants to look over Carlo's shoulder once a month to make sure everything stayed on the up and up.

Carlo hated the micromanagement but had to accept it. It became obvious early on that Carlo had a gift for the restaurant business. The Appean Way started out popular, then catapulted into superstar ranks, where reservations were required for dinner every night. He'd had to enlarge the bar and dance floor twice. When one of the mob accountants had complimented him on the consistently improving gross, Carlo said, "Ain't rocket science. Hire the best chef and pay him good. Hire the second-best chef, too. Hire good bands. Make good drinks. Keep an eye on the bartenders. Simple. See?"

Carlo made a habit of sending more money back to New York than they expected. He still had some tiny hope that if he consistently performed above the line that Sal would forgive him. Not completely, that would be impossible. But enough for him to maybe visit his daughters once or twice a year. He never said anything, just sent the extra money. Penance. The extra money he sent came from his personal income. What did he need money for, anyway? He spent two-thirds of every day at the restaurant where he ate and drank for free. His only recreation was taking in an occasional Dodgers' game and talking with Trey.

After three years, Carlo's feelings for Trey were stronger than any he'd ever felt for another human being besides his own flesh and blood. And he was sure Trey felt the same way. He found himself wishing he could have known Trey when he was a youngster. No. What he really wished was that he could have been Trey's father. The only time Carlo ever approached happiness was when he was talking with Trey at the bar.

So it was a terrible shock to him on the night when Trey told him he was moving away.

"My mother is not going to last more than a month, Carlo. My sister has essentially hidden in that house for the last 12 years. And I'm doing a job I was doing as a 17-year-old in Vietnam. I'm bored to death. We need a change. I'm thinking about Missoula, Montana. Going to college there. Starting over. Doing something else. I need some excitement. I miss the SEALS and the missions. My sister needs a new life." He smiled and shook his head, as though he were confused.

"Know what you mean," Carlo had said. And he did. Sometimes he missed New York so bad it hurt. He missed the constant threat of police informants, of attacks by other gangs. He knew what it was to miss the *excitement*. But he was shaken to the core by Trey's announcement. Somehow his life had become wound around Trey. The young man had replaced the roots sheared by his forced departure from New York. Carlo wasn't sure he could survive the loss of their late-night talks, their friendship, their connection. He kept talking but his brain was not engaged. He muddled through the rest of the night, then went home and stayed for two days. He spent that time sitting in his overstuffed chair, moving only when forced by bodily requirements. An observer would have suspected a sudden onset of catatonia but Carlo was simply focused, his mind working at warp speed. He considered and discarded dozens of ways to convince Trey to give up his plans to leave. It wasn't until the afternoon of his second day in the chair that Carlo came up with a plan. It was crazy. It was perfect. But it was dangerous, too. If the kid said no, Carlo would be in a bad spot. He didn't sleep for the rest of the night.

****

The target did a few laps with a crawl, switched to the breast stroke, then side stroke. He switched to the other side and finished up with a couple butterfly laps. He was a good swimmer, Trey saw. After the butterfly, he rested with his arms up over the rim, talking with the big bodyguard. Both men smiled and laughed; it was obvious they had a good relationship. I'll have to kill him, too. And right away. The target turned away from the poolside and pushed off strongly underwater. He stayed underwater for two full lengths of the pool. Good wind, too. Finally, he came to a stop at the end of the pool closest to the house.

This should be it. Trey took two slow breaths. His finger curled around the trigger, once again. His left hand cradled the forearm, pulling it gently into his shoulder. He looked through the scope.

The target hung on the pool gutter, let his face hang in the water, cooling off. He raised his head and put his hands up on the pool deck, preparing to push up out of the pool. The bullet hit him in the back of the head. Moving at 2,900 feet per second, the 130-grain bullet deformed partially as it penetrated the heavy skull, then passed through the brain, creating incredible hydrostatic pressure. Brain material might have expanded out through the ears, eyes and nasal passages under the pressure, but before it could do so the bullet exited through the face and alleviated the pressure. It came out just below the target's left eye and shattered against the poolside. The concrete shattered, sending dozens of sharp pieces flying backwards into the target's face, creating deep lacerations.

The target's head bounced backward from the poolside shrapnel, and then his body slipped quietly below the surface. The big bodyguard reacted quickly and well. He grabbed the target by the hair and physically yanked him halfway out of the pool. Trey was just chambering another round when the bodyguard got his hands under the target's armpits. The lift of a dead man from the water was almost Herculean. Trey was amazed, and would have cheered…but he was pulling the trigger again. The second bullet hit the target in the head again, within an inch of the initial wound, but this was purely accidental. Trey was aiming at the midpoint of the bodyguard's chest, and with only an already shattered skull to slow the bullet down, the second round was still doing over 1,400 feet per second when it hit the big man's chest. The bullet, already partially deformed by its trip through the target's skull, pancaked completely on its way through the bodyguard's sternum. The impact knocked him backwards and into the framework of a poolside bar, where he sat heavily, the thoroughly dead target stretched across his lap. The slug had slowed markedly by the time it penetrated his chest, but still had enough inertia to tear the pulmonary artery connecting the heart to the lungs. He would have bled to death in short order but didn't get a chance to—Trey's third shot hit him in the forehead.

The smaller bodyguard turned out to be slimy. He was crouched behind a lawn chair with his gun in his hand. His head was flat on the ground; his butt was in the air. No part of him was actually protected. Trey could see his body shake. "What are you thinking?" Trey asked aloud, and then put his fourth shot into the man's ear. "You call yourself a bodyguard. You couldn't wipe your friend's ass."

Trey raised himself into a kneeling position, pulled a Baby Wipe out of a small package in his pocket and wiped down his rifle. He put the wipe back in his pocket, along with the package. With a quick look down to the house to make sure no reinforcements were coming out, he moved rapidly up the hill and into a small stand of trees, leaving the weapon and cartridge casings where they lay. The rifle was a Remington Model 700, a common sporting rifle, bought two years earlier at a garage sale and then filed to remove the serial numbers. The ammunition was stock, purchased in Montana during a fly-fishing trip.

Trey stripped his camouflage clothing, gloves, face mask and hat off, revealing a jogger, outfitted in black shorts, tan T-shirt and black running shoes. He stuffed his clothing into a sand-colored runners backpack. He dripped water from a plastic jug over his hair, down the front of his shirt and down the back. He splashed a few drops on his face. Then he pulled a San Diego Padres baseball hat down low over his face, donned dark sunglasses and went jogging down the trail to his car, rented for this day with a fake credit card. He drove six blocks to a previously scouted wide spot in the road, where he stopped, changed into a short-sleeved polo shirt and put his T-shirt and baseball cap in the backpack. He removed his jogging shorts and replaced them with a pair of L.L. Bean six-pocket hiking shorts. His running shoes came off and were replaced by leather sandals from Birkenstock. Five minutes later Trey was driving along a carefully planned route through extensive suburban neighborhoods, wearing sunglasses and a wide-brimmed hat and working his way north before he jumped over to Highway 5. He returned the car to the small, local rental and walked a few blocks to his own vehicle. He dropped the clothing, backpack and shoes off at a Goodwill Store in Oceanside. He was home before 3 p.m.

Chapter 17

Having come up with a recommendation that would keep Trey in Long Beach, Carlo worried for the next week about the second half of his problem…helping Trey's sister, Tri re-establish her life. He knew it would have to be a package deal; Tri's future situation would be at least as important to Trey as his own. Carlo made numerous phone calls, then found what he thought would be the perfect solution. Call in a favor here, make a promise there, and pretty soon he was ready.

Trey didn't come in for a couple nights, but when he did, Carlo was ready. He handed a highball glass half-full of Makers Mark to Trey as the young man sat down.

"Howz it goin', Carlo?"

"Good. You?"

"No complaints. Thanks for the drink."

"You bet. Been thinkin'."

"Yeah? Any permanent damage?"

"Not so far. Got an idea, though."

"See? That's what thinking will do for you. You should be ashamed."

"I am. So, I think I found a job for Tri."

"A job? Tri's never worked."

"So? She can start. Be good for her. They'll train her. It's good work. Travel agent. After a while she'll get to travel, too, pretty much for free. She'll learn a lot. Be around nice people."

Trey hesitated. The idea sounded perfect. If the people were friendly and supported Tri as she learned the ropes, it could be the best possible thing for her. "It sounds great, Carlo. It might be exactly what she needs, but she and I need to stay together until she gets on her feet, and I'm committed to heading up to Montana."

"Got another idea 'bout you."

"Another idea?"

"Yeah. Come with me." Carlo led him back into his office in the back of the restaurant. Trey had never been in the office before.

"Close the door." Trey did.

"Why are we here?"

Carlo sat down heavily. "No bugs. I have it swept."

He pointed to a chair directly across from him. Trey sat.

"You have it swept."

"Yeah, you know…swept."

"Yeah, I know what it means. What I don't know is why you would bother… or who would want to listen in on your conversations."

"Probably nobody. But you never can tell. I know some people. We do some business. You know… from the old days."

Trey caught on quickly. "You're connected? What? From your days in New York?"

"Sort of. Yeah."

Trey laughed. "I should have known. You never did really talk about New York. You could have told me, you know. I would never talk."

"I know. I'm telling you now."

"Well, thanks for the vote of confidence, Carlo, but I don't have any interest in working for the Mob. I cheat a little on my taxes, but that's about it. I wouldn't know how to embark on a life of crime." Trey smiled.

"Oh, it's not so hard."

"No, I guess not."

"This job is a little different. This is about being a trouble shooter."

"A trouble shooter."

"Yeah."

Trey took a drink. He looked for a long time at Carlo, who leaned back and stretched. Tilted his head, one conspirator to another.

"Trouble shooter."

"Yeah."

"You're not talking about a trouble shooter, are you?"

"No."

"You're talking about a shooter. A hit man."

"Yeah, you could be good."

"I am good, I'm better than good. I've already punched that ticket. It was fulfilling but not very lucrative. And I did it for my country. It was war."

"I know."

"I'm out of that business, Carlo."

"I know."

Trey took another drink. Waiting for the rest. He knew Carlo enough to expect more. This was completely out of the blue and Carlo didn't do things out of the blue.

Finally, Carlo spoke. "We can set it up so nobody but me knows who you are. Nothing can come back at you. Orders come through me. You refuse any job you don't want."

"Why me?"

"You could be good."

"You said that. Why me?"

Carlo rubbed his face. Put his meaty hands on his knees, but not before Trey noticed the shake. For the first time Trey could remember, Carlo did not look directly at him when he spoke. His voice was throaty, shaky in a way Trey had never heard.

"I don't want you to leave, kid…I don't have much left. I can't go back to New York. I can't ever see my girls again. You're the family I got now." He looked up at Trey, blinked twice and stood up quickly, turned toward the window. "Montana wouldn't be good for Tri. She needs stability. Let her step out slowly from a place she knows. She'll love the job. You need variety, excitement. This work is exciting. You know that from before. And you'll make a lot of money."

"Jesus Christ, Carlo. I've never heard you talk that much in all the time I've known you."

"Fuck you, you little punk." Carlo smiled as he turned back toward

Trey. "The thing is, the people you'll be taking care of are scum. Thieves, snitches, killers." Carlo looked away momentarily. Trey saw something there; embarrassment maybe, but when Carlo looked back it was gone. He continued, "These are culls. You'll be doing society a favor."

Trey sat silently for a long time. Carlo got up and freshened both their drinks. Trey was trying to put all the pieces together. He was not surprised Carlo had ties to the mob.

The fat man had always slipped around direct questions regarding his former life, even as he explored all the details of Trey's past. He was just so smooth, and so friendly. And he was right about Tri. A move to Montana would likely be traumatic. Giving her a chance to move carefully back into a normal lifestyle from her lifelong home made a lot of sense. Montana had always been more about Trey, about his desire for something new, something else, but he'd already begun questioning the sense of it. Could he give up the Southern California lifestyle, the beach? He could, sure, but would it be better if he found a way to inject excitement into his life without leaving? Maybe.

But how did this make sense? If Carlo really cared about Trey, and he had no doubt it was true, why would he recruit him to be a hit man? Is this what Italian mobsters did with their favorite kids? Probably comes in a close second behind priest. No, it didn't make sense unless…unless…aww, shit.

Trey turned his attention directly to Carlo. "So, you know, don't you?"

To his credit, Carlo made no attempt to lie. "Yes, I know."
"How?"
"I sent a man out to put a beating on that little squirrel. He was checking him out when he noticed you doing the same thing. He came back and told me. I told him to get back out and do the job before you had a chance to get your tit in a wringer. But he wasn't fast enough. The next night he watched you follow the guy in. Two days later they found him. End of story."

Trey leaned back in his chair and took a pull on the bourbon. So, someone had seen him enter the scumbag's apartment. That was stupid. Sloppy. That's the kind of incompetence that gets you killed. But he'd been so mad; he'd wanted to pull the son-of-a-bitch's throat out. He thought back to the event; what was it… six months ago? He'd been getting ready to leave for work when Tri had knocked at his door.

"Trey, can I come with you to the Appean Way tonight?"

Trey was practically speechless; although Tri had been getting out of the house more and more recently, her forays were confined to shopping and school. Her refusal to take part in recreation of any type had been so long and so steadfast that Trey had finally given up trying to include her. She no longer surfed or even went out for dinner or drinks. She read, took care of their mother and occasionally watched television. Her showing an interest in going out at night was so alien that Trey realized his mouth was hanging open.

"Wha? I mean… sure, sis. That would be great. I don't get off my shift until 11, though. Do you want to go that late?"

"I think so…er, yes. Absolutely!" She smiled brightly; but Trey could see the uncertainty in her eyes. She shook her head, as if willing her own insecurity into a locked compartment. "I want to go… please!"

"Of course. I'll pick you up after work. But Tri, it's Friday and it's going to be crowded and loud at the Way."

"It's OK, Trey. I'm ready."

And so he'd picked her up after work and headed for the Appean Way. He'd introduced her to Carlo, who fawned over her, introduced his staff and gave her a tour of the facilities. Tri seemed overjoyed at the attention and at the happy energy of the crowded establishment.

Then, as they sat watching the dancers, Tri had been approached by a hesitant young woman.

"Tri? Tri Cannon? Is that you? Oh, it is, isn't it? I'm Jamie Riley. We were in middle school together. Oh, it's so good to see you."

To Trey's utter amazement, Tri stood up and hugged her old friend. In a few moments, the two young ladies were huddled together, talking and laughing like the long-lost friends they were. Trey could hear just enough over the din to realize that Jamie Riley was a remarkably adept and sensitive young woman. She expressed sorrow for the loss of their sister but didn't dwell on it, emphasizing instead the positive, how wonderful Tri looked, how fashionable her clothes were, there was even something in there about what a hunk her brother had grown up to be. Tri laughed at the ridiculousness of the notion.

"Trey," Jamie turned to him. "I'd like to take your sister over to meet my friends; it's just a group of us girls from work out for drinks and dancing."

Tri stood up. "I'd love to, Jamie." She reached over and pulled Trey's ear. "And I don't need my brother's permission." She leaned down and put her face close to his. "I'll be fine, Trey. But don't go too far away, OK?"

Trey squeezed her hand, "Sure, I'll just go over and shoot the bull with Carlo for a while. You guys have fun."

At first, Trey kept a close eye on his sister. The group of girls closed around her at first and two more of them seemed to recognize Tri. They must have attended the same school. Trey had attended the school as well but his memories of those years seemed to have been burned away by the events of his life. He could no longer remember any of his school friends or teachers. His life seemed to have started over on the day he'd enlisted in the Navy; everything before that was a blur, except for the slope-shouldered man. He was crystal clear. Occasionally, Trey would be approached by someone who'd known him in middle or high school. There was always an awkward attempt at reconnection but Trey never responded with the interest or excitement people seemed to expect, so after a few minutes of discomfort, those hazy phantasms from a barely remembered existence drifted off.

For the first time in as long as he could remember, Trey envied his sister. She was obviously enjoying herself. Now comfortably ensconced within the group, she was no longer their center of attention. Her new friends were sometimes talking at the table, sometimes dancing with young men. It was the typical nightclub scene; the crime was that Tri had never been able to experience it before. She was 28 years old and had lost the last 16 years of her life. As difficult and dangerous as Trey's own life had been, at least it had been exciting and fulfilling. Tri had spent those years taking care of their mother, hiding out, watching the world go by from her room. But now she seemed engaged, happy and outgoing. Then she was up and dancing. Trey leaned forward to get a closer look. Her partner was a bit older than Tri, in his mid-thirties, with a narrow, pock-marked face, but still darkly handsome. He seemed happy and friendly. He was not a regular at the Way.

"Nope, never seen him before either," Carlo offered without being asked.

Trey shook his head and laughed. "Oh, you're good, aren't you?"

"You bet. So, this is a good thing for Tri, no?"

Trey laughed and nodded. "Sure seems to be. I'd love to see her reconnect with society. She deserves a second chance."

"She does that."

The two friends sat at the bar for the next hour or so, Carlo occasionally getting up to help at the bar or answer a question from the waitresses. With closing time approaching, Trey leaned toward Carlo.

"Hey, would you mind if I used the staff restroom? I may be a few minutes and I don't want to fight the crowd."

Carlo nodded. "Of course. You don't need to ask."

Trey was having a bit of intestinal trouble and spent longer than he expected in the stall. He was half way out to the dance floor when he heard the commotion. A man yelled; a woman screamed. Tri! Trey moved fast. He stepped into the lounge in time to see Tri standing with her back against a wall, her hands held out as if to ward off an attack. She was obviously frightened and crying, but she was just as obviously angry and it looked to Trey like she was prepared to deliver more than just defensive blows.

Her former dancing partner was advancing on her, fists clenched. His face was flushed a deep crimson under his swarthy complexion. He was screaming obscenities. "You fucking cunt! Think you can take my drinks and tease me all night long and then drop me? Do you? I'll fucking show you…" Trey started across the floor, readying his left arm for the slash across the man's throat that would teach him a lesson about how not to treat women in general and Trey's sister in particular. It would also have an excellent chance of killing him.

As Trey approached Tri's assailant, two things happened simultaneously. The first was that a pair of Carlo's bouncers grabbed the man from both sides. The one on the right administered a short, powerful and unobtrusive shot to the solar plexus that put an immediate end to the man's tirade and rendered him cooperative. The second was that Trey suddenly found his arms pinned to his side and his feet lifted from the floor. He had just begun a response when he heard Carlo's voice in his ear.

"Don't be stupid. We've got this handled. You need to stay out of it."

Trey stopped struggling almost immediately, though his eyes never left the man's face as the bouncers led him from the building.

It took a while for Trey to piece the events together. Primarily because Tri was so little help, though not for the reasons he'd expected. He'd thought she would be cowed and frightened by the experience, but he was wrong. His sister was mad, so mad she couldn't put together a coherent sentence. It wasn't until her friend Jamie stepped in that things began to make sense.

"Tri wasn't doing anything wrong, Trey. She was just dancing and having fun. That asshole," she jerked her thumb at the door through which the troublemaker had been led, "just got more and more possessive the more he drank. He started pawing at her and Tri just told him to pack sand and came back to our table. He came over and grabbed her by the arm and started yelling and yanking her around."

"Thanks, Jamie. Do you know his name?"

"Sharla said it was Alan Dupree. She's seen him around at other clubs. Said he was a first-class jerk at other places, too."

The next morning, Trey began his research. He avoided some of the more obvious sources. He didn't want to leave any trace of his search. He learned where the man lived, then traced his employment history. Dupree was an investment counselor, new to Long Beach. He'd come from a three-year stint in Arizona and before that he'd lived in Florida. His work history petered out after that and after a little more probing Trey learned why. Dupree had spent six years in prison in Virginia for aggravated assault and attempted rape. After a little more digging Trey uncovered similar, though less violent activities in each of the locations Dupree had lived. In Florida, Dupree had been the subject of a restraining order protecting a former girlfriend and he'd been briefly jailed when he violated it.

In Arizona, he'd been accused of the use of Rohypnol in an attempt to take advantage of a female coworker, but the police had been unable to prove that he'd been the one to introduce the drug into the woman's drink at a well-attended party. His work supervisors had no such burden of proof, however, and let him go. And now here he was in Long Beach. Trey sat back at his desk, looking over the paperwork he'd amassed. He'd planned a painful lesson for Mr. Dupree. Now, as he looked at the man's record, Trey was revising his plan.

During his off hours, Trey began to follow Dupree. The man seemed to work hard at his job but as soon as the workday was over, he headed to a bar. He drank heavily until dinner, then ate some kind of fast food and headed out to a lounge. Dupree worked hard at getting laid, and was successful once or twice a week, but always with a new girl. He tended to visit different establishments as well. When he could find no female companionship he sometimes closed the bars, but just as often he bought a bottle of vodka and nursed it until the wee hours at home.

A little more than a month after his assault on Tri, Dupree was just opening the door to his apartment after another late night, when he heard a footstep behind him. Before he could react, he found himself pushed gently but firmly into his living room.

"What the fuck?" he cried.

The man who'd pushed him raised his hands as though to apologize. I just want to share a drink with you Alan. Maybe we could chat. I brought some of your favorite." He displayed a fifth of the same brand of vodka Dupree typically used. "Here, have a drink."

Dupree was very drunk, but he was still relatively observant. "Why are you wearing gloves?"

His unwanted visitor held up his hands. "I burned them in a campfire and the doctor said to leave the gloves on to fight infection."

Dupree nodded. It sounded plausible. "Who are you?" he wanted to know.

"My name is Mickey. I just thought we could have a drink together."

"I don't think so. You need to leave."

The stranger pulled a small pistol from his pocket. "I don't think you understand, Alan. That was not a request."

Two hours later, Trey stepped out of Dupree's bathroom. He turned to take a last look around. Dupree's naked body was sprawled across the bathtub. His bloody head and most of his torso were under water. A nearly empty fifth of vodka lay open next to the toilet.

Trey had not had to do much; after one look at the gun, Dupree had become downright thirsty. A few swallows into the bottle and Dupree seemed to have forgotten the existence of the gun. A few more and he treated Trey as a long-lost friend. They talked, laughed and told stories. After two-thirds of the bottle, Dupree was practically comatose. Trey only had to suggest a bath and the drunken idiot started the bathwater and threw off his clothes. It was a simple matter to knock Dupree off balance and guide his head into the tub faucet. He'd been unconscious before he hit the water and unable to save himself as his head went beneath the surface. It was over in a couple of minutes.

After making sure he'd left no indication of his presence, Trey pulled his hat down over his face and left by the front door.

****

Carlo, is this blackmail?"

"No, kid. I would never do that to you. That son of a bitch deserved what he got. I would never use it against you. If you make the decision to go to Montana, you go. Nobody will ever know about that scumbag. But you did it, which shows you've still got the nerve…and the attitude. And you did it like a pro, which means you've still got the skill. If I hadn't known about him, I would have tried something else. Offered to get you a job in banking, or sales, or something to keep you around here. But if you turn me down, you don't ever have to worry about that other… never."

Trey sat silent. Carlo got up and went to the restroom. His hands had stopped shaking, but he was sweating. He palmed water over his face. Dried off with a paper towel.

Jesus! Couldn't the kid see he was playing it straight? He was offering him a deal that could fix him for life. Yeah, but it's a hard life, and the kid's smart enough to know it. Still, with Carlo's help, the kid could be set up without any connection to the people who would be hiring him. They would never know his identity, which was the only way to ensure a long life.

Carlo leaned on the sink, his heart pounding. He forced himself to stay there for several more minutes, until his heart rate slowed. Then he went back into the office. Trey was gone.

Chapter 18

At first Carlo thought Trey was just thinking things over, that he'd come back with an answer. But days stretched into weeks and Carlo began to worry the kid had been so disgusted by the offer he had severed their relationship. He came close to calling but Carlo instinctively knew that would be wrong. After three weeks Carlo began to grieve. It had never occurred to him that Trey might find the offer so insulting he would stop coming around. In some ways, the pain of this loss was even worse than his banishment from New York and his daughters. At least he could remind himself that leaving New York was the only way to save his own life. The breakup of his family was necessary, but losing Trey's friendship was not. He could have tried a dozen different ways to keep Trey close besides offering him a job as a hired killer. But was it so great a leap to think Trey might be willing to do the same kind of work he'd done in the SEALS for more money than he could ever imagine? Evidently it was. And now here Carlo sat, 58 years old, overweight, diabetic, with high blood pressure, and a heart condition and he no longer even had someone to talk to at night. Shit. What a great way to end a life. Shit.

And then there was the knowledge thing. Now Trey knew of Carlo's tie to the New York Mob. He knew that Carlo arranged murders. He knew enough to make things bad for Carlo and the Family just by making a phone call. Carlo's stomach became queasy. He lived only at Sal

Corrarino's pleasure. If Sal became displeased, Carlo's remaining days would be short and painful. Jesus.

But Carlo trusted Trey. He would never talk. He's as loyal as they come… and as tough. Besides, and Carlo felt scummy about even having this thought, but there it was, Trey had been seen pushing the shithead into his house the night he was killed. Carlo's enforcer could never testify, but a phone call to the right Long Beach Police detective would put them on Trey in a hurry. *Jesus H. Christ. What sort of man thinks thoughts like these about his son? Shit.*

Chapter 19

As it turned out, Carlo was giving himself ulcers without reason. Trey had not abandoned him. He was simply caught up in troubles of his own that consumed him totally. His mother was in the last days of her life. The cancer was eating her alive and the pain was beyond anything she could bear. In one of her last moments of lucidity she'd looked at Trey and Tri and said softly, "Please find Trip. Please find your sister." After that, the pain had increased swiftly until clarity was not an option. If the level of painkiller in her body was reduced enough to let her think clearly, the pain left her screaming, thrashing and demented. She now spent her time asleep, or so lethargic as to be dead to the world. At the slightest indication of revival, either Trey or Tri gave her another dose of morphine. Her breathing became labored and tortured, she lay with her mouth open. Trey expected each day to be her last, but she just continued to live, in a horrible half-dead state that tortured her children as much as herself.

Trey was in the kitchen when Tri came out from their mother's bedroom. "She wants to die, Trey. She has thrush growing in her mouth and she wants us to help her die. You need to get some more medicine."

Trey looked at his sister, his shy, sensitive, emotionally damaged sister. She was a beautiful waif, with blonde hair and clear blue eyes, but her beauty was delicate and no one could look at her without knowing how fragile she was. Any decent man would see her weakness and want to protect her, but some, like that poisonous squirrel who'd hurt her at the Appean Way, derived strength from her pain. Well, he'd learned. But now here Tri was, standing up straight, looking directly at him, telling him what their mother wanted, giving him orders. He knew she was right, but he also knew that something had shifted in her; some stone had settled in more tightly on her emotional foundation. Somehow she was more secure, more certain. He'd been thinking the same thing, of course, and had begun scarfing morphine over the past several months from the ambulance. It was hard to get but when added to the stuff the Hospice nurse provided, it would do the trick and then some.

"I've already got it," he said. She nodded and motioned for him to retrieve it.

Their mother died peacefully in her sleep that night. After the funeral home workers came to take the body, Trey called Carlo and they talked for a long time. The funeral was three days later. Carlo attended and he and Trey got together afterwards for a talk that lasted late into the night. Sometime before dawn they shook hands on an agreement that gave Carlo reason to smile every day for the rest of his life. Other people, not so much.

Chapter 20

Carlo was the contact. All requests came through him. Fifty percent up front. Fifty percent when the contract was complete. No one in New York knew who Carlo's high-priced hitter was. At first, the contracts were sporadic, and usually in Southern California or Las Vegas. But gradually, as the successes mounted, he received contracts around the country, and then around the world. Trey's trademark, at Carlo's urging, was nearly infinite patience. He would take weeks and sometimes months to set up the perfect hit. He simply turned down contracts with timelines attached.

"This guy," Carlo told the people from New York, "he won't rush. Won't do it. Says rush means risk."

But when Trey took the contract, the result was guaranteed, no matter how long it took. It was obvious, right from the first, that even simple assassinations took longer than he could afford while working a regular job, so after a great deal of deliberation with Carlo, Trey quit his job with the fire department and bought a small book store in a trendy section of Long Beach.

"You'll have to show a way of making money," Carlo said. "Stock the right books and you'll have business. Sponsor book clubs. Bring in authors. Have readings. You'll do well."

Trey was nearly speechless. He didn't know much about book stores but it sounded like Carlo had just outlined a successful business plan.

"You can hire a couple people to run it when you're not around. The biggest problem is going to be accounting. Got to have someone you can trust. Someone who can work the records. The people I know can do it but you need to stay completely separate from them. They're connected, too."

"No," Trey said. "I think I've got that covered. I think Tri can do it." Tri had been taking accounting courses by mail for several years, and with her newfound confidence from the travel agency, was continuing evening classes at Long Beach State. When Trey approached her about it, she signed up for classes with the Small Business Administration.

"More real-world stuff," she said. "They can teach me the nuts and bolts."

The SBA also assigned a retired businessman to guide Tri through the initial process of setting up their record keeping.

"He is a treasure," Tri said of the bald, bespectacled man who spent hours helping her establish their bookkeeping system. Within three months, Tri was capable. In a year she was excellent… just in time, too, because by then Trey needed to begin laundering money from his new enterprise through the store.

This was less of a hurdle than Trey had anticipated because Tri was so psychically connected to him. It wasn't something they talked about, primarily, Trey suspected, because doing so pulled the scab off of their sister's disappearance. The bond between the girls had been far stronger than that shared with their brother, but both girls had been capable of reading Trey's thoughts with relative ease since they were young. Trey didn't think Tri had a grasp of the details of his profession, but at the least she understood the need for an alternate method of bookkeeping for him and willingly provided the necessary expertise. In her mind, it was simple, as she told him one day. "You need help. I'll help you."

A year or so later, the book store began to make money, a particularly serendipitous event because it made money laundering easier to conduct and hide. Within three years all their enterprises were up and running well. Tri was a successful travel agent and took care of the store records on evenings and weekends. Trey ran the book store and took extensive trips to find books, both domestic and foreign, during which he would occasionally kill people.

Chapter 21

One evening, several years after Trey began his partnership with Carlo, the fat man invited Trey into his office behind the restaurant. Although not rare, the office visit was uncommon. He poured them both a Maker's Mark.

"So, things going ok?"

"Sure, yeah. No complaints. You?"

"I got lottsa complaints. Nobody listens." He waved his stubby hands. "What can you do?"

Trey chuckled.

"We gotta think about the future."

"Okay. How?"

"You been getting your contracts from me, right? Alla background information, too. That's fine, long as I'm around, but what about when I'm not?"

"Haven't thought about it much."

"Yeah, I know. But see, the money people don't know you. I tell them you work anonymously. Period. But both of you need a way to contact the other, or you don't do business. See?"

"Yeah, I see. But…"

"Yeah, but. The big 'but.' They're always after me to tell them who you are. They want to know. They want something on you. But if they know who you are, they can find you. If they find you, they can whack you. You don't want that."

"No, I don't want that."

"So we got to design a system so they can get hold of you, without knowing who you are."

And they did. Potential employers would first place an ad in the sales section of the *Los Angeles Times* Classifieds for a "Size 14 Rock Climbing Shoes, worn twice." It would then give a fictitious phone number. Trey would add two to each of the digits to decipher the true phone number. He would then call the resulting number, which would connect to a public phone booth, at 10 p.m. on the following day to receive the necessary information. His call sign was Alonzo.

"Why Alonzo?" Trey asked.

"Why not," Carlo answered. "Amos Alonzo Stagg was a famous Italian guy."

"Oh, yeah. Of course."

"Wiseass."

"Sorry."

In the event photos and maps were necessary, they were delivered to a dead drop Trey designated in different locations within Los Angeles. He took great care in the reconnaissance of the drops, but he had never once suspected any attempt to follow or identify him.

Trey was given the phone number in New York which he suspected was the home of a low-level flunky. In the event he needed further information, he was to call and ask for Myrtle. He would be told there was no Myrtle there; he would apologize and hang up. The next day a classified ad similar to the first would show up in the LA Times Classified section, with a new phone number. He would call that night.

"Why Myrtle? Another famous Italian name?"

"Shuddup. So, you can see this is a little... ahhh... difficult, right? Takes time, yeah? But it's the best way to keep you safe. Sooner or later, they're going to give you a contract they would like to seal off completely, you know? No connections. But if you don't know who they are, and they don't know who you are, there are no connections to worry about, right?"

"Yeah, I understand. But I'd like to know who they are, Carlo."

"Sure you would. But I'm not going to tell you... at least not yet. If you're any good, you'll be able to figure it out, doncha think?"

"Yes. Probably."

"Yeah, you will. But you'll never, ever say the name out loud. Never. Unnerstand?"

He nodded. "Yeah. OK. I understand."

"Good. So, one other thing. When I tip over, you'll probably feel an urge to come to the celebration, or wake, or whatever the hell they decide to put on."

"Yes, I will, though I also expect you to live another 15 or 20 years."

"Well, no matter when it happens, you can't attend."

"Why?"

"Cause the people who pay you will be there looking around. OK? They will be looking for you. In this business you never say goodbye. Goodbyes are dangerous. Got it?"

"Got it."

As it turned out, when Carlo died two years later, his daughters collected his body and returned with it to New York, where the service was held. Trey's celebration of Carlo's life was held on a stool at the bar of the Appean Way, where he sipped one last glass of Makers Mark and thought about his friend. He finished the drink, walked out the door and never went back again.

Chapter 22

After the San Diego hit, Trey took a shower, then relaxed in the hot tub for 30 minutes with an iced tea. When Carlo was still alive Trey would have waited until midnight or so and then joined him at the Appean Way for a celebratory drink. But Carlo'd been gone for a while now and Trey still missed his truncated language, cynicism and absolute loyalty. Carlo had been the only true constant in his life since his father had been killed.

He also was the reason Tri had recovered as well as she had; the work as a travel agent he'd arranged had helped to bring her out of her shell. Oh, she'd had to struggle for the first several months to overcome her fear of strangers, but gradually she'd become more and more confident, more and more at ease. She was still shy and soft-spoken, but she was smart and detail-oriented and her clients loved her. Carlo had smoothed each transition. Tri's boss at the travel agency was nice to her and when one of the girls got snippy with Tri, that girl was gone the next day, transferred to a sister agency in Oxnard. Carlo's fingerprints were all over it.

Thanks to Carlo, life was good for both of them. Trey had just finished the last hit he would ever do. The people who hired him had no idea who he was. He had just over $6 million in offshore accounts and $2 million more in cash in the safe downstairs. One of his recent contracts had been a drug dealer who'd been on his way to a deal when Trey intercepted him. Trey had seen no reason to leave the briefcase, so he'd simply taken it as the spoils of war. He'd also purchased a villa in the south of France. He and Tri would move there after an extensive renovation was completed. Tri was doing well. No boyfriends—and no girlfriends for him, either. They did all right, just the two of them. He sank back into the warm water, lifted his iced tea once again in a toast to Carlo. He set the glass down and closed his eyes.

He could tell something was wrong by the footsteps. He'd expected Tri to call out with her bubbly little laugh like she almost always did when she came home from the travel agency. "Treyyyeee, where are yeee? But there was no happy call now, just a cat-footed, careful approach. Trey reached into a nearby cabinet and brought out a stainless steel, Walther PPK .380 semi-automatic. He held it outside the tub, out of sight. Tri came around the corner, pale as a ghost, eyes bright, shiny and scared.

"Is she here?"

Trey leaned back behind the door and set the pistol on a chair. "Is who here, Tri?"

She stood there, wringing her hands. "Don't play with me, Trey. Is Trip here?"

Trey's heart pounded in his ears. "No, of course not, Tri. You know she's…gone." *What is wrong with her? It's been sixteen years. But then, Tri knows things. Feels things.* "What is it, Tri? What's going on?"

"She's alive, Trey! Trip is alive and she's close by! I can feel her! I think she's trying to talk to me, Trey. She's trying to tell me where she is!"

The few next hours were a blur. Trey finally got Tri to sit down and relax. They held each other, talked about Trip and their lives before *the night*. The more Tri relaxed, the more she seemed able to derive from whatever signals she was receiving. Finally, she went to bed. Trey sat in the living room for hours, watching the water, thinking about Trip. He had absolute faith in Tri's ability to sense her sister. He had seen the otherworldly ability to communicate they'd shared with each other and their mother. In fact, Tri's inability to feel Trip for all these years since *the night* had convinced them that the kidnapper had killed Trip and dumped her body.

The fact they were communicating now might mean Trip had simply come back into range. What would their range be? How far will I have to look? Is Trip going to be all right? What has that monster done to her? How shall I kill him?

He fell asleep in the chair and the nightmares came back with a vengeance. He experienced the ominous feeling of prescience again, saw his young boy's body in the bed, eyes wide with fear. Heard the screams. Ran downstairs into a room splashed with blood. His father dead, his mother being humped into submission, her eyes glazed, his sisters taped to a chair, screaming soundlessly. He attacked and fought and fought and fought, but his efforts meant nothing. The rapist was unstoppable, implacable. The man got up off the floor and cuffed him in the head.

"Julian."

The rapist hit him again. He was groggy, couldn't get up fast enough. Hit again. Lights flashed and dimmed.

"Julian, Trey."

Trey kept swinging, scratching, but the man was kicking him now, and Trey could feel consciousness leaving him.

"She's in Julian, Trey. Trip's in Julian. We need to go get her."

"Tri?" He was foggy. Why was he out here on the chair? What was Tri talking about?

"Trey, let's go get our sister. TREY! I know where she is!"

He came out of the chair fast that time, and within half an hour they were on the road to the mountain village of Julian, 50 miles east of San Diego. They would have been gone sooner, but Trey had to gather up a few tools of his trade. Including a shovel.

Chapter 23

—·‹‹(●)››·—

"Hurry up," Tri yelled at him, as Trey negotiated the road leading up toward Julian. "She's worried!"

"We can't get stopped by the cops," he yelled back, nodding toward the trunk, where he'd stashed a rifle, pistol and shotgun. "What do you mean, worried?"

"I'm not sure. It's been so long since I've felt her, it's hard for me to tell whether she's scared to death or just a little uneasy." She smiled brightly, smiled in a way Trey hadn't seen since *the day*.

"Can you get us to the right spot, or just nearby?"

"I'm not sure. I think I'll know it when I see it, but I don't think I can give you exact directions. How big is Julian?"

"Not a lot of residents, but it's real touristy. And people live pretty much all over the hills. Do you think she's in the town itself?"

"I don't know. It's just a thought she sent. Julian. Like a place to start, maybe."

As it turned out, the closer they came to Julian, the stronger and clearer came the messages from Trip. Soon Tri began to receive images; a bridge, a barn, a broken-down shack, a rotting tree house. She passed them along to Trey, but none of them appeared.

"What direction should I go," Trey asked at one intersection.

"I don't know," Tri said, "but I think I'll know if it's right or not." And she did. Within a few minutes of making a turn, Tri could tell him whether or not they were going in the right direction.

After an hour of circling around Julian, Trey was both frustrated and amazed. "You're like a cross between Simon Says and a directional antenna," he complained. That was just before they crossed a bridge and looked over to see a fallen tree house in the yard of an old, broken-down shack. Just past it was a rundown double-wide trailer house and a barn that was last painted in the Depression.

"Stop! That's it! Turn there! Please, she's right there!" Tri was screaming, almost beside herself.

"Quiet!" Trey roared, and continued to drive past. "We can't just drive in there. What do you think that asshole will do if he sees two people drive up who look just like Trip? Don't you remember what he's like?"

Tri became quiet but she was quivering with excitement.

He pulled off the side of the road and into the woods.

"What are you doing? What are we doing here?" She grabbed his upper arm so hard it hurt. "We have to go get her, Trey. I think she's in danger. I think he's going to hurt her!"

The urgency in her voice unleashed a new fear in Trey's mind. What if he kills her now, after coming so close? What will happen to Tri? What will happen to us? His fear overwhelmed his native caution and he jumped out of the car, opened the trunk, put a holstered Ruger .22 Magnum revolver on his belt and slung a 30-30 lever action Winchester Model 94 over his shoulder. *Just looking for a place to target shoot, officer.* He closed the trunk.

"You stay here," he told Tri.

"She pinned him with a glance colder than he thought possible. "I am NOT staying here. I want a gun."

Trey shook his head, opened the trunk, grabbed a little .32 auto. He chambered a round, dropped the hammer, put the safety on. "Leave it in your purse until we're at the house. Try not to shoot the good guys." She turned to hurry off. He grabbed her by the hair, pulled her back, put her face inches from his. "You stay behind me, goddammit! Or stay in the car! I do this…never mind."

"Okay, okay! I'm sorry, Trey." She stopped pulling away, put her hand on his arm. "I know what you were going to say. You were going to tell me you do this for a living. I know what you do, Trey. I can hear your thoughts. She pulled his head down and kissed him lightly on the forehead. "I can see your dreams."

He closed his eyes. She held him close and for just a moment, they both breathed deeply. And then they were off.

Trey moved quickly through the brush and widely spaced pines. He could tell when they were approaching the house by the increasing amount of trash. He hesitated briefly just outside the clearing, perhaps 50 yards from the trailer.

"Are you sure she's in there?" he asked Tri.

"I'm sure. It's like I can feel her heart beat."

"Can she hear you, too?"

"I think so. I'm trying to tell her we're coming."

"Well, then, tell her to open the door and come outside, now!"

"I'll try."

"OK, I'm going to get up to the porch. If she opens the door soon I'll go on in. If nothing happens after a few minutes I'll go in one way or another. You stay here." He looked in her eyes. "You stay here."

"I'll stay here until I know she got the message; then I'm coming in."

Trey exhaled disgustedly. "O.K. Jesus. But move fast and stay behind something. Please." He squeezed her upper arm. Then he took off at a run toward the house.

He'd run just like this after he'd heard the scream, 16 years earlier. He'd hurtled into the room, taken everything in and attacked the slope shouldered man. But surprise wasn't enough and he'd let everyone down. He passed through the gate, slowing as he neared the house. Surprise might not be enough this time either. He needed to know something before he charged in. He stopped at the house, moved quietly around to the end and glanced in the window. A man stood facing away from him. Trey could tell it was the slope shouldered man and his breath caught in his throat. The man was speaking in a loud voice, angrily.

"Because I say you can't. Now get the fuck away from the door! Hey! Didn't you hear me? I said…"

Trey moved back toward the door, slid silently along the wall toward it. He was crouched two feet away from it when the handle turned, followed by the sound of a blow on flesh, an involuntary exhalation.

"Triiiip!" Tri was careening through the back yard toward him, her pistol waving wildly from her hand. Trey ignored her, spun and pulled the door open. The slope-shouldered man was bending over a fallen woman, pulling her blonde hair, preparing another blow. He stood as Trey entered. The face was the same, fleshier, but this time the eyes weren't gleaming with anger and lust, but with fear. "What the…" and then his nose broke as Trey's boot drove it into his face. Before he hit the floor, Trey was on him and Tri was through the door, cradling her sister's body in her arms.

"Is she ok?" Trey asked as he tied the unconscious man's arms behind him, using plastic slip ties.

"I think so," Tri said. "Trip, honey, Trip. It's Tri and Trey. We've found you. You're safe again with us. Please, Trip, please." Tri was crying uncontrollably. Trey dragged the unconscious man across the small living room and into a tiny bedroom.

Trey went to the sink, soaked a paper towel in cold water. He bathed Trip's face. She looks pretty good, he thought. She looks a lot like Tri, but bruised up and older and harder. But she's alive, she's alive.

A minute later, Trip began to awaken. She tossed her head from side to side, attempted to protect herself with her arms from blows that had long since fallen. After she'd oriented herself, she focused on Tri's face, then Trey's. She reached for Tri and hugged her tightly. "I want to kill him," were her first words. "You haven't killed him yet, have you?"

Trey hesitated, considered, then knelt, cradled her in his arms and lied. "Yes," he said. "He's already dead, Trip. I'm sorry." Trip cried then, too, deep racking sobs that shook her entire body. Trey enfolded them both and all three cried for a long time.

An hour later, Trey had his sisters ready to leave with what little Trip wanted to keep.

"Trip, does that car out front run pretty well? Good. Looks like a piece of junk. Is it hot? No? Great. OK, here's the deal. As far as I know, the cops never had any real clues about who your kidnapper was, Trip, so as long as we can keep his disappearance under the radar we can just announce that you were able to escape. I'll fix it so nobody finds him and

I doubt if anyone will connect him to this trailer. I'm assuming he uses, ah, used aliases a lot." Trip nodded, looking down. "You guys have been living off the grid, no real connections, paying with cash?" Trip nodded again. "Have you been in Mexico all this time?"

"Yes," Trip whispered. Put her hands to her head, rubbed her temples. "Until just a couple days ago."

"OK. We'll say you escaped from a place in Mexico. Good." He rubbed her back. "Living like that made it impossible for anyone to find you, but now it will make it much easier to get rid of him and bring you back without much of a ruckus." He looked at Tri. "Here's what I need you to do. Take the car and drive to Oceanside. Can you do that, Tri?" She said yes, and gave him a look that warned him not to question her ability in front of their sister again.

"Great. There are a bunch of malls and things close to the highway there. Exit 54C. Oceanside Harbor Drive. Got it? OK. Get a room at the Holiday Inn. The Holiday Inn. Go in separately. Don't be seen together. Let Trip get cleaned up there while you go buy her some nice clothes and things. And get her a dark wig or some hair dye. Stay in the room. Order room service. Get a good night's sleep. I need you to come pick me up at the Dennys Restaurant at six tomorrow morning. Dennys Restaurant. OK? It's that same exit, on the same side of the highway. Don't go in the restaurant. Stay in the car and I will get in. Trip, you wear your wig. We can go home then and let you relax for a few days before we have to bring the police into it."

Trip shifted, started to speak. Trey interrupted, "Now, don't worry. We'll work up a story the cops will buy, no problem. OK, got it?" The girls agreed, and after a few last-minute questions and answers, Trey watched them disappear into the woods toward the car.

He went into the bedroom to the unconscious man on the floor. Trey had chloroformed him twice to keep the girls from realizing he was still alive but now he was coming around again. Trey removed the gag. A ragged scream came from his mouth. Trey slapped him hard and the scream stopped.

"Don't whine." The sounds diminished to a soft, choking gurgle. Trey slapped him again.

"Don't blubber, either." The sounds stopped, replaced only by a wet, lathery breathing sound of air whistling through a broken nose.

"I've dreamed of killing you my entire life, but now the time is here I am not nearly as excited as I should be. I should probably have let my sister kill you, but I think killing you would be just one more thing she'd have to deal with and she's already got plenty of those, thanks to you."

Trey pulled the man to his feet and pushed him onto the bed. He looked everywhere but directly at Trey. He sniffed constantly but blood continued to drip from his ruined nose. "I...please...I didn't..."

"Shut up. There's nothing you can say." Trey threw him a towel. "Here, clean up your face."

The monster of all Trey's dreams sat before him, a sobbing, pathetic wreck. His once-powerful upper body had softened and sagged. Trey wanted nothing more than to be rid of him, to put everything behind him and his sisters. But he couldn't do that easily.

What were the options? Leaving the man alive was out of the question. Trip would never forgive him and as pathetic as the son of a bitch was now, he could still be dangerous. They still lived in the same house where he'd attacked them. And besides, Trey could never forgive himself. Turn the killer into the police? An option, sure. But then the cops would be all over Trip; they'd want to reconstruct every place she'd ever lived, everything she'd ever done. It was entirely possible the shithead had gotten Trip involved in illegal activities and he'd sell her out for sure. And then there was his own little problem. Trey didn't think he'd ever been a suspect in any of the assassinations he'd conducted but you never knew. Police poking around, television and print journalists taking pictures...people could make connections, connections could lead to identification and identification could lead to death, for him and everyone close to him.

So, the logical decision was the same as the emotional one. The slope-shouldered man had to die; it was just a question of where. He could kill him here and burn the trailer down around him, thereby eliminating evidence that might connect Trip to the trailer or to the man, but if a body was found in the ashes the entire site would be investigated carefully. It would be much better if the body simply disappeared. Then a simple trailer fire would be just written off as an unfortunate mistake or sloppiness. The stove and heating system were powered by propane from a tank on the end of the trailer. Perfect.

"Get up, asshole. We're going for a ride."

The man's eyes darted from side to side. Trey stepped forward and slapped him again. "Here's the deal. I can see you looking around for something to help you escape. Don't bother. Nothing and no one will help you now. We're going to a place I know in the desert. You can cooperate and stay healthy and happy for a while longer and I'll remove those slip ties from your wrists. Or you can try to take me, or escape. If I think you are going to do either one of those, if you give me the slightest reason to worry, I'll make you regret it. I don't like to torture people… but I know how. I will first use a hammer to crush your ankles, knees, fingers, wrists, elbows and shoulders. Then, when your body is like jello and you can't even turn over, I'll cut off your dick and stick it in your mouth and let you choke to death on it." He grabbed the man's hair and jerked his face up to look directly in his eyes. "So, what's it going to be?"

The choice, as it turned out, was easy, and a few hours later, the two men stood in the desert. The only illumination came from the stars and a gibbous moon. In the desert it seemed almost like daylight.

"Hands behind your back." Trey slipped another plastic tie about the killer's wrists, pulled it tight and maneuvered him sideways.

"Please don't…I'm sorry…I…"

Trey pushed him backward into the four-foot-deep hole they'd spent the last hour digging. The slope-shouldered man hit hard, knocking the wind out of him. He lay on his back, his eyes wide with fear, his mouth moving soundlessly.

"That's unfortunate. Can't catch your breath, huh? Well, I'll give you time."

Trey began shoveling dirt onto the man's feet and legs. He kicked madly, trying to get the dirt off. Some fell off to the side, the rest flew into the air and came back down on him. Trey continued to shovel. The man's legs were almost covered when he recovered his breath and began to scream. Trey's next shovelful hit him in the face, as did the next, and the next.

By 4 a.m. Trey was parked in the WorldMark Resort parking lot. He spent 30 minutes wiping the car down, then left it unlocked with the keys on the dashboard and walked through various parking lots to the Dennys. He washed up in the bathroom, then went out and had a three-egg omelet with a side order of biscuits and gravy and a large orange juice. He was reading the Los Angeles Times and watching the sun rise when his sisters drove up. His sisters. Plural. Two of them.

Chapter 24

Two days later the San Diego Union ran a page six mention of the trailer fire near Julian. The owner wasn't clear, it reported, and the trailer was a total loss. The main thrust of the story was just how lucky the community was that the fire had been contained.

Trey and Tri took turns staying with Trip nonstop for the first three weeks after her return. During that time she stayed indoors almost constantly. She took two or three showers each day, ate like a horse and watched television. It took more than a week for her to talk openly with her siblings. Nearly two weeks went by before she wanted to tell them about her experiences, and once she started, she could not stop. She talked for 12 hours and then slept for 20 more.

The slope-shouldered man, she called him Arman, had taken her into Mexico in the trunk of his car and they'd been down there ever since. At first, he'd been oddly decent to her. Treated her like his daughter. But as she grew older, Arman began to take an interest in her. She was fourteen when he first assaulted her. After that, their relationship became confused. He started telling her he loved her; how much he needed her. He became more and more dependent on her. As time went on she recognized the degree of control she had and began to exercise it. They became, over the years, "more and more like a weird married couple, except I always hated him and wanted to kill him. But I had no idea how to get away. I guess there are some married people like that, too."

Over the years they moved throughout Mexico; her kidnapper became involved in the drug trade. Finally, only a few weeks earlier, Arman had done something bad enough to make his boss very mad. "I think he stole money or drugs," Trip said. "All I know is that he was terrified. He came home one night, grabbed a few clothes, threw me in the car and raced for the border, looking behind us the whole way. It must have been really bad to send him back up here. As soon as I crossed the border I started thinking about you, wondering how you were and then I felt Tri reaching out to me…I knew you would come for me then."

She shook her head, covered her eyes with her hands. "I think Arman could tell we were communicating. At least he knew something was wrong. He was really scared and every little thing set him off." She looked at Trey. "You walked in when he was really losing it. I knew you wanted me to open the door and I was going to, no matter what. And then you came."

Two days later, Trey heard her laugh for the first time. He looked at her closely. Her eyes were bright, her skin clear, she was starting to look much more like Tri.

The next week they brought in the cops. "It was a miracle," Trey told them. Trip had called from the border just a couple days earlier. The police were amazed. Then a detective came who had been assigned to the case sixteen years earlier. He was almost tearful to see Trip come home. She told him the truth, except in her version, she'd taken off alone when she'd learned Arman had double-crossed the Mexican drug lord. Trip doubted he had survived. You know how those Mexican drug cartels work.

The detective was now within a month of retirement. This case had been one of his early ones, a high-profile, vicious crime that shocked the entire state. He had failed to find the man responsible or his victim. But now she was back. She was still alive. It was almost as though his career had come full circle and God had put a nice cherry on his retirement cake. It took him days to quit smiling. The whole thing just made him feel good, so good he didn't bother questioning the girl more aggressively even though he knew she was lying through her teeth. He figured the kidnapper was rotting in the ground somewhere and he'd give odds the girl's brother had something to do with it. Sounds like justice to me, he thought. He went into retirement a happy man.

After the cops stopped coming by and the hubbub surrounding her return subsided, Trip quit watching television, "Didn't really miss much, did I?" and started to read. She began by devouring the news magazines Trey and Tri had lying around, but became frustrated and quit. That night she sat down at the dinner table and announced, "My education ended in the 7th grade. I don't understand half the damn words I'm reading. It's time I did something about it." At that point Trip began what Trey described as a 'full body dip into high school." The same woman who had tutored Tri, a Mrs. Cullins, still lived in the area, and though she had retired two years earlier, agreed to come out of retirement for this special case. She worked with Trip almost full time for three months, when Trip took and passed the test for her GED. Then the tutor gave notice, sort of.

"I'm going to quit coming over to give lessons to Trip," she said. "But I'm going to start making three or four day trips each week to different places where I can continue my own education. I'd love to have some company. I think Trip and I can both learn a lot."

Although Trip was nervous about being out of the house, the excitement of learning new things helped overcome her fear, and their 'educational field trips' began. Day after day, she and Mrs. Cullins took off in the elderly lady's Volkswagen Beetle. They went to museums, displays, presentations. They attended concerts and storytellings. Every other week or so the duo did something just for fun, Disneyland, Universal Studios, horseback riding and once they went fishing on a charter boat. Mrs. Cullins' second childhood coincided with Trip's first and each was seized by a thirst for knowledge that practically made them glow.

"I'm jealous," Tri said to Trey one evening, as they listened to Trip sing in the shower following a day spent at a car show.

"So am I," Trey laughed. "But no one deserves this more."

"I think she's going to be all right," Tri said, hugging him.

"Yeah. Me too," Trey said, mussing her hair. I think we're all going to be all right."

But that was before he read the classifieds.

Chapter 25

Misty spent the next three days working in recovery and a lot of that time was spent with Tony Corrarino.

"What happened last night?" he'd asked as soon as he had the chance. "I remember being really upset and I know you were involved but I can't remember any details. I hope I wasn't obnoxious." He was obviously sincere, and worried. Misty tried to re-assure him.

"Mr. Corrarino, you were fine. You just had a fever from the infection and you got a little delirious." She should have left it there, she knew, but she couldn't. "You were apologizing for something you've done in the past. You kept saying you didn't mean to, that you had no choice…"

She tried to will him to explain, but he turned away and closed his eyes. Misty left wondering if she'd ruined any chance at meaningful communication. She didn't pretend to understand human nature but it was obvious that Tony Corrarino had caged a secret that was eating him from the inside out.

Misty had the next day off and so didn't see Corrarino until the following night. She was surprised to see that his condition seemed essentially unchanged. If anything, his eyes were more sunken, his skin more sallow. He brightened when he saw her, though, and made an obvious effort to make up for his rudeness earlier.

They chatted a little as Misty cleaned up and changed medication. Then Corrarino cleared his throat. "I'm sorry about just shutting down the other night."

"It's ok, Mr. Corrarino. I was intrusive."

"No… you weren't. I wanted to tell you. I want to…it's like a boil that needs to be lanced. I can't think of anything else. It's been like this for years. I can't stand it, oh…" he put his head in his hands and began to sob.

Misty started to tear up, herself. "Mr. Corrarino, perhaps I should call a counselor. We have people on staff who are trained…"

"No, please. I don't want someone like that. I don't want strangers to know… I can't…" Corrarino stopped, raised his head. Misty could hear his teeth grinding. Somehow, he controlled himself.

"It's ok," he said. "It was unfair of me to put such a burden on you. I'm sorry."

In that moment, Misty came close to walking away. Counseling was not her job and she had plenty more to accomplish that night. But Corrarino was distraught and his emotional state was obviously affecting his physical well-being. She was a nurse because she wanted to help people. Misty decided to help Tony Corrarino, and her decision sent waves of change through everyone she knew.

"You can tell me, Mr. Corrarino. I'm listening." Corrarino's eyes filled with tears and he began to talk.

"I killed a boy," he said, his lips quivering. "I killed a little boy. I killed him with my knife."

Misty was dumbfounded. She considered calling the police, but then she thought better of it. Corrarino was sick, with a high fever and certainly no risk. Probably the best thing she could do was to hear him out, then contact the police with information they could use. Besides, she could simply not believe this gentle, quiet man was a murderer.

"When was this, Mr. Corrarino?"

"I killed him."

"Yes, but when did it happen?"

"1970, sometime between August 3 and August 22. I can't remember."

A light came on for Misty. "Were you in the war, Mr. Corrarino? Were you in Vietnam at the time?"

"Yes, but that didn't matter. He was a boy. My God. A boy. He was scared and shaking. I told him to be quiet, but… oh, my God! Please! Oh!" Tony covered his face and became utterly still.

Misty's hand went out to him. She stroked the back of his head down to his neck, then almost physically recoiled at the touch of the scrabbly, scarred up flesh across the back of his neck. She forced herself to continue.

At her touch, Tony began to relax. He took several deep breaths, then started talking anew.

He'd never gone to another fire crew after Dean left school. In fact, Tony had only lasted one more quarter before he'd walked, zombie-like, into the Army recruiter's office and said he wanted to fly helicopters. He'd been thinking of nothing else ever since Dean left their room. In some strange way, Dean's faith and commitment had infected him. The extent of the infection scared him because it overcame even his growing infatuation with Dean's cousin Raven. They'd spent every possible weekend together, either in Ashland or Eugene since they'd first met and she was shocked to learn he was signing up. To Tony's relief, Raven made no promises to wait for him. She simply asked him to be careful and get in contact when he returned. Then she made their last night together memorable. "So you don't forget to come back," she said. As it turned out, Tony's memory of Raven played a big part in his ability to return.

****

"It wasn't like I changed my view of the world or the war," Tony told Misty in halting sentences. "I think… I think… I loved Dean and I wanted more than anything else to be like him. I just believed in him and trusted him more than I distrusted the government and their propaganda about the war."

Tony had followed Dean through basic training, and then on to helicopter flight training in Fort Rucker. He hadn't told his parents until he was already enrolled in flight school. His mother had been devastated, his father furious. Sal had come personally to Fort Rucker and they'd talked in his father's limousine just outside the main gate.

"What is this shit?" Sal had asked. "You don't care about your family at all?"

"I owe the country, too, Dad," Tony said.

"There's lots of ways of paying back the country, Tony. We don't play in their stupid wars."

"You mean the ones that don't involve Italy?"

Sal was nonplussed. This was a new Tony. He sat in the car and looked directly at his father as an equal. His hair was short, which emphasized the corded neck and ropy arms. Tony was still slight, he had a distance runner's build, but his slightness masked a muscular density that hadn't been there previously.

"I can't get you out," Sal said, then continued over Tony's angry interruption. "But I can get you assigned stateside, to Fort Dix, in Jersey. Listen to me. Your mother will not allow…" he stopped when Tony's voice reached a roar.

"No! You listen to me! If you do anything… if my orders out of here are to anywhere but Vietnam, I will never, ever have anything to do with you or Mom again. I will never set foot in New York City." He shook his head in fury. "I swear to God, Dad. I swear to God, if you get into my business with the Army you'll never see or hear from me again."

Sal sat silently. For one of the few times in his life, he had no idea what to do. Tony was not bullshitting. Sal was certain of that. If he backed off, took the congressmen off the hook, Tony's orders to Fort Dix would be cancelled and sure as hell he would go to Vietnam. Sal had no leverage once the boy got there. He couldn't make sure Tony would be assigned to Saigon, or something out of the line of fire.

As if he had read his father's mind, Tony continued. "I'm going to a combat unit, Dad. I'm going to the Air Cav. If you mess with my life even a little bit I will call Mom to tell her why she's never going to see me again." He stopped momentarily, then leaned over toward his father and spoke quietly. "Listen, Dad. One of the things you learn once you start flying is that nobody's got a string attached to your ass. Once you strap that bird on, it's all up to you. Nobody else can keep you alive. It's all you. I like the feeling. That's how I want my life to be now. I want to be on my own. You need to let me. I need your word you'll stay out of it." He put his arm on his father's shoulder.

"Jesus, Tony." Sal closed his eyes. "What do I say to your mother?"

"Whatever it takes, Dad. I think she'll understand."

And so Tony was left to finish flight school and Sal had gone back to New York, chastened and subdued. Letters from Tony's mother were sad but understanding and after a while, his father began to write a few paragraphs on her letters as well. It wasn't The Brady Bunch, Tony realized, but it was the best he could expect.

Chapter 26

At Fort Rucker, Dean and Tony crossed paths on an irregular basis. Dean was doing well. His solid, dependable personality meshed well in the Army mold and he had shown a real ability to fly.

"You've got to do well in flight training," he told Tony. "If you finish at the top of your class you'll get your choice of which unit to join when you get to Vietnam." They both had laughed at that, but only a little, because it wasn't so much funny as deadly serious. Nonetheless, Tony had worked hard and excelled in the academic portion of flight training, but he'd struggled a little in the cockpit, where he found the actual stick and rudder work to be "even harder than working a drift boat down through a fast, rocky stretch." After a couple setbacks he caught on, though, and by the time he received his wings Tony was a capable young helicopter pilot.

He'd joined up with Dean in an Air Cavalry unit in South Vietnam. They were both assigned to fly UH-1 Huey slicks, meaning they had no forward firing rockets or guns. Their primary defensive weapons were door-mounted M-60 machine guns fired by the crew chief and gunner. The slicks were used primarily as troop movers. Tony had been amazed at the change in his friend. After only five months in country, Dean was a highly experienced combat pilot who looked and acted the part. Not that he was pretentious; pretense had no part in Dean's makeup. He was just hard, hard and far more abrupt than he'd been in college. Dean had taken fire on numerous occasions and had been shot down once.

"My wingman came right down and got us," Dean had said, smiling. But Tony knew better. He'd heard the real story from other pilots in the unit. Dean had been shot down in inaccessible terrain and had carried his badly wounded co-pilot half a mile uphill through the jungle to an extraction zone, while his crew chief and gunner provided covering fire as they followed. All three men were shot during their retreat; the gunner had died in the rescue bird. The co-pilot in the field hospital. Dean and the crew chief, a 19-year-old Kentuckian named 'Wash,' were back flying two weeks later. Since then, the two were inseparable. If Dean was flying, 'Wash' was his crew chief.

That experience took a lot of the fun out of Dean, Tony was told, and left a pretty serious guy. 'No bullshit' was the way Tony heard the crew chiefs describe Dean and Tony had to admit, it fit him to a 'T'. The outgoing friendliness and happy-go-lucky sense of humor were no longer in evidence. In their place was a hard-eyed young man who did obsessively meticulous preparations for his almost daily flights into combat.

The first time they flew together, Dean kept him in the Operations tent for two hours. "Every time you strap one of these machines on, you've got to have a plan, Tony," he said. "You've got to have a good plan that takes into account all the best intelligence. Then you've got to have another plan for when all the best intelligence turns out wrong and your first plan turns to shit. And it's not enough for your flight leader or your section lead or your aircraft commander to have the plans. You've got to have them… in here" he pointed to his head, "as well as on your maps. You can't tell when you'll be left on your own." He turned away, but kept talking. "I fumbled around for a while when I went down. If I'd known more… if I'd done things faster, maybe a couple guys would still be alive."

Dean arranged to have Tony assigned as his co-pilot for most of his break-in hops, and Dean made sure that Tony got plenty of experience in the right seat before he started signing for aircraft himself. Tony's last scheduled flight as a co-pilot was on a patrol extract. Dean had him take the pilot's seat on the right side of the aircraft. Tony would be expected to make the decisions during the flight as though he were the aircraft commander.

Artillery and gunships prepped the zone (and several others, so the enemy couldn't identify the actual extract location) just prior to the pick-up. Dean and Tony were flying dash-2 behind their company commander. Everything went well until they were on final approach, when heavy machine guns opened up from the jungle just outside the LZ. The lead aircraft exploded in the air. Dean grabbed the controls, yelling "I got it" and yanked hard to the right. Both their machine guns opened up, but the gunner, on the left side, went suddenly silent. With only one machine gun firing, Tony could distinctly hear the sound of bullets hitting his aircraft. A quick look into the cabin showed the gunner lying dead across his machine gun. Wash, the crew chief, behind him on the right side of the aircraft continued to fire steadily. They had nearly completed their 180 degree turn away from the LZ when there was a bright flash from the cabin.

"Fire! Fire!" came the scream from Wash. The machine gun stopped firing. "Put it down! Put it down! Oh, God! Get…" Then there was unintelligible screaming. Tony looked behind to see Wash in flames, hydraulic fluid spurting from ruptured lines down onto him and into the cabin. Flames were licking across the cabin deck and up the transmission compartment.

"Oh, fuck, Dean, we've got to land. We're going to blow."

"I'm landing, I'm landing. Checklist." Dean's voice was calm. Tony at that moment knew everything was going to be all right. Dean had everything under control. He began the landing checklist. A rapid spattering sound said they were taking small arms fire. Wash was still screaming when he threw himself out of the flaming cabin. Dean grunted. The aircraft tilted hard, then righted itself.

"…hit. You've got it." Dean slumped in his seat, blood spreading across his chest and down his arm.

Tony took the controls and continued the steep glide path Dean had established toward a small opening in the jungle. He was two hundred feet above the zone when he felt hot liquid soaking his flight suit above his shoulders. He couldn't figure it at first; then, in the instant it ignited he knew. It was hydraulic fluid from yet another severed line and it was burning his flesh like napalm. A Nomex flight suit provides a fair level of protection from flame, but the hydraulic fluid had soaked the skin on his neck between his helmet and flight suit and was burning as it traveled down across his shoulders and back. The pain was instantaneous and overwhelming. Under most circumstances landing a helicopter requires two hands, one for the collective and one for the cyclic. Tony was screaming with pain as his back fried and flapping first one hand and then the other back toward his neck. The Huey slopped lazily through the air, almost fully engulfed in flames. All communications lines had melted in the heat, their only hope for communication was to yell back and forth but Dean was practically unconscious and Tony was out of his mind with pain. Only his high-backed steel seat was keeping him from being fried alive and it had become so hot he thought it might be melting. He looked over at Dean one last time as he raised the collective to cushion their descent and pulled back on the cyclic to reduce their speed. The collective flipped loosely in his hand, the control cables and tubes having melted. The knowledge he had no way to land the helicopter was Tony's last rational thought. As he looked down at the useless control in his hand, he was engulfed in flames and the aircraft smashed into the ground.

******

Screaming. Someone is screaming. They should stop screaming. Good. Now they are quiet. It's peaceful.

Thirsty. I can't swallow. Throat hurts.

Hurt. My neck hurts. Ow. Everything hurts. Make it stop.

DEAN! WHERE IS DEAN?

Tony sat up fast. The movement scraped scorched cotton and nomex across torched flesh on his neck and shoulders. The pain made him almost pass out. He vomited instead. DEAN! He rolled to his knees and then stumbled to his feet. The lap belt from his seat belt fell away from his waist, the lower part of the shoulder straps still attached at the locking mechanism. The ends of all four straps were burned completely through. He'd been ejected from the helicopter. He must have been thrown through the windscreen of the Huey when they hit. The cabin and cockpit sat burning 30 feet from him. Where is DEAN? He could have been ejected, too. Tony pitched forward toward the cockpit. The heat made it difficult to get close, the smoke made it hard to see. A quick breeze parted the smoke and Tony saw a sight that would haunt him for the rest of his life. Dean's body was fully engulfed in flames in the co-pilot's seat. It was twisting and curling as it burned. The flesh was blackened and crisp, hands were shrunken claws, the shoulders, arms and helmet-covered head were twisted in and around the torso.

Tony sobbed twice, then cried, his voice a high keening sound he didn't recognize as his own. He moved away from the heat and dropped to his knees. He sagged forward until his helmet touched the ground, then rolled onto his side, in a tight fetal position.

He awoke to the sound of Vietnamese being spoken nearby. *Oh, shit. Oh, fuck. No ARVN around. It's the bad guys! Where's Dean?* A glance at the Huey answered that question. His stomach heaved and he turned away, shutting his mind to the tragedy. *Got to get away. Shit, they're close. Coming from the direction of the LZ. My God! What about that patrol we were going in to pick up? Got to go!*

He got to his hands and knees, then scurried away from the voices and into the jungle. Getting to his feet, he practically sprinted a quarter mile up the mountainside, following a game trail of some sort, before he collapsed, totally winded. He lay with his face in the mud until his breathing returned to normal. Got to think. Can't just run. Think. Jesus, Dean is dead. Dean is dead. How can I ever tell his mother? Think. Got to live through this first, or I'll never have a chance to tell her anything. Christ, I've still got the helmet on. I ran all that way with my helmet on. He took it off and tossed it into the undergrowth.

Gradually, Tony gathered his thoughts. The first thing he did was inventory his survival vest. As he looked through it Tony remembered how Dean had made him add more stuff than the standard issue. "You need a good map of the operating area in your vest," Dean had said. "You can't count on bringing the one from the aircraft with you. And you've got to keep it updated with friendly and enemy units, just like you do with the map you'll use for flying." And so Tony had done so. He'd also gotten rid of the standard pilot-issue .38 revolver and replaced it with a

.45 caliber semi-automatic pistol. At Dean's urging he carried extra water, medical supplies and food.

"For Christ's sake, Dean," he'd complained, "My vest weighs more than my mother."

"Yeah," Dean had growled, "but your mother won't keep you alive."

Tony choked back a sob as he went through the survival vest. So much of what Dean had made him include seemed vitally important now. Dean had done so much for him; taught him everything. This vest was his final gift.

He was almost finished repacking his vest when he heard movement on the trail behind him. Goddamn it! How could they track me so fast? His first impulse was to get up and run, but he suppressed it quickly. No more panic. Not today. Those assholes killed Dean. He knelt behind a tree, pulling the vest in with him. He grabbed some dirt and rubbed it in his face, then looked carefully through dense leaves down the trail. The Vietnamese soldier seemed to be alone, but he was probably just the tracker for a patrol coming up behind. Tony was pinned. His heart was pounding hard but his breathing was controlled. He'd already seen the worst thing in the world. Now he was going to do whatever it took to survive. This man would kill him if he could. That made the choice easy.

Tony braced his left hand against the tree and trained the sights on the soldier's chest. The soldier took a step and stopped, alert. Tony squeezed the trigger. The .45s report shocked Tony, but not nearly as much as it shocked the soldier, who took the round in his stomach. The impact folded him almost in half and pushed him back into a tree. Instantly Tony threw on his vest and began to run again, waiting for the bullets that would smash his spine. But there was no return fire and he was out of sight in seconds. This time he ran carefully, thinking, breathing, stopping for water every hour or so. He ran up the hill and took a break in a small opening. From that point he could see the landing zone where they'd taken fire. This would be the place the Dustoff rescue choppers would land. He could see people moving around in the zone; they were Viets.

The entire patrol he and Dean had been sent to pick up must have been wiped out…or they were on the run like he was. He could wait up here for someone to come looking for him, talk to them on his radio and control their fire as they wasted the gooks around the zone. Then he could waltz down there and get on a helicopter. That would work nicely. He was looking around for a place to hide when a bullet 'snicked' as it zipped past his face. He dropped instantly to his belly and wiggled into the jungle. As soon as he was screened from sight Tony leaped to his feet and began running. He thought about staying on the ridge but doing so would keep him in range of the LZ and now they'd likely be sending troops up to aid in the search. He needed to clear the area.

And so Tony left the trail and crossed the ridge into a completely new drainage, running as he did so. He ran for the next 19 days, stopping only for brief snatches of sleep and to relieve himself. Vietnamese soldiers seemed to be on his trail non-stop. He ate candy bars and other snacks while he ran. Most of the time he had only the barest idea of his location. The jungle was so thick that he usually couldn't get a clear view of either the sky or the ground. He tried to stay off well-traveled trails but moving straight through the jungle was backbreaking work, and far too noisy. He tried repeatedly to head for American firebases and established landing zones that showed on his map, but each time the Vietnamese seemed to anticipate his movements and cut him off so he would have to take off in a different direction. He had enough food for three days and he kept going for two days after that, but finally hunger drove him into a small village where he hid until dark and then stole food from an untended hibachi. He was only one hundred yards away when he heard the alarm sound. By that time, he'd already eaten the stolen food. He took the time to fill his canteen in a small stream, dump in an iodine tablet. Then he doubled back, got in the stream and ran downstream for a quarter mile before he crossed over into a rocky area where he hoped his footprints would be hidden. He continued to steal from villages, hoping his thefts would be undiscovered, but realized how unlikely that sort of luck was. When you have as little as those people, any loss would be noticed.

Stealing from villages, Tony knew, simply alerted the soldiers of his presence and ensured they would always be on his trail. But he had no options; he had to have food. Already he estimated he'd lost 15 or 20 pounds and he'd been relatively slender when he started. He gave thanks every day for his long-distance running experience and endurance. Remarkably, his feet held up, even though his steel-toed aviation boots were certainly not designed for this sort of treatment. He tried at first to travel at night but after twice taking dangerous falls he resigned himself to daylight travel. He was tired all the time, but could not afford to stop and rest for long. Only after it became fully dark did he dare to stop and then he was careful to move away from trails and into dense thickets before he lay down. Twice, patrols came within a few feet of him in the dark.

On his 10th day on the run, which he knew because of the daily scratches he'd put on his canteen, Tony got sloppy in his food collection and grabbed an entire pot off a fire. A woman screamed just as he picked it up but Tony continued to run with it. He stopped after a few hundred yards and began shoveling the wonderful rice, fish and vegetable concoction into his mouth by the handful. He was only halfway done when two men with rifles burst into view. They were not soldiers, but simple farmers and their weapons were old single-shot and bolt-action rifles that looked to be left over from World War I. The first one brought his rifle to his shoulder and pulled the trigger but evidently had forgotten to take the safety off, and he hesitated for just a moment as he struggled with the safety lever. In that time Tony raised the .45 and touched off three quick rounds, one of which caught the farmer high in the leg, near his groin. He went down hard and groaning. The second farmer knelt behind a tree and shot back blindly. Tony ran, then circled around behind the farmer. When he approached he saw the man dragging his wounded friend back toward the village. Tony approached from behind and shot the man in the back of the head. The wounded man lay unconscious on the ground where his dead friend had dropped him, his rifle across his chest. He seemed completely out. Tony started to walk away, then turned back, remembering another time. He leaned forward and touched the end of his pistol barrel to the man's eye. Faster than thought, the farmer screamed and pulled the rifle up and toward Tony, who simply pulled his trigger. The man's head erupted in a fountain of blood and brain, his body arched and went still.

"You were right, Dean," Tony whispered. He ran back to his pack, stopping just long enough to drop the empty magazine from the pistol and replace it with a full one. He took a few more bites from the pot. Then he was off and running again.

Tony stayed away from trails for the next two days. He slowly forced his way through the dense jungle, often on his hands and knees. The bad news, he reflected, was that he was probably going only two miles each day. The good news was that he was relatively safe; the chances of being discovered in the thick vegetation were low. He used that relative safety to catch up on his sleep; he took a nap virtually every time he was forced onto his knees by the vegetation. When he was moving, Tony focused completely on staying alive, but in those few periods of wakeful resting, he was thinking about Raven. Her face became a valued companion. He considered and practiced the first words he would say to her on his return. At the end of two days Tony was well rested, but he was also starving. He'd been able to fill his canteen in small springs but other than a few grubs, he'd eaten nothing. He needed a village.

He took the next trail he crossed and followed it to a small mountain village, no more than six or eight homes. Although he'd planned to wait until after nightfall to make his move, his hunger had become an all-consuming need; he headed into the village as soon as there was no one visible. He grabbed a chicken roasting over an open fire and ran through the village, taking care to keep the houses between him and the farmers working their small gardens. He ran a few hundred yards into the jungle and sat on a downed log to cut the chicken apart with his survival knife and eat. He was halfway through the chicken when a soft noise behind him made him turn. Less than 10 feet away a small Vietnamese boy was watching him solemnly.

For the rest of his life, Tony would wonder what would have happened if he'd just kept his wits about him; if he'd just offered the boy a bite of chicken. If he'd smiled and rubbed his stomach, pantomiming happiness. If he'd done any one of a million things instead of what he'd actually done, which was to leap up and go for the boy. His movement startled the youngster and he took off running for the village. Tony missed with his first lunge and dropped his chicken in the dirt. He then had to chase the boy who was in full flight and screaming at the top of his voice.

Tony caught him inside of 30 yards, but it took all his strength to hold the boy down. He covered the boy's mouth with his hand, wrapped his other arm around the boy's arms and squeezed, listening intently for pursuit. Nothing. Then a yell from the direction of the village; a name. The boy leaped in his arms struggling mightily. He raked his head back and forth, back and forth. Somehow he worked his face free from under Tony's hand and bit down hard on his thumb. The pain was beyond anything Tony had ever felt and became worse as the boy ground his teeth down, farther and farther into both knuckles of his left thumb. Blood was flying everywhere; Tony could actually feel the knuckle bone being crushed and the sensation sent him out of his mind. He stopped worrying about pursuit; only one thing mattered in the world, stopping the pain. He let the boy go, shoved him back in the direction of the village, but the boy didn't go. He held on to Tony's arm and continued to bite. Tony was insane with pain and rage. He pulled the boy back into his grasp, clasping his small body to himself with his left arm and began hitting him with his right, smashing his right hand back into the boy's chest again and again. The boy struggled and cried with the first few blows, then went limp, but Tony continued to hit him until the boy's teeth fell away from his thumb.

Tony sagged to the ground, coming to his senses only when he heard running footsteps. He opened his eyes to see a group of five or six men and women staring at him from across the small clearing. He struggled to his feet to face them, only realizing as he prepared to meet their charge that he still held his survival knife in his right hand and it was soaked from point to hilt in blood.

The villagers, armed only with hoes and shovels, were stricken by the apparition that faced them. It was soaked in blood; eyes and teeth glittered through the dripping redness. It waved a razor sharp and bloody knife at them as it stood above the slaughtered form of their village boy. Even the boy's parents were stilled at the sight of the frightening form before them. There stood evil incarnate, raging at them, beckoning them forward to be torn apart. The villagers cringed and hid behind one another.

Tony backed up slowly toward his survival vest, taking in as he did so the sight of the dead boy. He had done that. Oh, Jesus, he had done that. No time to think about it now. Now he had to live. He had to live. He picked up his vest and backed slowly into the jungle, turning to run as soon as he could, trying to shut out the wails that filled the air behind him. He put the boy out of his mind. He ran. He was getting good at compartmentalizing memories now. He would just run. It wasn't until he stopped to drink and wash off an hour later that Tony noticed the gashes in his chest. It took him several minutes to realize they had come from his own knife. The knife thrusts that had killed the small Vietnamese boy had gone clear to the hilt, leaving one-half inch of blade to penetrate whatever was behind him, which happened to be Tony's chest. While killing the boy, Tony had stabbed himself in the chest eight times.

It was impossible to ignore. The boy had whimpered when Tony covered his mouth. He'd been so afraid. Tony tried to call up Raven's face. Impossible to compartmentalize. The boy had growled as he bit Tony's thumb. He was so brave, to fight so hard. Each time Tony breathed, the chest wounds hurt. The boy had writhed with pain each time he was stabbed. Each time his thumb throbbed he saw the boy, felt the bite. *Please Raven. Please God.* He knelt beside the stream and cried.

None of Tony's wounds had reached vital organs, but all were painful and bleeding. His thumb was real trouble. It was crushed, bleeding, throbbing and swelling fast. It was essentially unusable. He took all his clothes off and washed them, as well as his body in a stream. Then he used Iodine and Bacitracin and the remainder of his bandages and tape to bind his mangled thumb and cover the knife wounds in his chest. He dressed himself again in his soaking clothes and walked on into the jungle, off the trail, thinking about the boy, thinking about his thumb, thinking about the boy. For the first time since his helicopter had been shot down, Tony walked aimlessly. He had no plan; he didn't care where the nearest firebase was. He'd completely forgotten about Dean. He was simply walking away from the village, away from the boy.

He walked and crawled all day and all night, and never once did the boy leave his thoughts. He tried over and over again to visualize Raven, to think of their last night together but it was impossible. His mind had no room for anything else. He had nothing to eat, and he forgot to drink as well. By evening he was dehydrated and dizzy. Several times he stumbled and fell and each time he forgot about his thumb and tried to break his fall with his hands. The pain was excruciating and left him gasping and moaning in the dirt. Even worse, though he didn't know it at the time, was the dirt that was driven into the wounded thumb with each fall. By mid-morning, when he finally passed out from exhaustion, the thumb was well on its way to infection.

Tony slept poorly and awakened repeatedly with nightmares about the boy. Although the dreams varied significantly, several versions included the boy pleading for his life in English, screaming and crying. Several times, Tony woke up thinking it had all been a dream, that he would never kill a child. But then he looked at his thumb and felt his chest; and the memories came flooding back to torture him until he fell back to sleep. He finally awakened just before daylight, so thirsty that even his revulsion at the boy's death was relegated to background noise in his mind. He set out to find water. The first water he came to was a muddy little stream and he used his last iodine tablet to treat his canteen after he'd filled it. It took every bit of his will power to keep from drinking the water straight from the stream. His thumb was throbbing painfully and he suspected the headache and fever he felt were related to the reddish flesh he could see peeking out from beneath the bandage. But he couldn't bring himself to unwrap and clean it right then. Maybe later. He drank the entire canteen, then refilled it from the creek and started off. His intake of water helped his thought process and Tony made the decision at some point to just head east. Didn't matter much anyway but who knew, maybe sooner or later he'd arrive at the South China Sea.

The days began to run together after that. It started to rain and within minutes everything he carried was soaked. It was impossible for him to keep his dressings clean and after a while he stopped trying. The best he could do was try to keep the thumb bandaged tightly because it seemed to hurt less when it was snug. This became a problem as the infection progressed and the thumb, and then the hand and arm, became more and more swollen. By the 16th day, he was no longer capable of monitoring the passage of time, Tony's infection had progressed to the point where his fever was causing occasional hallucinations. He dreamed that he'd bumped into a small patrol on a trail and had a gunfight, killing two of them and putting the rest to flight. He was never sure if it had actually happened, but he found out later that there were only two rounds left in his pistol magazine when he was carried into the hospital.

His thoughts were so disconnected by then Tony didn't really understand what was happening when, on the 17th day, the stomach virus took hold of him. His bowel movements became loose, watery and totally uncontrollable. He would be walking along when his bowels let go, soaking his pants down to his boots in watery shit. At first Tony tried to wash off by wading in the streams along the way but it happened so often he just quit worrying about it. He pretty much quit worrying about everything.

His arm was swollen by now to twice its normal size and Tony had begun talking to it. "No, it's not gangrene. Bullshit! You are trying to scare me. It's just a little infection. It will get better. You'll see."

Then he began to sing. "You're going to kill me and I don't care, you're going to kill me and I don't care," to the tune of Jimmy Crack Corn. Sometimes Raven sang along.

By the 19th day Tony had forgotten the words. He was sitting on a log, humming Jimmy Crack Corn when someone began playing the drums in accompaniment. It pissed him off.

"Too fast, Goddammit! Too fast for the fucking song!" He raged at the drummer for some time until he finally realized the sound was not drums, but rotor blades.

Tony could no longer remember why he cared about helicopters but he was pretty sure he did. He looked out through the trees to see 10 or more Hueys approaching an open meadow less than a quarter mile below him. He took off running, or he thought he was running. In truth it was just a shuffle, and far slower than his normal walking speed. He arrived at the meadow just as the last of the Hueys was departing. Tony waved, but it was no use. They were gone. He lay down in the meadow and cried, though he wasn't sure why.

An hour later he was still in the meadow when the Hueys returned. The meadow where Tony lay was one of several fake landing zones the helos had used en route to their real drop-off spot in hopes of confusing the enemy. They were coming in again as part of their second delivery. Tony didn't hear them at all until all the aircraft had landed around him. They were staying on the ground for a full minute to simulate a complete drop of people and equipment. When the sound finally made its way through to Tony's brain, he stood up shakily, scaring the hell out of the gunner in the second aircraft, third flight, who opened up with his M-60 machine gun and put a round into each of Tony's legs. The entire flight leaped into the air when the pilot called enemy, enemy and it wasn't until they were more than a mile away that one of the troops involved claimed the man in the field looked like an American wearing a skuzzy flight suit. The ensuing conversation resulted in the release of a section of two Hueys to return to the LZ and check out the situation. An hour later Tony was delivered to a field hospital where the first medic to see him exclaimed, "Jesus Christ! This guy looks like he was shot at and missed and shit at and hit!"

"No," said the surgeon who was cutting Tony's flight suit away. "He was hit by both shot and shit, though I don't see how. The poor guy is so skinny I don't think he would throw a shadow. What's his name?"

The medic checked Tony's dog tags. Chief Warrant Officer Anthony Corrarino."

"Well, if we could ever figure out how to bottle and sell survival instinct, this guy would be the best possible donor. There's no telling how long he's been out there alone. He's been shot in both legs, stabbed multiple times in the chest, his left thumb has been crushed and cut, maybe bitten and is so infected it's gangrenous, and he has a terrible burn across his neck and shoulders that somehow escaped infection. On top of all that he obviously has been starved and has dysentery, possibly malaria. I wonder… just what would it take to kill this guy?"

Just then Tony woke up long enough to say, "My arm thinks it has gangrene, but it's lying. Don't cut it off. I'd rather die than have my arm cut off." Then he passed out again.

"That's what they all say," said the doctor, and he removed Tony's arm just below the elbow.

Chapter 27

Shane was patching one of his rafts when the phone rang. It was Cliff Martin, down at the Riverhouse Bar and Grill. Cliff, a classmate of Shane's, was the bartender and night manager there. The former center on the football team, Cliff had opened holes for Shane and protected Jared for years as they progressed through the various levels of football together. Blocky and strong, Cliff looked like he could do those jobs even better now. He'd spent three years after high school in the Air Force as a parachute rigger, before coming back to Grangeville and buying a part interest in the Riverhouse. He was as solid and dependable now as he had ever been. Police calls to the Riverhouse, which had historically been numerous, were far less so when Cliff was around. He simply took care of most of the problems.

"Hey, Cliff."

"Howdy, Shane. How goes it?"

"I'm doing fine, buddy. You?"

"Doin' great. Just sellin' beer. You know. But there are a couple guys out here I think you should come see."

"Yeah? Who?"

"Two Marines who served with Jared. They are telling all kinds of stories about their time in Vietnam with him."

"We're pretty well past that, now, Cliff. Jared's been gone for two months."

"I know, Shane. You weren't the only one hurt by the way he treated all of us. I always thought the sun pretty much rose and set on Jared McCauley. But the stories these guys are telling are worth listening to, Shane. Old Jared was even better than any of us realized. You do not want to miss this."

And so Shane headed to the Riverhouse, where Cliff introduced him to two young men sitting at a table. Andy, a rangy South Dakota farm boy, had been one of Jared's squad leaders. Amos, a massive, dangerous-looking black man from Detroit, had been Jared's radioman. Cliff had obviously been providing free beer and it took little encouragement for them to rehash a few of the stories from their days in Vietnam with Jared. Shane was seized with an almost uncontrollable urge to ask if the two men were really named Amos and Andy, but the closer he looked at them the more he thought it would be a bad idea.

"He showed up as a replacement lieutenant when our platoon was providing security for a forward artillery base," Andy explained.

"Fuckin' new guy," Amos growled.

"He was pretty green," Andy continued, "and he came into an outfit that had been demoralized by several straight months of combat. We also had a real bad race relations problem." He grinned and jabbed a thumb at Amos, who made a half-hearted attempt to grab it.

"So this baby-faced white boy come into our world and he tell us what's what and how it goin' be. We got 10-12 brothers been takin' shit from that cracker Jones…"

"Our platoon sergeant," Andy explained, "and a world-class bigot."

"…and all the time we been takin' fire from Charley and we ain't in the mood for more of his honky shit."

"So the Lieutenant listens to people bitching…" Andy said.

"And this is his first time…" said Amos.

"And he turns to Staff Sergeant Jones…" Andy continued.

"That fuckin' bigot, and he look him in the eye and he say, real slow, 'P'toon sar'n't, we will not have any men treated differently in this p'toon. We are all green. Do I make myself clear?' Hah! 'Do I make myself clear?' he say. An' then…"

Andy jumped in. "And then he looked at Amos, who was the biggest, baddest black power panther in the Crotch and he…"

"An' he say, 'You goin' be my radioman, startin' now. Go get your shit.'" Amos shook his head in wonder, as Andy howled. Shane and Cliff smiled and nodded. It fit.

"'Go get your shit,' he say," Amos repeated, wistfully. "So that night, Charley pounding the hell out of us; me and the Lieutenant making ourselves real small in the foxhole, shells goin' off all roun' us and he leans over to me an' he say, 'You know, Amos, a lot of people never get to do this kind of thing.'"

"So, what did you say to him then, Amos?" Cliff asked.

"I said nothin' 't all. I figured he too crazy to talk to."

All four men laughed, and Cliff ordered another pitcher.

After glasses were filled, Andy continued. "So they pounded us all night and assaulted at dawn." He took a long drink. "The lieutenant hadn't been in country for two days, he only knew four or five people's names, and his position was hit by a company-sized assault. The artillery commander was killed right out of the chute so they were pretty disorganized; the Lieutenant got them to depress their tubes and fire some point blank flechette rounds and those thinned the dinks out a good bit, but there were still several dozen coming across the wires. A couple Huey guns showed up and worked them over but a bunch of them still made it into our camp. That's when things got interesting."

"So the fuckin' dinks are comin' across fast and they in the camp, so it don't do no good to stay in your foxhole, 'cause they just walk up behind and kill you but the men, they don't know it. But the lieutenant, he figure it out right away and he jump up and say, 'C'mon Amos!'"

"I say 'Shit, I ain't that stupid, Honkey!'"

Andy laughed and picked it up. "So I looked across the line and I see the lieutenant and Amos come sweeping in, killin' bad guys as they come, screaming, 'Out of the holes, out of the holes!'"

"Where was your platoon sergeant at this point?" Cliff asked.

"That honky prick caught a mortar round in his foxhole early in the fight, but we din't know it at the time," Amos said.

"That was a big part of our problem," Andy said. "Jones would normally have been coordinating between the squads, so we were a little crossed up. And as big an asshole as he was, Jones was one helluva fighter. Not having him there let the air out of us, if you know what I mean. So when the dinks came in through our lines we were close to coming apart completely. That's when the Lieutenant and the Black Avenger here came screaming through the smoke, swinging e-tools…"

"Things was happening fast, too fast to tell, when that crazy Lieutenant take off out of the hole. He shootin' his .45 like they give officers, and when that runs out of shells he picks up an M-16 and when that's empty he picks up an e-tool and I tell you what, the Grim Reaper ain't got nothin' on that boy. He killin' everythin' that moves with that little shovel. He the devil himself, his eyes so big they shine, sparks coming off that fuckin e-tool. He givin' off his own weird light and it scare the shit out of the dinks."

"Of course, it's not just him. Amos is right behind him, all swelled up even bigger than normal, with that old M-14 and a bayonet way out in front of him, making noises no human should make, big eyes and white teeth smiling in the dark, covering the Lieutenant's six.

"And the whole time the Lieutenant is screaming for the men, getting them up and out of their holes, getting them organized, moving them around to fill the gaps in our lines. It was unbelievable."

"Unfuckingbelievable," Amos said, and the two men went silent.

"A shovel," Cliff whispered.

"Fuckin' A," Amos agreed. "A shovel."

"Good time for a head call," Andy said, and headed for the door. All four men took a break.

Shane joined Cliff at the bar while he checked with the bartender and reviewed the sales. "What do you think?" Cliff said.

"I don't know, Cliff. It sounds pretty much like what I'd expect from Jared, don't you think?"

"Oh, yeah. Sure, but that's not what I meant. I'm talking about the situation, how bad it must have been. Makes riggin' parachutes seem pretty pathetic."

"Not pathetic, Cliff. Just a little more, um, subdued."

"Yeah, subdued. Tell me something, Shane. Do you ever wish you could have been there, living through that kind of fight? Ever wonder what you would have been like?"

"Sure I do. I think every young man does. And I'm sure each one of us wonders if we would have been brave, too. I know one thing."

"What's that?"

"You would have been right there with Jared, as tough as him and all the rest."

"I like to think so, Shane. Thanks. I think the same about you. Well, here they come again. I'm ready for Act II."

The two young Marines were quieter as they sat down. They were tired, and more than a little tipsy. Still, Andy seemed committed to telling the story.

"So, we get through that fight and it's like the Lieutenant is some kind of God. The whole thing was surrealistic anyway, and the way he saved us…"

"And Jones is dead," Amos interrupted. "So it's the Lieutenant's p'toon. Nobody else's. And he starts making it over just the way he wants it. Gets a good man in at p'toon sarn't and starts treatin' people right. No bullshit. Just plays it straight. And he stood up for people too, din't let nobody mess with us."

"But you didn't want to screw up, either, because the Lieutenant didn't mind fucking with you until you wished you were dead."

"So the whole p'toon is decorated and the Lieutenant gets a bronze star, which is a crock of shit. If there'd been any officers alive to see what he'd done, he'd a got a Medal of Honor, or at least a Navy Cross."

"In fact, Amos got a Silver Star out of that fight," Andy explained.

"Yeah, right. The Lieutenant wrote it up, but he din't say shit about me following him the whole time." He shook his head.

"So they moved us back to the rear for a while and brought in some replacements and we got pretty squared away, but it wasn't long before they sent us up to run security patrols around a fairly large base."

"We were also supposed to disrupt transportation of Vietnamese soldiers and supplies along a series of trails nearby, so we did a lot of nighttime ambushes."

"We got pretty fuckin' good at it," Amos laughed.

"That had to be scary," Cliff said.

"Real scary," Andy agreed, "but I'll tell you what, it was scarier for the dinks. The lieutenant was a creative son-of-a-bitch when it came to setting an ambush."

Andy suddenly laughed out loud at a memory. "And he got everyone involved. You remember the night he let the doc fire the Claymore?"

Amos smiled. "Oh shit, oh dear, yes. Turned that youngster into a hellion, for sure."

Andy continued. "We had a Navy Corpsman, 'Doc' we always called them. Blonde, surfer kid about 18, looked about 12. Really a nice kid, knew his stuff and he was absolutely fearless. Helped a lot of us out when we were hit."

"Tough guy, too," Amos said. "Scary tough."

Andy continued, "Never had a bad word to say to anybody, you know. Everybody liked him. But one time while we were in the rear a couple REMFS..." at Shane's quizzical look Andy explained, ... "'Rear Echelon Mother Fuckers'...gave him some shit and the next thing anybody knew those two guys were down and down hard."

Amos added, "Doc knew jujitsu or some shit."

"So anyway, one day, Doc asks the Lieutenant if he could do some shooting in the next ambush. Lieutenant knows about the fight of course, and he says 'Sure, you been saving enough lives. It's time to take a few.'"

"He let the Doc carry a rifle and blow the Claymore when the dinks come into the ambush and it works out great except..."

Amos continued, "Except we sprung the ambush on the lead element of a big fucking group and they come after us hard. Couple guys got hit and we couldn't get clear. All hell broke loose."

"Amen. Well things were looking pretty bad until the Doc turns into Captain America and conducts his own flanking maneuver on the bad guys."

"Shit. We all scratching ourselves a place in the dirt and the Doc is up and running at them, firing as he goes. He is rippin' those assholes up."

Andy: "Soon as the Lieutenant figures out what is happening, he gets the rest of us up and we charge." He laughed out loud. "He actually said 'Charge.' I never thought I'd hear it."

- 215 -

"I damn sure never thought I'd do it," Amos said, chuckling. "So we run through the dinks and whip 'em bad. And then the Lieutenant calls in arty on the ones running away."

Andy: "So, after that the Doc gets to carry a rifle on every mission; course he had to carry his medical stuff, too. The chief corpsman bitches and moans about him being a non-combatant but the Lieutenant ignores him…says there are no non-combatants in this war and just keeps giving him a rifle. The doc was one of our best men until the lieutenant got hurt, then they yanked him out of the platoon."

"Tell me about how he got hurt?" Those were the first words Shane had said.

"He got hurt twice," Andy said. "Twice badly. Both on the same hill."

Amos shook his head slowly and cursed under his breath.

Andy continued, "He'd been nicked a time or two before that but nothing big. The first time we were taking the hill. It was a major operation, battalion-sized. The dinks were dug in well. There was a whole series of tunnels and bunkers across the upper part of the hillside. We were moving up slowly, letting arty and air support soften them up ahead of us, but then we stumbled into a fortified position and things got sticky."

Amos spoke, "Machine gun opened up and killed two guys like right now. Lieutenant starts moving people, fire and maneuver, gets somebody out to flank the gun. Bad times, then Andy here takes out the machine gun with a LAWW and things settle down."

"At least we thought…" Andy said. "Then four or five more NVA pop up out of a tunnel we'd missed and start shooting. Two more guys are killed and though we didn't realize it right away, the Lieutenant was shot, too. We kill those guys and we're getting our men set out into defensive positions when somebody notices the Lieutenant is bleeding bad. So the Doc heads over there and is patching him up when two more dinks appear out of nowhere and come right down on them. The Lieutenant is lying flat on his back and he's pretty weak from loss of blood but he kills one of them with his .45 before the other runs right into the Doc."

Amos jumped in. "Well, the dumbass could have picked any one of us and been better off but he had to jump on the Doc, who knows about a million ways to kill people. He kicked and slashed and stomped and punched and pretty soon the little dink was dead. But it turned out he'd knifed the Doc pretty bad and we had to wrap him up and dump him in a Huey with the Lieutenant."

"We spent two nights on that hill," Andy explained, and then went back to our base for security patrol. The Lieutenant and Doc were out about three weeks, didn't even get sent back to the world. Spent their time on a hospital ship and then came back together three weeks later."

"Just in time to take that fuckin' hill again," Amos snarled. "They hadn't been back a week when the word came down we were going back up that motherfucker. 'You shittin' me?' we say. 'Get somebody else. We already lost four men on that piece of fuckin' rock.' But the Lieutenant, he say it don't matter. 'We got it to do,' he say. 'An' we goin' do it.' Well, shit." Amos shook his head again, slowly, thoughtfully. And went silent.

Andy stepped in. "It wasn't a picnic, but it wasn't as bad as the first time. Our part of the hill wasn't as well defended…but then we ran into another machine gun nest, in steep ground, where it could control almost the entire slope. Some guys worked their way up, from directly below the gun—it was so steep the gooks couldn't depress the gun that far—and our guys got pretty close. That's when the grenade came out. It was thrown too high and hard. I could see the Lieutenant wasn't even worried about it. But then it clipped a tree branch and fell straight down behind him. I was screaming, but he couldn't hear me and that fucking grenade went off right below him."

"By rights he shoulda' been blown to bits," Amos said, "but only one fragment hit 'im. Shoulda been even luckier. He deserved to be luckier."

"So the Lieutenant is hurt bad and he's screaming and rolling down the hill," Andy said. "Amos grabs him and wedges him up against a stump so he doesn't go all the way down and the doc gets there. And I can see the doc is crying but he's doing the job just the same. He and the Lieutenant were really close, especially after they spent their time on the hospital ship together. And the doc still wasn't 19 so he felt like the Lieutenant was his dad or something. Then I see Amos shedding his radios, and he's swelling up and he's roaring like that time when we were overrun. I know he's going up the hill and I know he's going to die but then the Lieutenant reaches up and grabs him."

Amos was quiet now, speaking softly. "He gets hold of my flak jacket and he pulls me close. He's hurt so bad he can't hardly breathe but he won't let go and he trying to tell me something. He whispers in my ear the same thing over and over. I can't understand at first and I keep trying to pull away but he won't let me go. And finally Doc leans down with me and he says, 'Smoke, Amos. He's telling you to pop smoke!' So I yell over to Andy and one of his guys pops some smoke and…"

"And Amos slides in behind the smoke, gets in close to the machine gunners…"

"An' that's that," Amos whispered.

Andy put a big hand on Amos' shoulder and to him alone he whispered, "It needed doing." Then to Shane and Cliff he said, "That was definitely that. As soon as the machine gun was gone the Viets diddied back into the jungle. We were able to get the Lieutenant up to an LZ and get him off in a '46."

"Last we ever saw of him, and he won't see us now." Amos said.

"He won't see any of us now," Shane said. "And we've known him all our lives."

Chapter 28

They'd already had Tony's funeral, so his parents were understandably confused when, for the second time in less than a month an Army Chaplain and a Captain appeared at their door. Maria went to church three times a day for a month. It took almost that long to get Tony recovered enough to return back to the states.

He spent two months at Walter Reed, putting on weight, recovering from the various diseases and letting his arm heal up enough to fit with a prosthesis. The doctors were trying out some new prosthetics, but for the most part, Tony preferred just the hook. Sometimes, he didn't bother with it at all, just wrapped up his shirt sleeve and called it good. He was thankful it had been his off arm. For the most part he could do everything he'd done before—just slower.

When the therapists weren't pestering him, Tony preferred to spend his time sleeping. Except for occasional nightmares, the hours he spent sleeping were the only peaceful time he had. If he wasn't sleeping or involved in something else, Tony was seeing flashback images of his time in the jungle, of Dean's body burning in the Huey, of the Vietnamese farmer who'd feigned unconsciousness in order to kill him, of the boy. The boy never seemed to leave him. He was always there in the background and if Tony stopped for a moment, if he tried to rest or relax, the boy came back. And he wouldn't be quiet. He would scream until Tony covered his mouth and then he would bite, and bite and bite.

His parents came to see him at Walter Reed. He enjoyed seeing them. It was nice to know they were healthy. But he had trouble connecting with them, or with any of his other relatives or friends who came to visit. They belonged to a life that had somehow been taken from him. He was outside their window and as much as they wanted him to return, he couldn't.

His father had been nearly speechless with grief and anger. He kept shaking his head. "I told you not to do this. There was no need." Tony wasn't sure any more that he wasn't right, but it made no sense talking about it.

"You need to come home," his mother said. "Let us take care of you."

"I've got to go back out to Oregon, Mom. Got to see Dean's family. I'll be back after that."

One day after he'd been at Walter Reed a while, an Army general showed up to present Tony with a few medals. The general seemed upset that Tony was not in his full-dress uniform, but no one had told Tony about the ceremony, so the general pinned the medals on Tony's hospital gown. As soon as he was back on his feet and functioning, the hospital discharged him and the Army informed him he would be retired with a 90 percent disability rating that would ensure a small but steady income for the rest of his life. He still had almost 30 days of leave remaining, so when they released him Tony put on his uniform and took a train all the way to Oregon. He wanted to get there, but he didn't want to hurry. The closer he got, the slower he went. He stopped for a day in Kansas City, two in Denver, two in Salt Lake and three in Portland. When Tony finally stepped off the train in Albany; he almost didn't have it in him to continue. He sat for a long while in the station. Finally, the station manager walked over to him.

"Where you goin', soldier?"

Tony almost couldn't answer. If he said the word, it would finalize his journey. He'd have to continue.

"Where you goin', son?" The manager asked again.

"Alsea." There it was. No escape now.

"Got kin there?"

"Not really, no."

"Nobody pickin' you up?"

"No, I... No."

A long pause. "It's a hard thing."

Tony looked at the old man for the first time. His face seemed to be one big wrinkle, but in between the wrinkles were two wise brown eyes. And in those eyes was a lifetime of understanding and compassion. The old man nodded slowly. "A hard thing."

Tony smiled slightly, looked away when his eyes teared up. "Yes, it is," he said. "A hard thing."

"I'm off in an hour," the manager said. "I'd be proud to give you a ride to Alsea."

"Thanks, but no. That would get me there too quick." Tony stood and held out his hand. "Thanks, mister. You've been a help."

The old man smiled. "One day at a time, son. One day at a time." He walked back toward his office and Tony noticed for the first time how he swung his right leg stiffly in a half circle with no bend in the knee.

Tony hitched a ride over to Corvallis. He walked through town and stuck out his thumb again when he hit Highway 34. A one-armed soldier carrying his duffle bag was a sure thing and he got a ride almost immediately. The driver lived in Waldport, but worked occasionally with Dean's older brother and knew the Taylors.

"You're Dean's friend, huh?"

"Yes."

"Betty will be happy to see you. I heard Brian talking about you the other day. They've been hoping to hear from you. Guess you dropped off the face of the earth. To be honest, I don't think they knew you'd been banged up like this."

Tony reached over to touch his stump. "I should have been in touch. I should have. But I…."

"Don't worry about it, pal. Betty's just going to be glad to see you. It'll be fine."

But Mrs. Taylor was not glad to see him, at least not at first. She was working in her orchard when Tony walked down the driveway. She looked at him as though he was an apparition until he was close enough to see the wrinkles around her eyes, then she threw down her pruning shears and ran silently into the house. Tony sat down heavily on the garden swing and wondered what he was doing there.

He closed his eyes and thought of Mr. Taylor's funeral. He remembered when the Taylor clan had gathered around Mrs. Taylor, how he'd marveled at the way they surrounded and protected her, how she'd drawn strength from them. A family. A real family.

He'd been sitting there half an hour when an old beater pickup drove up. Brian Taylor got out, a big smile on his face.

"Welcome back, Tony. Aw, shit. Your arm. Mom didn't say anything about it."

"She might not have noticed, Brian. I think she was a little shocked to see me."

"Yeah, she's having a little trouble absorbing you…"

"Would it be better if I just left? I don't want…"

'Hell, no, Tony. We all want to see you. She just needs to get used to the idea. Don't you move an inch. I'll go in and check on her. I'll bring you a beer."

"That'd be good. Thanks."

When the beer came, it was Mrs. Taylor who brought it. She walked carefully, slowly, as if she was walking on unfamiliar ground. Her hair was thickly shot with gray, her eyes sunken and shadowed. She'd lost a great deal of weight and looked much older than the last time he'd seen her. She handed him the beer, sat down across from him. Tony took a sip and set the bottle down.

Tony waited, hoping she would speak but finally he spooked. "Mrs. Taylor, I'm so sorry, I…"

"You were with him?" It was not really a question. "Tell me." Her voice was demanding, her eyes beseeching.

"Mrs. Taylor, I …."

"Tell me the truth, please Tony."

"Mom," it was Brian speaking up from behind his mother. "You've got to remember how hard this whole thing has been for Tony. He might not be ready…"

She turned on him with fury Tony would not have believed possible. "You just be quiet, Brian Taylor!" she hissed. "You just shut up! I'm asking

Tony a question that's none of your business." She turned back to Tony, her face still contorted with rage. "You tell me about my son, now, Tony. You tell me about his last day," she choked then and hesitated, drew an anguished breath. When she spoke again it was with a soft, sorrowful voice. "My Dean wasn't much of a letter writer. The Army won't tell us anything. If you won't tell me I won't know anything at all. Please."

He'd always known it would come to this, and until he opened his mouth Tony didn't know how he would handle it. In the end, he told the truth. He told her what a fine pilot Dean had become, how carefully he planned his missions, how he had helped train Tony as well. He talked about the way people looked up to Dean and how his crew chief wouldn't fly with anyone else. Then he explained the mission, how they'd taken fire and tried to turn away. He told them how Dean had made a right turn, leaving himself on the side closest to the machine guns and how he'd been hit and collapsed on the controls. He talked about the fire in the aircraft and how he'd been thrown clear when they crashed.

"And then I ran for a long time until I got picked up," he finished.

"His body was burned beyond recognition," Mrs. Taylor said. "They only knew it was him because he was on the controls. They thought for a while it was you because he was in the co-pilot's seat."

The unasked question hung between them for several moments. Tony had another of a long line of many flashbacks. In the few seconds before he answered Tony could again hear the screams as he lay semi-conscious outside the Huey. He even remembered wishing to himself that the screamer would simply quit; it was so unnerving. It had been Dean screaming; he knew it now, but he couldn't think of one good reason why anyone else should know, least of all the man's mother.

"I never saw him move again, Mrs. Taylor. I think he was killed on impact."

Mrs. Taylor sobbed and seemed to shrink to a fraction of her former size. "He was a good boy," she cried. Tony went to her without thinking, wrapped his arm around her. "He was an even better man, Mrs. Taylor. The best I've ever known." They were both crying when Brian put his arms around them both and for the first time in his life, Tony knew what it meant to belong, to be given strength by the people who love you.

Tony stayed at the Taylor's place for three more weeks. He helped Mrs. Taylor around the house and talked a little bit with Dean's many friends and relations who came to visit when they learned he was there. Raven came, too, and told him in the nicest possible way that she had met the love of her life in Ashland and they would be married soon.

"It's OK, Raven, I understand," Tony said.

But Raven wasn't letting him off that easily. "No, you don't, you dummy. Wait a minute! You don't think this has anything to do with your arm, do you? I liked you a lot, Tony. But I LOVE him. It has nothing to do with your arm. Besides, I'm really fond of stumps! Let me feel that thing!"

They laughed for a long time then and left as friends, but Tony's disappointment in losing Raven cut deep and figured strongly in his decision to go back east. Brian came to talk with him one day while he was weeding the garden.

"The place looks one hundred percent better since you've come back, Tony."

Tony leaned back from his knees and into a sitting position. "Thanks, Brian. I appreciate it. It's been really good for me, too. I appreciate your mom letting me hang around."

Brian scoffed. "Heck, Tony, you're family. Mom wants you to stay forever. We all do. Have you noticed how much better she looks than when you first came home? She's putting on weight again and the circles under her eyes are almost gone. You've been great for her." He hesitated. "I don't know what you plan to do now, Tony, but we could sure find a place for you in one of our businesses. Someone in the family is involved with construction, surveying, real estate, fishing, banking…and we're all relatively close. We're all in western Oregon. With you here it would almost be like having Dean with us."

Tony looked up from the tomatoes to see Mrs. Taylor standing behind Brian as he spoke. Her eyes were brimming with tears as she nodded. "Please stay, Tony."

Tony stood and walked over close to them. "I doubt that you know how much you all mean to me, but I haven't even gone home yet, and I promised my mother I would. I'll be back someday; I promise."

Two days later Tony boarded the train in Albany headed east. This time there were nearly 20 members of the Taylor clan along to see him off. The old man with the bad leg was there and sold Tony his ticket.

"Things going a little better for you, I see," he said as he slid the ticket over.

Tony couldn't place him at first, then recognized the crinkled face around warm brown eyes. Tony smiled, "Yes sir. Quite a bit better. Like a wise man once told me…it's one day at a time."

"There you go, son. There you go." Tony reached into the booth to shake his hand.

It was hard leaving, especially since Mrs. Taylor kept hugging him until he climbed on the steps. Brian had to put his arms around her; she was sobbing openly.

Tony turned in his seat and closed his eyes as the train pulled away.

Chapter 29

Tony's visit to the old neighborhood was a different experience altogether. Lots of friends and family and good cheer but instead of the heartfelt appreciation he'd felt in and around Alsea, Oregon, he was greeted in New York by old friends and relatives who couldn't understand why he'd put himself in a position to be hurt so badly.

Carlotta Giovanni, a schoolmate with whom he'd been involved during their junior year in high school, and the daughter of one of Sal's lieutenants, put it succinctly: "Jeez, Tony. Why'd you have to go over there and lose your arm? You didn't have to join up! Everybody knows that. Nobody else who was connected had to go, ya know?"

Tony didn't begrudge the loss of his arm, the bullets in his legs or even the ugly burns on his neck and back, but the killing of the Vietnamese boy still tore at him night and day. He was aloof and distant even as he smiled and laughingly took part in many get-togethers and celebrations. His mother sobbed as he patted her back and attempted to console her.

"I'm fine, mom. Really, I'm going to be all right." But she knew better and Tony knew she could see right through him. He began to avoid her. He tried going to church but the act of confession confounded him. Even Father Bagliori, who had baptized him and been a part of his whole life, couldn't get Tony to confess, or even discuss his experiences while he'd been on the run in Vietnam.

One weekend, a few young men from the neighborhood decided to go down to Atlantic City for a weekend of gambling and partying. Tony despised Atlantic City but agreed to go just to get out from under his mother and all her pushy, well-meaning friends.

The boisterous group of young Italian men attracted a lot of attention in Atlantic City, including that of a beautiful, red-headed dancer, Brenda Piazza. It wasn't long before she'd been drawn into the group and was soon attracted to Tony. He was handsome but horribly thin, brooding but friendly in an open, casual way. Her attraction to him deepened when she learned the men were all part of the New York mob and that Tony was the son of a powerful New York crime boss. She was aggressive. Tony was vulnerable and in three months they were married. Tony told Brenda repeatedly of his break with his father and his commitment to build a life for himself outside the mob, and Brenda always said she understood, but she knew how strong his family ties were and she fully expected him to be pulled back into the fold within a few years.

Brenda knew how the wise guys live. She'd been involved with a couple of them during her time in Atlantic City, and she wanted another taste of that life, the high living, the pampered existence where other people think about what you need before you need it, and make sure everything is just like you want it. Not until after they'd been married for several years and had a son did Brenda finally understand just how serious Tony was about not being a part of the mob. Her disappointment began then and became more concentrated as the years passed.

Tony and Brenda bought a house in Bowie, Maryland; 'far enough away from New York to be insulated from the flare-ups and close enough to visit when we want,' Tony said. He finished his degree in American Literature at the University of Maryland and took a job at a small publishing house specializing in historical fiction just outside Washington, D.C. He found the job tremendously rewarding and over the years he worked his way up to Editor-in-Chief.

Brenda didn't work outside the home; she didn't want to work at all, but even if she had, the high school GED she finally finished at age 20 wasn't the best preparation for good jobs. The constant disappointment of Tony's refusal to move up in the world, to be a part of the mob, grated on her every day, and gradually broke down the veneer of sophistication and good cheer she'd been struggling to maintain. To make matters worse, Brenda felt her good looks slipping away and the sense of loss accelerated her descent into bitterness. Her once beautiful high cheekbones became angular and sharp. Her once sparkling eyes glinted. The mirror showed a woman whose features had hardened into the classic look that announced having seen and done too much. Brenda was well on her way to becoming shrewish; she knew it and hated it but was powerless to halt the process.

One day, after a three-martini afternoon Brenda joined Tony on the couch when he came home from work.

"Tony, Sweetie, I just want you to compare the way we live and the way your relatives live. They have big houses, lots of servants. We've got this," sneering as she swept her arms wide, encompassing an upper middle-class ranch-style home. "You could be someone special in the Family, Tony. You're smarter than all of them. We could have it all." She breathed the last few words into his ear, at the same time running her hand up his thigh. It was a move more appropriate for a hooker in a smoky downtown dive and Tony wondered, not for the first time, about Brenda's life before they had met. He couldn't help feeling repulsed and his response, to stand up quickly, telegraphed his feelings to Brenda more accurately than if he had explained them. Her reaction was predictable and emphatic.

"What? Are you disappointed in me? You shithead! Goddamn you! That's what disappointment feels like, you sorry asshole! Don't you think I'm disappointed? I'm disappointed in you every goddamned day!"

Tony lowered his head; he hated loud confrontations with Brenda. He tried again.

"We live well," he told her, quietly. "We travel, we have a nice, 2,400 square foot house, a wonderful baby. We've got plenty of money. What more could you ask?"

"I want it all!" she screamed, waving her arms. "I want it all! I don't want this pissant little middle-class life. I hate this boring, fucking housewife-mother gig, where my time is spent picking up after a spoiled brat, cleaning toilets and cooking dinner. I can't believe you are satisfied with this shit! We could be so much better."

Tony walked over to pick up the baby, who'd begun to cry as his parents' argument grew louder. "Anthony Dean," he said in a soft voice. "It's all right, it's ok. I've got you. Daddy loves you." The baby quieted in short order, and Tony held him in what remained of his left arm while loading up a stroller with diapers, wipes and a bottle.

"You know what my father does, right?" he asked Brenda. "And my brother? Do you want to raise Anthony Dean to that life?"

"Yes! Why not? Yes! It's a great life. Think of the money, for Christ's sake! He could have everything he ever wanted."

"They push dope, Brenda. They run hookers. They run protection rackets. They hurt people who don't go along and kill anyone who causes trouble. Do you honestly want Anthony Dean involved in those things?"

She lowered her voice in a last-ditch effort to convince him. "Tony, someone is going to do those things and make money at it. If it's not your family, then who? No, don't talk to me about what's legal, what's legal is what a sharp lawyer can convince a jury is legal. What's right is what we can take for ourselves."

Tony shook his head and headed for the door. "We're going for a walk, Brenda," he said.

"You can just keep walking for all I care," she shot back as the door closed.

That argument marked a fundamental change in their relationship. Brenda essentially stepped out of her role as a mother, one which had never fit her well anyway. She signed Anthony Dean up for a babysitter and from then on had little to do with him. She spent less and less time at home; going to the gym was a big part of her daily life, as was shopping. She was frequently out late in the evenings 'visiting friends.' She stopped cooking meals; on those few occasions she had anything to do with food, pizza or Chinese foods were delivered.

Tony ignored her steadily worsening behavior; he simply took up the slack. He got up to make breakfast for himself and Anthony Dean, then took him to the babysitter, all before Brenda got up in the morning. He arranged to come home earlier than normal so he could pick the child up from the babysitter, then went home and cooked dinner. Although the workload was drastically increased, Tony found the routine pleasant, if for no other reason than the elimination of complaints and screaming from Brenda. He no longer loved her, if he ever had. He no longer cared what she was doing in her time away from home.

The only time Brenda took any interest in Anthony Dean was when Tony went on business trips, which he had scheduled on a once-per-month basis. Even then she complained loudly about the need to care for the baby; "I've got things to do, ya know?"

Only twice did something happen to disrupt the stable, if unhappy, goings on. The first was when Tony received a Master Card bill for $10,900 of purchases in one month. Livid, Tony confronted Brenda that night.

"Those are things I need," she responded.

"You needed more than $10,000 of clothes, jewelry and makeup?" Tony asked, in a voice that Brenda had never heard before and one that unsettled her, but she put on a brave face.

"Yeah. I needed it. I wanted it. I deserve it. If you worked with your father that bill would be chump change."

"But I don't and I won't and it's not chump change. It's money that will have to come out of our retirement account and Anthony Dean's college account." He looked directly into her eyes and Brenda wasn't sure she knew the man who was looking at her, his words sliding together in a low growl that frightened her deeply. "It's not going to happen again. Never. OK?"

She nodded. There was nothing else to do. He took the credit cards out of her purse and scissored them. "You pay cash or write a check and you pay attention to the stubs. I will not have you bouncing checks."

Tony began taking on more and more duties at home, in addition to his work at the publishing house, but the effort was too great and gradually, he began to fray around the edges. His work suffered and finally, in order to protect his job, Tony was forced to hire a full-time nanny for Anthony Dean. Brenda didn't like it, but after two or three blowups, one of which sent the nanny out the door, Tony gave Brenda the choice; leave if you want, but if you stay, it will be quietly and without rancor. The rancor part of the deal was shaky; bitterness fairly dripped from Brenda, but she kept silent and lived her own life, all but separate from her husband and son, neither of whom seemed to mind.

As his son began running and laughing, Tony was reminded more and more frequently of the Vietnamese youngster. Sometimes, when he traveled, Tony couldn't remember his own son's looks; the face he saw instead was the Viet boy, covered with blood. Anthony Dean and the Vietnamese youngster became entangled in Tony's mind and memory until finally, in one horrific dream, it was Anthony Dean who screamed for help, Anthony Dean who bit his thumb and Anthony Dean who died at his father's hand.

Unable to bring himself to seek professional help or even talk to his wife about his feelings of guilt, Tony began to drink. In the space of a year he became dependent on a nightly dose of nearly one-half a fifth of bourbon. The alcohol dulled his memory, allowing him to laugh and enjoy himself but Tony soon learned the price. When he was drunk enough to make the memories fade, he was also a boorish slob. Brenda, a heavy but controlled drinker herself, had no sympathy for Tony and arranged to videotape his actions during a particularly ugly night. The next afternoon, she played the video in front of Tony and Anthony Dean. Tony was appalled at the video but even more shocked when Anthony Dean looked up at him and said, "Sometimes you're not a nice person, Dad."

Tony never had another drink of alcohol. He settled gradually back into a routine consisting of career and Anthony Dean. Brenda lived a parallel but essentially disconnected life. Over time, each of them learned to co-exist in this sterile, unfeeling fashion. Over time, they learned to consider it normal.

Chapter 30

Jared awoke slowly and late, revived most cruelly by nature's call. The horses were stomping and snorting on their line. They were used to being turned out or fed earlier than this. He stuck his head from the sleeping bag and was disgusted to see Shane still sleeping peacefully in his bag. "There is no justice in the size of our bladders," he reflected, then forced himself out into the frigid air. His foray through the tent flaps exposed him to some serious cold, but soon enough his business was done and he returned to what now seemed to be a warm and comfortable tent. He cleaned out the ash from the woodstove and started a fire, cursing all the while at Shane and his oversized bladder. In moments the tent actually was comfortable and Shane made his appearance.

"I don't feel at all well," Shane said. "I wonder if it was something I ate."

"I'm sure it was," Jared mumbled. "I believe I ate the same thing. It was that damned ice!"

"What ice? We didn't have any ice."

"That's it! We didn't have any ice! Give you a headache every time."

"Today's a meat day, headache or not," Shane offered.

"Yeah, I know. So let's get going, bladder boy, you're burning daylight."

After a quick breakfast of oatmeal, toast and cold water, they rigged up two pack mules, saddled their horses and headed out to collect the meat from their two bulls. They headed to Shane's animal first; since it was closer and would be a good warm-up. Shane's horses and mules were experienced mountain animals; they were just as comfortable making their way through thick timber as along the cleared trails. Shane led the two mules to within 20 feet of the carcass. The mules had done this many times, they weren't worried by blood or the scent of death. The men put the hindquarters into panniers on the larger mule, a male named Sam. Backstraps, as well as liver, heart, and associated loose meats were divided into equal portions and added to two bags containing the forequarters; their total weight approached that of the hindquarters and these bags made up the load for the smaller mule, a female named Sissy.

Shane used a small saw to remove the top half of the elk skull and attached antlers. They were lashed across the top of Sam's back, with the points held off his flanks by a stout branch that spanned his wide back. Back in camp by 9:30, they spent two hours trimming the meat and then hung the quarters in the open air to let the outer sheaf of skin harden into a protective glaze. That afternoon they would put the glazed meat into heavy canvas bags and hang them from the covered meat pole.

"Time for lunch!" Jared cried. His headache was gone and he hadn't worked as hard for many years as he had for the past two days.

"Yeah, I'm hungry too," Shane said, "but let's just cram some sandwiches and stuff into our saddlebags and chew on the trail. Your bull is quite a bit farther away than mine and the sky's looking a little squirrelly. I'd really prefer to be back in camp before any kind of storm hits."

They chewed their way up the 30-minute ride to Long Ridge, and were well satisfied by the time they had to navigate up the slope that had done such damage to Jared's leg. The horses and mules did a much better job of picking their way through the exposed roots than he had; in short order, they made their way to Jared's bull.

"Phew, you weren't kidding about that bull, were you?" Shane said. "He is a big critter."

"He is that," Jared said. "Body-wise he's a real stud, but I don't think his antlers are as long as yours."

"No, but look at that mass." He grabbed the base of the antlers; his hand, and he had large hands, was two inches short of encircling it.

"Damn. You were right. He is massivest."

Jared smiled and loosened the panniers, making way for the meat. It was same and same again with the quarters, though they were much heavier and more difficult to load. It was also obvious to Jared that the carcass of his bull had quite a bit more meat left on the bones on it than had Shane's. It was not nearly so well taken apart. *I haven't even opened up an animal in 15 years,* he said inwardly, *and Shane has done dozens, if not hundreds in that time.* Still, he wished he'd taken more time with the knife. Shane said nothing about the quality of the butchering, but he praised the size of the animal repeatedly, and asked Jared to replay the entire event. "Where were you when the bull came up the hill? Where was he when you shot him?" The conversation revitalized Jared and helped to solidify his burgeoning sense of self-worth. He knew Shane was trying to help him but he still appreciated it… and he felt better for it.

Dark clouds were climbing into thunderheads by the time Shane and Jared finished the pannier knots and tied the antlers across Sam's back. "I hate it when they get all muscular," Shane said, nodding toward the sky.

"How long you think we've got?" Jared asked.

"Hard to tell. I expect it will hit somewhere real soon, but it might miss us completely. I'm sure you remember how mean some of the thunderstorms get up here? If it will just wait until we get the meat all taken care of and the horses fed, I'll be happy to take my chances in the tent with a nice drink. Let's hustle on out of here."

They hustled right along, even trotting when the trail allowed it, though trotting was hard on the pack animals when heavily loaded.

By the time they pulled into Dry Meadow the sky was dark and threatening, clouds so thick they could no longer pick out individual thunderheads. They tied up their horses; Jared took care of the saddle horses while Shane tied Sam and Sissy and loosened their pannier ropes. Both men were moving fast now; there was not a moment to lose. The air was brittle with tension, a few scattered drops fell, whipped sideways by a ripping wind that shifted direction without warning. Needles and small branches slanted across nearby. Even the mules were nervous, eyes rolling, stamping their feet and swinging their heads.

Having removed and settled the saddle horse tack across a downed log, Jared hurried over to help Shane. They unloaded Sissy first; she was getting seriously spooky, then he walked her over and tied her to the line. Then they went to work on Sam. Thunder boomed in the distance. Electricity sizzled in the air.

"Shit," growled Shane.

"Almost done," Jared said, as much to calm himself as for any other reason. Shane smiled across the pack saddle, steadying the opposite side while Jared lifted the pannier on his side; it held one of the hindquarters. He turned to carry it to the meat pole. The world brightened suddenly.

Jared was choking. He couldn't breathe. He was drowning. He fought against death, slashing his arms, screaming but unable to move. He came awake suddenly, lying face up in a heavy rainstorm, water gushing from an unfortunate fold in his cowboy hat directly into his open mouth. Once he was able to tip the hat aside he could breathe more easily, but after spending a few moments catching his breath he still couldn't move. It took some time to realize that the pannier, complete with 80-pound hindquarter, was lying on his chest. He forced it off, then struggled over to his hands and knees, where he stayed for a minute or so. Then he stumbled to his feet. The meadow was dark with heavy rain and low-hanging clouds, but he couldn't tell how much time had elapsed since he and Shane had been working on Sam.

Shane. Where was Shane? His ears rang so loudly it was painful. He heard nothing but the ringing. Jared turned in a slow circle, trying to orient himself. There was the meadow. The horses and mules were still tied to their line. But all were visibly trembling.

"Shane! Shane!" he called out.

Jared stumbled, first left, then right, unable to keep his balance. The tent was standing but the rainfly had been blown off and was hanging from the front guy line.

"Shane. Shane." There was no response. He continued his wobbly circle, his feet sloshing in the mud, eyes blinking in the steady downpour. There was Sam, but he was on his knees. No, his knees were driven into the mud, his hind legs leaned forward, creating a steep slant from his rear to his front, to which his head and neck were no longer well connected. They hung on a crazy angle; his blank, open eyes stared at Jared. Blood dribbled from the gaping wound where his neck had once attached and steamed thickly into the rain-filled air.

No. That was not all steam. The pack saddle and underlying blanket were smoking, still burning, even in the rain. Fire hissed and sizzled along the hair bordering Sam's great wound.

Lightning! This was all about lightning. Jared's mind began to reassert itself. He and Shane were unpacking Sam. Shane was on the other side. Startled by the suddenly conscious thought, Jared stumbled around the rear of the mule to find Shane, on his back with arms thrown wide, and beset by tremors across his entire body.

"Shane!" Jared walked quickly, his mind and body coming together as he moved. By the time he knelt by Shane, Jared was close to coherent thought. He evaluated the problem and was prepared to deal with it. For the second time in two days, bitter experiences from a former life came flooding back, shoring him up, putting him into a heightened sense of awareness and preparation. This time, though, he avoided the reflexive descent into the past. He stayed in the present and worked to help his friend.

"Shane." Jared put his hand on Shane's chest. Beneath the trembling muscles Jared could easily feel the uncontrolled and arrhythmic racing of his heart. Shane's eyes were open but his eyeballs turned wildly in their sockets, unseeing. His mouth opened and shut. Jared couldn't hear anything, but he was nearly positive Shane was making no noise, there was no exhalation of air. Jared tried to blow into Shane's mouth but it was impossible, with the continual open and shut motion. Shane was not breathing. His heart was totally uncontrolled and racing, buddabuddabudda. Jared grew more and more frantic. He knew Shane was dying. He couldn't breathe and his heart was not working. He should shock Shane's heart. Impossible. Shane's body arched and shivered, aching for oxygen, dying. Jared knelt there, remembering… remembering… something about hearts. What had his corpsman done in Vietnam to poor Haines after he'd been shot by a sniper? Oh, yes. The doc had hit his chest, hard. Haines had died, but the doc said with a shrug, "Sometimes it works."

Jared slammed his fist into Shane's chest. Nothing. He hit him again. No change. Screaming, he raised both hands over his head into a single, great fist and brought it down with all his strength into Shane's chest. And again. The tremors stopped. Shane's eyes closed. He was dead. Jared dropped his head onto his friend's chest and sobbed, devastated.

And then Shane coughed, and coughed again. Took a few massive breaths. His eyes fluttered, closed, opened. Scared. "Wha? Wha?"

"Shhh, shhh. Easy. Don't talk, Shane. Settle back for a minute."

He covered Shane's face from the rain and closed his own eyes. They both lay there for a long time. Finally, the rain cloud passed overhead, leaving a patch of brilliant blue. Jared stood up shakily and dragged his friend toward the tent.

Neither man moved from his cot until the next morning. Jared was still sleeping deeply when he heard Shane croak, "Oh, I shit myself. Oh, no. I pissed all over myself, too. Oh, fuck me to tears."

It was nearly a minute before Jared could collect himself enough to talk, he was laughing so hard.

"It's not funny, Jared. I swear to God I will kick your ass from here to Mexico if you don't stop laughing…oh, shit my arms, my shoulders, my neck. Oh Jesus, Jared. My muscles hurt so bad I can't move, will you please stop fucking laughing?"

"Shane, dead people shit themselves and piss themselves, too. And you were as close to dead as it's possible to be, my friend, nearly as dead as poor Sam out there and he set new records for being completely and totally dead."

Shane collapsed back on his side.

"C'mon, pal. Let's get you outside and get you cleaned up and into some new clothes."

It took Jared two full days to get the camp straightened up. He hung the elk quarters from a second meat pole, then spent hours trimming the meat ruined by lying overnight in the puddles of rainwater. With great difficulty, he hooked Sissy and another mule into a semblance of a team and dragged Sam to a downwind corner of the meadow. "Sorry we can't do better by you, Sam," he said as he untied the tow ropes. "We're going to have to let the bears and coyotes and ravens and vultures fight over you. I suspect you'll be pretty popular for the next couple of weeks. You were a fine mule."

Three days after the lightning strike, Jared came in and sat next to Shane's cot. "Well, we're pretty much cleaned up and ready to pack whenever you feel up to moving around. If we don't get out in the next few days I think we're going to lose the meat. It's been fairly chilly at night but it's getting warm during the day. We're short one mule…"

"Our best mule," Shane interjected.

"Our best mule, so we'll have some trouble packing out."

"We'll leave the tent," Shane said. "I can send someone up here to get it. We should be able to get everything else out."

"OK. But what about you? Will you be able to ride out? I could run you down to the Chamberlain Airstrip and call a plane for you."

"No, I think I'll be ready soon. I can already walk out to relieve myself…"

"Yeah, and I appreciate getting out of that job," Jared added, smiling.

"Do not make me laugh. Every part of my body is still sore. What in the world did that electricity do to my muscles? Did it just make them contract? Could that have made me so sore I can barely move? I live in fear of a sneeze or cough." Leaning back, Shane took a few deep breaths and collected himself. "If you will start getting things ready today, I think we can pack up and get out tomorrow."

"OK, I can do that."

With directions from Shane, who began hobbling around, Jared burned all their accumulated trash and started putting things in order. He packed canned goods and non-perishable items into a waterproof sack and suspended it in a tree, a cache for the next season. Meanwhile, Shane packed pots, pans and cooking utensils into their kitchen box. By the next morning they were ready to begin the serious and difficult phase of loading meat and gear into panniers and then onto the pack animals. Shane was still sore but he was also young, strong and in excellent shape. He responded well to the exercise and by the time they were ready to begin the trip he was loose enough to swing into the saddle with little discomfort.

It was a long trip down the mountain. Sam the mule had been a calming influence on the pack string. In his absence the other animals, especially Sissy, were flighty and nervous. They had to make several unplanned stops to retighten the panniers and top packs but they made it down to the trail head in the mid-afternoon and back to Grangeville by dark.

Chapter 31

A burst appendix is a mean and ugly condition, spewing poison throughout the abdominal cavity and into the bloodstream. Effects on the body are always severe and often life threatening. Worse, they are completely unpredictable. For more than a week, Tony's life was in real danger; only massive amounts of antibiotics kept the infection and resulting fevers at bay. For days afterward, new and smaller infections would spring into existence after a period of normality and his planned return home would be delayed… again. The on again-off again nature of his hospital stay was difficult for everyone concerned; even Tony, kind, thoughtful Tony, became irascible and snappish—except with Misty. By the end of his first week in the hospital, he and Misty were friends. After ten days, they had begun to share hopes and dreams and even secrets.

For the first time since Dean died Tony had found someone he could confide in and he was amazed to experience the pleasure of talking with someone who understood, or if she didn't understand, at least was not judgmental. Tony found himself almost blurting things out to Misty. He told her about his family, about Dean and what their friendship meant to him. He told the story of his first elk and of his time learning to row on the McKenzie River. Misty, who had grown up around elk hunters and had handled boats and rafts herself on white water, spoke the language. She understood. Her comments were insightful and accurate and she was invariably supportive. Tony felt no need to embellish the truth; there was no need to… Misty accepted everything. After all, Tony realized, she already knew his deepest, darkest secret; everything else paled in comparison. If she could deal with his slaughter of an innocent child, she could deal with anything. It was several days before Tony realized how much her approach had meant to him. Her knowledge of his horror—and acceptance of it—were not just measures of their burgeoning friendship, they were therapeutic in ways Tony Corrarino had never dared to dream. He literally felt as if a weight had been lifted from him. He began to sleep through the nights without nightmares. It occurred to him during his many hours staring at the ceiling that if Misty could forgive him so completely, maybe, just maybe, he could forgive himself.

For her part, Misty found the discussion therapeutic as well. Although she'd initially wanted only to help a troubled patient through a rocky emotional period, she found herself interested, then intrigued and finally captivated by the tale that unfolded before her. Tony's story seemed utterly unbelievable. Son of a mafia don goes to Oregon and becomes an outdoorsman, wildland firefighter and then a combat helicopter pilot in Vietnam. And his experiences after being shot down were simply impossible to comprehend. And yet she believed without question that every word of it was true.

Tony's story struck a personal chord with Misty as well, because his heart-rending, personal tale, his overwhelming need to be heard and understood contrasted so completely with the closed, bitter reticence that had characterized her husband's communication since he'd returned from the war. At that moment in both of their lives, Tony's desperate need of forgiveness dovetailed perfectly with Misty's own need to be needed.

As Tony's personal demons began to loosen their hold on him, Tony began to smile and laugh… and talk. He told Misty about his life in New York and the Taylors, about Raven and about fighting fires, he talked about his favorite classes and about races he'd won and lost. One night, in the midst of another story, Tony stopped suddenly, shook his head and said, "My God! I haven't shut up since I met you. I'm so sorry."

"It's OK, Tony. I enjoy it. You've had an interesting life and it's obvious how brave you are. I love it that you've shared it with me. Please don't feel like it's an imposition."

"Thanks, OK. But I'm still going to stop talking for a while. It's your turn now. I'd like to hear about your life."

And so, each time Misty came into the room she would tell him something about her past. Her responsibilities with other patients kept her on the move except late at night, but each time she came back Tony would give her the last part of her last sentence, so she knew where to start. She was surprised that he cared enough to remember each detail.

Tony was well into his second week of recuperation, and almost well enough to go home when Misty leaned over his bed to fix his IV and he looked directly into her eyes. She had eyes like Raven's, only brighter, livelier. It was like she was dancing inside. Until that point he'd been talking and listening to a sympathetic young nurse. From that moment on he was affected in a way he couldn't, and really didn't want, to explain.

As Tony gradually began to recover, Misty spent as much time as she could with him. Several times she even stayed past the end of her shift to sit and talk with him. As he requested, she shared much of her life as well. Tony learned that she lived in a Bowie subdivision less than a mile from his own with her husband and five-year-old son. He told her about his son, also five, and they talked about letting them play together some day. She was a runner, and was impressed to learn that Tony had once been (sort of) on the same track team as Steve Prefontaine. She told him about her running habits; they often ran at the same tracks and around the same neighborhoods.

They shared this information in small pieces that were glued together as each new piece made its appearance. As time went on, each of them became more comfortable with the other. Misty felt drawn to Tony, not sexually so much, though it was impossible to discount the underlying physical attraction she felt to him. What she felt more strongly though, was the kinship she'd experienced all those years before with Shane. Suddenly she realized that she hadn't had a true friendship with a man since she'd left Idaho.

As much as she loved Jared, his injury had forever changed the emotional dynamic between them. When his wound had healed, the portal to his soul had sealed over as well, shutting her out from the innermost thoughts they had shared so completely before he'd gone to

Vietnam. She could tell that her conversations with Tony had helped him; the effect was obvious in his demeanor. But what was less obvious was how much their relationship was helping her. The simple sharing between a man and woman was somehow… comfortable. Her liaisons in other cities were short and, at her requirement, strictly sexual. She had shared nothing of consequence with her partners, nor had she ever met any of them again. She had missed, more than she'd realized, the honest communication between friends of the opposite sex.

She shared a great deal of her life with Tony, as well, but she'd not been nearly as open as he had been with her. She didn't tell him about her illicit affairs, nor did she explain the nature of Jared's injury. Several times she found herself thinking about how much Jared and Shane would like Tony.

Misty met Tony's son, Anthony Jr., several times when he came to visit with the nanny. Anthony was a delightful youngster, with dark, reddish-brown hair and a slow, disarming smile. He was not openly, overtly happy, like many children, but he was certainly well cared for and loved being around his father. Tony's wife came only once, and that was more than enough for Misty. Brenda came in one afternoon just after the nanny and child had arrived; she stalked along the hall in a tight, short skirt and high heels, looking more like a hooker than a wife and mother. She was the type of woman, Misty saw, who worked hard to maintain the come-hither sensuousness that had come naturally in her youth.

"Definitely a boob job," Misty thought to herself, even as she acknowledged a tendency to be a little catty about those women more well-endowed than she.

"I'm looking for Tony Corrarino," Brenda said imperiously.

"Room 216," Misty said smiling and trying to be nice.

Brenda turned to the room without comment and walked away.

"Slut," Misty whispered, and made as if she were writing entries. Surreptitiously looking in from the nurse's station, Misty saw the nanny pull away toward the corner of the room and the youngster climb quickly onto the hospital bed and into Tony's arms when Brenda entered. Tony looked up at his wife without smiling and though Misty could not hear their voices, she could read Tony's lips. "Hello" and "Fine" were all he said. His wife left soon afterwards. Although she tried hard to be gracious, Misty smiled inwardly at the nearly open display of hostility between man and wife.

Tony was not quite smitten… but he was certainly captivated by Misty. She wasn't sexy, or even really sensual; she had a lean runner's body with few of the curves and softness classic beauties possess, not to mention a funny gap between her front top teeth that gave her an urchin-like quality. But she had the most beautiful, dancing eyes he'd ever seen. He simply could not look at her without smiling. When the doctor finally told him he could leave the next day, Tony's initial response was disappointment, a reaction that had him shaking his head in wonder.

That night Misty brought it up first. "So, I guess you're finally leaving us," she said, as she busied herself with his IV. It was everything she could do to keep from saying "I'm sure you're excited to go home." Fishing for a compliment, some indication that he cared for her like she did for him.

"So they tell me," he said. "I'll miss you." There it was, lying out there all alone. Simple and unaffected.

She stopped her work and turned to him, cheeks burning. "I'll miss you too, Tony." She was reaching to touch his hand when her pager went off. She turned quickly, embarrassed, as though caught in a crime. She hurried to the door, pausing to turn before she left.

"Maybe we'll run into each other when we're, umm, running." She grinned that elfish grin, turned and went through the door.

Misty never got back to see him that night. She was transferred down to the Emergency Room to help care for the victims of a multiple car collision and couldn't break free before Tony was released. He was deeply disappointed and found himself repeatedly looking back from his seat on the wheelchair hoping to see her until he was put in the car and driven away.

As a pleasant place to recover, Tony's house left a lot to be desired. The nanny did everything she could to help but Anthony took most of her time and she was inexperienced with medical matters anyway. Brenda made a short-lived effort but after another failed attempt to convince Tony to become part of his father's crime family, she retreated to her previous schedule of self-absorption. She only rarely looked into his room. Tony's recovery was long and inconsistent. One day he would feel much better, the next he could barely get out of bed. Five days after going home Tony was hit with another fever and it began to look like he would have to go back in the hospital. He didn't have the strength to take care of himself and he wasn't getting any help. Finally, in desperation, Tony called his mother and asked for assistance. Maria came swooping in, full of mother's love and hot soups and took over Tony's care with a gleeful thankfulness. Finally, he could relax and concentrate on getting better and soon began doing so.

The only pothole in the road to Tony's recovery was the presence of his brother Charley. Their father had sent his younger son south with his mother over her strenuous objections.

"Sal," she had hissed to him during an argument in their bedroom before she left. "Bowie is only four hours from here. I don't need Charley to babysit me."

"I know, Maria," Sal had said, unmoved. "But I'll feel better if you have someone to watch over you and besides, it will do Charley good to get away from the business for a while."

Maria looked at her husband for a long while. She realized this was about her younger son. "Is Charley going to be all right, Sal? She hesitated. "I mean, in the business?"

She was not asking about Charley's future in the business at all. Sal looked at his shoelaces, and Maria knew his next words would be a lie.

"Sure he will, Maria. Charley's going to be fine."

She steeled herself, taking strength from her husband's hesitancy. "Don't brush me off, Sal. You know as well as I do there's something not right about Charley. He worries me and I know he worries you."

Sal breathed heavily. He knew far more of the specifics of Charley's depravity than Maria did, but probably less of the pure truth. Maria sensed things, felt things that Sal only guessed at. She would not be surprised, he knew, to learn the things Sal could tell her, but she would be devastated, any mother would, in a way she only guessed at now. How could he begin to explain to the boy's mother that Charley was universally reviled within the Family and would likely survive only as long as his father did… not one day longer? Or that, had they not been related by blood, Sal would have killed Charley with his own hands long ago.

"We've all got our demons, Maria. I know I've contributed more than my share to both our sons. Charley's struggling, it's true, but he's going to be all right. I'm going to help him." Maria came to him then and he held her close, hoping his lie helped her. Maria knew he was lying and loved him for it, but it still didn't help her overcome her own disgust for her second son.

Maria was met at Tony's house with appreciation and happiness from Tony, Anthony and the nanny. Predictably, Brenda interpreted Maria's presence as a personal attack on her suitability as a wife and mother. She responded by trying to re-establish herself as the primary caregiver. Just as predictably, she tired of the sham after only one day and went back to her habits of sleeping until late morning and then leaving again until late evening. This schedule also appealed to Charley and he was quick to accept Brenda's invitation to join her.

Charley was even more surprised at Brenda's invitation than Brenda herself, which was considerable. She'd asked the troll, which is how she always thought of Charley, on a whim and almost regretted it, but as they drove downtown Brenda had a little more time to reflect; and she now recognized several benefits to having Charley along. First, he was by all accounts, heavily involved in the Family operations and so offered a potential connection to big money in the increasingly likely event her marriage to Tony ended. Second, he was besotted with her. Her casual sensuality, short skirts and low-cut blouses kept Charley in a perpetual sense of low-grade excitement and as slimy as Charley was, she enjoyed knowing she still 'had it.'

She sensed she could get Charley to do anything she wanted. She laughed to herself about the hard-on Charley was wearing whenever he was around her. She was right. He got hard just thinking about the color her face would turn while he squeezed her windpipe closed as she thrashed and bucked beneath him.

They spent more time together in their own separate fantasies as Maria nursed Tony back to health. Neither was a gifted conversationalist; Charley had no interests outside the Family business, but that was fine with Brenda, who had no interests besides money. Now that the opportunity presented itself, she wanted to learn everything there was to know about mob operations and so she listened, understanding, supportive, as Charley's stories began to include detailed explanations of the business. Several times he realized he was talking too much about sensitive, even dangerous subjects, and attempted to change the course of the conversation but each time her interest waned and she stopped paying attention to him. He couldn't stand it; he was feeding on her interest in him, and although he knew she was drawing him on for her own purposes, he loved the way her eyes wandered up over his face, across his body. And sometimes, when she really wanted to show him how well she understood, how much she agreed with him, she would reach out and touch his leg with her hand and the electricity would make him shudder.

In Charley's fantasy, Brenda would gasp for breath as he pounded inside her…then, at the last moment, he would release her throat and she would suck oxygen deeply into her lungs, wheezing as she felt her life return. And at that moment, just when she realized he was going to let her live and her body shuddered with the life-giving breath, his ejaculation would occur, and it would feel like the top of his head exploded. After that, he knew, she would never want anything to do with him again—they never did. But he doubted she would tell Tony and based on the way they seemed to interact, Charley doubted if Tony would care much anyway.

"How's everything going with you and Tony these days, Brenda?"

Brenda almost stripped a gear in the BMW at Charley's audacity. They were on their way to a mall in Chevy Chase and Charley had, until that moment, been discussing the various city councilmen and lobbyists he knew on a first-name basis. Somehow, Charley seemed to know everyone in New York on a first-name basis. She hesitated a moment before answering and came close to telling him to mind his own business, when she thought, What the hell? Why not? Maybe I can plant a seed.

"It's not going great, Charley. We've been arguing a good bit about connecting with the Family. I'd like for Tony to work with you and your father, be part of the organization, but he won't even consider it."

Charley felt the bile rise in his throat and he stiffened. The last thing in the world he wanted was for his brother to return to the fold; he himself would be shunted even farther into the background than he already was. Still, he'd asked the question and now he had to respond.

"That's too bad," he pretended to commiserate, "but Tony's always felt the same about my father's work. Chances are he'll never change."

"I've finally figured that out," Brenda said, wondering if she should go further, let out more line. "I don't know. His vision of our future and mine are a lot different."

Charley let the silence draw out between them, unsure how to set the stage without taking a step too far. Finally he said. "Well, maybe now we know each other a little better we can help each other mold our own futures." He wasn't sure what the hell it meant, but it seemed to fit the occasion.

Brenda seemed to think it did, too. She touched him on the leg again, letting her fingers linger this time.

Chapter 32

Shane threw his hat on the couch, then thought better of it and picked it up again, carried it over and hung it on the hat rack.

"Good idea, Sheriff," said the female voice behind him. "You're learning." He smiled without turning around.

"Yep," he agreed, as he unfastened his belt. "I'm a regular quick learner. Only 16 years and I remember most of the time." He removed his service revolver and carried it over to lock it in his safe, stopping along the way to give Lacy a long and satisfying kiss. "Sorry I'm late."

"It's ok," she said. "How's your dad?"

"About the same," he hesitated. "Maybe a little worse. He's getting pretty negative." In fact, Ben Larrimer was in the depths of a terrible, years-long depression, broken only by his increasingly frequent descents into a dementia-ridden fog.

"It's a pretty sad state of affairs," he said to Lacy as he grabbed a beer from the refrigerator, "when the only time a man can be happy is when his mind fails him and he forgets who he is."

"It's been getting a lot worse since your mom died," she said, leaning her head against his chest.

"Yeah, she was his anchor, and who'd have thought she would go first? But I'm not really sure if it was her death or just the normal progression of the disease that sent him down this road so fast." He took a long swig. "I'm going to sit outside for a minute. Where are the kids?"

"Marshal and Craig are still at school, soccer and band practice. Julie and Jessica are down at the creek, exploring. Just ring the dinner bell when you want to be disturbed. I'll finish dinner."

Shane sat on the porch, a wraparound Lacy had demanded for the old house when they first bought the place. He'd argued about the need at first, but now was glad she'd held fast. The porch was his refuge and he regularly sat on different sides of the house, depending on the sun position, weather and the kids' location. Right now he was sitting on the west side, where he could watch the sun go down way out across the Palouse, and listen to the laughter of his daughters in the creek bed.

In truth, the visit to his father had been truly unsettling, the old man drifting in and out of coherence. But one of his periods of lucidity lasted almost 10 minutes and had shaken Shane to his core.

"Shane," the old man had said. "We don't have much time, you know?"

"It's OK, Dad. I'm not going anywhere."

His father grimaced, grabbed Shane's upper arm. "I don't mean that, boy. I mean me. I keep forgetting. I need to tell you something and you need to promise to help me."

Shane looked down at the shrunken, wizened old man whose legs were not quite as big around as the arm he was holding. "Well, I'll try, Dad. I'll do the best I can."

"Not good enough." His father's eyes were sharp and clear and angry. "You have to promise."

"Dad, I can't promise for sure until I know what you're going to ask, but I will do my best. You just have to trust that it's enough."

His father looked away, then slowly back again.

"OK. I need you to get me a gun. I'm done. I want to be with your mother."

Shane stiffened. "Dad, you've got my whole family here who loves you. You need to think about your grandchildren."

His father leaned toward Shane's face, the gray, wispy hairs on his head silhouetted in the light. "I'm thinking about them, but I need to be selfish now. I have a right to be a whole person when I die. Sometimes when I come back to myself I've pissed my own pants. It's getting worse all the time. Bring me a gun, Shane, please."

Shane waffled some more and in a few moments his father had drifted off again, to a place where logic, language and serious thoughts didn't exist. Shane sat with him a little longer, then went home.

"You know, don't you, that he's happy most of the time?" Lacy had come out on the porch behind him. How did she move so silently in this house where so many of the floorboards squeaked? She put her arms around his neck, pressed herself to his back. He thought back to the first time he'd seen her at the Sheriff's office, how flustered he'd been. And how happy his parents were to meet her. His father had caught him alone in the kitchen that night. "Looks like a keeper to me, son," he'd said.

"I'm sure going to try, Dad," he'd answered, and they'd both laughed for a long time.

"Lace, the only time my father is happy now is when he's off in never-never land, when he doesn't even know us. I don't really think that being in a demented state is the same thing as happiness."

He turned to face her and they held each other for a long time.

"You know what he asked me today, Lace?"

"Knowing him, I bet I can guess. He wants you to help him kill himself. What did you tell him?"

Shane look directly into her eyes. "What would you'd think if I'd said 'yes'?

She looked at him calmly and Shane was reminded again of the quiet strength his wife possessed.

"I'd think that your father put you in a terrible spot."

"And?"

"And he's so caught up in his own problems now that he can't see what the cost is of his request."

"What do you mean, cost, Lace?"

"I mean you have to live with yourself whatever you do, Shane, and you have to live with us. Lives have been ruined from much smaller things than that."

Shane released her and turned to face the woods. He spoke while looking away.

"How many times did he stand up for me, Lace? Cover for me? Take my side? Is there anything he wouldn't have done for me?"

"He's asking you to take his life."

"Are you sure, Lace? Or is he asking me to save it?"

She put her hand on his right shoulder and gently turned him around to face her. "I love you, Shane, and I'm going to love you no matter how you handle this. My grandfather had Alzheimer's, so I know how bad it can get. I also know what a good man you are, and I'm not sure how you'd come through it if you do what he's asking of you." She rubbed the back of his neck and he leaned over on her shoulder.

"Let's call the kids," she said. "You'll feel a lot better with them around you."

Shane tried to put the issue out of his mind after that and for a couple weeks he was successful, but only by stopping the visits to his father. As long as he could keep his father out of his life, he could control his thoughts as well. He focused on work, his children and on things that needed doing at the house. Only once did Lacy bring up the subject of his father, and Shane's response left little doubt that he wanted no part of the subject. She didn't bring him up again, though Shane was sure Lacy was visiting his father without telling him. He was glad for that, and beholden to her. She'd always been close to his father and although he chose not to spend time with his father now, Shane was thankful Lacy did.

The estrangement couldn't last, of course, and it ended for Shane when the nursing home called and said his father was becoming agitated whenever he was lucid. He'd become abusive to the aid workers and was often angry. This kind of behavior was completely out of character for him. The nursing supervisor assured Shane that it was becoming worse and that if it continued he would have to be restrained.

"It's not the normal progression we see, Sheriff," the supervisor said. "Usually, if Alzheimer's patients are going to become violent, it occurs when they are in a dissociative state. When they are connected to the real world, we'd expect their actions to be more in line with their natural personality, and you and I both know that your father's natural personality is that of a kind, gentle man. This is different; he is very angry about something and it is showing through when he is in our world, when his brain is working properly. He is deeply unhappy and his unhappiness seems to be focused on you."

Shane shook his head. "OK, I'll talk to him."

"Thanks, Sheriff. I think that's a good idea."

When Shane walked into his father's room, he knew right away it would be bad. The old man was sitting in his LaZ Boy reading. His features were alert and sharp. He was 'on his game' as Shane usually described it to Lacy and the girls.

"I never thought you were a coward, Shane," were his father's first words.

Shane closed the door to his father's room. "What have I ever done to make you think I was a coward, Dad?"

"It's what you're not doing, son. I need help. You're not helping because you are afraid."

"How can you ask me to kill you, Dad? How can you ask that of me?"

"You don't have to kill me, Shane. Just get me in position to kill myself."

"How could I live with that? You're my father, for Christ's sake."

"Is that what you're worried about? What effect it's going to have on you? You worried about a little guilt? Well, tough shit." His father spread his hands to encompass the room, the nursing home, his life. The question is, "How do *I* live with this?"

Shane almost staggered. The emotion, and the truth, of his father's words hit him as a physical blow.

"Dad, I..." He couldn't finish the thought.

"You'll be doing a good thing, Shane. What's to live with? How many times have you put down a horse or a dog rather than let them suffer? I'm only asking for equal treatment. It's the right thing to do. I've never asked for anything from you, your mother and I... we... found... shake. A fish? Are you? Hmmm."

Shane watched his father's eyes go dull and blank. His posture relaxed as he sagged back into the chair. His mouth formed words, sometimes soundless, sometimes whispered. A slender ribbon of spittle formed at the corner of his mouth. Shane sat for a long time watching his father, waiting for him to come back, but even after an hour there was no change. The nurses said he rarely was lucid more than a couple hours a day now, and his periods of clarity were decreasing fast.

He was just getting up when a sharp tang in the air grabbed his attention. He looked down, but already knew what he would find. A dark stain of urine was spreading across his father's lap. The old man smiled vacantly into space, blissfully unaware of his plight. Shane turned to look out the window for a long time. Then he left the room.

"I'm sorry," he said to the floor nurse as he passed by in the hall. "My father had an accident." He lowered his head and walked quickly to the door.

The next day he called and made arrangements to pick up his father on Saturday for a fishing excursion.

"I'm going to take my father fishing on Saturday," he told Lacy that night in the kitchen. She was washing lettuce in the sink, her back toward him at the time. He saw her shudder, her shoulders sag. For nearly a minute she didn't move, didn't speak. The water continued to run. Then she roused herself, took a breath and shut off the water. She turned to face him, her hands enveloped in a dish towel. Her face was white, its normal ruddy, healthy glow given way to a wax-like shimmer.

"The kids will want to go," she said.

"The kids can't go this time." Silence avalanched into the room.

They stood looking at each other, electric thoughts flowing between them; unspoken questions asked and answered. Silent fears quailed and calmed. Trembling weaknesses stiffened.

"What do you want me to do?" she asked.

He shook his head. "I don't know. Nothing you can do, I don't think."

The back door burst open and their oldest son burst in, "Hi Mom, Dad. How's it going? What's wrong?"

Just like his mother, Shane thought. Way too intuitive for my own good. "Nothing's wrong, Marsh. How was practice?"

"It was fine. I think I'm going to be a starter, soon. But what's wrong? And don't tell me 'nothing'."

Lacy stirred, took a breath. "We're just trying to figure out our weekend, Marsh. I think you and I will take the little ones up to Spokane to go shopping on Saturday."

"Great! I've been wanting to go to the big city. Aren't you coming, Dad?"

"No, I'm just going to hang out with Grandpa."

"Well, you don't need the whole day for that. He's only around for 10 minutes at a time."

"Show some respect, Marshal." His voice had an unfair edge, they all joked about the old man regularly.

Marsh looked at him, hurt, certain only that something was wrong here but unsure what it was.

Lacy came to the rescue. "Dinner's in 15 minutes, Marsh. Could you collect the youngsters from down at the creek?"

After their son left the room, Lacy walked over and leaned against her husband. He put his arm around her, pulled her tight. Shane could smell the clean, fresh scent of her hair. She could hear his heart through his chest. They held each other until they could hear the approaching rumble of their herd. Lacy patted his chest and moved away. "We'll go to Spokane," she whispered, and moved toward the stove.

****

The fishing spot was as secluded as it was possible to drive to. His father could still walk, but shakily, and only for short distances. Shane parked along the Clearwater River and removed a folding chair from the back of his pickup. He set it up near the water and returned to the truck for his father. He helped the old man walk to the chair, then returned again for his fly rod and vest… and the pistol. It was his father's gun, an ancient Colt .45 single-action revolver, one of the models made famous by cowboys and gunslingers. Shane kept it in his safe and still loaded underpowered ammunition for it. Underpowered by today's standards, but still just as hot as the shells that killed so many people a century before.

His father was lucid and had been for several minutes when Shane set the holstered pistol on his lap. "Thanks, Shane," his father said simply.

"I can't thank you enough."

"I love you, Dad."

"I know, son. I love you, too. Now you'd better hurry. I don't know how long I'll be around."

Shane clasped his father's hand and escaped upriver. He didn't go far. There were several decent holes close by. He spent a couple minutes rigging his rod and tying on a fly. His stomach was churning. Having made the decision to help his father commit suicide, he was now focused on legal problems he was likely to face. In order to establish a reasonable facsimile of an alibi, he'd stopped by the house after picking up his father. The rest of the family was gone. He'd taken his father in, so anyone nearby could confirm that the old man had entered the house where he might have picked up the pistol. There were no nearby neighbors but Shane knew how many times criminals were tripped up by an unanticipated, unseen witness who could give testimony that crumpled the story they'd bet their freedom on.

By the time Shane had tied on an elk hair caddis, his hands were shaking. It had already been five minutes, why had there been no pistol shot? Much longer and the chance his father was still in control of his facilities would drop to near zero. Shane started back toward the pickup, but couldn't bring himself to go. He was deathly afraid of seeing his father's death take place. He went back to the stream, flicked the caddis a few feet away, into a swirling eddy. "Always fish the close water, first, Shane," his father had taught him. "No reason to drag your line over perfectly hungry fish while you demonstrate your ability to cast a long way. Catch the close ones first."

He roll-cast the next one, the fly landing just on the seam between the current and the eddy. The fly bobbed along the seam, ducked in and out of a small whirlpool and was slurped downward to disappear. Shane set the hook on a nice 12-inch rainbow and for the minute or so it took him to land it, he did not once think of his father. Once the fish had been released, though, thoughts of his father came racing back. He hooked the fly onto his reel and headed back toward the clearing where his father sat. His heart sank; the old man's head was bobbing, his feet were shuffling beneath his chair. He'd checked out again before he was able to pull the trigger.

Shane walked up behind his father. "Dad?" No response. The revolver sat heavily in his father's lap.

Shane squatted by the chair for a long time. He was roused from his reverie by a dripping sound. His father had pissed his pants again, and worse. This time it was accompanied by the sick smell of human feces.

An accident. My father had an accident. Like some kind of three-year-old who's only been potty-trained for a year. My father, my proud father, who shaved every day of his life because he didn't want people to see him at any less than his best, is now having accidents, messing his pants.

"Jesus, Dad." Shane stood quickly and turned to walk away, disgusted. Three steps and he stopped, hesitated and turned back. He walked swiftly to the old man and in one smooth motion, picked up the pistol, placed it in his father's right hand, carefully pointed it toward the old man's right temple and pulled the trigger.

Chapter 33

Maria stayed with Tony for a month. She wanted to stay longer; Tony wasn't completely well yet and she loved being with her grandson, but her relationship with Brenda, despite her best efforts, was becoming toxic. Brenda did nothing for Tony or her son and did nothing around the house but still she resented everything Maria did. It wasn't that Brenda was actively obnoxious; she seemed to alternate between active dislike and smarmy, fawning, sucking up, which was even worse.

Maria recognized the symptoms—she'd seen them many times over the years. Brenda wanted to be a player in the Family and Tony wouldn't have it. Her efforts at winning over Maria were sporadic at best; most of her time was spent on Charley, and their budding relationship was a major reason Maria decided to leave when she did.

Brenda had graduated from regular get-in-shape visits to the gym to a full-blown body-building regimen. She'd hired a personal trainer and spent the biggest part of each day at the gym working out. She'd invited Charley and he'd accepted instantly. Charley had always been powerfully built and he loved displaying his muscular torso. Here, in a new gym, the people didn't know who he was. They didn't know of his humiliation at the hands of an effeminate black man.

Brenda was like a bitch in heat, Maria thought, cursing herself as she did so for her venality. But venal or not, Maria knew she was right. Brenda might as well have been giving off a scent, and Charley might as well have been a *pathetic, driven male dog, trying hard to get close enough to hump her. Brenda was all coquettish, if a woman who dressed and acted like a hooker could be coquettish, and Charley was soaking it up, reveling in it. They laughed together at private jokes, they whispered and at least once a day, they sat down for a serious, extended conversation. Maria figured that was when Brenda was trying to set herself up for the future. All the time spent together, the familiarity, the overt sensuality, was just her way of keeping a connection to the Family. How stupid could the bitch be? Does she think I am powerless? Does she think I will allow her a place in New York without Tony? Puttana!*

Tony seemed to be oblivious; either that or he just didn't care. Maria suspected the latter. He rested when he needed to, which was far more than he wanted or than he accepted graciously, and spent the rest of his time with Maria and his son. The absence of Brenda or Charley simply never came up and Maria noted, with a pang in her heart, that never once did the boy ask about his mother's whereabouts. What sort of terrible mother would not have her-five-year old son come running to her whenever she was around?

So Maria left for home, taking Charley with her. He'd tried to work out reasons to stay but for once Maria was adamant and Sal had a car pick them up the next morning. The house took on a preternatural quiet after his mother's departure and Tony soon found himself struggling with depression. There simply was no one around to talk to. In the short time he spent in the hospital, Tony had become attached to Misty, primarily because she was such a good listener. Now, he found himself carrying on extended conversations with his son, and with her nanny. Any pretense at a real marriage with Brenda, poor as it might have been, ended with his mother's departure, and they simply went their separate ways. It was, Tony realized sadly, a much nicer, stress-free way to live.

His son was now spending a half-day, three days a week in kindergarten, during which the nanny would get out of the house, run errands and spend some personal time. During those lonely hours, thoughts of Dean and the Vietnamese boy dominated his mind. Surprisingly, he was able to revisit their memories with only a trace of the recrimination and regret he'd lived with for the last 14 years. Was it just a result of his talking with Misty? Or had he finally lived long enough to forgive himself? The sense of guilt and loss would never go away, he knew, but maybe there was such a thing as just getting past it. Maybe it was possible to reach a point when you've experienced enough pain that you have paid your debt. Or maybe, sometimes you just get lucky enough to meet an angel like Misty who can touch your forehead with her cool, tender fingers and pull the guilt out of you. Maybe someone like her can simply make you well.

Tony got out of the La-Z-Boy and headed to his bedroom, where he put on a pair of running shoes. He headed out the door.

It took two weeks of walking before Tony was able to start running, and another month before he could do much more than jog. Infections, fevers and enforced slothfulness had done their work. He took pains never to run in the areas where Misty told him she usually ran. He didn't know why, but he lived in fear that he would see her and she would invite him to accompany her on a run…and then he couldn't keep up.

Gradually, as time went on, his leg muscles began to tighten, his lungs began to fill and soon, instead of worrying that he might see Misty, Tony began to relish the thought of seeing her again. He altered his running routine time and again, changing the routes, the timing, destinations, in hopes of crossing her path. It took weeks, and he began even entertaining the idea that he should just call her home, or go over there, or maybe go to the hospital and try to meet her there. But he dismissed those ideas as demeaning.

Finally, Tony had to go back to work. It was a welcome change in every way but one; he could no longer run at any time of the day or night in hopes of meeting Misty. So he did the best he could. He ran in the early morning several times a week and then in the evening on other days.

When Tony finally saw her it was within a block of his house. He was so glad he ran to her, swept her up and hugged her tightly. "I missed you," he whispered. She pushed him gently away. "Me too, Tony. I ran all the way over here to see if you were still alive."

They ran together regularly after that, agreeing on one day on the location to meet the day after. They ran comfortably, without pushing hard, talking as they went. Tony realized about one mile into his first run with Misty that he was not quite in as good a shape as he had hoped. But he said nothing and as soon as his breathing became somewhat labored, Misty adjusted her speed just enough to make it easier for him. She said nothing about it and neither did he, but he said a silent thank you.

They ran together two or three times a week after that; and as they became more comfortable with each other their conversations became more wide-ranging, especially on Tony's part. Because their friendship had begun with Tony's admission of a killing, and because his tortured memories had seemed to ease following those hospital conversations, Tony was well disposed to continue his open, uncensored dialogue. There were essentially no aspects of his life he didn't share with Misty. She soon knew about the difficulties of his relationship with Brenda, though she'd already surmised it from their meeting in the hospital, his relationships at work, and the details of his family in New York, including his concerns about his brother, Charley. He still thought of Misty as his personal savior and although he never told her or anyone else, he regularly referred to her in his own mind as 'my angel.' The relief from his torment was so wonderful, so complete, that it was astonishing. He loved her for it and would certainly have loved her far more completely; except that she made it clear early on that their relationship could never become physical. He'd hugged her again on their second run and held it a second or two too long. She'd pushed him away again, saying "No, Tony. We both live here."

What she didn't say, Tony realized later that evening, was that she didn't like him. Rather, she made the pragmatic statement that no kind of relationship could exist in the fishbowl of their own neighborhoods without explosive and tragic consequences. She was right, and Tony backed off, helping her to maintain a close personal friendship that never progressed farther.

Although she never said as much, Misty was at least as disappointed as Tony with the truncated development of their relationship. A part of her was sorely disappointed that Tony did not more forcefully pursue a love affair with her. Had he done so, she knew, she could not have resisted. But over time she realized how much Tony cared for her. He didn't push her because he couldn't take the chance of pushing her away. Gradually, because they both realized that taking their relationship further invited tragedy, each made peace with simple friendship and as time went on, simple friendship became more and more comfortable. Misty, who'd grown up with male friends, found herself enjoying Tony's company immensely. He filled the place left vacant by the absence of Shane and the earlier, happier Jared.

For his part, Tony loved Misty in an open, clear-hearted way. Although he was happy to spend time running and talking with her, he didn't try to kid himself; he loved her, and he would do anything she asked without hesitation, including leaving his wife, selling his house and starting over somewhere else. Of course, he would bring along his son—Brenda certainly wouldn't care, as long as she got enough money. But Misty would never leave her husband; Tony knew this without asking, so he was left to hope on a regular, if somewhat impersonal way, that her husband would find some way to die early and leave her free. He always felt guilty for thinking such thoughts, but never guilty enough to stop thinking them.

Chapter 34

Jared came back from his Idaho elk hunt with a new-found strength and vitality. It had helped, he knew, that he'd improved his attitude and physical conditioning before the hunt, but there was much more to it than that. He'd done well in the wilderness, and the knowledge gave him a sense of confidence and power he'd completely forgotten in the years since Vietnam. He'd called in a mature bull elk to within 25 yards, then killed and field-dressed it. He'd overcome a lightning strike, saved his best friend's life and gotten them both out safely. In spite of his tendency to understate his own accomplishments, Jared couldn't help but feel damn good about himself. It was as though he'd been swimming through molasses for the last 15 years. He could tell himself (and did repeatedly) that he was no less a man than he'd been before, and believe it, at least intellectually, but emotionally, he'd never been able to accept himself as whole. An undercurrent of sexual inadequacy ran through him that manifested itself in uncertainty. That uncertainty was in constant war with his natural self-confidence and resulted in a bitter, self-indulgent, self-pity. Now, as he felt himself coming out of the pit, he was able to look behind and see how deeply he had sunk. Each day seemed brighter, each voice clearer. The molasses was disappearing. He was swimming through clear water, now.

He called Shane every evening for a week after getting back, checking on his recovery.

"Finer'n frog hair," Shane told him, when asked how he was doing. "Doctors say there're no residual effects from the lightning strike, but he's making me take a full two weeks off and get a fitness-for-duty physical before I can go back to work. Lacy's pretty tired of me. How about you?"

"I joined a gym," Jared told him. "I need to improve my endurance and my upper body strength, especially if I'm going to have to keep carrying you out of the woods when we go hunting."

"Ha! I'll try to keep that a one-time thing, but hey! That's good news about the gym."

"Yeah, I'm trying to go five times a week. They've got a day care, so I can take Josh with me. Misty isn't real interested in the gym but she's running five or six miles a day, so she's staying in great shape. You know, I really enjoyed meeting Lacy and the kids. You sure have done well for yourself."

"Thanks. I have no complaints; of course, you got the real royal treatment, since you saved their father's life and brought him safely home, but they're not always so well behaved."

"They seemed great to me. Listen, thanks again for letting me go elk hunting with you. I know you had other things to do."

"Sure, I always plan other things during elk season. I've already blocked out the time to go elk hunting with you next year, too, so don't make any other plans. Lacy and I would like it if Misty and Josh could come out and join us for a few days after the hunt."

"Are you sure you want Lacy and the kids to hear all the stories Misty is likely to remember?"

"I'll take my chances. You just protect the last two weeks of September. Jared?"

"Yeah?"

"I'm real glad you're back."

"Yeah. Me, too. Thanks for everything, Shane."

"Sure, but you're the one who saved my life, remember?"

"I think maybe you did the same for me, pal."

"Stay in touch."

"I will, you do the same."

Jared hung up the phone and shook his head.

How could he have gone for so many years without contact with Shane? Jared wondered. *He tried and tried to talk; he practically begged me to communicate, but I just ignored him, over and over again. What kind of man can completely cut off contact with his best friend, and everyone else as well? Someone in a whole lot of pain, I guess. But that pain seems to have subsided. I still don't have any nuts, but I think I've found a way to live without them.*

He walked over and picked up Josh, turned him over and gribbled his stomach. The boy held tightly onto his father's neck, laughing with a bubbling happiness.

Jared's new physicality began to manifest itself in at least a partial return to his old aggressive approach to life. His once thunderous handshake began to firm up, his stride regained most of its former bounce. And he began handling Misty in ways that spoke wordlessly of desire.

She was shocked the first time he came up behind her, pulled her close and fondled her small runner's breasts.

"Jared!" she gasped.

"Hello again," he said. "It's me. I'm back."

"You certainly are," she said, turning to face him.

They held for a long time, then he led her upstairs to the bedroom, where they explored some new and exotic methods of making each other happy. Jared was uneasy at first; he no longer felt the mind-numbing urge to complete the sex act that he still dreamed about, but gradually he relaxed. He was willing to take chances now and he was driven to help Misty achieve her own completion and he made that his sole focus, with considerable success.

In the coming months, Jared's life changed remarkably. He looked forward to going to work, and even more to coming home. He and Misty resurrected a habit they'd long since given up, that of touching each other as they passed in the house. It was a small thing, Jared reflected; he would pat her bottom, she would caress his upper arm or back. The actual physical contact was usually less than a second, but each touch reinforced something Jared didn't realize he'd lost. It took Jared several days to realize what it was. It was happiness.

Sometimes now, when he was holding Misty, his mind would drift uncommanded to her former lovers. What had she felt, when they were touching her, entering her, fucking her? Could she ever really be happy with him, penis scarred and flaccid, searching in his clumsy fashion for ways to keep her happy? But those thoughts were fleeting now, they no longer incapacitated him as they'd done for years after his injury. Misty gave every indication of loving him now as completely as she ever had. Their relationship was strong; they shared thoughts, they talked. Jared was a man again, and if he weren't completely whole…well, how many people really were? Everybody had problems, physical, mental and emotional. He could deal with things now. He could be a good husband and a great father.

He hadn't told Shane, or Misty for that matter, but he was taking a self-protection class at the gym. Three days a week he was learning how to kick and punch and gouge. He wasn't sure why but the class made him feel even better about himself. Maybe he was just kidding himself, trying to inhale strength, endurance and self-confidence doing things that had been easy in his youth. He'd killed multiple elk before he'd joined the Marine Corps, but this year's elk filled him with self-assurance. He'd saved many lives, most in combat under horrific conditions, but he was inordinately proud of his actions to help Shane. He'd been a powerful and dangerous fighter as a combat Marine, and yet he rejoiced in the simple, physical pleasures of kicking and punching a bag, of sparring at half-speed with men younger than himself. He smiled to himself. What he'd done before no longer mattered. This was the beginning of a new life. New man. New father. And especially, new husband, one whose wife would love only him.

Chapter 35

Her newly resuscitated relationship with Jared created ripples throughout Misty's life as well. She enjoyed work and her co-workers much more. She looked forward to coming home and found herself cooking more intricate dinners and doing much more sewing. "Good grief!" she thought to herself one day as she loaded a carefully prepared chicken casserole into the oven. "I'm becoming my mother." But no matter how careful her self-examination was, Misty could not escape the realization that with her new-found happiness came an inexplicable desire to nest. For the first time in her life, Misty was taking real pleasure in housewifely activities.

Josh was a big part of that, of course. At five years old, Josh was what Misty described as a 'well-behaved hellion.' His round Korean face seemed to have been designed for a smile, and was rarely without it. Like many Asian children, Josh's physical maturation was occurring more rapidly than among his Caucasian friends, and he was far more athletically advanced than they. Both characteristics endeared him to his adoptive parents, but the aspect of his personality that most appealed to Jared was his sense of humor. Josh loved playing jokes on anyone nearby and although they were not always appreciated by neighbors or passersby, Josh always laughed. "He's exactly like you were at that age," Misty told her husband, with something less than deep appreciation.

Jared maintained his connection to Shane and the two couples talked over the phone every couple of weeks. It occurred to Misty, with just a touch of jealousy, that Jared's remarkable emotional recovery had as much or more to do with Shane than it did with her. The reason for it didn't really matter, though, as long as the real Jared was re-emerging after all these years. It sounded to her as though Shane could use some support now. His father had killed himself in the early spring and evidently Shane wasn't dealing well with the tragedy. Jared and Shane would talk at length after their wives had gotten off the phones and Misty had wondered several times why Jared felt the need to speak so softly during those private conversations. When she'd asked, though, Jared had pooh-poohed her and deflected the question on to something else.

But now, as the casserole's smell wafted through the house and Misty put the finishing touches on a fruit salad, she reflected on how much better her life had become in the months since Jared had returned from his elk hunt. They were a family, with all that meant. She and Jared scheduled a babysitter and were going out on 'dates' once each week. They also tried to do new and creative things with Josh each week, too, but Josh's choice began and ended with the Smithsonian Institution. At five he could identify and give details about every dinosaur exhibit in the institute and most of those pictured. He was like a sponge, absorbing and regurgitating the new information he learned... constantly.

Even her relationship with Tony was better. They were friends and running partners, and Misty gave silent thanks for the 200th time that they hadn't allowed themselves to become more involved. It wasn't as though there was no sexual tension between them; there was. But it was way, way under the surface, and they successfully ignored it. They talked about anything and everything except their own feelings about each other. In fact, they'd made plans the week before to let their sons play at each other's houses one afternoon each week. Jared had been supportive of the idea. "Josh needs to play his tricks on someone his own age and besides, I'd like to meet this running partner of yours."

Misty had told Jared about Tony and how they'd met but she'd never gone into much detail, recognizing a bad idea immediately.

The first play date worked well. Jared and Tony liked each other and Misty breathed a sigh of relief. Misty's only concern was leaving Josh at

Tony's house when Brenda was around. Tony assured her that Brenda would not be a problem with the boys, "The nanny is going to handle the boys and besides, Brenda couldn't care less about her own son, much less yours." Nonetheless, Misty refused to let Josh go over there unless Tony was going to be home.

Just as Tony had promised, Josh's play date at the Corrarino home went just fine. "They have an all-the-time babysitter named Jenna, Mom, and Anthony's dad is really fun. He said I could call him Winklepuss, but Anthony had to call him King of All That is Right and Good. But we both just call him Winklepuss."

The second time Anthony was scheduled to visit the McCauley home was on June 30. Jared was leaving that day on a short business trip and was upstairs packing his suitcase when Tony and Anthony drove up. He didn't hear the car enter his driveway; he felt more than heard the car door slam and looked out to see Tony unstrapping his son and helping him out of the car. He almost turned back to the suitcase, then, but inexplicably stayed at the window and watched as Misty greeted Tony and accepted a bag with the youngster's change of clothes. Then, as though it was the most natural thing in the world, Tony reached over and patted Misty on the back while she rubbed his arm. The only thing missing from the happy couple was a quick kiss goodbye. Then Tony got back in his car, backed out of the driveway and drove down the street. Misty was standing in the driveway watching when it suddenly occurred to her that she might have been observed. She glanced quickly up to the bedroom window, where Jared stood in plain sight. She ducked her head involuntarily, shocked and embarrassed. Then, thinking more clearly, she looked up again, forced a smile and waved. Guilty as charged, Jared thought, but he waved back, smiling thinly.

Jared continued standing at the window; the scene replayed itself over and over in his mind. There'd been nothing remarkable about the interaction and perhaps that's what was remarkable. His wife and some guy were so close, so comfortable with each other that they touched intimately, lovingly, without thinking of it. Granted, he didn't pat her bottom and she didn't run her hands lovingly across his chest. Still, their touch was far cozier than would be expected between simple running partners. In Jared's mind, Tony had stolen the best, the most intimate part of his relationship with Misty, the soft, unobtrusive loving touch.

How could this happen? Everything had been going so well. Jared was happy; he'd thought Misty was happy. But obviously, she wasn't, at least not with him. All his positive energy for the past several months, ever since the elk hunting trip, really, had been built on his newfound relationship with Misty, and that relationship now seemed to have been built on lies. His reconnection with Shane, happiness with Josh, and his wife. He'd been so happy for the passing touches, but obviously they meant nothing to her, at least nothing more than she would share with her pump of the week. What was that he'd said to Shane back in Idaho? At least Misty is always discrete. Yeah. Discrete. In my driveway, probably in my home, in my own fucking bed. Yessir. Discrete.

So when it came down to it, he simply wasn't man enough to keep her happy. She was going to the stiff dick, every time. He should have known better. His mind was swirling. He couldn't concentrate. He should have seen this coming. He should have hardened his heart, protected himself. Where were the clues? She had ACTED so happy. Had she been laughing at him for the past six months? At his pathetic limp-dicked attempts to be a lover? Did she talk about him with this Tony? Did he pity me, shake his head understandingly, even as he reached for my wife? Oh, Jesus. Fuck. Fuck. Fuck. Suddenly he choked, choked again and found himself crying, sobbing openly as he sat on the bed.

"Jared? Jared, honey?" Misty was coming up the stairs. Shit. She was not going to see him cry. He locked his suitcase and lifted it; grabbed his briefcase in the other hand and headed out the door. They met in the hall; Jared did not slow down. He lowered his head and continued forward; Misty had to duck into the bathroom to keep from being run over.

"Jared. Jared. Don't be mad. There's nothing…" He continued down the stairs and out the door. Josh and Anthony were playing in the front yard. "Hi, Dad!" Josh yelled. Jared looked at him blankly. He couldn't remember why he was leaving or where he was going but… that was Tony's kid, with Josh. Tony had a kid of his own, because he has two balls and a stiff dick. Misty probably wants a child of her own. I can't give her one but Tony could. Lots of sperm. Live seed. Humping. Fucking. Sweating.

He was in the car and it was running. How did that happen? He pressed the garage door opener and began backing out. He checked the rear-view mirror. Misty was behind and to the left standing just off the driveway. The boys were behind her, still playing. She was talking to him, pleading with him but he kept the windows up so he couldn't hear her. He turned the air conditioner up full speed. It didn't matter that the fan was simply blowing scorching air…he wanted no noise from Misty. He backed up the slight grade toward the street.

Jared couldn't believe Misty would do this to him. Not now, not when things were going so well. He was getting back to his old self. They have a son. Why couldn't it be enough for her? And with a guy in the neighborhood? Using our kid as a connection! How could she do this?

Jared hears a yell from somewhere outside of his consciousness, and the yell turns to a horrible soul-wrenching scream, just as he feels a bump. In that instant, Jared knows he has killed his son. Poor, beautiful Josh, the light of his life. Jared is at once devastated and frozen. He knows what faces him. Now there is non-stop screaming from outside the car, but he cannot bring himself to open the door to look. He has seen so much death…how can he bear to look at his dead son's face?

And then there is Misty, a terrified, tortured look on her face, pounding on the window of his car. She is screaming something, but the sound is muted by the closed window and the air conditioning fan. He can't make it out. Doesn't want to make it out. Jared is holding on to the steering wheel with both hands.

"Jared, pull forward. Pull forward! My God! Get the car off of him." Jared looks around, sees neighbors running toward him. He's got to react! He steps on the gas to pull forward, but the car is still in reverse and it powers backwards fifteen feet, nearly crushing one of the neighbors and sending the front wheels rolling up and over the still body lying in the driveway.

"Oooo," it is a gurgling, wet scream. Misty, now in front of him and in his direct view, collapses into a heap next to the crushed body. Jared's vision collapses in on him. He is vaguely aware of people pounding on the car, of people running around in his periphery. And then he sees Josh standing off to the side. It is Josh. His son. He's wearing his bright yellow

Winnie the Pooh T-shirt. It's Josh! He's alive!

Jared jumps from the car to embrace his son. The car, still in reverse, backs slowly out of the driveway and into the side of a neighbor's car parked across the street. No one notices. All attention is on the small, lifeless body in the driveway, except for Jared, whose happy embrace of his son is totally out of place.

Misty, hysterical with grief, runs to her husband's side, screaming "Jared, you killed him! My God! You killed him! You ran over him twice! What is wrong with you?"

And in that moment, Jared realizes that although Josh is all right, someone else is not. The little boy, Tony's son. Tony, the man involved with Misty. For one brief instant, Jared feels a sense of vengeful elation. The man who has hurt him will be hurt even more. But then Jared's basic decency reasserts itself and he is suddenly devastated. He will regret that brief moment of exultation for the rest of his life.

The rest of the day is a blur. Ambulances come and go. Police take statements and want interviews. One of their neighbors has taken Josh downtown with her daughter to see a movie. She will bring him back for dinner. One of the medics has given Misty a sedative and she is upstairs in bed. Jared sits in his living room, strangely disconnected from his surroundings. He can feel his skin tingle, his heart beat. He can feel the breath come into his body and the oxygen feed his blood. But he can't connect with the world around him. He is separate from everything else. He has answered the questions asked by the police and they have gone away. The neighbors have gone away. The dead boy has gone away. Jared knows he will soon need to go away. But first he will have to go to the dead boy's house and apologize to his parents. He doesn't know what he will say. He can't bring himself to think about it too much. He can feel the rough texture of the chair on his arm.

Misty doesn't wake up until the neighbor arrives with Josh. Jared is still sitting in his chair. He doesn't respond to the doorbell. Misty tries hard to maintain a cool exterior but she continually breaks into tears. Josh wants to know what happened but neither parent will talk to him. He cries through their vain attempt at dinner.

Later, in the kitchen, Jared tells Misty he is going to visit the

Corrarino's home to apologize.

"What will you say?" Misty wants to know. "What can you possibly say? Oh my God! Tony adored that boy. He's going to think it's all his fault, because of the boy he killed in Vietnam."

Jared nods his head slowly, without knowing the details, he understands in his heart that having such knowledge about another man shows a deep level of intimacy and confirms his worst fears. Theirs is not just a physical liaison. Misty cares deeply about this Tony, and about his now dead son. Jared's feeling of desolation reaches deeper, chilling the depths of his being. Misty is gone to him now. He can see the disgust in her eyes when she looks at him.

Even in its deadened state, Jared's mind seeks a solution. But the only thing he can think of is suicide. It is the only way to stop this pain. His wife has discarded him. He has killed a five-year-old boy. All his efforts to rebuild his life since Vietnam have been ripped apart, in the cruelest possible way. He can't remember all the details; everything is a haze—but details don't matter. Excuses don't matter. He killed a young boy right in front of his own son. What kind of horrible effect will the memory of this day have on Josh? What did the poor boy ever do to deserve this? Jared can hear his own breathing, his heartbeat. He can hear his eyes blink. When he kills himself, these sounds will be silent. Everything will be silent. His jaw hurts and Jared realizes he's been gritting his teeth for hours.

Misty looks at Jared but doesn't see anyone she recognizes. *Who is this calm, straight-faced automaton? Where is his sense of guilt and despair? Where is the Jared who wears his heart on his sleeve?* Misty is overwhelmed by the fear that Jared killed Tony's son on purpose. Jared was mad when he came out of the bedroom. Misty knew he'd seen her with Tony and although he'd interpreted their relationship inaccurately, his sense of their emotional intimacy was correct.

Did Jared back over Anthony Dean on purpose? Did he want revenge so badly he would kill a five-year-old child? No. Jared wouldn't do that. Besides, Anthony Dean ran directly behind the car at the last minute. Misty had watched it happen. But then Jared had stopped with the left rear tire on top of Anthony Dean's chest, as though it were on purpose. Could he have done that by accident? And then, when she screamed, he backed up fast, running over Anthony Dean again with the front tire. If the poor child weren't dead at that point he certainly was shortly afterwards. No. Jared simply wasn't capable of such an action, certainly not against a child. But why won't Jared talk to her? Why doesn't he show any emotion?

Jared stands up slowly, an uncertain look on his face, as though he is unsure what to do with his hands. "Where do they live?" he asks Misty. He does not make eye contact.

"Who?" Misty asks, before she has a chance to think. Jared's tortured face gives her the answer. She gives him the address off the top of her head, reconfirming Jared's suspicions once again, but Jared's suspicions are far away and unimportant now. It doesn't matter any longer what she did with Tony or anyone else. The only thing that matters is putting a stop to all this pain.

"You can't go over there, Jared."

"I have to. I have to own up to what I did."

"Jared, Tony's father is a Mafia chief from New York, Sal Corrarino. I don't want you to get close to him."

Sal Corrarino. Mafia. That's where he'd heard the name before, but…"You had our son playing with a Mafia kid?"

"Tony's not involved with the family, Jared. He works in publishing. Listen, you should at least wait to talk with them until tomorrow. Let them deal with the shock, figure things out a little before you go over there."

She's right. They'll need some time. Jared nods. He'll need to apologize before he ends his life, but it can wait until tomorrow. He wants to hold Josh one more time as well. He lifts Josh in his arms, the boy still snuffling, and walks slowly up to bed. Two hours later, when Misty comes upstairs, Jared and Josh are lying together in the boy's bed, Josh's arms wrapped around Jared's neck. Misty steps softly into the room. Although Josh is sound asleep, Jared's eyes are wide open, tears streaming silently down his cheeks.

"You should come to bed," she whispers, but Jared doesn't respond at all. Finally, Misty turns and pads out the door.

Chapter 36

—·((•))·—

When the policeman showed up at Brenda's door the first thing she thought was that Tony must have been killed or badly injured in an accident. And she was glad. She hoped she didn't give it away but who really gave a shit what the cop thought? Even as he made his way into the house and asked her to sit down, "I'm afraid I have some bad news for you, ma'm," Brenda was thinking about life without Tony.

With him gone, the Family would have to absorb her. They wouldn't leave me out in the cold…not as long as I've got Anthony Dean. They'd move her up to New York and once she was settled she could make her way into the circles of power. She would have to be careful not to step on toes, but she knew how to ingratiate herself, make herself indispensable. After all, that was how she'd gotten Tony to ask her to marry him. Anthony Dean would be a pain in the neck, but he was now the key to everything Brenda wanted. With Tony out of the picture, his mother and father would shower their love on their grandson and anything that came to Anthony Dean would come through her. Babysitting would not be an issue; Brenda knew that Tony's mother, Maria, would jump at the chance to keep the child as much as she could. And if not her, then one of the aunts would do it; there were always shirt-tail relatives hanging around the Corrarino house. She'd have to grieve properly, of course, let his family know how much she'd loved Tony. If she was patient and careful, she would have everything she ever wanted, everything that shithead Tony kept from her.

Why didn't the cop hurry up and leave? What was he muttering about, anyway? There must be some mistake. He wasn't talking about Tony, but about some kid who'd been run over. What did she care? Had Tony run over someone? Wait! Was he talking about Anthony Dean? Was her son hurt? Or dead? Is that it? Oh, God! No. No. What would she do, now? What was she supposed to do now?

****

Tony was in the boarding area when they announced his name over the loudspeaker.

"Mr. Tony Corrarino, Mr. Tony Corrarino, please pick up a white courtesy phone for a message. Mr. Tony Corrarino."

He hurried down to the phone, certain it was his secretary telling him about something he'd forgotten. He identified himself to the operator and was told to call his home. He knew then that something terrible had happened.

"God help me," he thought, as he dialed the number, "but I hope it's Brenda and not Anthony Dean."

A policeman answered and with a kindness and brevity Tony would always appreciate, told him of his loss. "I'm sorry Mr. Corrarino, but your son Anthony has been run over by a car." He hesitated, but only briefly, while Tony's life fell out from under him. "Your wife is taking it pretty hard, sir. I think she needs you to come home as soon as possible."

"Yes. Yes, I will." Tony was surprised at his ability to speak. "I'm coming home now."

He hung up the phone and went back to the chair where his overnight bag lay. He sat down heavily next to it.

Anthony Dean. Dead. Run over by a car! How? He must have run into the street in front of Misty's house. Oh, Jesus. Tony tried to stand but wobbled and sat back down again. He thought of his son, his sweet, dead son. His baby face flashed like a neon sign into Tony's mind. Anthony Dean, dead! How could he be gone before his father? He was only five. Dead! No more Saturday morning cartoons. No more crazy stories and foolish songs to make him laugh. No more guided missile-boy crushing hugs when he came home from work. What sort of terrible guilt must Misty be feeling now? She was responsible for him. How could she have let this happen? Now Anthony Dean is dead. Dead like the little Vietnamese boy Tony had stabbed so long ago. Ah, Jesus. The Vietnamese boy! His face! His face! Contorted with pain, blood-spattered lips, body shuddering as death took him. He was somebody's son, too. He died a horrible, unnecessary death, just like Anthony Dean.

But the Vietnamese boy didn't just die, Tony had slaughtered him. And there, once again, was his face. Tony had not seen him for months, not since the appendix operation; not since Misty had saved him. Misty, his guardian angel, had helped him find serenity, but obviously, serenity was not enough. If God wants to punish you, you'll get punished.

He'd always worried about Anthony Dean, and in the grip of his horrific nightmares had sometimes transposed his son's face over the Vietnamese boy's. Now, for the first time, Tony wondered if Anthony Dean had been taken in payment for his actions in Vietnam. An eye for an eye. A son for a son. He was seized with an urge to scream, to rage against the injustice of the death of an innocent boy, but the Vietnamese boy had been innocent as well. Innocence is no guarantee of anything. Fairness does not exist. There is only justice, a vicious, blind and bloody justice, a justice that punishes the son for the sins of the father. What goes around, comes around…in spades.

Had he not prayed enough for forgiveness? Had he not suffered enough with his nightmares? The answer seemed plain. No. No forgiveness. No escape. No end to the torment.

Shaking, Tony got to his feet and headed out on the long walk to the airport entrance. He could think of nothing he wanted to do less than go home and share his grief with Brenda. But where else could he go?

****

Misty wakened instantly, but incompletely, her mind still foggy from emotion and the remains of the sleeping pill she'd taken earlier. She'd heard something but she wasn't sure what it was. She stayed where she was, checking from the corner of her eye to see that Jared had not come to bed. He must still be in Josh's room. A light knocking at the door alerted her to the presence of someone outside. It must have been the knocking that woke her, the visitor was trying to be courteous, not ringing the doorbell, hoping to get someone up with a minimum of noise. She looked through the curtains of the bay window and was at once horrified and overjoyed to see Tony standing on the front porch. She threw open the door and hugged him.

"I'm so sorry, Tony."

He hugged her back. She led him into the house.

"I'm so sorry, Tony," she said again.

"I know. Thanks. They caught me at the airport; I haven't been home yet." Her breath caught.

"You don't know?" she breathed.

"I know Anthony Dean was…. I don't know anything else," he shook his head. "But I was worried about how you must be feeling." Misty started to sob. He didn't know any of the details. Didn't know her husband had killed his son. But he was worried about her. Worried about how she must feel. Oh, God! How was she going to tell him? She reached out and took his hand.

Tony loved the coolness of her skin on his but couldn't deal with it tonight. His senses were overwhelmed. The thoughts, guilts and fears were shooting through his head so fast they were coming out the pores of his skin. He pulled away.

"Tony, I…"

"I know, Misty, I know. Do they know what happened…who did this?"

Misty choked back a sob. "They… he… didn't mean…"

"Yes, Tony. They know." Jared stood at the foot of the stairs, stark as death, with eyes burning from the depths of a tortured soul.

"He didn't mean…" Misty tried again.

"Tony, I backed the car over your son."

The words were only confirmation. Tony had known what he would say the moment he heard Jared's vacant, pain-filled voice. Jared stood there, tall and strong. His shoulders square, giving the worst news a parent can possibly receive. Your only son is dead… and I killed him.

Tony received the news like a physical blow. He staggered back a step, then recovered. Misty watched as he processed the information. His dark eyes flashed with rage, then grew contemplative. She could see him consider all the possibilities. The silence continued. Tony stared into Jared's eyes. Jared looked straight back, but his eyes were focused on something else entirely. Something only he could see. The two men faced each other silently.

Tony glanced toward Misty, caught her eyes. She responded instantly. "He didn't mean to, Tony. Anthony Dean ran…" She stopped in mid-sentence as Jared raised his arm toward her without taking his eyes off Tony.

The physical act of raising his arm seemed to destabilize Jared. Tony began to notice aspects of his son's killer he'd not noticed earlier. Jared's rusty red hair stood out sideways, a horrible case of bed head. And although Jared's body seemed straight and solid, Tony now noticed a sort of shimmering, which he realized was a kind of shaking, almost a palsy. But the most telling aspect of Jared's appearance was his eyes. They were not sad so much as haunted, stricken. Not terrified so much as hopeless. Tony knew that feeling and he knew then with certainty that Anthony Dean's death was an accident and nothing more, an accident that would torture Jared for the rest of his life. Jared emanated a look of shattered strength, an aura of defeated invincibility. Jared was, Tony realized, holding himself together by strength of will alone.

Tony walked slowly toward Jared and put his one good hand on Jared's shoulder.

"I know," he said. "I know."

Any semblance of control or strength Jared had managed to convey collapsed under the weight of Tony's kindness and he began to cry, short sobs at first, then deep, racking, pain-filled moans. Jared sat down hard on the stairs and lowered his head between his knees, his shoulders quaking. Tony stood, unsure of what to do. Misty moved between them quickly, and knelt beside Jared, taking his head in her hands. She looked up at Tony with grateful, tear-filled eyes. She mouthed the words, "Thank you. I'm so sorry." He nodded and left the house quietly.

Chapter 37

When Sal first heard of Anthony Dean's death he and his advisors interpreted it as the beginnings of an attack on him and his family. They went into combat mode. Soldiers went to the mattresses, women and children went into protected fortresses, leaders went to previously established war rooms. His was a modern operation and he understood that everything came down to intelligence and communication. It took his people two hours to determine that the child's death had been a terrible accident and nothing more. But it took six more hours to ensure that none of the other competing organizations were trying to use the Corrarino tragedy as a springboard for an attack. The preceding years had been difficult for Sal. His organization was, in a word, declining. His top two lieutenants had died in the past two years. Paul Mirabelli had choked to death on a shrimp at his own daughter's wedding and Dom Petrino had died following a stroke at a Yankees game. Even now, Sal had no one who could replace them. Oh, there were competent young guys, but Sal had no real history with them. He knew they were ambitious but their loyalty was not well established.

And then there was Charley, his deviant son. By rights, Charley should have been stepping into Sal's shoes, but instead he was shunted into a nothing job that paid his bills and kept him out of everyone's way. Sal had hoped his son would change but reports indicated Charley was still involved in subterranean deviant sex. Thus far there'd been no proof and Sal was doing his best not to find any.

As a result, Sal had no trusted advisors to fall back on when his only grandchild was killed. It took every bit of his self-control not to fly down to Bowie and take care of the bastard who had killed Anthony Dean with his own hands, but Sal had to think of the rest of his family as well as the organization. He stayed in hiding until the all-clear was given. By that time, Maria was becoming increasingly unstable; she actually screamed at him in front of their assembled relatives.

"By what right do you keep me from my son at a time like this, you son of a bitch? I'm going now. RIGHT NOW! Do you hear me?"

Sal had acquiesced and they'd chartered a small jet right then. Sal, Maria, her sisters and Charley. Sal didn't like having Charley along; Maria had shared her sense of Charley's relationship with Brenda, and although he hadn't told her, Sal knew even more. He'd had people keeping tabs on Brenda and Tony ever since they'd been married.

"It doesn't matter if Tony doesn't want to be part of the family," Sal had told Dom and Paul, when he'd ordered the surveillance. "He's got the blood and he's got the name. Somebody wants to hurt me, they know they can do it through him. I want to know what's going on in his life." Surveillance was sporadic; Sal would order increased vigilance when change was in the works or when something just seemed to be up. Sal knew that Brenda had never sealed the deal with Charley, but seemed to be leading him on. He knew that Tony was spending a great deal of time with this nurse, whose husband had killed poor Anthony Dean. It didn't sound like Tony was involved with her, either, but Sal knew what jealousy could do, whether it was rooted in truth or not. It didn't really matter, Sal thought to himself as they jetted south, whether the nurse's husband meant to kill the boy or scare him or just didn't see him. No one could injure or kill a Corrarino. The only question was when and how payment would be made.

His temper flared silently at Brenda. This was all her fault, the slut. Does she think I can't see her for what she really is? Does she think I don't know that she's made my son's life a living hell and she doesn't even take care of her own house? Her own son? If she'd been any kind of wife, any kind of mother, Tony wouldn't have been spending time with the nurse and Anthony Dean wouldn't have been at her house, where her husband could run over him with a car.

When the plane landed, Sal would be getting the complete dossier he'd demanded about the nurse's husband. He consulted his notebook. Jared McCauley, ex-military, real estate agent, generally good guy, according to the quick and dirty rundown he'd gotten before he left. But none of that mattered. Intent didn't matter. Not a goddamned thing mattered except that he'd killed a Corrarino.

Chapter 38

Brenda was having trouble keeping everything together. Surrounded by the various members of the Corrarino clan, neighbors and Tony's friends from work, she was trying hard to be the person she needed to be, a grieving mother. She needed to control her emotions but still show the depth of her bereavement.

She didn't much care about the rest of them but Tony's family had to be convinced of her love for her son. Anthony Dean had been her ticket to riches. Even if she and Tony divorced, she would have gotten at least partial custody of the boy and even partial custody would have ensured a consistent flow of cash. God! What was she going to do now?

She sat on the edge of her bed, squeezing a little more time away from the well-wishers downstairs. She'd begged out of the gathering a few minutes earlier, with tears brimming. Everyone had said, "Take as long as you need. Take care of yourself, first." Actually, the only ones who said that were neighbors and friends. Tony's mother had simply stared at her blankly when Brenda had explained her need to collect herself.

Maria, that bitch. She'd been all over them just a few months ago, after Tony had come home from the hospital. Making meals, taking care of her son, cleaning the house. She damn near never went home. Watching, always watching. Like she and Charley had been hiding their time together. The bitch probably thinks she and Charley had been hooking up on the side. Like she would really let that muscle-bound little dwarf jump her bones. No need. She could just string him along. He'd already do anything she asked him to.

"Damn it!" she hissed aloud. *Why couldn't it have been Tony who died? Everything would have been so much simpler had Tony been the one to die, but now she was going to have to move carefully. Her marriage was over. Tony as much as told her so the night he'd come back from the airport, just after Anthony Dean had died.*

She'd precipitated his response, she knew, because she'd been hysterical when Tony came home.

As Tony opened the door, the policeman who'd delivered the news to her shook his hand, said "Sorry for your loss," and practically ran out the door.

Brenda stood in the foyer, hands on her hips. Her hair was wild but her makeup was unblemished. *No tears*, Tony thought to himself. *No tears.* He made an effort to reach for her, hold her, a natural, human response for comfort, even though her body language warned against it. She screamed, and shoved him backwards.

"This is what happens when you let your little nurse bitch watch my son?" she shrieked.

Tony shook his head, hunched his shoulders, and continued past her to the kitchen. She followed him closely.

"How could you? How could you put him in the control of someone who hates you?" Her voice scratched across the walls, ricocheted off the windows; it had a witchy, bitchy quality that Brenda recognized but she didn't care. She'd been building up to this moment for two hours and nothing would stop her now.

"Anthony Dean was just playing in the yard and the son of a bitch ran over him; ran over him twice. Did you know that? Do you even care?"

Tony washed his hands under the kitchen faucet, then caught water in his cupped hands and took a drink. Afterwards he washed his face. Dried it with a paper towel.

"Yes, Brenda. I know what happened. Anthony Dean ran behind the car as Jared was backing up." He sat on a tall stool near their island, facing away from her.

"That's what they say. So, why did the bastard run over him twice? You tell me that?" She moved around the island so he could not escape looking at her face. "Tell me!" She picked up a nearby glass and flung it against the refrigerator. It didn't break and its continued survival upset her even more. She pursued it with her feet, finally stomping it into pieces when she trapped it against the dishwasher. Then she turned to him again, eyes wide and staring. She was nearly unhinged.

"It wasn't an accident, Goddamn you! That asshole got tired of you putting the pork to his wife and paid you back by murdering your son." Tony's head came up and swiveled toward her. He uncoiled slowly up from the stool and Brenda was reminded for the second time in her life that there was a limit with Tony and crossing it put her into the realm of the unknown.

She backed up and to the side, turned her face to the refrigerator and sobbed deeply. She hated the color of this refrigerator and had been planning to replace it. Now that would have to wait. She could hear Tony sit back down on his stool. The dangerous moment had passed. She turned and resumed her attack.

"Well, what are you going to do about it? He was your son, too. What happens now?" she said. "What are you going to do about it?"

Tony looked down at his hands, then up at her. He breathed deeply. "What is there to do? I'm going to bury our son. Then I'm going to try and keep living. That's all there is to do. That's all either of us can do. Go on living."

The way Tony looked at her chilled her to the core. It was disgust she saw in his eyes. Disgust and loathing. The knowledge sent her over the edge. "That's not enough!" she screeched. Her arms flapped wildly. "That's not nearly enough! Think of our loss. They've taken everything away. They…"

"Shut up!" Tony roared. He leaped to his feet. "Shut your fucking mouth!"

Brenda stopped in mid-sentence, staring. Tony rarely cursed and never raised his voice. They stood, looking at each other.

"The only thing you ever did for that boy was give birth," he snarled. "The only thing you ever saw in him was a meal ticket. So don't…" his voice caught. "Don't…" He sat back down again.

There it was. Out in the open. There was no reason to dissemble.

Brenda stood for a few moments longer. Then she sank to the floor, sobbing into her hands. "What happens to me? What am I going to do?"

At last, Tony thought. *Some true emotion.* "I'm sure you'll think of something," he said, and wandered up to his bedroom.

****

Tony hadn't spoken to her in the five days since then. He'd simply gotten up the next day and started taking care of things. He was strong; she had to give him that. Anthony Dean had been his whole world and the boy had wanted to spend every waking moment with his father. His sense of loss must be horrific, and yet he continued on. It wasn't as though Brenda didn't like the kid. She did, but that was all she could muster up. She tried, but couldn't imagine the emotional pain Tony must be feeling. She wished she could. She'd always wanted to feel love and caring like other people. It simply wasn't there, and never had been…so the hell with it. She needed to take care of herself.

Tony made all the funeral arrangements and dealt with the phone calls and visits. He sat straight and unflinching beside her at the church service. He was the one standing straight and tall at the burial. She'd tried to hold his hand there and he'd pulled coldly away. She didn't look up but she was sure other people must have noticed. She hoped the attempt had gotten her some points with the family. She was trying. They could see she was trying.

Of course, Tony was the one down there now, acting the perfect host. Of course, his mother Maria, the bitch of all bitches, was overseeing the house, handling the food, supervising the caterer, although God knows why they had a caterer. Every neighbor within sight had brought food, as well as everyone Tony worked with. How could he possibly have so many friends? There were people here from Oregon, for Christ's sake. An older woman who sat with Tony for hours the day before the funeral, holding his hand, rubbing his back. Brenda had walked by at one point and heard the woman say, "I feel like I lost him twice." Then she broke down and Tony had turned to fold her into his arms, their roles reversed. Another man, obviously the woman's son, had sat silently in a nearby chair as Tony and his mother comforted each other.

Most of the others probably just wanted to rub elbows with the Mafia, although she knew for a fact Tony never, ever mentioned his connections to the New York crime family. They probably just figured there had to be a connection and came to see. Jesus Christ. They'd probably all expect a thank-you note. Maybe Maria bitch will take care of those, too.

God, she'd been upstairs almost an hour. She needed to go back down. People would notice. There was a change in the tenor of the conversation buzz coming from downstairs. Someone was arguing at the front door. Maybe she'd check it out but first she needed to fix her face. She moved into the bathroom.

Chapter 39

Jared had spent the previous five days in a living hell. He'd had an average of two hours of nightmare-filled sleep each night and had lost 15 pounds. He'd stopped shaving and showering. His eyes were wild and streaked with red. He would break down and cry at the slightest provocation, most dependably whenever his son came into view. For the first three days, he'd sat motionless in silent rooms, erupting in anger whenever Misty turned on a radio or television within his hearing.

Although she initially thought having Josh nearby would be good for Jared, she'd begun to fear his unpredictability, and now never let the boy near his father unless she was there. Jared recognized what she was doing but didn't hold it against her. He wasn't all that sure of himself, either. He was just marking time, for the most part, waiting for the funeral.

Jared had started out for the Corrarino's house the day after Anthony Dean's death, but police detectives had come and kept him answering questions most of the morning. He was two hours into the interview when he finally realized the cops considered him a murder suspect.

They'd finally taken him down to the station, where they kept him in a room by himself for the entire afternoon, occasionally one or both of the detectives coming in to question him. After two more hours of it one of the detectives asked him if he wanted to call his lawyer. Jared shook his head. Said it didn't matter. The detective looked sharply at him and Jared realized the man recognized his misery, and suspected the depth of his depression. If he wasn't careful, Jared realized, this policeman would take steps to keep him from committing suicide. The thought that someone might keep him from his goal was too horrible to contemplate.

He smiled wanly at the detective, shrugged his shoulders, said, "It was an accident. A lawyer can't help me tell you it was an accident and he can't make you believe it."

Jared could almost see the man's antennae relax. They kept him another hour after that but Jared could tell their hearts weren't in it; they were going through the motions. Just before they turned him loose the detective who'd been concerned leaned in close and said, "Just a piece of advice, Mr. McCauley, you'd best stay away from the Corrarinos."

Jared started to tell him that he had to apologize, but the detective waved him silent. "I know, I know. You feel bad. But the Corrarinos aren't regular folks. Know what I'm saying?"

"Yes, but…"

"No buts, Mr. McCauley. You could wind up in real trouble. If you have to talk to them, you should do it at the funeral, when there are a lot of other people around. And then you might want to consider a long vacation, change of job, change of name. Understand?"

Jared nodded dumbly.

"The funeral is scheduled for Saturday at 2 p.m. Maybe after that would be a good time, OK?"

Jared nodded again, then, as the policeman turned to go, he had another thought. "Detective?"

The man turned, "Yes?"

"Is my family in danger?"

The man shook his head emphatically. "No. That's not the way these people do business, but you…." He shrugged meaningfully, turned and walked out the door.

Jared nodded to himself and set his sights on Saturday.

****

Jared had gotten pretty well cleaned up on Saturday. He'd showered, shaved, put on a suit. Granted, it looked like he'd stolen it from another, better-built man, but at least he would be respectful.

He drove to the Corrarinos' house in a fog. He didn't know what to expect, he just knew he had to look Tony and his wife in the eyes and tell them how sorry he was. He owed them that and he owed it to his own family. After he was gone he wanted them to remember him as a man who didn't shrink from his responsibilities.

A burly, dark-haired man was standing by the door on a raised porch when Jared walked up the stairs.

"Thanks for coming," he said. "Please come in."

Jared didn't want to go inside and mix with the crowd. "My name is Jared McCauley," he said. "I wonder if I could speak to Mr. and Mrs. Corrarino out here."

At the mention of Jared's name, the man flinched. His body language, facial expression and stance underwent a slight, but unmistakable change. He was no longer a friendly doorman, but something else entirely. He looked at Jared for a long time, as though committing his face to memory, then said curtly, "Wait here." He turned and walked into the house.

A few minutes later, a slightly built older man, with mostly gray hair appeared in the doorway. "I'm Sal Corrarino," he said flatly.

"Ah, Mr. Corrarino. I'm sorry, I'm looking for your son, Tony."

"Yes, I know. But you got me."

Jared stuttered, hesitated. He hadn't anticipated this. He didn't know what to do. Flustered, he simply said the words he'd been practicing for five days. "I'm so sorry for your loss, Sir. I'd give anything to bring your son, er, grandson back."

Sal stared at him and Jared thought he'd never seen such reptilian eyes before.

"Mr. McCauley," it was a woman's voice. "I'm Maria Corrarino, Tony's mom." Obviously Italian, she was strikingly beautiful, only slightly younger than her husband, with long dark hair just starting to show gray. She moved smoothly toward Jared and held out her hand. He took it thankfully.

"Thank you for coming, Mr. McCauley. I know how hard it must have been for you."

"Yes, I…" Jared's voice caught and he sobbed once, as though in surprise, it having been torn from him without warning. He collected himself.

"I'm so sorry, Mrs. Corrarino. I don't...I can't...I..." He was babbling. "I hope you can forgive me."

Glancing to the side Jared could see Sal Corrarino shift his stance, raise his head as if to speak, but Maria leaned over and placed her hand on his arm, as she smiled sadly at Jared.

"Of course, we forgive you, Mr. McCauley. It will just take some time. This has been difficult for everyone. And now we must get back to our guests. Please excuse us." She took Sal's arm and maneuvered him back through the front door. Sal's head swiveled to watch Jared, even as he turned and disappeared.

Jared backed down the stairs and stood there uncertainly. He'd come to see Tony and his wife, and he was unwilling to leave without doing so. Now there were two bodyguards standing on the porch, looking down at him. As he waited, another, shorter man appeared in the doorway. He whispered a question to one of the bodyguards, nodded at the answer, then stepped off the porch, coming to a stop close to Jared. He was muscular and hard and more openly cruel looking than either of the bodyguards or the older patriarch.

"I'm Charley Corrarino, Tony's brother. This ain't going to save you, ya' know?" His voice was loud, grating. He was playing for a crowd, though the only people around to impress were the bodyguards

"Sorry?" Jared said, uncertain how to respond.

"Coming here to apologize isn't going to save you. You killed my nephew and you're going to pay. Understand now?"

They'd have to be quick, Jared thought to himself, if they intend to beat me to the punch.

Jared lowered his head. He understood loss, but this man showed no sense of loss, no sadness. He only cared about putting on a show. His nephew was the last thing on his mind. Still, Jared would do anything to avoid conflict here. "Yes, I understand," he murmured. "I'd just like to speak with your brother and his wife, please."

"What the hell makes you think they want to talk with you, asshole?" said the tough guy, his voice up yet another octave. He was rocking back and forth, from one foot to another, visibly pumping himself up. His attitude and body language were becoming more and more intimidating. Even in his dismal state, Jared recognized the threat. He was disgusted. He would end his own life in the manner of his own choosing but he would not allow this scumbag to browbeat him.

"Enough," he said, without looking up.

"What's that?" the mouth said. "Enough? You think you're giving orders here, shithead?"

He rolled his eyes for the benefit of the two bodyguards, then took two steps forward, which turned out to be one step too far. Jared's right hand shot out and grabbed Charley's throat, with a death grip on his windpipe. With a strangled gasp, Charley flailed with both hands, trying desperately to break Jared's grip. But Jared's thumb and fingers were practically meeting in the soft tissue behind Charley's windpipe and the more Charley struggled, the more excruciating the pain became. He couldn't take a breath. The bodyguards were alert and moving, but they did not seem to be moving with any real urgency. Jared wondered, in a detached sort of way, what the mouthy guy had done to make these gorillas willing to watch him be humiliated, and perhaps badly hurt. He leaned down until his mouth was near Charley's ear.

"I said enough. Enough is what I meant. I owe you nothing." He released Charley's throat, pushed and stepped away as the shorter man fell hard to his rear.

The bodyguards picked up their pace now. They were going to do damage. Jared backed rapidly away, hoping to get a car to his back.

"Hold on," came a familiar voice. Tony stepped out from the side of the house. He must have come from the back yard. The bodyguards stopped. Tony looked at them and waved his hand dismissively. "Not necessary," he said without heat. The two men relaxed and retreated to the porch, still watching attentively. Tony came to a stop next to Charley, who was still seated and trying to take a complete breath, but he ignored his brother and said only, "Hi, Jared."

"Tony, I…I wanted to apologize in person. Is your wife available?"

Tony smiled slightly. "Probably not a good idea, Jared. I will pass along your message." He stepped forward, reached out to shake Jared's hand. Jared took it hungrily and held on. "I'd give anything…"

"I know, Jared. Believe me, I know. But there's nothing you can do except learn how to live with it. Misty and your son need you now." He disengaged his hand and pushed Jared's shoulder gently to make him turn and head back down the walk.

"Wait! Stop! Is that him? Did he come here?" Brenda was on the porch, flanked by the bodyguards, her voice a shriek. "Why are you talking to him? He killed my son! Why is he still standing? Why is he still alive?"

Tony turned to her and raised his hand. "Stop. Shut up. Go inside." One of the bodyguards opened the door for her but she ignored him. She pointed a long finger at Jared. "I hate you! Hate you!"

Jared raised his face to her. "I don't blame you, Mrs. Corrarino. I'm sorry." He turned and walked slowly out to the street.

Tony reached down to give Charley a hand as he struggled to stand. "Help her inside," he said to the bodyguards and they moved a sobbing Brenda through the door.

"The sonofabitch," Charley gasped. "I'll kill him."

"No, Charley, you won't. You will stay far away from this. This is not about you. Next time, he'll probably really hurt you."

It is possible, though unlikely, that Charley might have learned to live with the humiliation of being manhandled by Jared McCauley. He had, after all, learned to live with the humiliation of his beating by the black ballerina. But the offhand, flippant comment by his brother sunk a barb in his heart and began to burrow in toward his soul, leaving a ragged track of pain on the way.

Tony the golden boy, who wouldn't take his place in the family business, who'd never made his bones, at least not here in the states, and killing gooks didn't count anyway, cracked wise about Charley. As though he was some punk who couldn't handle himself. His brother, the one-armed cripple, had warned Charley off. Well, bullshit to that. Charley Corrarino didn't take orders from his brother. The cocksucker who'd killed his nephew had gotten in a lucky punch and made him look bad, but that was just for a moment. There are lots of ways to hurt someone and the last man standing wins.

Chapter 40

Trey had always been careful with his money, even during his time in the Navy, and he was more careful now. The bookstore made legitimate money, though not nearly as much as it received credit for. After his first few contracts, he and Carlo realized there was no way to camouflage as much money as he was making in a small business. They set up a numbered Swiss bank account, and then another in the Cayman Islands. As time went on and Trey's reputation grew, Carlo advised him to hike his prices. "It's all about marketing, Trey. The folks who hire people to do your kind of work usually want the best, you know? So, you're becoming known as the best on the west coast. You need to set your prices like you are the best. Know what I mean?"

So he moved his price up to $100,000, then $250,000 where the price leveled off. After a few years, Trey was given a contract on a Mexican drug lord, a hit that involved months of effort and a one-man seaborne assault straight out of the SEAL cookbook. For that, Trey charged $500,000. Then something happened to make Trey's services worth even more to his employers. A lifelong member of a competing New York crime family, a man who had been involved in hundreds of illegal activities and dozens of killings, made a deal for immunity with federal prosecutors. He gave testimony that put many of the higher-ups in the organization in prison for periods up to and including life. His decision to break with the tradition of Omerta, or silence to the law, shattered the invulnerability of the Mafia and ultimately destroyed his crime family, whose territory and activities were taken over in their weakened state by competing families. Suddenly, no Family felt safe; and hired killings, which continued to be as necessary as ever, were potentially as dangerous to those who ordered them as to the targets. It became safer to contract with freelance killers without any connection to the organization. And safest of all was someone like Trey, whose identity was as unknown to those who contracted with him as theirs was to him. The demand for his services increased markedly, and at Carlo's urging, so did his fees. His regular fees jumped to $400,000 and increased from there according to the difficulty, danger and time necessary.

"You know, the money really stacks up fast when the average take for each job is nearly half a mil," Trey told Carlo one afternoon. "I'd like to give you some of it. Now, don't argue. Wait a minute. You set these jobs up for me, and if you don't want it you could give it to your daughters."

"Thanks, kid, but I don't need it and neither do they. Besides, just because you get paid four or five hundred grand per hit don't mean that's what you make. You're spending a month or more setting up these hits, living in hotels, paying for food, buying used cars, putting out bribes. You're going to need a pretty good nest egg, you know? You're going to want to get out of the business someday and when you do, you'll need to get out of the area, too. That takes cash, lots of it."

Who is this guy who does so much talking? Trey wondered. What happened to Carlo of the truncated sentence structure? But he knew, and smiled inwardly at the thought. The short, pronoun-free sentences that had marked Carlo's speech in the early years were an affectation that had become so ingrained as to become a habit. It was how he communicated with acquaintances and friends. But this new pattern of speech was something very different, something far more involved and descriptive. This is how he communicated with his son.

"What do you mean out of the area?"

"I mean out of the country. You can never tell when a new witness is going to show up or some new piece of information will put the cops on your trail. You need to be out of the country for several years."

"What if I don't want to go out of the country?"

"Your sisters live with you, right?"

Trey's eyes became flat and emotionless. Carlo shivered despite himself. This was the last thing dozens of men had seen in their lives.

"Yeah. That's what I mean. The cops aren't the only ones who would like to know who you are. And the others wouldn't mind using Trip and Tri against you. You disappear to some remote Polynesian island or South American ranch, dye your hair, grow a beard and after a few years you'll be home free."

It made sense. So, after some reflection, Trey began a search for his sanctuary. He approached it in the same careful, detailed way he planned each aspect of his professional life. He researched weather patterns, demographics, topography, real estate values and taxes. Finally, after several trips to Europe, he made an offer on an old estate close to a small village outside of Narbonne in the south of France. Near the foothills of the Pyrenees Mountains, his home was in the shadow of one of the ancient Cathar castles where those breakaway Catholics holed up in an unsuccessful attempt to escape the efforts of a series of Popes and French kings to bring them to heel. Trey was impressed by the history of the Cathars, and liked the idea of settling in their footsteps. They'd held out for one hundred years and sold their lives dearly. His purchase was an ancient stone building with high, frescoed ceilings, six bedrooms and five bathrooms that had been renovated in the 1960s. It had 20 hectares of grapes and five hectares of olive trees, 10 hectares of fenced pasture and a large garden. It was a perfect place to live…a perfect place to disappear. Over several years he sank quite a bit of money into the place.

His sisters had been involved in the decision and Trey had always assumed they would both accompany him, but Tri decided to stay in Long Beach. A shy young man named Darrell she'd first met in accounting class had suddenly become an insatiable reader and for the last several months had been a near-constant visitor to the bookstore. During that same period, Tri decided she needed to do most of her bookkeeping at the store and soon the two had begun eating lunches and dinners together. "They aren't dates, Trey," she'd told him. "We're just spending a little time together." But gradually, the two began to be comfortable with one another and comfortable with other people thinking of them as a couple. For his part, Trey couldn't have been happier for his sister; he'd almost given up hoping for a real life for her. He owed that to Carlo, as well, he knew. Carlo had set her up in the travel agency where she first began coming out of her shell and it was his idea to buy the book store. Then, too, it was Carlo's idea for Trey to become a hit man, a recommendation that Trey found harder to be happy about, though it had paid off handsomely.

Trip struggled with Tri's decision to stay in the States. The two had nearly reestablished their once supernaturally close relationship and—given the right conditions—they could essentially read each other's thoughts. That returning ability was what convinced Trip to accompany Trey to France. "For one thing, it's not that great reading your sister's mind when all she thinks about is some guy. Besides, the things she thinks about doing with him are just crazy. Do you know that she is seriously entertaining the idea of…?"

"Stop. Just stop, Trip," Trey said, laughing. "Give her a break. She deserves a chance at some happiness." He moved closer to her and put his arm around her. "You had it bad, I know. But Tri suffered terribly, as well. And she is only now coming out of it. She can come over and visit any time, you know? And you can always come back here."

"I think I'll be fine in France," Trip said. "It will be a great chance for me to learn something new, and to be honest, I'm really not too interested in guys right now. Tri and I have decided it's my turn to take care of you; I've got the second shift."

"Second shift, huh? I suppose it's a second shift for all of us, isn't it?"

The call from New York had come, though. Against his better judgment, Trey had taken the job and he worried his decision would change his life and his future, irrevocably. He hoped it would not change his sisters' lives as well. As luck would have it, Trey had recently finished the final arrangements for their move. He'd completed a trust with Tri and Trip as his successors and put both their names on his accounts. Finally, he'd given Tri the choice of selling the bookstore and keeping the money or continuing to operate it. She didn't hesitate. "I'd love to own it, Trey. Darrell and I have several ideas about incorporating a coffee shop and deli. Thank you so much."

"Tri, it's not like it will be a big change. You've been running the store for years, now."

"I know, but it will still be different. And Trey, Darrell and I are thinking about getting married in September. Will that work ok for you?"

Trey sighed deeply and shook his head. "No, I'm sorry Tri. I'm going to be tied up for the next month or so on one last job. Then, I'll be leaving direct for France. I've only got a couple more days here."

"Oh, my God, Trey! I can't get married without you!" She sat, thinking. She knew better than to ask Trey to change his business plans and she knew that once he left for Europe he probably wouldn't return for several years. She nodded to herself, smiled and hugged her brother around the neck. "I'll talk to Darrell. I don't think he'd mind getting married a little early."

Tri was right. Darrell jumped at the chance to be married early, though he asked that it be a secret civil ceremony so his family could still enjoy the big September hoorah. His family was all in the area, and they loved Tri. The next day Trey gave his sister away in a small ceremony before a justice of the peace. As part of their wedding gift Trey gave them the deed to the bookstore and a blank check for wedding expenses.

Chapter 41

Lacy got the kids off to school and sat down with her morning cup of coffee. She responded to the daily creaking noise from beneath the floorboards of her kitchen nook like the greeting of an old friend. In the quiet she'd always believed she could sense the life of her family through the creaks and groans of this old house. It was a moderately crazy thought, she knew, and she never shared it with anyone, even Shane. But she and Shane had done much of the rebuilding work themselves; replaced the toilets, fixed the leaky pipes, installed new windows, refinished the floors. She knew it intimately, from the studs, pipes, and wiring out. She talked to this house, and sometimes it talked back.

Lacy and Shane had raised their children here and cared for his father until his needs exceeded their abilities. She'd loved that old man; in him she saw the elderly gentleman Shane would become, and she was glad of it. She and her father-in-law had been close and she felt his spirit now. He was at peace, she thought, much more so now than when he was fluctuating between lucidity and dementia.

Shane was taking it bad. He wasn't sleeping and he'd become snappish with her and the kids, something he'd never done before. She'd tried to talk with him about his father's death, tell him that it was all right, that he'd done the right thing. But she couldn't bring herself to say the words. Lacy had been raised to believe suicide was a sin, and the idea that Shane could basically empower his father to kill himself was difficult for her to comprehend. And that was just the story for public consumption. She was fairly certain Shane had actually killed his father. She'd heard him talking to Jared late one night. She hadn't been eavesdropping but as she walked by his office she'd heard him say, "Well, at some point, someone had to pull the trigger." The sadness in his voice told Lacy everything she needed to know.

How could she help him to feel better about such a terrible act? Lacy couldn't go against everything she believed on Shane's behalf. But she was not an innocent bystander. She'd known what would happen when she'd taken the kids to Spokane that day. She'd given tacit approval. But afterwards, when she should have held her husband and let him know she was with him, body and soul, she'd pulled away, avoided contact. Shane hadn't begged; he hadn't asked for her support, even though they'd always supported each other throughout their marriage. In this, the hardest decision he'd ever had to make, his wife had abandoned him, left him to carry the burden alone.

Now, on top of that terrible load came the news about Jared's accident. He'd actually killed a little boy! Misty had been almost out of her mind with grief when she'd called, asking Shane to talk with Jared. But Jared had refused to get on the phone, despite numerous attempts on Shane's part.

"Shutting me out again, like he did after Vietnam," Shane said. "Why won't he let me help?"

Just like Shane, Lacy reflected. Even though he's overwhelmed by his personal turmoil, he worries most about those he loves. And where am I, during his struggles? I'm standing over here, playing holier than thou. He deserves so much better.

Overcome by grief and guilt, Lacy put her head in her hands and sobbed. She cried for several minutes, for her father-in-law, her husband and for herself. She cried until an especially loud groan issued from the open beams above her head. She smiled and nodded. Then she made plans for the evening.

****

"I'm OK, Babe. Really."

Lacy wrapped her arms around her husband and shook him lightly.

They were both naked and slightly sweaty from a session of afternoon delight she'd arranged when he returned from work. She'd given the kids enough money for pizza and a movie and sent them on their way after school, earning her an amused and all too understanding look from the two older ones. Oh, well, she thought. Can't keep kids innocent forever. Besides, she had more important issues now.

"No, Shane. You're not. You haven't been OK since your dad died."

He stiffened and rolled away. He would never look at her when they discussed his father. She moved up behind him and put her arms around him. She lay her head across his shoulder blades. "Shane, I know there are things about your father's death you want to keep secret." He broke her grip at his chest and turned quickly to face her, his face drawn.

"Lacy, I…"

"No, Shane. Listen to me. You don't need to tell me. I know enough. I know you are a good man. You did what had to be done. I've been wrong about this whole thing. I'm your wife. You can count on me no matter what. Do you want to talk to me about it?"

Shane pulled her close and kissed her forehead. "No, Lace. I don't. I can't tell you how much I appreciate your help here." He chuckled throatily and ran his fingers across her breast. Then he turned serious. "But this is my cross to bear."

"OK, I understand. You don't have to talk to me about it, but you need to talk with someone."

"Lacy, I'm the sheriff in this county. I can't talk with anyone here."

"You've been talking with Jared."

"Yes, I've been talking with Jared, but that was before this situation with the little boy occurred and he's completely shut me out since then."

"Maybe you should take a few days and go visit him. Maybe you can help each other."

He pulled her in a little closer. "Hmmmm. Maybe I should. Maybe I will. Thanks."

He rested his cheek on Lacy's chest and held her silently, listening to the muted creaks of the old house.

Chapter 42

Jared hung up the phone, his shoulders slumped. He couldn't believe his father's phone call. Jared had planned to end his life tomorrow. He'd spent the last three days with Josh, and he'd made sure all his papers were in order. He'd cleaned and fully loaded his pistol, though he only needed one round. But now his parents were coming.

"Your mother's cancer has come back, Jared. She really needs to see you again."

Jared's mother had been dealing with a mild form of cervical cancer for the past eight years. It was so low on the radar that they rarely talked about it. Jared had a strong suspicion their visit was an orchestrated attempt to bring him out of his depression. Bringing up his mother's cancer was just a lever. His father had always known how to poke the softest spot. Jared had tried to squirm out of it, saying that this was not a good time, but in the end Jared did not have the strength to refuse them. He resented it deeply, but he knew how much he owed his parents.

Besides, he thought, I should see my parents again before I go away for good. My suicide will cause them a great deal of pain. Pain like mine, he realized. They will be losing their own child. But without the guilt. They won't have accidentally killed me. They won't have backed a car over me in a fog of jealousy and hatred. Oh, Jesus! How could I have been so stupid?

His face contorts in agony. *I want this to be over. I want it to stop!* All thoughts of his parents disappear in a flash of self-loathing so bright it makes every other thought in his mind disappear. Jared turns his chair around to the desk, reaches into the top drawer and retrieves a key. Moving fast now, he uses the key to open the lower-right drawer, from which he pulls his 1911 Colt .45 service pistol. He has a sense of urgency, of focus, all outside stimuli are gone. He seats a magazine and racks the slide backwards, chambering a round when it snaps forward. He moves the pistol up by the side of his head, twists it to point directly at his temple. This is a problem. He can't twist his wrist around fully enough to keep a tight hold on the grip while pointing it at his temple. One of the 1911's safety features is a depressible plate on the back of the pistol grip. Without a firm handhold, the pistol will not fire. OK, there are ways around this.

Jared twists the pistol so that his thumb goes through the trigger guard and his fingers curl around the grip. Now he can do it—he just needs to make sure it is pointed the right way. He doesn't want to kill Josh or Misty, or some other innocent person accidentally with the bullet after it passes through his brain. That would be … God! He turns so the bullet will pass out through the wall and toward the garage. The garage should stop the bullet, so no neighbors will be hurt. He needs to be careful of the electrical box in the garage. And he needs a towel or something. There is no reason to spread skull and brain around for Josh and Misty to see. It's already going to be bad enough for them.

Shit! Jared's concern pivots momentarily back to his wife and son. His own death, especially here in their home in such a violent fashion, will devastate them. He cries inside thinking about the impact on Josh. But his own pain soon reasserts itself and Jared focuses back inside, to that selfish, me-first spot where all suicides ultimately dwell. *They will be better off without me.*

There is no towel in his den and he isn't going to break his train of thought again with a trip to the bathroom for a towel. He reaches around and removes a windbreaker he'd hung carelessly on the back of his desk chair, winds it carefully around his head, ties the sleeves together; it stays there nicely. He arranges himself carefully in the chair. He doesn't want to fall out of the damn thing and be lying there in a heap when Misty comes in. Ahh, that will be a terrible thing. I wouldn't do it to you, Misty, if I had any choice at all. He feels sad for her and for Josh, but peaceful. Things will be better, soon. He closes his eyes and raises the .45, turns it around in the unnatural position and looks around one last time.

"Dad? Are you in there? Dad? I need help. Can you help me? Daddy?"

Suddenly cold and frightened, Jared begins to shake. When Josh tentatively opens the door, his father is sitting with his face in his hands, crying. Instinctively Josh runs to him, puts his arms around his father's head. "I love you, Daddy," he says. And his father cries harder.

Chapter 43

It didn't take Charley Corrarino long to find out that his brother had moved into an apartment in a neighboring township. And even less time to act on the knowledge. He'd been calling Brenda on a daily basis to 'check in' and she'd been keeping him informed. Keeping him hot, too, if the truth were known. God, he'd never felt so aroused as when he was around her, and talking to her on the phone was almost as good. He'd practically come in his pants the last time they talked. She seemed to be dealing pretty well with the loss of her son, and the breakup with Tony seemed not to bother her at all. Brenda was getting on with her life, Charley thought.

She was indeed. In fact, Brenda thought of Tony only rarely, and then only when she was thinking about the high life she deserved but could not have. She thought of Anthony Dean even less often. He was part of her old life, one that no longer existed and she needed to move on. She was focused now on Charley; she knew he was attracted to her, and she saw him as her ticket into the Family. Not permanently. No. That would be too weird, even if he wasn't a muscle-bound psychotic dwarf. But he could introduce her around New York. She could accompany him for a while, just long enough to meet a few men with a lower dirtbag quotient, men with potential and a future in the Family. If she could get close to that kind of man, she could take care of the rest, but she would need Charley to open those doors. There would be a price, she was sure, and she didn't look forward to Charley doing the collecting, but now that Anthony Dean was dead and a divorce was in the offing, she had few options and time was not on her side.

Dealing with Charley was the cost of doing business. An investment in the future. Besides, there was one other thing she wanted done and she suspected Charley would enjoy the work.

Charley left word for his father that he'd decided to go down to Atlantic City for a week and drove south. He actually did register in his favorite hotel, but never unloaded his suitcases. If his father checked he'd just assume Charley'd gotten lucky and shacked up with a girl somewhere. He headed further south to Bowie, Maryland. When he knocked on the door Brenda came to him like a long-lost lover. She clung to him and kept her face close to his. Only when he began to respond in kind did she pull away, taking him by the hand and leading him into the house. Charley could hardly breathe.

He stayed for several days, each one more achingly sensual than the last. They spent a lot of time working out at the gym together. Brenda found things for him to do around the house to help. Sometimes she lightly squeezed his bicep; occasionally she would run her fingers through his hair. At night she kissed him lightly on the cheek, then left him steaming, heart pounding and muscles taut. Afterwards, Charley would lie in his bed, down the hall from Brenda's bedroom, and listen for the sound of her feet coming to his door, for the handle turning. He knew how to react if she came to him, but couldn't bring himself to take the first step. And he still wasn't sure about Tony. He didn't want to be in Brenda's bed if Tony came home. It would be different, he told himself, if Brenda was in his bed. It would show that she'd been the aggressor. He'd asked her several times about Tony, but Brenda brushed the questions aside, saying they were separated, as good as divorced. Several times, he thought she was ready, his time had come, but then she'd suddenly pull away.

One morning, Charley was drying off from a shower following their workout at the gym when Brenda came into the bathroom, wearing only a towel. Charley covered himself and flushed. He was completely off balance. He was never comfortable with women unless he was in control, and he was never in control with Brenda. She leaned against the counter, obviously distraught. "Oh, Charley, I'm just such a terrible person!"

"Why? Why do you say that?"

"It's Anthony Dean. I feel so bad about him. And, and...I just want to hurt the people who did it."

"Don't worry," he breathed, painfully aware of her proximity and the marginal coverage her towel provided. He was swelling beneath his own towel. "We're going to take care of that son of a bitch."

"I know you will," she said.

You will. She said 'you will.' She expected Charley to do the work personally. She was depending on him. He felt a thrill of pride that she thought so highly of him. But at the same time, he remembered the feeling of utter helplessness as Jared McCauley had choked him down. He could feel himself becoming flaccid beneath the towel.

"But I want him to feel the kind of pain I feel, Charley. I want him to feel the loss. Is that wrong? Am I a bad person?" She peered out at him from beneath her curls.

"No, of course not." He took her in his arms, becoming strong again in all the right places. This was it. This was it. She was going to feel it like never before. He'd give it to her so she never thought about Tony again. He reached for her towel. And she slipped his grasp, sliding out the door. She stopped and turned. "I count on you, Charley. I count on you too much."

Charley turned back toward the counter and leaned across the sink. He exhaled completely, fogging the mirror.

That night he lay on his back, wondering how to proceed. Brenda wanted more than just McCauley's death; that was obvious. She wanted vengeance. He understood vengeance, although he wouldn't have thought of including McCauley's wife and kid on his own. The more he considered it, though, the more it appealed to him. In the aftermath of his father's dire warning, Charley had had to curtail his activity in the world of extreme sex he loved. But Sal couldn't know everything and after several months of abstinence, Charley had linked up with a shadowy group that provided women and occasionally children for an exorbitant fee. The fee was particularly high because the people they provided were expendable;

throwaways, they called them. He found himself getting hard, just thinking about the possibilities.

The next morning Charley and Brenda went to the gym early. While he was doing chest presses, Brenda leaned down to him and whispered. "What are we going to do about McCauley, Charley?" He stared into her bountiful cleavage and almost forgot the question.

"I've got an idea," he said. "I'll be doing some checking."

Chapter 44

Gino Marlotta was eating lasagna at Carlucci's when the call came from Charley.

"Come to Bowie, Maryland and don't tell anyone about it," he was told.

"But I thought you were in Atlantic City, Charley," he said.

"Never mind about where I am, Gino. Just get down here and come prepared." Gino looked sadly down at his lasagna. Charley was in Maryland putting the meat to his brother's wife. God, what a can of worms. Life had been nice since Charley had gone to Atlantic City and Gino wasn't looking forward to going back to work, although working for Charley Corrarino did have its benefits. He was a part of the Family, even if it was an outlying, looked-down-upon segment of the Family. He'd been Charley's assistant for several years now and it had turned into a decent job. For the most part, he was just a bodyguard and he liked it that way. Nobody ever really messed with Charley and Charley almost never messed with anybody else either. Not anymore. That black boxer had broken him of the habit. Charley just worked the books, now. He stayed holed up in an office without windows most every day and when he called for Gino, it was to tell him to pick up lunch or something. It was a soft gig, Gino knew, and he liked it. Even in the evenings, Charley pretty much stayed home, drank wine and watched movies. But not always. Sometimes, Charley went out late and stayed all night. Sometimes, he didn't come back the next day. On those occasions, Charley told Gino to go home and wait for his call.

The first time Charley told Gino to take the night off, Gino complained.

"I shouldn't do that, Charley. I'm supposed to be watching over you. If something happens and I'm not around, Sal will have me skinned. You know that, Charley."

"No, Gino. He won't. He knows you'd never give up on me. He knows you'll always follow orders. Besides, nothing bad is going to happen. I just want to get a little nookie without you looking over my shoulder. You wouldn't want me looking over your shoulder, would you?"

"Um, no." In fact, Gino could think of nothing he would like less than having Charley looking over his shoulder while he was with a woman. Even if he hadn't heard the inevitable rumors about Charley's proclivities, Gino had seen the way Charley looked at women, heard his pathetic come-ons, then his muttered imprecations when they turned from him in disgust. He knew, despite what Charley said, that Sal would have him killed if something happened to Charley when he was not around. He would take the chance. He was not going to be around Charley on his late-night forays no matter what the price.

Gino took another bite of lasagna, chewed without gusto. He started to put the fork down and leave, then thought better of it. He took another bite and smiled. The staff all knew him and he knew them. There was no reason to make them feel bad and if Gino Marlotta left the table without finishing his food they would be devastated. He smiled again as he swallowed. *God damn Charley Corrarino.*

Gino leaned back expansively and saw his waiter smile. He remembered a fantasy book he'd once read about dragons and their riders. In the story, the dragons and riders were a team for life and if the rider died, the dragon would die as well. He was the dragon, Gino knew. He would live only so long as Charley lived. For one of the few times in his life, Gino wondered what it must be like to have a regular job, like people had who weren't connected. He'd always considered those people chumps but Gino wasn't so sure anymore. Maybe the chumps knew something he didn't. He was pretty sure they weren't killed if their bosses died. Gino sighed and finished his dinner. He left his customary big tip, waved to the waitress and chef and headed out to pack.

Chapter 45

Charley couldn't remember ever having been so excited. He could actually feel his ears burn. And even better, for the first time in years he was not afraid. The absence of fear made colors brighter, sounds more clear. And it made his appetites stronger, too, as his thickening manhood reminded him whenever he thought about his schedule for the upcoming night. By rights he should be terrified; after all, he was going to kill a man who'd already proven himself dangerous. But what happened before didn't matter, now, because he had a gun, two guns really, because Gino would be there. Gino was no brainchild, true, but he was street smart and pretty quick on his feet. He was also fearless, loyal and steady when things got rough. If anything at all went wrong, Charley knew Gino could fix it.

Charley'd had Gino arrange with a local mob affiliate to bug the McCauley's living room under the guise of checking for a gas leak, and the bug had proven invaluable. By listening to conversations, they'd learned that Jared's parents, who'd been visiting for the past week, were leaving on a red-eye flight tonight from Baltimore International. Jared was taking his parents to the airport and Charley intended to be waiting for him, wife and son in hand, when he returned.

Charley was absolutely confident McCauley would be no problem once he saw his son was threatened, and once McCauley gave in, the fun would start. Charley's only regret was the knowledge he would have to cut short the festivities well before daylight. He wished he could have another day. He always arranged to have two full days with the throwaways. But he couldn't count on being safe for a long period of time in a suburban house in an upscale neighborhood. Way too many things could happen, especially during daylight, so Charley could only count on four hours of uninterrupted bliss before they had to leave. Luckily, the McCauley's home bordered a wooded area, so he and Gino would have a relatively secure way in and out.

One potential problem came from his own family. His father hadn't given the go-ahead on hitting McCauley, but then again he hadn't specifically forbidden it, either. As long as there was no screw-up that got the police on his ass, Charley was convinced his father wouldn't be upset, and would actually be glad Charley had taken the initiative. The more Charley thought about it, the more certain he was that Sal would see his action as proof of his leadership skills. He might move Charley into management, instead of a glorified accountant. He was more concerned with Tony's response. Tony HAD specifically forbidden Charley to take action and though he technically had no role or power in the Family, he was probably capable of causing trouble. Not any real trouble, though. Tony had one arm, for Christ's sake. No, the only real threat was the police. As long as he and Gino took the necessary precautions, though, he had nothing to worry about. Necessary precautions and no witnesses.

Chapter 46

—·《●》·—

Jared left the house at 10 p.m. with his parents. Their flight was scheduled for a 1:15 a.m. departure from Dulles and although Jared had tried hard to get them to change their flight to a more reasonable hour and from a closer airport, Simon McCauley had refused. "We saved $300 on these tickets," he'd explained, and though he didn't say so, Jared and Misty knew his parents were on a tight budget. So Jared had acquiesced.

The previous week had been good for everyone concerned, Jared knew. His parents had completely changed the dynamic in the house. Within hours of their arrival, Misty and Josh were smiling and laughing as if the weight of the world had been lifted from their shoulders. Even Jared found himself chuckling occasionally. To his great relief, neither of his parents made any effort to have a discussion about the recent tragedy. They seemed content to simply spend time with Jared and his family. Their easy acceptance and gentle laughter helped Jared begin to let his mind wander, to start thinking about things other than a dead child. After a week with his parents Jared could almost imagine, though he couldn't yet see, a life that didn't end with his own bullet in his brain.

As much as he had expected it, Jared was still surprised when, the evening before they were supposed to leave, his father leaned toward him as they wandered around the back yard and said softly, "So, are we going to see you again, Jared?"

Shocked, Jared stared at his father open-mouthed. He couldn't respond.

Simon McCauley shook his head and smiled. "Do you think I don't know how you must feel? How bad you must want to make the pain stop?"

"Dad, I…" Jared stopped and looked away.

"I told you about what I did to the Japanese soldier, right?"

Jared nodded, looking down.

"But I don't think I told you how badly it affected me. For quite some time after that I considered taking my own life. The thing I had done was so cruel, so inhuman, I couldn't see a way I could continue to live."

"How did you get past it?" Jared whispered.

"I didn't. I just kept living and gradually the memory scarred over to the point it didn't hurt so bad."

Jared was quiet for a long time. Then he looked up. "I don't know, Dad. This thing…the boy… it's all too much for me. It's too much for a man to bear."

"I know, son. I hate that you're going through this but you've got to do just that, go through it. There are professional counselors out there who work with similar problems all the time. They can help you. And then there's this…God wouldn't give you more than you can handle."

Jared looked up quickly. He had never before heard his father refer to God, any god. "I'm not sure, Dad. It's better since you and Mom have been here, but, Jesus Christ, why couldn't I have gone more slowly, or looked more carefully, or pulled forward like Misty was trying to get me to do?"

"Jared, you could have done things differently; we could all do things differently. But the little boy died because he ran behind your car without giving you time to respond. It was an accident. An accident! Now, I'm going to ask you one more time, will we see you again?"

Jared had leaned his head back against a dogwood tree. "I don't know, Dad. I just can't give you an answer right now."

That conversation still ran through Jared's mind as he sat, holding his mother's hand at the airport departure gate. *How could he leave his parents, his wife and son so abruptly? But how could he continue to live with this pain?*

Chapter 47

Before making their move, Charley and Gino waited an hour after the upstairs light went off at the McCauley house. They'd learned from their listening device that Jared was planning to stay with his parents until they boarded the plane before returning home. They had at least until 2 a.m. before Jared returned; plenty of time to secure the woman and boy and prepare the stage for what Charley described as 'fun and games.' They made their way through the woods that stretched between a church parking lot and the McCauleys' back yard. There was no dog and the guy who'd planted the bug had not seen any indication of a security system.

Staying to the shadows, they came through the gate in the wooden fence. Charley took care not to let the latch snap when he closed it again. He hated the plastic gloves they were both wearing, but it was the price of doing business.

Charley worked the lock on the sliding glass door easily but the bitch had braced it with a piece of wood so he couldn't slide it open. Shit. He moved to a nearby window, attached a suction clamp and then cut out a circle around it. He reached through to release the window lock. He wanted Gino to be first into the house; this was a dangerous time, but Gino was the size of a small rhinoceros and would certainly break something on the way in. Charley slid through silently onto a couch, then stepped off into the living room, which was conveniently lit by a strong night light. He removed the wooden brace from the sliding glass door and let Gino in. He pointed down the hall to the master bedroom and mouthed the words, "Get the woman!"

Gino turned away, pistol in hand. Charley pulled his pistol as well and moved smoothly up the stairs. He took the steps without hesitation. The fake gas repairman had not been able to go upstairs but he'd said it looked like young boy stuff in the bedroom closest to the street. Charley expected to hear the muted sounds of a child's breathing as he stepped into the room. What he didn't expect was to have a screaming, nightgown-clad banshee hit him in the chest and drive him backwards through the door. The woman was as tall as Charley and rangy strong. She had her hands on his face and was trying to scratch his eyes out as she simultaneously tried to knee him in the groin. After the initial charge, Charley was able to fend her off, but she was moving too fast to get hold of her, so he couldn't bring her under control. And her screams, Christ Almighty, now she was starting to fight like she knew what she was doing. She poked stiff fingers toward his eyes and followed with strong kicks to his knees. If one of those hit he'd be crippled. Charley's back was to the railing and now he was in danger of falling over backwards. He could hear Gino coming on the run but he wasn't sure he could hold out that long. Then the woman stumbled as she advanced and her head went down slightly. Charley reacted instantly, grabbing her by the hair and pulling her toward him, then over the railing. She screamed non-stop until the instant she hit the floor, but she didn't sound afraid to Charley. All he could hear was hatred and rage.

Gino watched the entire sequence from halfway up the stairs. The woman went over head first and hit her face on the slate flooring. The sound of her neck snapping sounded like two pieces of bamboo hitting. She crumpled in a grotesque parody of the human body and didn't twitch.

Gino's heart trembled in his massive body. *Oh, shit…shit … shit.* He was devastated to see the woman die, but even more disappointed that it hadn't been Charley going over that banister. Gino thought she'd had him. God help him, despite the near-certainty of his own ugly death should something happen to Charley, Gino still wished Charley was the one piled up on the floor.

"Charley was breathing so hard he could barely speak. "Is that… is that her?"

"Yeah, I think. No one downstairs."

"Why's she…?"

"Dunno. Maybe sleeping with the kid."

They both looked at the bedroom from which the woman had emerged. A small Asian boy stood there, a tiny blanket clutched in his hand and a look of horror in his eyes. "Mommy? Where's my mommy?" Then he stood as tall as he could.

They all stood there, watching each other. Charley's eyes took on a feral glint. "Change of plans, Gino. You go back to the car and wait for me. I'll finish up here and meet you."

Gino looked at Charley. He was still breathing hard, but he'd lost the panicked, jittery look. Now he just looked mean… and hungry. The little boy had begun to tremble, his bravery melting away in the face of the predator before him. "If you hurt her I'm going to tell my daddy."

He started to cry. "Mommeeee!" he screamed and ran for the stairs, oblivious to the massive presence of Gino before him. Charley was on him before he made the first stair, grabbing him up just before Gino could get to him.

"Go back to the car, Gino. I'll be there shortly." Charley turned and headed toward the bedroom.

"No."

Charley reversed course and stared. He'd never heard Gino refuse before.

"We didn't come here to hurt women and children, Charley." Gino's voice rumbled and rasped. Charley realized the big man was crying.

"We came here to do what I tell you, Gino. Go and wait for me."

Gino began to walk up the stairs. He seemed to grow larger with each step. Suddenly Charley was unsure how this would play out.

"C'mon, Gino. Go back to the car. It didn't work out the way we planned. Without the wife, we're not going to have the leverage we need with McCauley so we need to get out of here."

"Then let's go."

"OK, I'm just going to take care of the kid. You go ahead now."

"No."

"You know we can't leave him to talk."

"Yes we can, he's a kid. He don't know nothin'."

"He knows our names."

Gino thought for a moment. Charley could see he was shaken. "I don't care," he said finally.

Charley was torn. His whole goddamn design was coming apart.

Did that dumb fuck Gino really think we were going to let the woman and boy go? Sure, Charley had described it like that, but only to make the plan sound more civilized. If they had succeeded in controlling the woman and boy and then killing McCauley, those two would still have seen and heard way too much. Shit. Nothing had worked right but that didn't mean it was over. We can still hit McCauley; just not tonight, not after this mess. And then there is the kid. He could have served a useful purpose. But no. Gino had to fuck it up. All right, Gino. You had to get in the way. Now enjoy it.

Charley shifted his left hand into the boy's hair, bent his head back, pulled a knife from his pocket and slit the boy's throat before Gino could even make a sound. Charley tossed the still struggling body over the railing and onto the floor near his mother.

Gino gave a strangled cry and ran downstairs to kneel next to the boy. The small body twitched, made a choking sound and became still. Gino screamed again and pulled his pistol, pointing it up at Charley. His eyes were wild and for a moment Charley thought he was a dead man. He tried to talk, tried to say "Gino, please." But nothing came out of his mouth. He held up his hands in mute supplication.

Finally, Charley found his voice. "OK," he said. "OK." His brain started to work again in fits and spurts. Maybe they should stay, just kill McCauley when he walked through the door. It would be a lot cleaner that way. One and done. But no, it wouldn't work. His nerves were shot and Gino was loony tunes. He had to get Gino out of there. Everything had turned to shit and he couldn't trust Gino to keep it together and wait for Jared to return. And Charley was not about to wait for him alone. They had to get out. He could take care of McCauley later on.

Charley moved slowly down the stairs. Gino was pulling at the boy, trying to wake him up, totally distraught. Charley walked slowly past him, toward the back door. "Gino, Gino, it's time to go." He wasn't sure what Gino might do. The big man still had a gun in his hand. Charley stopped at the door.

"Gino." Finally, Gino laid the boy gently back to the floor, got to his feet and walked toward the back door, his back bowed. He walked past Charley and out the door.

Chapter 48

Jared was late getting back from the airport, but he was curiously happy. His father was a good guy and his mother, well, she'd always been the sun around which the rest of the family rotated. Maybe things would work out. Maybe he could recover.

Jared knew the instant he opened the door from the garage that no one would ever recover. The snaky smell of blood slathered the house and there was a sense of stillness that crushed his heart. He took a few running steps through the kitchen but saw the bodies and came to a stop. He fell to his knees 10 feet from them and crawled slowly forward. He cradled his son, shocked beyond feeling when he saw the slashed throat. He put his face into Misty's hair, reaching around, trying to pull them both to him. He stayed there almost an hour, but when he got up he was no longer crying.

Chapter 49

—·◦(●)◦·—

Gino stood under the trees outside Tony's house, standing guard. Tony's house. Tony's wife. In there laughing and scratching with Charley, celebrating the murders of a woman and a baby.

"Nothing's going to happen tonight," Charley had said, after they'd left the carnage. "Just watch over the house 'til daylight and go on back home. You'll get good money for this, Gino."

Gino didn't think so. Didn't think he'd get any money. Didn't think Charley would be around to pay him. Didn't think the silent wraith moving toward the house was likely to be forgiving. Gino thought about his job, his responsibility, his life and decided that after this night's work not one of them was worth much, and he didn't care. He moved further back into the streetlight shadows, leaving the phantom to approach the house undeterred.

As Jared McCauley slipped through the door to Tony's house, Gino began walking down the street. Going away, from the house, from Charley, from the life. Suddenly, as though surprised, he stopped and vomited, again and again until there was nothing left to expunge. Unsurprisingly, it didn't make him feel any better.

Chapter 50

Charley was as close to heaven as he ever expected to get. Brenda was as good as her word. She was working him over in ways he'd only dreamed about. Unbelievable to think that Tony was getting this for free all these years and was willing to throw it away. Charley was working up to his third orgasm and had become progressively more physical. He had entered her and had his hands around her throat, steadily increasing the pressure. Brenda had taken part in rough sex before meeting Tony but she was a little out of practice, and the decreasing airflow was making her frantic, causing her to slam and kick and try to fight Charley off. Her efforts only served to excite him further, though and he tightened his grip. He was just beginning his climax when a soft voice from behind said to him, "Go ahead, Charley. You need to finish it."

Charley would not have dreamed it possible for a stiff dick to go limp so fast. He released his hold on Brenda's neck and started to turn.

"Don't turn around and don't let her go. If you want to live, you need to kill her."

By now Brenda was beginning to recover, gasping and choking. Charley put his hands around her throat again.

"I can't..." he said.

"Why not?" the voice asked. "You killed my wife and son. What's the difference?"

"I didn't mean... it was a mistake. Gino... Gino did it."

"I've been here for a while Charley. I heard you talking with this slut about what happened. It was foreplay for you. But you told her you killed me, too, didn't you? Now, stop letting her flop around like that, Charley. If you don't kill her right now I'm going to shoot you in your lower spine… first. Now, do you want to live, or don't you?"

Brenda was strong and motivated, but she was already weakened and Charley was between her legs. Once he tried to let her breathe a little but he felt the gun barrel on his tailbone and he squeezed with all his strength. Brenda's eyes rolled back in her head and her bowels voided.

"Ughh, ughh," Charley tried to move away, but still the gun barrel pushed him back.

"Messy, huh?"

"Now, pick up the phone, Charley, and call your father."

"What? What?"

"Call your father. Hurry up. I want to talk with him."

Charley reached over to the phone and dialed the number. He was sobbing when his father answered the phone.

"Who is this?"

"Dad, I…"

"Charley? Charley?"

Jared took the phone. "Mr. Corrarino, this is Jared McCauley. You remember, the man who killed your grandson"

"What are you doing with Charley? Charley?"

"Do you remember me, Mr. Corrarino?"

"I remember you, you son of a bitch and if you hurt my son nothing will save you."

"We're way past that, as you well know. Way past it."

"What do you mean? Let me talk to my son. Charley!"

"Are you telling me you don't know what Charley's been doing? You want me to believe you didn't send him?"

Sal hesitated. *What had Charley done? Oh, my God, what has Charley done?* "Listen, you. I don't know what the fuck you're talking about. You'd better explain it to me now."

"I'll do better than that, Mr. Corrarino. I'll let Charley explain it to you. Tell him what you did.

"He's having a little trouble, Mr. Corrarino, lying as he is in the piss and shit of his brother's wife. And of course, her body. Charley killed her a few minutes ago. Hey! Charley. Tell your father about your night. Tell him now or I'm going to shoot your nuts off."

"Dad, Dad! I'm sorry. It wasn't me. Gino got carried away. This guy's wife and kid got killed. Now he's here and he made me kill Brenda and…"

"Give me the phone, Charley. Now lie back down on your belly, hands behind your back. Mr. Corrarino, are you still there? You need to listen carefully. I told Charley I'd let him live if he killed Tony's wife but he's not going to be nearly as pleased with the deal as he thinks right now. I'm leaving soon. I'll call you and let you know where to find me. You got that? I hope you will come yourself, but I doubt you have the balls. And speaking of balls…"

He covered the .45 with a pillow and shot Charley in the scrotum. Charley screamed and rolled over, pulling himself into a ball, holding himself with both hands. Then, aiming carefully between Charley's extended arms, he shot Charley low in the gut. Charley vomited blood, his eyes bulging.

"Mr. Corrarino? Still there? Don't worry, Charley's still alive, just like I promised. There was a long pause. "Fuck it. I lied." Jared shot Charley through his open mouth.

"See you soon, Mr. Corrarino."

Chapter 51

Shane sat in his office staring at the wall. He could hear the office staff outside, the comings and goings of his deputies, but he couldn't quite bring himself to talk to anyone. He should have listened to Lacy. She'd told him to stay home today.

"How can you hope to be worth anything today?" she'd asked him. "You haven't gotten over your father yet and now this thing with Jared and Misty... Shane, please take a few days off."

"I can't, babe. He'll come here. Jared will come home. I have to be there."

"How do you know he'll come? Every cop in the country is looking for him. You've told me many times before how hard it is for someone to stay hidden when all of law enforcement is looking for them. And now it sounds like the mafia is looking, too. Stay home, Shane. Let me take care of you."

Shane looked in Lacy's eyes for a long time. "Jared is my best friend. Like a brother. Even after all those years when he wouldn't see me. He's still my closest friend. I always believed, we all believed, that he could do anything. Then everything turned bad for him. But he was doing better; he was happy again. Then he ran over the boy and now, to lose Misty and Josh. This shouldn't be happening, to Jared of all people." He swallowed twice and looked away. He wiped his eyes across a sleeve.

"But he won't come to you, Shane. You are the Sheriff. You are the law."

"No, but he'll let me know; he'll contact me somehow and I have to be at the office, so I can control things."

Lacy looked up at her husband for a long time. He was such an open book to her; such a solid, honest man. But not today, today there was something else behind his eyes, some shimmering tension in his bearing.

"You don't just want to control things," she said. "You are going to try to protect him. Aren't you?" She put her hands on his chest and leaned against him, speaking into his shirt. "You know it's gone too far, don't you? There's nothing you can do. And you are an officer of the law, Shane. You are responsible for apprehending criminals, not helping them get loose."

"Jared is not a criminal, Lace."

Lacy's eyes flashed. "He's killed at least two people, babe. How many does it take?"

Shane turned away then and walked over to the sink. He drew himself a glass of water, then turned to look at his wife.

"What if it were you, Lace? What if your world turned upside down like Jared's and you were on the run? Do you think I'd let the law keep me from helping you? Do I seem like that kind of man? Jared is my brother. I'll do anything for him. Do you understand? Anything." He relaxed a bit, drank some more water. "Realistically, there's probably going to be nothing I can do. He may not even make it here, but if he does, and if there is any way at all, I'm going to do it."

"You could lose your job; you could go to jail."

"I'm not an idiot, Lace. I'll consider everything and I'll be careful. But if I have a chance to help Jared McCauley, I'm going to do it."

The phone rang at his desk, startling Shane back into the present. "Sheriff?" It was the receptionist. "Chester Wewa is on the phone for you."

"Tell him I'll call him later, please."

"Um, sir? Chester said to tell you it was important…he never says that, sir."

"OK, put him through. Chester? What's up?"

"Shane, I thought you'd like to know… an old friend showed up yesterday."

"I'm busy, Chester. Can we talk about this later?"

Chester went on as though he hadn't spoken. "This friend, he didn't have a lot of time to spare so he asked me to give you his best."

"Well I was around yesterday. Why didn't he just call me? Why didn't he…?" Shane's heart began to tremble. "Chester, who was the friend?"

Again, Chester ignored him. "I lent him a horse and two mules and sent him up to Dry Meadow. We haven't pulled the gear from that camp yet and it sounded like just the kind of place this friend was looking for. In fact, he was adamant about that location."

"Jesus, Chester, was it…?"

"He said to tell you that he was sorry, not being able to see you in person but that you would understand. He wanted you to know he was thinking of you, but that you should stay away from him and Dry Meadow."

"Shit, I've got to go get…"

Chester overrode him. "He was adamant about it, Shane. He said that under no circumstances should anyone come near him. It would be dangerous."

"He would never hurt me."

"I don't think he was talking about himself. I think he's expecting company. He took a rifle and a shotgun, too."

"Jesus, do you suppose he told the m…, er, those people where to find him?"

"Lays out like that, doesn't it?"

Chester, what do the terms 'aiding and abetting' mean to you?"

"Not nearly as much as the term 'friendship.'"

Shane was quiet for a long time. "So, it sounds like we had a break-in."

"Not to my knowledge, but then I don't always check on the stock or the equipment as often as I should. I probably won't count horses or inventory gear for quite a while."

"Yeah. I see what you mean. Could be a week." Shane was quiet for a long time. Chester, as was his habit, said nothing. Finally, Shane sat up straight in the chair, looked skyward and shook his head slightly. "Chester, I know we're shorthanded, so I think I will agree to your request that I head into the mountains and take down the Dry Meadow camp. It's too late to leave today, so could you set up a string for tomorrow morning for me? Saddle horse and three mules. I'll need one of the big trailers. Gear and food for five days."

"Already done."

"What do you mean already done?"

"I mean the tack is loaded in the trailer, panniers are full and loaded in the trailer, horses are cut out and resting in the small corral. What did you think I meant?"

"How long have you…?" Shane closed his eyes. "You've known since yesterday. You've been delaying telling me so he could make it up to the high country and get set before anyone could catch up."

"Don't know what you mean."

"But how could you know that I would go up?"

"I couldn't, but I was pretty sure. Then again, if you had refused to go, I would have. By the way, Shane, what does aiding and abetting mean to you?"

"I must have missed that class at the academy. I've got to go set up my vacation time and talk with Lacy. See you in the morning."

Chapter 52

Jared put hobbles on his saddle horse and turned it loose into Dry Meadow to join the two mules he'd already hobbled. The name was misleading at best; there were only two or three truly dry places in Dry Meadow and Shane's large canvas wall tent was sitting on one of them. Most of the meadow was covered by sodden marsh grass and there were few visual clues to identify where the ground was simply wet and where it was a mudhole waiting to devour unsuspecting boots. Although the meadow looked level, it was covered in small ridges and ditches, most of which were hidden by the grass and impossible to see until they were stepped in or on. That was good, Jared thought. Anyone coming into the meadow would find it difficult to move without making a lot of noise; and that's if they weren't already given away by the ever-suspicious pack stock. Of course, any attacker with half a brain would approach the tent through the woods which bordered the tent on three sides. He'd have to set up a few noisemakers in those woods. Too bad he didn't have any claymores or det cord.

Even as he went through the motions of setting up his camp and making preparations for a fight, Jared felt like he was moving in slow motion. He was unable to concentrate and so forgetful he had to re-do every task at least once. He'd barely slept since leaving Bowie. Memories of Misty and Josh swirled through his brain unbidden as he laid out his sleeping bag, filled the lanterns, started a fire in the woodstove. All the times he had visited Misty's house while they were in high school; the various places he'd sneaked kisses, and sometimes a little more; their utter happiness during their camping trip after Basic School. The excitement they'd shared during their trip to Korea to adopt Josh. But the pleasant memories couldn't hold back the carnage of two days earlier.

His mind flashed repeatedly to the picture of Misty and Josh lying on the cold stone floor in a pool of Josh's blood. After the hour he'd spent crying over their bodies, Jared had reverted to a cold, emotionless automaton. Somehow, he'd separated himself from reality and functioned as though he were cleaning a kitchen after dinner. He'd cleaned his wife and son carefully, wiped up the blood, changed Josh's clothes and put all their bloody things in the washer. He'd carried them to the master bedroom and laid their clean bodies out together on the bed he'd shared with Misty, folding her dead arms around her son. He tied a blue kerchief around poor Josh's ruined throat. He covered them both with a sheet and wrote a note; "Sal Corrarino did this." He didn't know how well the cops could put things together but it didn't really matter. He was going to settle things up as well as he could and then he just wanted it all to end. End.

By the time he arrived at Tony's house Jared's brain was on fire, his thirst for revenge palpable. But as he'd stood quietly outside the bedroom and listened to Charley and Brenda rutting in the bed, whispering details about the murder of his wife and son as though they were flirtatious comments, his disgust and loathing turned his hatred into something cold and implacable. He'd stood there until the time was right and then moved in. He felt no remorse for the things he'd done to Brenda and Charley, though the manner of their deaths was something he could never have imagined only a few weeks earlier. Now, he just didn't care. And if his actions came back to haunt him, it wouldn't be for long.

After killing Charley, Jared wrote a note. "Partial payment for my wife and son. Jared McCauley." He placed it between Brenda's toes, one of the few places on the bed that was not blood spattered. As he drove out of the neighborhood, Jared noticed a large man walking purposefully down the street toward town. He looked vaguely familiar but Jared couldn't place him. He continued on to the Baltimore Airport. He rented a car using Charley's credit card and headed for Idaho. He didn't think they'd figure out Charley's credit card was missing until he was way out of the area. He waited until reaching Boise to call Tony's house and tell Corrarino where to find him. As he expected, the phone was answered by someone who knew right where Sal was and in minutes he was connected.

"Yeah?" Jared would have recognized the voice anywhere.

"Corrarino, it's me again. The man who killed your son and daughter-in-law and oh, yeah, your grandson, too."

"You are a dead man."

"I thought you were smarter than empty threats, Sal."

"You might think you are ready for death, but I promise you you're not ready for the kind of death I'm going to arrange."

"Enough of your bullshit, Sal. I'm going to be in the Frank Church River of No Return Wilderness at Dry Meadow, just north of the Chamberlain Basin. I'm sure you can find it on a map. I hope you can come yourself, Sal, if you're not too old and decrepit, but I'll look forward to meeting whoever you send.

"But one thing, Sal. Try not to be too long. Sooner or later the cops will figure out where I am and then you'll lose your chance at me."

"I can get at you wherever you are, cops or no cops."

"You really are a blowhard, aren't you Sal? Now I see where Charley got it. Remember, Dry Meadow, just north of the Chamberlain Basin in the River of No Return Wilderness."

"I'll cut your liver out!" Sal screamed into the phone, but he was already talking to a dial tone.

Chapter 53

—·((•))·—

Tony had been half asleep in his apartment when the phone rang, but his father's hysterical voice had wakened him rapidly. Someone had attacked Brenda and Charley. Sal had men on the way but they had to come from Virginia so Tony could get there sooner. Take a gun, his father said. Tony leaped into action, even as his mind struggled with the decided lack of information his father had provided. How had the old man known what was happening? Who was involved? But, OK, time for action now and questions later. Tony grabbed the little Walther PPK .380 pistol from his nightstand and raced over to the house he'd shared with Brenda and Anthony Dean. He moved carefully through the front door and padded quietly around the first floor.

Just outside his old bedroom the stench of blood and urine and shit gave Tony an idea of what to expect. He flipped on the light and saw the butchery, then turned it off again. The split second of light had frozen the image on his brain. He checked out the rest of the house carefully, then sat down on the front porch and watched daylight ooze through the morning haze.

This didn't make sense. Who would have done this? One of his father's enemies? Someone Charley had treated badly? But what could Charley, or Brenda for that matter, have done to anyone to deserve this? If anyone had reason to kill them it was me, as I'm sure the police will make clear. Wait. No. Could this have anything to do with Jared McCauley? No. Jared is overcome by grief. If he hurts anyone it will be himself. Unless. No. His father would never allow retribution against women or children. But Charley... and Brenda was vicious. If she had enticed him...

****

Tony was still sitting on the front porch watching dawn break when his father's men arrived. After a brief moment of uncertainty when he thought they might shoot him, they became business-like. They led Tony into the house and took his pistol from him. They looked into the bedroom and then made a phone call. The discussion centered around what to do with Tony. Finally, they decided it was too dangerous to take him away from the house. Too many neighbors could have seen him; it was better to have him make the call to the police and then wait for them. One of Sal's responders took all three of their guns and left to dispose of them; no sense giving the cops something else to worry about. He returned just before the first police cars arrived.

****

The next two days were a blur for Tony. He'd been right in expecting the police to consider him suspect number one for the deaths of Charley and Brenda, but the note Jared had left between Brenda's toes had sent investigators to the McCauley house right away and their discovery of Misty and Josh had thrown everything into chaos. For 24 hours, the cops hadn't known what to think. Their initial suspicion of him was ameliorated by Tony's willingness to answer every question…and by his refusal to accept the help of a lawyer his father had dispatched to help.

Finally, things began to fall together in the investigation. Blood found on Charley's clothes was identified as Josh's. Skin under Misty's fingernails was identified as Charley's. And a handwriting expert confirmed the notes found in both sites belonged to Jared. The chief detective had apologized to Tony and released him, saying, "We'll find McCauley, Mr. Corrarino. Don't worry."

****

Tony sat on the couch in his living room. People were walking all around him. Most had tried to engage him at some point but, though he'd been polite, he simply wasn't interested in conversation or being made to feel better or, in his father's case, assured of vengeance. He'd been so unresponsive that people gradually began to ignore him, to conduct conversations in the same room as though he weren't there. In many ways, it didn't seem like his house. The police crime scene tape had been removed that morning and the cleaners had left just an hour before. The door to Brenda's bedroom remained closed though, and he had no intention of going in it.

He'd been out of the house for weeks since Anthony Dean was killed and any feelings remaining for Brenda had been incinerated in the blistering conversations they'd had after the tragedy. If, as now seemed to be the case, Brenda had used her sexual favors to persuade Charley to kill Misty and Josh, then he couldn't bring himself to care what had happened to either of them. He missed Anthony Dean, but he'd begun to come to grips with that loss, terrible as it had been. The murder of Misty and her son, at the hands of his own brother, was simply too horrible to contemplate. What could Charley and Brenda possibly have been thinking? The uneasy, ill-defined sense of wrongness he'd felt whenever he was around Charley seemed all too concrete now. And the vicious hatred emanating from Brenda should have set off warning bells all around. But Tony had wanted nothing more than to get away, to escape the devastation of his marriage and the loss of his son. So he'd taken the apartment not far away and settled into a muddled obscurity.

This living room was where he'd read books to Anthony. He and the boy had wrestled on the Persian rug at his feet. One-armed men are not great wrestlers and the boy had quickly learned to attack Tony's left side. Tony always took his prosthetic hand off to wrestle, but he still had enough arm left below the elbow to use it as a hook, with which he could grab the boy and bring him in, where he would squeeze until Anthony would giggle breathlessly and squeak, "No squishing! No squishing!"

Tony heard the phone and was dimly aware of a conversation going on, but it wasn't until his father's maniacal scream about livers that Tony actually began to pay attention. It was the first time he'd ever heard Sal scream and the first time he'd ever heard the word 'liver' cross his lips. There'd always been rumors of Sal's flair for dramatic punishment, but only rarely were they given voice near his sons.

Chapter 54

Sal hung up the phone and stood there, his chest heaving and eyes flashing. Two of his bodyguards stood close by, waiting for orders, unwilling to approach him without direction. Tony remained on the couch, watching but saying nothing. His father's outburst, uncharacteristic as it had been, had awakened his interest. The numbness of his mind and body was receding. For the first time since his son died, Tony wanted to know what was going on. He waited, wondering what to expect. Finally, Sal seemed to relax slightly. His shoulders squared and he turned to the closest bodyguard. "Write this down. Dry Meadow. Chamberlain Basin. River of No Return Wilderness in Idaho. Get me Vito back in New York. He needs to make some calls for me."

The man who'd written down the information moved quickly out of sight, presumably to make the phone call. The other one moved unobtrusively to the side, to lean against the wall in the deceptively coiled stance of the professional bodyguard.

"What's going on, Dad?" Tony stood up from the couch and moved toward his father.

Sal looked up, startled. "What? Oh, Tony. Nothing. Nothing much going on."

"Dad." Tony put his hand on his father's shoulder. "I was listening. You were talking with Jared McCauley?"

Sal looked directly into his son's eyes. "Yes. I just had the last conversation that son of a bitch will ever have."

"What was he supposed to do, Dad?" Sal turned and began to walk away. Tony reached out to grab his arm. "What was Jared supposed to do?" Sal turned faster than Tony would have believed possible, breaking Tony's grip and grabbing him by the shirt front.

"He was supposed to look where he was driving, so he didn't kill my grandson, your son. YOUR SON, GODAMMIT! YOUR SON! He's a dead man for that alone. But now he's killed two more of us and not by accident this time. Oh, no. Not by accident at all. And he's bragging about it. Throwing it in my face. But not for long! Oh, no. He's going to pay and keep on paying."

"Dad. Dad! You know what Charley did, right? You know he killed Misty and Josh. You know what Charley was, right? And Brenda? In some ways she was worse. Dad? You know that, right?"

Sal's face went through multiple expressions, from grief, to sadness to guilt, but when it stopped, the only expression recognizable to Tony was rage, a heartless, all-consuming rage. His face was splotchy, contorted and when he spoke, spittle sprayed across Tony's face.

"Yeah, I know it all. I know everything. I know Charley was a Corrarino! And so was Brenda! And so was Anthony Dean. I know those things, even if you've forgotten. You go back now to your couch, Tony. You sit and twiddle your thumbs or whatever the hell you've been doing all these years while the rest of us have been keeping our family on top of the heap! You never wanted to be a part of us. You never wanted to get your hands dirty. Well, you just relax and let the rest of us do the job that should be yours to do. You should be the one to hunt him down and skin him alive. You should be out of your mind with anger. But no. You sit back on the couch and watch the world go by, pretending it doesn't apply to you. And you make excuses for the man who killed your wife and child. Who killed your brother. Well, I got news for you, Tony. It doesn't apply to you, not any more. Nothing this family does applies to you anymore. Get out of here! Go somewhere else and change your name! You are not a Corrarino. You are not my…"

"SAL!" Maria came into the room quickly. She walked up to Sal and looked him square in the eyes. She was an inch shorter than Sal, but right then she looked several inches taller. "You be quiet right now. You have no right to speak to your son that way. YOUR SON, DO YOU HEAR ME? You have no right."

She took a deep breath and put her right hand on his chest. "Enough, Sal. Enough."

She turned from her husband and went to her son. "I'm sorry for this, Tony. Your father is upset. He didn't mean it."

Tony looked closely at his mother. She was strong and regal and gave nothing away, but how hard this whole thing must be for her. He took her hands and spoke.

"He meant it, Mom. You know it as well as I do. He meant it, and he was right. From his perspective, he was right." He turned to look directly at his father, who appeared to regret nothing he'd said.

"You're a mobster, a criminal and from a mobster's point of view you need vengeance. There can be no forgiveness. But you seem to have forgiven Brenda, who went to bed with her husband's brother and you have evidently forgiven Charley, who murdered a fine woman and her five-year-old son! You are a forgiving kind of guy, aren't you, Dad? There's only one person who can never be forgiven for this entire mess… YOU, Dad! You made all this happen. You made Charley into a career criminal. He never wanted anything except your approval. You rewarded his meanness and toughness until he thought those were the only important things. And when Jared McCauley accidentally, ACCIDENTALLY killed Anthony Dean you made it clear he was going to die, too.

Charley knew what you wanted and even though you probably didn't give the order, Charley knew you wanted it done. You made him into a monster, Dad, and then you sent him out to kill. Oh, you talk about the family but we never had a family. We had a mother, and a mobster who lived with us. I'll keep the name, Dad, because someone has to live in a way that doesn't bring shame to the name, but you are right about the family, Dad. It no longer applies to me. And I won't be leaving. You will. This is my house, bought with my money and no help from you. Get out of my house, now. Go back to your mob family, the only real one you've ever had. I want you gone."

Sal stood there, his eyes having gone wide with the effrontery of his son's outburst, then narrowing as the bitter assault continued. Tony was unsure if his father would attack him and he rolled forward onto the balls of his feet in anticipation. The moment stretched; the entire house went silent as guests and others overheard the heated exchange. Everyone but Maria had moved out of sight to other rooms; only she, the bodyguard, Tony and Sal were there.

Finally, Maria shook her head as if awaking from a bad dream. "You're right, Tony. It's time for us to go. Get our coats," she said over her shoulder to the bodyguard, then she took Sal's arm, pivoted him in place and marched him out the front door. Sal moved mechanically, as though some synapse was failing to fire. A few seconds later, both bodyguards came on the run, carrying two extra coats. Shortly afterwards the remaining guests trooped through the door. One or two tried to talk with him but Tony ignored them and soon they were gone.

Suddenly, Maria came back and put her arms around him. "I'm sorry, Tony. I'm so sorry for all of this. I don't know how this is all going to work out with your father, but I promise you this, you are not going to divorce yourself from me. I am your mother, and from now until forever you are my son. Your father can't change that and neither can you."

Tony smiled and patted her shoulder. "OK, Mom. OK."

She gave him a quick kiss on the cheek and disappeared through the door.

Tony sat back down on the couch, his father's words ringing in his head. *He's right, of course. I should be raging right now. But Anthony Dean was an accident and God help me, I would trade Charley and Brenda in an instant, if I could bring Misty and Josh back.*

Tony put his feet up on the couch and stared at the ceiling for more than an hour. Then he took a deep breath and sat up straight. He stood up and went into his den, where he pulled out his US Road Atlas and a state map of Idaho.

Chapter 55

After Carlo died, it became increasingly important to Trey to find out who his employers were. Without Carlo's experienced and cagey view of the world Trey felt far more vulnerable than before. He needed intelligence. He needed to figure out who his friends were, in case they someday became enemies.

And over the years, Trey did figure it out. Not by a sudden unmasking of identities, but by gradual answers to small questions. He always did careful research on the people he was contracted to kill. Before he took any action Trey knew everything possible about his intended target, primarily from legal sources: newspaper stories, court records, school transcripts, magazine articles, public police records. On occasion, he would pay for phone, bank, credit card and doctors' reports. Usually, those efforts let him develop a short list of people who might wish the target ill. Occasionally, the target himself provided good information. Twice he'd had to kidnap his targets before killing them. Both times, the men pleaded for their lives, offered money, explained that Sal Corrarino had it wrong. It wasn't them that stole, or ratted. They would never cross Sal. There must be some mistake. Two of his other hits were the subjects of posthumous newspaper articles that tied the dead men to the New York mafia, specifically to the Corrarino family.

Trey thought the articles were excellent, well-researched and written. The writer used his facts to develop theories, and, at least as far as the killings were concerned, he was unerringly accurate. It bothered Trey to know someone could reconstruct his actions so completely. Knowing it was possible made Trey even more careful. After reading those stories Trey began using makeup and disguises. He made a practice of reading the writer's work from that point forward and was never disappointed. The writer, a man named Philip Malom, was remarkably thorough.

Trey came to deeply admire the kind of careful exploration and ability to fill in the gaps that Malom exhibited in the development of his articles. In some ways, Trey felt he and Malom were partners; with Trey leading the way, doing the initial investigation and Malom coming along behind, putting the pieces together into a cohesive whole. It was not lost on Trey that Malom's cohesive whole could contribute to his own identification and capture, but he couldn't help but admire the man's work. It troubled Trey a great deal when the contract came to kill him.

Trey kidnapped Malom as he left the newspaper late one night and drove to Topanga Canyon, where he knocked him unconscious and sent his car careening off a cliff. That was the first time Trey had admired one of his targets. Up to then they had all been slimy, in one way or another, but the newspaperman was something else entirely. Malom's death was a watershed event in Trey's life and not a good one. Until that point, he'd worked hard to see his contracts through the lens that Carlo had initially provided: "These are culls. You'll be doing society a favor."

It was no longer possible to see them in that light. Malom was a good man, a contributor to society, a husband, a father. His killing meant that Trey was nothing more than a murderer, a distinction he'd hitherto worked hard to avoid. Each subsequent contract had been progressively more difficult to justify and harder to fulfill.

The classified ads he read the day after he and Tri had talked so optimistically about their sister had another notice for him but he'd already made the decision to quit. Thanks to Carlo's plan, all he really had to do was ignore the ad, don't make the phone call. Sooner or later they would give up on him and find someone else. But what the hell, they'd been good to him. The least he could do was let them know he was out of the business.

That night he drove to Glendale and used a pay phone at an all-night market.

"Alonzo," he said to the voice that answered.

"Ready?" asking if he was prepared to copy the information.

"No. I'm retiring."

Hesitation. "Not a good time for that. This one's major. Major, major."

So the money would be big, but Trey didn't need money. He needed out.

"Sorry, I'm done."

"Wait a minute, wait a minute." A note of panic filled the man's voice. What is with this contract? "We'll double the usual fee."

Holy shit! That's $1 million, without even quibbling. They must want this guy really bad. Or it must be really difficult.

"OK, I'll listen. No guarantees." He listened halfheartedly until he heard the name. From that point forward he took careful notes. Halfway through the conversation Trey began to shake his head softly from side to side. He was still shaking his head when he said, "I'll do it," into the phone. He stood by the phone booth for a long time after he hung up, his shoulders hunched. "Jesus Christ," he murmured. Jesus Fucking Christ."

Chapter 56

Trey sat on a decaying spruce log just inside the woods at the southern end of Dry Meadow. From his location, he could watch the tent, as well as the trail approaching it, and the entire length of meadow. Jared's horse and two mules grazed contentedly, following each other in the easy herd character of domestic livestock. He'd been there an hour, and had watched Jared emerge from the tent several times to set up perimeter booby traps, or at least a warning system. Trey was surprised at the change in Jared. He seemed heavier than during his days in Vietnam. Trey remembered him as a lithe, muscular man, possessed of a fine mind and indomitable will. Today's Jared looked soft, but not egregiously so, more like he was tired, sluggish. It was understandable, based on what Trey had heard from his New York contact and on occasional national news reports as he traveled to Idaho. If he had lost his wife and child and then killed the people responsible and successfully evaded the law two-thirds of the way across country, Jared had a right to be tired.

None of it made any sense to Trey. Killing women and children was not the mob way, but it sounded like the man Jared killed was Sal Corrarino's second son and the woman his first son's wife. He'd had little time to do the sort of in-depth research typical of his work. He'd left two days after receiving the mob phone call and he had far too little information to develop a working theory. It didn't keep him from trying, though. People were endlessly fascinating for Trey, plus it gave him something to do while he waited. It also kept his mind off the fact he was doing the stupidest thing he'd ever done in his entire life, putting himself and all he'd worked for, as well as his two sisters, at terrible risk… for a man he hadn't seen in 16 years.

Ah, but what a man he was. Trey remembered when the lieutenant had first taken over the platoon. Trey had only been there for two weeks, and though the Marines always took care of their corpsmen, he was still a newbie, with no close ties to anyone. He and the lieutenant had hit it off right away. Trey was a bit of a wise ass, in that gentle, not quite respectful way some bright enlisted men adopt around young officers. Their mannerisms are often offensive to the least confident officers, but self-confidence was never lacking in Jared McCauley and he recognized in his new corpsman a kindred spirit. Probably because he never thought he'd have to order Trey into battle, 2nd Lieutenant McCauley treated the "Doc" more like a little brother than an enlisted man in his command. Hospitalman 3rd Class Trey Cannon, who desperately missed his own father, adopted Jared in his place.

Trey remembered when the lieutenant had shit all over that asshole platoon sergeant, what the hell was his name? And then stared down that big-ass black panther, Amos. Made him his radio man and foxhole buddy. Shit. Should have been me. Lots of platoon commanders buddied up with their corpsmen. I would have gladly dug the foxholes and put up our tent. He should have chosen me. Shit. Amos was a good man, though. And tough. Jesus. Choosing him was a great move on the lieutenant's part. Let the air out of the black panthers in a hurry. Got everybody moving in the same direction. It was a great political move. Still should have been me. Maybe if it had been me he would have agreed to see me when I came all the way to Idaho that time. Probably not, though. He wasn't seeing anyone. What the hell am I going to do now?

He'd been as careful as possible. He'd chartered a plane from Boise instead of nearby Grangeville, hoping to make it more difficult to follow his tracks. The plane had dropped him into the US Forest Service airstrip in the Chamberlain Basin. Although motorized vehicles, including airplanes, were usually forbidden in established wildernesses, this strip had been grandfathered in when the River of No Return Wilderness was established. It was either that or have no wilderness designation at all.

Upon landing Trey had grabbed his gear and moved quickly away from the aircraft. He didn't want any Forest Service personnel to be able to recall his face or describe him in any meaningful way. He shouldered his pack and hiked north along the two-blaze trail. Five hours later, having covered 12 miles, he settled in to watch his old platoon commander, the man he'd been hired to kill.

Chapter 57

Smokey Stover rocked in the saddle and watched the horses and mules ahead of him. He and Shane had crested the hills above Trout Creek and were following Three Blaze Trail toward Dry Meadow. They'd left Grangeville early but would still be lucky to make it to Dry Meadow before sundown. They'd stopped only once on the way up from the Whitewater Trailhead, just long enough to haze a pissed-off old rattler who hadn't been impressed enough by the approach of a 700-pound saddle horse to move off the trail.

Smokey watched Shane roll smoothly ahead with the gait of his horse. Even now Smokey occasionally felt jealous of Shane, but any more it was quickly extinguished by a feeling of thankfulness. Shane had earned his respect years before in the parking lot of the River House and his eternal gratitude years later with a job and increasing responsibility.

"He sure didn't have to hire me," he'd told Rand, that night when Smokey came home to tell him about the new job.

"Of course, he did," Rand laughed. "You are the best there is and you're on your way up."

Smokey had laughed then, and squeezed Rand's shoulder. It embarrassed him to hear Rand talk like that, but it made him feel good, too, because he knew Rand believed it. Of all the changes in his life, having someone truly believe in him was the best of all. Smokey ran his hand down the side of Rand's face, felt the tortured, palsied skin, the patchy whiskers. He'd been a nice looking young man once, Smokey knew. Almost beautiful, from the pictures from before. But Smokey hadn't made his acquaintance until Rand had been lying bloody and broken in the bank. Smokey had cold-cocked Case Olden when he'd attacked Rand and then protected Rand with his body when Case's cousin Dyke started shooting. The ensuing gunfight had been brief and way too close. Dyke had fired four times from a distance of 12 feet without effect. Smokey had fired twice, both bullets hitting low in Dyke's belly. Even now Smokey couldn't remember having aimed.

He was still holding Rand in his lap when the cops arrived. Rand was twitching and arching himself uncontrollably and Smokey couldn't stop crying and saying, "I'm sorry. I'm sorry." Those horrified blue eyes had looked out at him as though he had all the answers, as though he would be all the protection the poor damaged man would ever need.

Smokey had gone to prison, but he'd changed that day, annealed in Rand's innocent blood. His new attitude, together with his actions in the bank, brought him a drastically shortened sentence. After six months in prison, Smokey received a letter from Rand. In it, Rand had thanked him for saving his life. The problem was brain damage from Olden's beating, he explained. It had manifested in stroke-like symptoms; a grotesque droop on the left side of his face and a drastic loss of strength and control in his left arm. But he was getting better, the letter explained, and he hoped for full recovery. Perhaps Smokey could come by and visit when he was released. Rand and his parents would like a chance to thank him in person. The letter was matter of fact, devoid of self-pity. Rand was obviously a man of great personal strength.

Smokey had cried then, cried for the damage he had done, for the life he'd led, for the young man whose life he'd helped to ruin. Then, he wrote Rand a letter of apology. And Rand had written back. Soon they were communicating regularly; Smokey sending congratulations for each step toward physical rehabilitation, Rand urging self-confidence and continued efforts toward a better life. Later, after they'd become close friends, each told the other how important those letters had been, how they had communicated strength and endurance and persistence, how much they'd helped in each man's journey.

When Smokey was released from prison, Rand and his parents were waiting for him. They took him home and gave him a place to stay while he tried to establish a life. Rand's father offered a temporary job in his paint shop with time off to look for something better. After dinner, Smokey and Rand would talk or play games with his parents. Rand's physical recovery was as complete as it was ever going to be. His face still slumped and his arm was weak, but he could get around normally and his voice only rarely betrayed him.

When summer came, Smokey got a job on a fire crew. It was a big-fire year and he'd stayed busy until the rains started in the fall. Then he planted Douglas fir seedlings on the steep coast range hillsides in Oregon. From there he'd headed to southeast Oregon where he'd worked on a ranch in the Great Basin. There, where few questions are asked about a man's past and a good hand can always find work, Smokey did the backbreaking work of fence building and haying, gradually learning his way around horses and laying the groundwork for his future success as a wrangler. He spent the next four years on ranches between McDermitt and Burns, and another five years in Alaska, alternating between crab fishing in the Bering Sea during the winter and salmon fishing in the summer.

Throughout those years he and Rand stayed in close communication, and he traveled back to California to visit whenever he was between jobs. During that period, Rand became the closest friend Smokey had ever had. Rand seemed to understand the confusion and fears Smokey experienced around people and helped to maintain his confidence. At one point during a visit, Rand put his hand on Smokey's shoulder and said, "No matter what else happens, I am on your side… and I always will be."

Smokey leaned on that statement many times. Whenever he felt left out or put down, feelings that had led to violence in the past, Smokey said to himself, *Doesn't matter what you people think, I've got a good friend who truly likes me.* That knowledge gave Smokey confidence and the confidence made him into a man other people wanted as a friend.

Smokey was in the Seattle Airport on his way north to take part in the winter crab fishery when he was paged. The caller was Rand, and he was sobbing uncontrollably.

"Smokey…. I need you…I need your help. Please."

"Of course, I'll help, Rand. What's wrong?"

"It's Mom and Dad," he said, and then broke down.

Smokey waited. Sometimes there's just nothing to say.

"A long-haul driver fell asleep and crossed the center line. He hit my folks head on. They're both…"

"My God! Oh, shit, Rand. I'm sorry."

"I'm having trouble keeping it together, Smokey. Could you come?"

"I'm on my way. I'll let you know as soon as I figure out my arrival time."

"Thanks, Smokey. I… sorry… I…"

"I'm coming, Rand. I'm coming."

Smokey stood by the phone for several minutes. It was the first time he could remember someone asking him for help. It felt good that Rand would turn to him in his time of need. And it felt even better, sort of, to realize he was about to give up a $40,000 share on a crab boat to help a friend. This must be what normal people do, he thought, though a part of him wondered how they could afford it.

His mind drifted between the pain of his friend's loss and a newfound sense of personal dependability until a gentle tap on his shoulder brought him back.

"Excuse me, but I have to use that phone."

Smokey apologized, then hurried over to change his reservation. His call to the crab boat skipper was more difficult. The man had taken Smokey on a few years before as a crewmember for $150 per day, which Smokey thought was great, until he'd done the job and seen what the deckhands with shares of the catch were getting. But he never complained and at the end of the season the skipper gave him a sizeable bonus and offered him a share during the next season. He'd been on shares ever since.

The phone call was predictably grim. After a serious dressing-down, during which Smokey's personal dictionary of curse words was significantly expanded, the skipper wished him well and offered him the same share the following season.

"You're a good man, Smokey. You'll always be welcome on my boat," the skipper said, and Smokey waited for his flight back to California feeling better about himself than ever before.

He spent the winter helping Rand wade through the intricacies of his parents' lives and business. In the midst of the grief and loss, the comfort Smokey provided became something a great deal more. He and Rand were drawn to each other and though each man expected feelings of regret after their relationship became physical, neither ever felt any. Their friendship had simply morphed into love, which gradually felt comfortable and right.

One night, after weeks of dealing with the details of his father's business, Rand said, "I don't want the business, Smokey; and I don't want to live here. I'm going to sell it all."

"But what will you do then?"

"Between the business and the house and the insurance settlement and my parents' policies and savings, I'm not going to need to ever work again, Smokey. I can live any way I want…or, we can live any way we want. Can we stay together?"

Smokey reached over and kissed his friend's forehead. "I'd like to stay together forever," he said. "But I'm not living on your money. Do you mind traveling a bit?"

And so they'd moved to Grangeville, which Rand recognized as an effort on Smokey's part to clean up a part of his past he regretted, to rewrite his personal legacy in the town.

****

Shane squawked a bit when he'd realized that Smokey had saddled an extra horse and was planning to accompany him.

"Thanks, Smokey, but I don't need help packing up the camp."

"I know this is not about the camp, Shane. I know I can't force you to take me but I feel like I owe Jared for the way I treated him…and talked about him. I'd appreciate it if you'd let me come along."

Shane shook his head and moved close enough to Smokey so he

couldn't be overheard. "There's more to it than just Jared, Smokey. There are people looking for him, and evidently he told them where to find him. These are not nice people."

"I know what's going on. Chester explained it. That makes it even more important for me to help. I have a lot to make up for…especially in this town."

"This isn't heroic, Smokey. I'm not going in to arrest him. And if we do the job right, we'll bring Jared out and no one will ever know what happened."

"I'll know. And besides, things might not go like you hope. If they don't, you're going to need some help."

"Christ, you're as bad as Chester. All right, let's load 'em up. And Smokey? Thanks."

Chapter 58

Shane and Smokey made the turn into Dry Meadow with two hours of daylight left. Shane stopped the horses a hundred yards from camp and yelled out, "Hellooo. Hellooo the camp."

Jared McCauley stepped out from behind a tree, lowering his rifle as he did so.

"I thought you were smarter than to come up here, you dumb fuck!" he yelled.

"You always overestimated me, Jared," Shane yelled back. "Now, don't shoot us, we're coming in."

"No! Wait! Don't move! Did you come to arrest me? Cause I'm not going in."

"No, Jared. I'm not even wearing my badge. I'm here as a friend."

"OK, good. I'll have to lead you in. There are a few surprises along the main trail you don't want to find." He walked out toward them.

"Oh, that's great. You booby-trapped our camp?"

"Nothing fatal. Don't have the right stuff. I could only manage a few noisemakers."

Shane dismounted and moved quickly to his approaching friend. He engulfed him in a bear hug. "I'm so sorry, Jared."

"I know. Thanks." Jared turned away, visibly struggled, then found a way to wall off his grief. "You should not have come, Shane. But thanks." He rested his hand on Shane's shoulder. "Listen, there are going to be people coming for me soon. You can't be here when they arrive. They are not going to care who you are or whether you wear a badge. You understand? And your friend here is going to be…is that Smokey Stover? Are you Smokey? For Christ's sake, Smokey, turn around and go back. Get out while you still can. You've got no dog in this fight."

"I'm just here to help, Jared. I don't plan on leaving."

"Well, fuck. Smokey Stover is here to help. Proof positive the world has turned upside down. Well, thanks, I guess. But only until tomorrow morning. You both have to be out of here by sunrise. Now stay close behind me and you won't have any trouble."

****

Trey lowered his binoculars and leaned back. This wasn't good. More people meant more complications. He still hadn't figured out what to do with McCauley but the addition of two more people, one of whom was evidently a lawman, introduced a level of uncertainty that was totally alien to Trey. He couldn't afford this, not with retirement so close; not with both his sisters counting on him. The smart thing would just be to kill McCauley. He was a dead man anyway. Or, if he couldn't bring himself to kill his old lieutenant, he should just walk away. Fly back to California, pack up and head to France. No one the wiser. But that wasn't going to happen, either. Professional pride. He'd never failed to complete a job once he'd accepted it. No matter how long it took or how difficult it was. He wasn't going to ruin that record by just walking away. He was going to kill Jared McCauley, but if he did it just right, maybe afterwards his old lieutenant could walk away to a new life.

****

It took an hour to unload and unsaddle the animals. Jared ferried their personal gear into the tent while Shane and Smokey took care of the tack. After the work was done and the animals hobbled, Jared and Shane moved into the tent and sat down. Smokey went out to give them some privacy. He walked out into the woods to retrieve a food cache the guides typically left hanging in a tree nearby.

Shane broke out a bottle of scotch and poured each man a stiff shot. Jared raised his glass, looked squarely at his old friend and said, "You've got a wife and four kids, Shane. These people find out who you are, they might be in danger. You know what they did to Misty and Josh. I don't want their lives on my conscience, too. Or yours."

"Reports I've seen indicate that it was just one sicko. I don't think the mob actually targeted your family."

"Doesn't really matter much, does it? The sicko you refer to just happened to be the boss' son. And Misty and Josh are just as dead as if they planned it. Doesn't matter much at all."

Shane looked carefully at his friend. There was a surrealistic calmness around Jared he'd not seen before. There was no extraneous motion; no scratching of hair, shifting of shoulders. He barely blinked, Shane realized with shock. And his eyes seemed devoid of feeling. Jared had always practically vibrated with energy; now, his emanation seemed to be of deadness or emptiness. He was not overtly sad. He just wasn't there.

"I want to bring you out of here, Jared," Shane said.

Jared took a small sip and narrowed his gaze. "Is that the sheriff talking?"

"No. No. I told you; I'm here as a friend."

"OK. So you want to take me out of here…as a friend. You're going to help me, right?"

"Jared, I know there are problems. But if we can get you down…"

"Just for the sake of conversation, Shane, what do you think will happen once I come down?"

"We could get you into a witness protection program…"

"I'm not a witness, Shane. I'm a murderer. The only place I can possibly go is to jail and once I'm in jail, Sal Corrarino will send someone to kill me."

"Then I can take you to Mexico. You can disappear."

"I know you don't believe that. I could maybe run from the law… or maybe from the mob… but no way could I stay ahead of both of them. And besides, I don't want to. I want this to be over. All I really care about is taking a couple of them out with me. I know you don't understand this,

Shane, but at this point, just being alive is more than I can bear. If I didn't have so much hate in me right now I'd make it stop, right here, right now."

Shane sat back on his folding stool and sipped his drink. Jared did the same. There wasn't much else to say. He should have known. Lacy had warned him but Shane couldn't imagine being unable to reason with his old friend. It was like talking with a statue.

Shane considered his options. *He could pack up in the morning and head down the mountain. Go back home like nothing had ever happened. Pretend he'd just taken a couple personal days off. Wait for word that some hunter or hiker had found Jared's body. Chances were that he could pull it off. Neither Smokey nor Chester would ever talk. No one had seen him at the trailhead and as long as he could get back to Grangeville without being seen, no one would ever know he'd come in the first place.*

Could he just walk away from Jared? And if he didn't walk away, what could he accomplish… take part in a gun battle trying to protect a man who didn't want to live? He couldn't do that, not with Lacy and the girls depending on him.

He sat quietly for several minutes, nursing his drink. Jared did the same. This was Shane's way, Jared knew. He'd sit and think on it for a while, get his thoughts together before he made a decision.

"I like to cogitate before I decide important things," Shane had told him years before. "It's what all great thinkers do."

"Bullshit!" Jared had laughed. "You just sit there with a totally blank mind because you can't think of anything else to do. Cogitate, my ass!"

Despite himself, Jared smiled at the memory. Shane was big and open and trusting and some people assumed he was slow. They were wrong. Shane thought things through from every direction and when he made his decision, he rarely made a mistake. Jared just hoped that Shane's loyalty to him would not cloud his thoughts. No one else needed to die up here.

They were still sitting quietly together when Smokey returned to the tent. Taking in the situation, he sat on a stool near the woodstove without speaking. Five minutes passed, then ten. Shane massaged his shoulder. Jared rested his face in his hands. Smokey sat without moving. Four years in prison had taught him how to wait.

"Sam died right out there." Shane's voice startled both men, coming without warning into the silence. "You saved me, Jared. Brought me down off the mountain. I can't remember a time when we weren't best friends. We were like brothers until you went to Vietnam…and then you took a few years off…but that didn't really change anything for me. Now you want to kill yourself—no, don't interrupt—no matter who pulls the trigger in the next few days, you are in fact, committing suicide. And you want me to walk away and let you do it. You think I should be OK with that. You think I can go back to my wife and kids and tell them I left my best friend up here to die. How am I supposed to live with that?" He fell silent again and closed his eyes. Jared took a deep breath and exhaled. Smokey sat quietly during the ensuing stillness.

"Bullshit, Jared. Bullshit." Just as quickly as he had begun, Shane stopped speaking. And the silence seemed to stretch forever.

"But I guess it's not about me. I mean, I know it's not about me—but it's not right for me to worry about the impact of your decision on me. You've lost so much—my God, Jared—this is so unfair. How could something like this happen to people like you and Misty and Josh? No! No. What I mean is this: I can't begin to understand what you are going through, what you've gone through since Vietnam. But you're right about your present situation; I…I don't see a way out of this for you. Not a long-term way. I wanted to bring you out of here, even if it meant turning you loose in Mexico. But that won't help you. The only way I can help you is to let you do what you want and do it alone." He took a deep breath and looked past Jared. "OK, Smokey, we'll head out first thing in the morning."

Shane stood up and put his big hands on Jared's shoulders. Jared stood up too and the men embraced. That's when they heard the booby trap bells ring.

Chapter 59

It didn't take long for Tony to find the Frank Church Wilderness on an Idaho map. He threw some clothes into a suitcase and drove to the airport. He couldn't get a flight all the way to Boise so he took one to Denver, hoping to get a standby seat the rest of the way. He got as far as Salt Lake City and had to spend the night. An early morning flight to Boise was canceled due to an electrical malfunction and the next one wasn't scheduled until that evening, so he rented a car and drove to Boise. There he stopped at an outdoor store and geared up: a day pack, light sleeping bag and tarp, flashlight, jerky and trail mix, a one quart-canteen and some water treatment pills. And a map for the Frank Church Wilderness, where he located Dry Meadow and the Chamberlain Basin.

"You understand this is wilderness, right?" one of the clerks said, when he'd asked about the best way to get to Dry Meadow. "Most all the people who go in there are hunters and almost all are on horseback." He looked carefully at the map. "Dry Meadow is 12 miles from the airfield and 20-something from the Whitewater Trailhead. That's a long way in and out."

"By the trail," Tony said. "It's quite a bit shorter on a straight line. Looks like the trail does a whole lot of back and forth from Whitewater up. "I could cut several miles off by jumping across the river at the trailhead and going straight up the hill."

The clerk smiled. "That's the Salmon River you're talking about 'jumping across.' It's probably 30 yards wide at that point and pretty fast. It's also snow melt. The reason the trail goes where it does is to use this bridge down here. Otherwise you're going to be a bit wet and cold. And all that 'back and forth' you referred to we call switchbacks. Trails in steep country are built like that to make it easier on the horses." He looked again at Tony and saw no wavering. "Having said that, a guy in good shape could probably put his gear on an inner tube, swim across the Salmon, change into dry clothes and hoof it on up the hill. You could intersect the trail here and cut off six or eight miles. After that you are going to be in thick timber so you'll want to stay on the trail, but you'll still save several hours."

Tony nodded. "So, can you sell me an inner tube?"

The clerk shook his head. "Nope, but I can sell you a dry bag, so your gear stays dry and I can sell you a life preserver, so when that water shrinks your nuts down to the size of peas and your lungs to the size of cherries you'll still probably survive. And I can point you to Les Schwab, and they can certainly sell you an inner tube. If it were me, I'd just get a flight to the airfield. It would be so much easier."

The clerk was right, Tony reflected, as he dressed himself on the far side of the river. His nuts were no larger than peas and he hadn't been able to draw a breath the entire way across the river. The inner tube and life preserver had been, quite literally, lifesavers. And flying into the Chamberlain airfield would have been quicker and easier, but the people his father sent would certainly go that way and he had no desire to cross paths with them. Just what he did desire was unclear to Tony. All he knew was that he had to get to where Jared was. And for now, that was enough.

He headed up the hill. It took a while to get his blood flowing again and breathe comfortably, but once he was warmed up Tony walked quickly across the grassy hillside. Twice he nearly stepped on rattlesnakes but they gave him plenty of warning and he went around easily. Once he intercepted the trail he sped up; when he got to the top he switched to running shoes and was able to alternate jogging and hiking.

His biggest problem was footing. Hoofprints on soft ground dried into rough, uneven ridges which were an invitation to sprained ankles. Heavy runoff sometimes overwhelmed the occasional waterbars and cut deep ditches into the trails. Better, he thought, than some of the country through which he'd bushwhacked while fighting wildfires, but back then he hadn't been running, running, running to catch up to the man who killed his son. And try as he might, he couldn't remember much about the footing during his 19-day nightmare escape in Vietnam. He remembered events and near misses, and his experience with the young boy was never far from his mind—but he couldn't remember anything about the footing. He'd spent a good part of his life trying to forget the entire experience; he wasn't overly disappointed now to not be able to remember.

The turnoff to Dry Meadow was easy enough to find but Tony was glad he'd arrived before the light was too dim. It would have been easy to miss in low light conditions. Once on the right trail he simply followed the horse tracks and within 100 yards he saw the light of a lantern through a canvas tent. He stopped for a moment in the trees and considered his next move. There wasn't much to consider, he thought, since he had no real idea what he was doing here. He'd get to within 50 yards of the tent and call out, so as not to surprise Jared. Unfortunately, the wire he tripped was set 60 yards out.

The clanging cans brought three men boiling out of the tent, each grabbing a rifle as he came. Tony stood still, waiting. He recognized Jared, though he looked thinner and more haggard than before, with several days' worth of beard. Jared's face went slack when he recognized Tony and he stumbled, almost falling. Although he recovered quickly, his demeanor changed noticeably; a sense of uncertainty replaced his stolid confidence. A small man with wispy, thinning hair moved quickly to a thick pine and began scanning the woods around the camp. A large blonde man walked side by side with Jared, taking the rough meadow hummocks in stride. He carried his rifle like a briefcase, but Tony had no doubt it could be brought to bear in an instant. The two men came to a stop, 10 feet away.

"Hi, Jared."

"Jesus, Tony… are you… are you the one they sent?"

"No. That's not why I'm here; but those people will be coming."

"But, why… why are you here?"

Tony hesitated, searching. "I…"

Shane broke in. "Let's talk later," he said. "Right now we need to get back undercover." He reached for Tony's backpack. "I'll take this." He turned to move, then noticed Jared still standing, looking at Tony as though he were a new species.

"Jared," Shane said, with a touch of asperity, "there may be others with him. We don't want to stand out here in the open."

Jared ignored him, pinning Tony with haunted eyes. "Why *are* you here, Tony?"

"I wanted to tell you I'm sorry about Misty and Josh. I don't know. I'm not here to kill you. I know that."

Shane was becoming visibly upset by their vulnerability. Scanning the trees around them he said, "Jared, even if he's telling the truth, the fact he's here means others could already be here, too, or be real close, anyway. We've got to get back in the trees. Go. Go. I'll reset your booby trap."

Jared turned on his heel and headed back to the tent, leaving Tony to follow.

"Christ," Smokey said under his breath as he watched the men returning, "turning your back on a guy who might be here to kill you doesn't seem all that clever." He watched Tony carefully as the two men approached across the meadow and stayed to cover Shane, as well, when he finished with the booby trap and returned. He waited until the big man came abreast and then asked him in a whisper, "What the hell is going on?

Shane shook his head. "I don't have a clue. That is the father of the boy Jared ran over."

Smokey whistled quietly. "Holy shit."

"Yeah," Shane agreed. "Holy shit. Maybe you'd better keep an eye on things out here for a while."

"Yeah, I got it. I'm going to move over by that spruce, though. It will give me a better view around the camp."

When Shane entered the tent he found Jared and Tony sitting in chairs on opposite sides of the wood stove, staring intently at each other. He sat down off to the side…and waited. There seemed to be no animosity between the two men; they were just studying each other.

After a couple of minutes, Shane grew restless. "Jared, maybe we should…"

"Why are you here, Tony?" Jared interrupted as though Shane was not there.

"Glad I could help," Shane whispered.

"I told you, I don't know. Except that…what happened to Misty and Josh…"

"What happened was that your brother murdered them."

"I know. I'm…"

"He threw my wife off the second floor."

"I'm…"

"He cut my son's throat and threw him on top of her."

Tony sat silent.

"Your wife? She egged him on. They were talking and laughing about it when I found them… in the bed."

Tony nodded as he looked at the floor.

"He was choking her when I walked in. She seemed to like it but I made him choke her until she died. Then I made him call your father. Then I…"

"Jared!" Tony spoke up loudly. "My brother was a monster. And my wife was worse because she manipulated him. I can't blame you for what you did to them. You lost everything; I know. But so did I."

Jared choked back a sob. "It was a mistake; it was an accident."

"I know. I know it was. I know how you feel. I once…"

"Misty told me; the boy in Vietnam?"

"Yes."

Both men were silent for a long time. Shane put a couple logs in the woodstove.

Tony broke the silence. "The question is, why are *you* here, Jared? I was in the room when you called my father. I've never seen him so mad. You must know what you're facing, right?"

"I don't care what I'm facing."

Tony looked around the tent. He rubbed the nub of his left arm. "I can tell you what you're facing. My father will send a professional killer, maybe more than one. If you're lucky, you won't know what hit you, but my father may have given orders to torture you…" he closed his eyes and shook his head wearily. "He may have told them to make your death as painful as possible. He… he has a history of that sort of thing."

Shane sucked air through his teeth. The other two ignored him.

"I'll try to make it hard for them to do that."

Jared's surreal calmness disturbed Tony and he looked a question over at Shane, who responded with an almost imperceptible shrug. Tony looked back at Jared. "But what is your plan, Jared? You can't just sit here and wait."

"My plan is for Shane and Smokey to leave at first light and for you to go with them, ah, no, let me finish. You've come all the way here to tell me something important. And you did. I appreciate it; you don't know how much. I'd give anything for none of this to have happened, but it did…having you forgive me for…for what I did… takes some of the pain away. But you have to understand, like Shane here… there is no place left for me to go. I have no future and I don't want one. So please leave in the morning."

Chapter 60

From his prone position under a downed pine tree fifteen yards from the tent, Trey Cannon smiled. Life would be so much nicer when the rest of them left. He pressed into the ground as the man he referred to as Baby Beard stood up from his lookout position and carefully scanned in all directions before sitting down again. It was nearly full dark; he'd soon be able to move away from the tent and relax until the lieutenant's friends left.

Inside the tent Shane couldn't remember ever being so uncomfortable. Jared and Tony sat there, looking at their food, looking at the woodstove. The only person Shane could possibly talk to was standing guard outside, and it was time he had a break.

"I'll relieve Smokey," he said as his got up from the camp stool.

Jared spoke. "You know, Shane, I don't think it's necessary to stand guard tonight. I can't imagine that hired killers from New York could get into the wilderness this fast, and certainly not up here in the middle of the night. It's not easy finding your way around here in the dark even if you've been here before. I think we can all sleep tonight."

"I think you're right," Shane said. "I'll go get Smokey."

Trey smiled again. They were probably right. It would take New York killers several days to get ready for something like this. But the mob doesn't always hire New York killers, boys. He almost wished he could walk into the tent right then just to see their faces. Almost. He didn't want to kill anymore.

He waited another hour after Baby Beard went in before he started to move toward his small camp at the upper end of the meadow; a lightweight tarp spread over a sleeping bag which lay across a poncho. It was a backpacking arrangement he'd used many times while hiking in the Sierras… and while fulfilling contracts in a variety of rural locations. He was 50 yards from the lieutenant's tent when he heard the buzz of a small plane. It was quite high, well above the 1,500-foot minimum over designated wilderness areas. Then he heard a slight change in the engine noise; reduced power. Trey listened carefully. As the plane drew farther away, he could make out a slight tearing noise, he recognized it, the sound of a parachutist reaching terminal velocity. Then the sound lessened. Maybe, he thought, maybe I'm wrong, but then he heard the dull fopp, fopp, fopp of parachutes opening. Three chutes. *Oh, shit! That son of a bitch sent a team in on top of me!*

There was no time to spare; Trey moved out of the trees and into the open meadow, where he could run. He avoided the booby traps and tried to stay quiet; he didn't want the lieutenant or one of his friends to kill him. Thankfully, the tent door was not tied, so he stepped in, looked right at an astonished Jared and said "There are three parachutists coming down right now to kill you. If any of you want to be alive in half an hour you'd better get your asses out and shoot these people before they hit the ground."

Shane was reaching for his gun, muttering "What the fuck?" Trey ignored him. Jared reacted the way Trey hoped he would, taking only an instant to recognize him, then jumping off the cot and heading for the door, grabbing a rifle on the way out. After a moment's hesitation, Smokey did the same.

"Jared, wait! We can't just trust this guy! We don't know him. Jared!" Shane looked ready to level Trey.

Jared stopped and looked back at Shane. "Yes, yes we can. I know him." He turned to go.

"Wait!" Trey hissed. "They will probably have night vision goggles and automatic weapons. Stay well behind the trees." Then Jared was out the door. Trey was right behind him, whispering. "I'll explain everything later. Please don't use my name."

Smokey and Shane stumbled after them. Jared led them into the trees where they stopped to peer upward. A thin, high overcast filtered most of the moonlight, but soon they picked up the chutists, shadowy against the night sky. Two were headed into the lower meadow, a third, even closer to the ground, was aiming for the upper meadow, not far from where they stood. As they watched, Tony drifted in behind them, carrying a pistol in his good hand. Shane glared at him. Tony shrugged and mouthed, "I'm here."

Trey took charge. "I've got the one closest to us; he should land first. Jared, you take the next one. Tony, you stay here and back up whoever needs it. Shane, you and Smokey take the last one down. Get as close as you can to where they are going to land and shoot them just before they touch down."

Shane nodded, but he was obviously uncertain. Trey grabbed him roughly by the shirt. "These guys are pros," he whispered. "They will kill us all if you give them a chance."

Shane slapped his hand away and looked questioningly at Jared.

"I wish you hadn't come, Shane, but here you are… and this is it. Are you in?"

Shane breathed deeply and nodded.

"OK, then. Let's go." Jared turned and led Shane and Smokey into the woods at a run as Trey burrowed under vegetation to take up a prone position behind a log. Tony moved back toward the tent, standing behind a tree outside the lantern glow.

Trey picked up the first jumper in his scope just before the man descended below the trees. A bit of good luck. A light breeze from behind Trey virtually guaranteed the attacker would be facing and moving toward him as he prepared to touch down. The same would be true of Jared and Shane. It would make their shooting easier. He flipped off the safety of his rifle, settled his cheek on the stock and waited. His target made a final low turn in toward him and pulled on his risers to slow his descent. Trey's bullet caught him full in the chest. He collapsed on his face without moving. The chute settled to the ground behind him. The second bullet took him in the top of the head. Trey got to his feet and began moving toward the lower meadow.

Jared acquired his target as Trey's shot shattered the night. The man in his sights responded by spraying the wood line near Jared with silenced automatic fire. Two of the rounds actually hit Jared's tree, making him think the man had seen him. But continuing rounds chuffed through the trees and brush on either side of him. Nonetheless, by ducking during the onslaught, Jared lost the chance to kill the man in the air. The attacker spun his chute 180 degrees and hit the ground running on the other side of the meadow, 60 yards away. Jared took aim and fired, just as the man dove for cover.

Jared stood up and steadied his rifle against the tree and waited. Within seconds he saw movement in the grass. The man was quartering away at a belly crawl. Jared's views of him were fleeting and unclear. No shot. Then the grass stopped waving. There was something dark rising above the grass. It seemed to have no form, just a dark, shadowy lumpish mass. Jared settled the crosshairs on the shadow and waited as it rose. Two inches, four, six inches above the grass. He squeezed the trigger. When he reestablished the sight picture the lump had disappeared and all he could see was something dark flopping in the grass. It moved for a few seconds, then slowed and stopped, settling out of sight again in the grass.

He ran toward the chutist, dodging and staying low. The man was very dead, with brain matter leaking from his watch cap.

Jared turned toward the lower meadow when he was nearly trampled by a running Trey.

Jared grabbed him and said, "What the hell is going on here, Trey? What are you...?"

Trey cut him off. "No time to explain. Don't use my name, remember? We've got to find those other guys. I haven't heard any shooting."

"Yeah, well, Shane is the sheriff in this county. I doubt he could bring himself to kill a man in cold blood."

"If he can't, I hope he's very good... or very lucky."

Shane was good... and lucky to have Smokey with him. As Jared had guessed, Shane was unwilling to shoot the man. Just as the attacker was landing, the firefight erupted at the other end of the meadow and while he was shedding his chute and looking in the direction of the shooting, Shane appeared behind him and said, "Hands in the air."

The black-clad figure froze, his body beyond tense.

"Don't… even think it." Smokey had established a full 45-degrees separation from Shane and was kneeling with the shotgun to his shoulder. It would be almost impossible for the killer to get them both before he was cut down, no matter how fast he was.

Still the man did not come out of his crouch. Shane's finger tightened on the trigger; he found himself regretting not having killed the man in the air, lawman or not. The man was obviously a professional killer. Why had Shane put himself in the position of having to make a perfect shot to keep the man from chopping him up with that automatic pistol? Which way would the man spin? Would he try to roll? Shane's finger tightened even more. Fuck this. I'm going to kill him where he stands.

Smokey spoke again, an air of finality to his reedy voice. "Double. Aught. Buck."

As though a button had turned off, the man relaxed, dropped his weapon and stood up, hands in the air.

"Get on your belly. Hands behind you." To himself, Shane's voice sounded quavery, frightened. He felt like he was going to throw up. "Keep that shotgun on him, Smokey, but stay close enough so you don't kill me, too if you have to shoot."

Shane was still frisking the man when Trey and Jared ran up. When Trey realized what was happening he was enraged. "The fuck are you doing? Didn't I tell you to kill him?" He stepped in front of Smokey, pointed his pistol at the prone figure's head and pulled the trigger. The explosion and flash occurred only a split second after Shane's left hand slapped the gun.

"No! No! You don't give orders here! I'm not killing people because you say so. This man is my prisoner!"

"You stupid shit! You have no idea what you are dealing with!"

Trey took a step back and raised his pistol as Smokey shifted the shotgun toward him.

"Enough! Stop!" Jared's hand on Trey's shoulder kept the situation from deteriorating even further. "He's down. He's not dangerous at this point. Let's get him in the tent and figure out what the hell is going on here."

"Goddammit!" Shane growled. "I didn't bring my goddamn handcuffs. Well, I've got some twine in the tent. I'll tie him up there."

"No." Trey was emphatic. "He needs to be tied up before he moves a muscle. Here." He holstered his pistol, handed his rifle to Jared and unsheathed a knife, which he used to cut long lengths of cord from the discarded parachute. "Don't take any chances with this guy… any more than you've already taken."

Shane took the cord and worked on the man's arms and wrists as the others watched silently. Finally, he was finished and he hauled the man to his feet. They made a strange procession, Jared leading the way, followed by the prisoner and Shane, then Tony who had come out into the meadow when he'd heard the arguing. Trey waved Smokey forward, but Smokey waved back with the 12-gauge and so Trey reluctantly went ahead, leaving Smokey to bring up the rear.

Chapter 61

Once inside the wall tent, Shane shoved the prisoner to the ground in a corner of the tent. The cots were stacked along one wall and four chairs were set out in a rough circle around the woodstove. Tony brought in an empty five-gallon paint bucket they used to bring water from the creek and turned it upside down. They all sat down.

They sat quietly for a few moments. Except for the prisoner, each man was still holding a loaded weapon in his hands, and all were staring at Trey. He looked at each in turn, and at the prisoner, whose black mask still shrouded his features. He was staring with equal intensity at Trey.

Suddenly Trey smiled, a dazzling grin that had disarmed friend and enemy alike for years. "Hey, I saved your lives! If it weren't for me, you'd all be lying dead in this tent."

"That's true," Jared agreed, his statement aimed primarily at Shane and Smokey, whose distrust of Trey was palpable. "I think we can trust him."

"You think we can trust him." Shane was not sarcastic often, but there was no question now. "He practically shot me a few minutes ago, Jared, when I refused to kill that son-of-a-bitch in cold blood. I mean, I understand that one," he pointed again at the prisoner in the corner. "He's exactly what we expected, just a little earlier than we thought. He's a contract killer. But who the fuck is this?" nodding toward Trey. "Where did he come from and how do you know him? I mean, he walks in out of the night, says we need to go out and kill a few strangers and you jump to like it's the most natural thing in the world. And he knows our names! Are you shitting me? What is going on here?"

Jared looked at Trey, who gave an almost imperceptible shake of his head. Jared sighed deeply. "I do know this man, but for reasons of his own, he doesn't want me to divulge his name. I'm willing to respect that."

Trey shrugged and handed his pistol to Shane, butt first. "I'm just here to help," he said.

"Maybe so," Tony said. "But it didn't seem like you expected him, Jared. Had you told him where to find you? And if not, how did he know where you were?"

Jared's brow furrowed. *Good God! What is wrong with my brain? How had Trey known where to find him? His appearance was nothing short of miraculous, ready to fight, armed to the teeth and with an even more deadly ability than he'd shown in Vietnam so many years before. But how had he known where to come? Jesus, the only person in the world who knew where I was going outside the Corrarino family was Chester. That must have been it; Trey told Chester of our time together in Vietnam and Chester had told him about Dry Meadow. But Chester was not a trusting person; was there any chance he would have told a stranger where to find me? No. Could Trey have tricked Chester, or tortured him for the information? I'm not sure of that, not after what I've seen tonight. But that wouldn't make sense; Trey did come here to help, that's obvious. But if he didn't get his information from Chester, that left the Corrarinos.*

"I think he and I need to speak in private," Jared said, rising from his stool. "You guys keep an eye on the prisoner."

As Trey rose to accompany him the prisoner began to speak. "His name is Trey Cannon. Trey Cannon and he was a 2nd Class Petty Officer in the SEALS. Trey Cannon is his name."

As soon as his name was mentioned, Trey moved quickly toward the prisoner. Smokey sat between them and the shotgun came up as the safety snicked off. Trey stopped, a troubled look on his face. He shook his head and sat back down on the stool. The prisoner chuckled. Jared walked back to his seat, his face a mask of puzzlement.

"Why does it matter, Trey?"

The prisoner guffawed. "The reason it matters, McCauley, is that you and your friends are now dead men. I have just pronounced a death sentence on all of you." He continued to laugh uproariously.

"Shut up!" Shane threw a pepper shaker at the prisoner, hitting him in the chest and silencing his laugh right away. Shane had not yet recovered from his follow-through when a blurred movement and a thudding sound to his right were followed by a shocking blow to his right temple.

"Hnnnh. Mlurff. Wha?" Smokey did not have nice breath. Especially when his face was so close. Bloody nose, split lip, swollen eye. Lying there on the tarp. So close to my face. On the tarp!

Shane attempted to jump to his feet, but managed only a stumble to his hands and knees before he vomited.

"Oh, yuck, Sheriff. We can't have that." A full roll of paper towels rolled over in front of his face. "Clean it up."

"Let me do it, Trey, he's hurt."

"No, sorry, Lieutenant. You need to stay where you are. He's a tough guy. He can do it."

Shane looked around the tent. It was still fuzzy but it was coming into focus fast. Next to him, Smokey was still laid out, but small neuromuscular twitches seemed to indicate he might awaken soon. In close proximity, Jared and Tony sat on chairs. The prisoner was still sitting cross legged on the tarp nearby. They'd all moved into the corner with the prisoner. But where was…" Shane twisted his head, feeling for all the world like a sick dog. He saw Trey sitting in the opposite corner, shotgun across his lap.

Isn't that Smokey's shotgun? How did he do that? Shane looked again at Smokey. Both of us? That fast?

"Please clean up the vomit, Sheriff." It was not a request, though it sounded like one, so Shane tore off a bunch of towels and got to work. Once he'd deposited the used towels in the hanging trash bag he felt well enough to seat himself on the paint bucket. Jared patted him on the shoulder. "Sorry."

He looked over at Trey, who seemed even more downcast than his prisoners. "What did you hit me with?"

"Shotgun barrel, I'm afraid."

"What did you do to Smokey?"

"Oh, an assortment of things. He was uncooperative."

"You were lucky, big fella." This from the prisoner. "I've seen him kill people in less time than it took him to put you two down. Of course, it's easier to kill than control. Anyway, you were lucky; he had you and the little guy down before One-arm and McCauley knew which end was up. McCauley might have had a play, but he didn't want to shoot Trey and Trey didn't want to shoot him. It's like a little love fest that makes this whole lashup so much more wonderful."

Shane looked at Tony, who shrugged. Jared avoided his eyes. Shane lowered his head to his hands. *None of this made sense. This guy Trey turns up to save the day but then turns nuclear when the killer mentions his name. Even Jared. How do they know each other? Wait. He said Trey was Navy. What was the story the two Marines told about the corpsman who served with Jared in Vietnam? He knew all kinds of ways to fight. Yes.*

Shane turned to Trey. "You're the doc."

Trey shifted his eyes to Shane, smiled sadly and shook his head. "If you'd only shot that son-of-a-bitch when I told you to… Where'd you hear about me?" He nodded toward Jared. "I thought he pulled away from everyone."

"He did. But a couple Marines from Jared's platoon came by to see him once and ended up at the Riverside telling stories. Big, mean looking black guy and, um…"

"A tall, gangly farm boy?"

"Yeah."

Trey chuckled. "That would be Amos and Andy. Remember them, Lieutenant?" Jared smiled, nodded. "Now, those two were a piece of work. They don't come a lot tougher." He shifted his gaze downwards; reached out with his left foot and pushed Smokey's boot. "I liked the way you stood guard and handled yourself with the shotgun. And you fought well, too. I'd consider it a shame to have to kill you now."

Smokey took a deep breath and pushed himself to his knees. "Worth a try," he said sheepishly.

"Sure," Trey agreed, "but your breathing pattern gave you away. Take a seat. You're Smokey, right?" Well, we all might as well get to know one another while I try to figure out how to handle this whole situation."

"Shit!" An explosive sound from the prisoner. "As though there's more than one possible solution for you! All these people became liabilities as soon as they knew your name. They all have to die, just like me!"

Trey's eyes got flinty and he leveled the shotgun at the man. "Maybe," he said. "But nobody has to die right now, unless you keep talking."

The prisoner stared right back at Trey, but he kept his mouth closed.

Trey continued. "Now, we've got several hours until morning and I don't think anything's going to happen until then. And I'm certainly not going to sleep so why not talk? I believe I'm just as confused as most of you about this situation. And that's no way to live…or die. So, I'd kind of like to understand how all of you fit together. Let's start with you, Smokey. How do you fit in this?"

Smokey moved slowly into one of the stools; the shotgun followed him. "I work for Shane."

"Hmm. But you came up here into an obviously dangerous situation; I doubt that you'd do that just because your boss asked you. And I doubt Shane would have asked you. You came for Jared. How do you tie in with him? Long-time friends?"

Smokey snorted.

"Ahh, not exactly friends. But something owed, some debt brought you here." It was not a question.

"You can still do it, huh, Cannon? Still look into people's minds?" the prisoner snarled.

"I never could do that, Shrike. Certainly not into that pathological dung heap that passes for your mind. I just listen to what they have to say. Now, keep in mind, I am interested in these people but I already know everything I care to know about you. The only reason not to kill you is so we don't have to deal with your stinking body fluids." He shifted the shotgun over. "That was a shitty thing you did, giving my name," Trey continued. "I didn't even know who you were at the time."

Shane noticed for the first time that the black face covering was gone from the killer's head, exposing a hard-edged face with deep brown eyes.

A heavy brow line gave his face a raptor-like look. It was not a face that promised mercy or understanding.

The prisoner shrugged. "Pulling out all the stops. You know. If these people know you are going to kill them, maybe they'll rush you and I'll have a chance to get away." He thought for a moment. "They said you'd be here. No. They said Alonzo would be here. Nobody knew who you were. I never dreamed it was you."

"Why'd they send you on top of me?"

"They don't confide their reasons to me, Cannon. But I suspect they want to be double sure this guy buys it." He jerked a thumb at Jared.

"No, that's not it. I've never missed."

The man called Shrike gave Trey a vicious grin. "Also, they mentioned you'd wanted to quit; you only agreed to take the job when they upped the ante. They don't like being squeezed and they don't like people retiring. Because you'd managed to go all these years without anyone knowing who you were, this was probably their only chance to retire you for good."

Jared looked up, his eyes bright with the beginnings of understanding. "Wait. Trey. Are you a professional killer? Did you come here to kill me?"

Trey continued to look at Shrike, even as he answered Jared. "I came because of you, Lieutenant, but I didn't come to kill you." He grinned again and looked directly at Jared. "Although I have to admit, the money was a big attraction. Three million dollars!"

Shrike gave a strangled cough. His entire team was only being paid $600,000, then swallowed it when he saw Trey laughing at him. He wondered, though, what kind of money Alonzo really did demand for a hit.

Chapter 62

Shrike had hated Cannon from the first day they'd met, during the workup for a combined Special Forces, SEAL insertion into Beirut years earlier. There were weeks of rehearsals and mock attacks. During those endless days and nights, Cannon became the one against whom the other team members were measured. He grasped the tactical concepts first, asked the right questions, made the best recommendations. His laid back, happy-go-lucky style was in stark contrast to his cold, professional demeanor when they got down to business. After only a few days, even the officers would defer to him or ask his opinion. Physically, he was not particularly imposing, but his almost supernatural quickness and remarkable grasp of various styles of hand-to-hand combat made him dangerous far beyond his bodily strength. Plus, he had that sixth sense, that ability to sense danger that gave him an edge, the ability to anticipate trouble and take steps in advance. He might claim he couldn't read minds but that didn't mean it was true, as far as Shrike was concerned. If you could sense danger, it was as good as reading minds. You could eliminate possible threats before they took any action. Of course it was that sort of thinking that had gotten Shrike crosswise with Cannon, and began his slide to the truncated end of a military career.

Shrike was on a sniper rifle covering their egress route on the operation, which was a rescue attempt of two CIA operatives, so he had a 14-power view of Trey's handiwork as he dispatched one, then another guard while the team made its way into the compound. Shrike had done the same thing several times and he recognized superior skill. He was impressed, in spite of himself.

The operation had gone smoothly, which convinced the generals to use the same combination of units in an operation into Iraq. That insertion had gone bad early and resulted in three separate teams running for their lives and trying to make their way to backup extraction sites. Shrike and Cannon had been forced to hole up in a small house, waiting until dark to move on. They'd immobilized a husband, wife and two daughters to keep them from sounding a warning and settled in. When it was time to leave, Shrike said, "I'll cut them loose. You go scout the way out."

Trey had complied without thinking, but he'd come running back shortly afterward—in his after action report he said he'd had a bad feeling—to find Shrike just standing up from slitting the father's throat. He'd made the man watch as he'd done the same to his entire family.

Shrike had never been so certain he would die. "C'mon," he said to Trey's mixed look of horror and rage, "You've done the same yourself; I've seen you. And we can't afford for them to tell we're Americans." Memory of that moment still made Shrike's bowels loosen. Cannon had looked at him with death in his eyes and his finger whitening on the trigger.

"We are all thugs, Shrike," he'd hissed. "This is a thug's business. But that doesn't mean we have to be psychopaths. Put your gun down and leave your knife here."

"But what if…?"

"If we are hit and need your gun, then we'll both die. Now throw down your backup pistol and knives."

They'd made it out without further incident, but Cannon had kept a gun on him the whole way and once they'd gotten back to the ship he'd marched him straight to the guardhouse and convinced the CO not to let him out. Shrike was on his way to the states and to a General Court Martial the next day.

That memory was one more bolt in the ironclad guarantee that he would die tonight. Not that Cannon would need any reason other than to protect his own identity. Shrike often wished he'd tracked down Cannon and killed him after he'd gotten out of the Army. It was the least he should have done; after all, it was Cannon's testimony that got him cashiered from the Army and sent him into the ranks of the mercenary world. But as many times as he'd thought about it, he always had a reason not to. It was fear, Shrike realized now. *He was scared shitless of Cannon. How do you deal with someone who will know in advance when you mean him harm?*

And now Cannon was the legendary Alonzo. A mob killer who'd made dozens of successful hits with never a failure. And he called me a psychopath. Well, if I was a psychopath, we all were, Cannon included. Not one of us didn't revel in the excitement, didn't pound our chests with the excitement of the kill. We talked about it after the ops. We drank beer and told stories, Cannon too. We did what the government told us to do, which was kill. Killers kill. No big surprise. And there's no crime in enjoying your work, taking pride in your work. Sure, there's a difference between actual combat and cutting the throats of four defenseless innocents, including a six-year-old girl. On paper there's a difference. But it needed doing. They would have given us away. And if it had to be done, why not enjoy it? Because the excitement, the heart-pounding sexuality of the wide, staring eyes, the abject and overwhelming fear, devolving into the certainty of their own death at your hands; the arms straining to fight and the mouth to scream, the spurting blood, spurting, spurting, spurt and then flow to a dribble, the gradual loosening of the muscles, the tapping of the heels, the release of the bladder and the sphincter, the glazing of the eyes…the excitement is the same. Though of course Cannon and the rest of the operators would never admit it. Well, no matter. What's done is done. I never expected to die of old age. But I sure don't want to die with my hands tied behind my back. I can feel a slight loosening in that cord around my wrist. But can I stretch it enough to make a difference? Who knows? Maybe…

Chapter 63

Jared shook his head, looked up at Trey. "You actually are a professional killer. You of all people. I never…"

"Yeah, it sort of surprised me, too. And I have you to thank for it."

"Me? How could I…?

"You set me up with my first claymore, remember? Gave me my first rifle. I did like it, I have to admit. It wasn't any more exciting than trying to pull people out of firefights and save lives, but there was something invigorating about being able to shoot back." He looked at the shock in Jared's face. "Just kidding, Lieutenant. You didn't set me on the path to being a killer. You gave me confidence in myself. You gave me something to believe in."

"What?"

"You."

Jared opened his mouth, then shut it again.

"And I would have walked away from it all last week, except for you. You have to admit, the whole thing has a kind of circular beauty to it. You introduced me to combat and then 20 years later, you bring me back into it."

"He didn't bring you back into it, you prick!" Shane was mad; a calm wave of the shotgun from Trey kept him on the stool but it didn't keep him from yelling. "You made your own choices, both times. And if you didn't come to kill him, why the hell are you here?"

"A good question, Sheriff. I guess you are the lifelong sidekick, huh? There had to be at least one. The lieutenant is the kind of man who creates strong loyalties, isn't he? Well, I'm like you too, in a way. I hope to take him away to someplace safe."

"We've already been through all of that, Trey," Jared said. You were probably listening to us while we talked, for that matter…"

Trey nodded. "In fact, I was. And you were right, as far as you went. You would never be able to avoid the mob and the FBI on your own for long. But I have assets and skills you don't have. I've been working on ways to disappear for years. I can get passports, IDs. I can fix it so you can be safe for the rest of your life."

"But I don't want to live, Trey. That's why I came up here."

"I know and I understand. That's how you feel today and maybe tomorrow. But a year from now, it will be different. Listen to me, Lieutenant, I can get you to a place where none of them can find you. You can heal, if it takes one year or ten. I know you've had tragedy in your life, much more than your share. But you've been around long enough and gone through enough to know you can recover. You can recover from anything."

Jared stood up from his stool, his face drawn with grief. Trey tightened his grip on the pistol but left it at that. "I might be able to recover from the loss of Misty or Josh, if I hadn't caused it, but I did. I caused their deaths, as well as poor little Anthony's. My God! I could maybe recover from the harm done to me, but never from the harm I've done! Three completely innocent people! Two of them children! And more are dying." He swept his arm toward the pasture where the two parachutists lay dead. "And now these good men are at risk, simply because they came to protect me, either from you or from more mob killers. The cost is too high, Trey. Way too high." He sat back down wearily.

Trey sat silently. No one spoke for several minutes. Shrike shifted position, moving his legs from one side to another. Trey tracked him with the shotgun until he reseated himself. Then the killer spoke, his face grim with the knowledge that every word might be his last, but not caring.

"I don't understand what your deal is, Cannon. This seems like such a no-brainer. You came to rescue your friend but he doesn't want to be rescued. He wants to die. The best thing you could do is help him reach his goal. We've both helped wounded friends end their pain. No difference. Then you could slick off the rest of us and be on your way, with no possible complications. You could even collect the money for doing McCauley on the way to your retirement home. What is wrong with you; lost your nerve?"

Trey looked at Shrike like he was a cockroach. "Ask your friends out there in the grass if I've lost my nerve." He leaned back, looked at the ceiling. Then back at Jared. "I'm tired of it. I don't want to kill any more. I know a little bit about how you feel, Jared. Can I call you Jared? Thanks. As a kid I ignored some warning signs and then I was too late to stop something very bad from happening to my family. I didn't cause it, but I have always known that I could have stopped it. If I'd paid attention to the feeling, if I'd gone to warn them…. but I recovered, just like you can. More recently, I killed an innocent man, a good man. I took the job before I realized who he was and what he had done. Then it was too late to back out. It was a first. The other people I've killed were scum; they deserved it. This guy was not like that. It took a lot out of me. Can't keep it up any longer and I don't want to."

Tony, essentially forgotten and ignored by the others, twisted in his stool and spoke, almost to himself. "I wonder sometimes what it takes to be a good man. I mean, I know that none of us are completely good or bad. But what tips the scales? Can we still be a good person if we've done one horrific thing in our lives? Even if it's by accident? I don't mean in the religious sense, because I know what the church says about sin and forgiveness. I mean how we feel about ourselves. I know that Jared is a good man. I know that my son's death was an accident. I know this, here." He touched himself on his heart. "I know because I can see into Jared's soul and I see the same pain I have felt since I killed a young boy in Vietnam." Every eye turned to him then. "I'd been shot down and I had been running for days. The boy surprised me and he was going to scream. I covered his mouth but he bit me and bit harder until I couldn't stand it. I couldn't stand it. I hit him and hit him again, but I was holding a knife and then he was dead. I don't think I knew I had the knife but I can't remember for sure. I don't think I wanted to kill him but the pain was so…excruciating. I wanted it to stop. I had to make it stop.

"I ask myself, what is the difference between me and Jared? Only an accident of our victim's births. The Vietnamese boy's parents were farmers whose lives began and ended in their small village. Anthony's grandfather is a mob boss whose life is built on violence and revenge. Everything else has derived from those differences. I've lived a life full of guilt and grief and fear that punishment for the crime I committed would be visited upon my own son. And so it was. Jared's guilt was leading him to self-destruction, even before my brother…did what he did. Now, after his own revenge, he sees no possible return to normality.

"Here's what I think, Jared. I think Trey's right; time will heal you, or at least dull the pain enough so you can go on living. And if you go on living, then the possibility still exists that something really good can happen, something that can truly save you."

"Yeah, but…" Shrike began speaking, even as he rolled his shoulders, shifted his legs again. Trey sighted the pistol toward his chest. His voice was flat, without inflection and more frightening for the lack. "Shut up. You've talked enough." Shrike readjusted his legs and was quiet.

"So, what if it's not an accident," Smokey asked from his seat on the paint bucket. He addressed Tony. "What if you're not even the one who did the damage, but it wouldn't have happened if you weren't there?"

Tony was puzzled. "I don't understand," he said.

Smokey shut his eyes, as though trying to get rid of the memories. "I was helping rob a bank. One of the guys I was with got crazy and beat a young kid, beat him real bad. Real bad. Brain damage. He's never been the same. It ruined his life. I was the one who pushed for the bank job. The other guys just wanted to do liquor stores and gas stations. But I wanted the big money."

"Wait a second," Shane spoke up, but Smokey talked right over him.

"No, it wasn't just that. I was a shithead all my life. I stole, I hurt people. I was in and out of reform school and jail and prison. Everything I touched turned to shit."

"That was a different life, Smokey," Shane said. "You were a different person. You saved that boy and you take care of him now. You've completely turned your life around."

"Yeah. I have. Thanks, Shane. But like Tony said, where's the balance? How much good do I have to do to make up for the horrible way I lived my life, for the damage I've done? Or can it ever be balanced out? Rand will never speak properly again. He will never walk right. How can I ever make up for that? Not everybody's like you, Shane. Not everybody's life is perfect. Not everybody has the perfect job, perfect wife, perfect kids. Not everybody…"

"I killed my father," Shane said.

"What?" Smokey was poleaxed. "No. He committed…"

"No. He wanted to commit suicide. He asked me to get him a gun for two years. The Alzheimer's was eating him alive. He couldn't stand the degradation of having other people take care of everything for him, clean him up. But by the time I worked up the guts to give him a gun and get him in a place where he could do it, his mind was too far gone. So I did it. I pulled the trigger. Then I made it look like he'd done it. So where's the balance there? Was killing my father good or bad? The church would condemn me to hell. The law would take my job and send me to jail. I don't know if my wife will ever forgive me and I'm afraid to ever tell my daughters. How's that for a perfect life, Smokey?"

Jared spoke up. "It's still a perfect life, Shane, or as close to perfect as it could ever be. You made a tough decision and did what was right for your father. He wanted to die, with good reason. Who else should make his decision for him? Some pastor who thinks life should be prolonged at any cost? Some district attorney who wants to enforce every law, no matter how stupid? You acted on his behalf, in accordance with his wishes. No way you should ever feel bad about that."

"It's true," Trey added. "There is a big difference between looking back and wishing something you'd done had not been necessary, and feeling guilt for something you know was terribly wrong. You'll feel regret for both of them, but only one puts you on the wrong side of Tony's balance sheet."

A sharp tang filled the tent. Smokey crinkled his nose disgustedly and looked at the prisoner. "For Christ's sake, you pissed yourself. What is the matter with you? Why didn't you just ask?"

Shrike grinned at him malevolently and nodded his head toward Trey. "He'd never have let you untie me. Ask him."

Smokey swiveled back to look at Trey, who answered without being asked. "It's true. He's not the type of person you want to have his hands free. Don't worry, you'll get used to the smell."

Tony cleared his throat and addressed Trey. "So let me see if I understand this. You are actually considering killing us all in order to protect your identity."

Trey sat quietly for a moment. "So you are Sal Corrarino's kid? The good one?"

Tony smiled tightly, nodded.

"And you are the one who refused to have anything to do with the family. You went to college out west. You volunteered for Vietnam, lost your arm and now you are here, essentially to tell Jared you forgive him for killing three members of your family. Is that right?"

Tony, grimacing, nodded. "Essentially."

"And you came anyway, knowing that your father was sending professional killers. You had to know that if you were here when those killers arrived, they would never give you a chance to say "I'm Tony Corrarino!" They'd just kill you before you opened your mouth, right?"

"Yes."

"Then why should you be surprised that I would kill you?"

"Well, you don't seem like the type."

Trey pursed his lips. Shrike snorted.

Tony continued, "And Jared doesn't seem to think you will, either."

"Jared doesn't know me very well anymore. And he sure doesn't know how important my anonymity is, or how hard it's been to develop and maintain. I should explain this to all of you, so you understand my predicament. Years ago, with the help of a friend, I developed a system of notification so I could receive job offers and respond to them without either of us knowing who the other party was. Over the years, because I stay up on the news, I figured out the Corrarino family was one of my primary employers and I researched them carefully, but they never knew squat about me. Because payment went to unnamed offshore accounts, the people who hired me never knew who I was or even where I lived. In my business, anonymity is the best kind of life insurance, because there always is a job somewhere, sometime, that they want to clean up completely, leave no trace. My first mistake was in telling them I was quitting, which I still don't understand. My second was taking the job after telling them, but when I learned who the target was I couldn't walk away. So, they sent a team in on top of me, thinking they could eliminate two problems at once.

"I have loved ones, too. I have made plans to protect them and provide for them, but if the authorities and the Corrarinos find out who I am, then none of my plans will matter. They'll track me down sooner or later. But, as Shrike said, if I just eliminate you people, I can walk away from here free as a bird, and demand payment for the job as well."

"But you don't want to kill any more," Smokey said.

"*Don't want to* isn't the same as *won't*. I don't want to wipe my ass anymore, either."

"But then you'd have to kill Jared, too. And you've gone to a lot of trouble not to do that," Tony said.

"Yes, that would be a problem, but again, *don't want to* isn't the same as *won't*."

Jared looked around at the people in the tent. "Trey, what if these men gave their word never to give you up?"

Trey chuckled aloud. "What? Bet my life on the word of three men I've never met, one of whom is a career lawman? Does that seem like a good idea to you?"

"You're pretty good at telling when someone is lying and means you harm, Trey. You're actually much better than good," Jared continued.

"Doesn't matter, good idea or not," Shane broke in. "Because I'm not going to give you my word to protect you. I'll give you my word to turn your ass in as soon as I get back."

Trey grinned sardonically. Smokey turned to Shane and spoke quietly, "I think the point is, Shane, that if we don't work with him, none of us will get back at all." Shane stiffened his back and looked away.

"I need to take a piss," Tony said.

"Yeah, me too," Trey said. "OK, here's how we'll do it; everyone who has not already pissed in their pants, get up and go outside. Stay in a small group. Shane, you carry the lantern. Go straight out of the tent about 10 yards, stay together and do your business. If any one of you tries to get out of the light, I'll kill you. And then I'll kill everyone else, too. When the rest of them are done, Shane, you can pass the lantern off to Jared and then he'll hold it while you do your stuff. Then all of you come back together. Keep in mind, this is a major act of faith on my part, don't make us all regret it."

Once outside, the group within the lantern light realized how vulnerable they were. Trey followed them out of the tent, but stayed in the darkness, unseen. As they relieved themselves, Jared spoke in a whisper. "Don't anyone be stupid. We have no chance."

"Thank you, Jared. That was smart." They all jumped. The voice came from the other side; somehow Trey had circled around without them hearing a thing. "Let's finish up, now. I don't like leaving Shrike alone."

As they all filed back in, Shrike spoke up. "Cannon, can I stand up for a minute, just to get my blood flowing. My legs are killing me."

Trey looked at him a long time. "Yes, get on your feet, but no walking around."

Shrike struggled, his legs were obviously asleep, but after a few seconds he staggered and stood up straight. Trey watched him closely but said nothing.

When the rest of the men were seated and quiet. Trey, still watching Shrike, said "Tell me about your extraction."

"You'll kill me if I do."

Trey pointed the pistol at Shrike's left kneecap. "Maybe, but maybe not. You can see I'm struggling with the whole aspect of killing. Depending on what the lieutenant decides, if he wants to go with me, I may just let the rest of you go. I can't let you be pulled out as planned, you understand, you'll have to walk out, to give me a couple day's head start. But I need to know the details to see what I can do with all of you."

Shrike tilted his angular head, considering his options.

"Look," Trey continued, "I want to avoid complications. If I know call signs and passwords and code, I can send them away without any further bother and I can let you go, too. You don't owe your employer any loyalty. But if you hard ass me, I'll start shooting at joints and I won't stop until you talk…of course by then it will be a little late for you."

Shrike took a deep breath. He hoped Cannon couldn't tell how frightened he was. There was zero chance Cannon would let him out of here alive, no matter what he said, but if he could work on the knots behind his back a little longer, he might still have a chance. As long as he was in one piece there was always a chance. He couldn't lie, though, Cannon would know. He'd have to just put all his faith in one last big move.

"Helicopter, first light. In the meadow."

"Frequency?"

"VHF, Channel 13."

"Code or password?"

"Call sign is 'Scarface.' Nothing encoded. Never saw the need. I'll just tell them it's clear. But I know the pilot. He'll recognize my voice and he won't come in, otherwise."

"Yeah. OK. Sit down."

Shrike dropped to his knees, leaned back on his toes, stretching. Trey studied him for a few seconds. Jared thought Trey was going to tell Shrike to drop back on his butt, but he didn't. Instead, he turned to Shane.

"You know, Sheriff, sometimes in situations like these, your decisions all come down to this… how do you want to die? Personally, I'm trying to arrange things so I can die many years from now, in my sleep. I've always thought that would be the way to go. Just go to sleep peacefully and not wake up. Now, the lieutenant there, Jared has made the decision to die hard. He wants to take as many people with him as he can, but they have to be bad guys. He doesn't want any collateral damage. Certainly not you, because you are his best friend. And not Smokey, because even though he and Smokey have never been friends, he feels a close kinship with a man who would risk his life in an effort to make up for things he's done in the past. And not Tony, maybe more than even you, because of all he has taken from Tony. So now Jared is reevaluating his plans, trying to figure out a way to keep you all alive, but still meet his own goal.

"And you, Shane. If you had your druthers, which seems a little farfetched right now, but if you did, how would you like to die?"

Shane grimaced, the last thing he wanted to do was talk with this guy. He could see Jared, nodding, egging him on. Who knew, maybe there was still a chance, if he just kept him talking. "In my bed, with my wife and daughters surrounding me."

"Ahh, yes. The consummate family man. But a dedicated law enforcement professional, too. Tough situation for you now, you feel like it's your duty to report the name and description of a mob killer, but you can't imagine not being there for your family and you're coming to grips with the fact that you probably can't do both. Of course, you could lie and promise not to give me up, but you are a man of your word, as well. It's not in you to lie. If you promise not to give me up, you won't, period. No easy answers, are there?

"How about you, Smokey? How do you want to die?"

Smokey leaned forward. He considered carefully. "I'd like a little lead time. I'd like to have some disease or cancer that moved relatively quickly, but not too fast, you know what I mean. Something that would give me three months, maybe, so I had some time to take care of things."

"What kind of things?" Trey asked.

"Make some things right. Do some apologizing. Let some people know I've been trying to do better."

"Uh huh. Tell me, Smokey. What if I decided to let you go, would you agree to never give me up, never mention my name?"

Smokey smiled. "I spent years in reform school and jail. Four years in the big house. I'm not a snitch, not for the cops, not for anyone. Not ever. Besides," Smokey tilted his head as though wrestling with the concept, "I don't see you as a bad guy. No, I won't give you up."

Trey smiled. "Thanks. How about you, Tony? If you could control your way of dying, how would it be?"

Tony took a breath, rubbed the stump of his left arm. "I have spent so much time worrying that I was going to die the next day, the next hour, the next instant, I don't know if I'm brave enough to deal with it again. I think I'd like for my death to be a surprise, no warning, no fear, no pain. Just an ending. I don't know, maybe a heart attack or something like it. Boom, all done. End of story." He thought for a moment. "Just so you know, I've never been connected in any way with my father's organization. And now, I'm totally estranged from him as well. Before I left, he disowned me and I did the same for him. After this, I'm on my way to Oregon, so as for ratting you out, I won't do it. The least I can do, if you let us all go, is to keep your name a secret. Especially considering what my father tried to do to you."

"Personally," Shrike interjected, as he rolled his neck and shoulders, "I don't want to die at all."

"Thanks for your input," Trey said dryly.

"Trey," A single word. An order.

He looked over at Jared. "Sir?"

"Do you really think you could get me to a place where I'd be safe?"

"Yes, absolutely. You'll have to spend a couple years pretty close to home and not wander about town too much, and get a little plastic surgery, but yes. You could be safe. You could live out the rest of your life."

"OK, I'll go with you."

"I'm glad to hear it, Sir, but that opportunity is still up in the air, pending a couple other developments. You understand."

"Yes, I do." It all came down to Jared's best friend and his highly-developed sense of honor. "Shane?"

"Jared, he's a killer. If we promise to protect his name he will get off scot free. No one will ever know him."

"Yes, Shane. But if we make no promises, he will get off scot free, no one will ever know him… and we'll all be dead."

Trey laughed out loud, a conjunctive throaty laugh. "I may be slow, but damned if I can see why this is a tough decision. But I'll tell you what, Shane. You go outside and look up at the stars, commune with nature, think of your family for a minute—no more—and then come back in and tell me what you've decided. Don't screw around. Any longer and I'll kill them all and then I'll find you. OK? Go."

Shane stood up slowly from his stool. He felt dizzy, out of sorts. He couldn't quite understand what was happening. It was like he had no free will at all. He had no real choice. The only other option was to make a run at Trey, try to take the gun away. But Trey kept his distance, and the shotgun tracked him at all times. Double-Ought-Buck. He wouldn't make two steps. Nothing for it but to go on outside. Maybe he could find another gun, or a tool, or something.

The hand snaked around his chin and backward so fast that Shane's inward breath was cut off. A second hand brought a small knife to his throat even as a hip bent him backward and held him immobile. His attacker hid behind him. Shane's head was held immobile but his eyes tracked wildly. Trey was up and pointing the pistol in his direction. All the rest were on their feet as well, but they looked lost, uncertain. Shane heard the voice behind him hiss, "I'm going outside, Cannon, free and clear, or he dies, right here."

Shane couldn't see the knife; his head was tilted back and his body was bent so far backwards that his feet had no purchase. He could feel Shrike's body nestle ever closer to his, denying Trey a shot.

Where had the knife come from? He'd checked the man himself for weapons. And how did he get his hands loose? Shane had done the tying as well. Oh, shit. Now he was going to die anyway, Shrike would slit his throat or Trey would shoot them both and eliminate two problems at once.

Trey said nothing, he was trying to get a bead on Shrike but Shrike wasn't giving him a target, even as he inched them both toward the door. Shane wanted desperately to shake the man loose, but Shrike's hold on him was so complete that he could gain no leverage. They were moving; Shane's toes danced across the tarp. He looked at Trey. Trey's eyes darted toward his leg. Trey nodded and Shane lifted his right leg off the ground. The shift in weight caused Shrike to sag backwards; but Shane's leg came higher.

The shot shattered Shrike's kneecap and, because of Shane's weight pressing down on him, caused him to collapse with a scream. The knife passed upward across Shane's cheek, just forward of his ear and into his scalp as he rolled away. Shrike screamed again, an inhuman cry of rage and pain. Trey stepped forward and put two more shots into Shrike's chest as he tried to rise. Shrike's scream devolved into thin, bubbling gasps. His hands fumbled at his chest, fingers straining to pull apart the clothing. His head slashed viciously from side to side, bloody saliva dripping down both sides of his mouth. He strained mightily to speak. "I... I... hate..." His movements grew slower and his head lowered slowly back to the tarp. Trey never relaxed his grip on the pistol; he kept it aimed directly at Shrike until the man's movements stopped completely and his eyes began to glaze. Then, he reached forward with the pistol and poked Shrike's dead, open eye. Tony shuddered. There was no movement at all.

Jared moved first, springing across the tent to aid Shane, who was writhing in pain, blood pouring from his face and head. Smokey grabbed a first aid kit from the kitchen utensils box and went to help. Trey caught Tony's eye. "Help me get this out of the tent." He indicated the body. Tony nodded and they dragged the body through the door and into the darkness. Trey put the pistol in his holster and picked up the shotgun as he went, carrying it in his off hand as they maneuvered the body.

When they returned, Jared and Smokey were both hard at work on Shane. If cussing was any indication, Shane was going to be all right, if badly marked. They were trying, without much success, to stem the flow of blood. The cut was deep and long, beginning at his jaw, across the top of his nose, between his eyes and continuing well up into his hairline. Jared was talking as he worked. "Jesus Christ, Shane. Talk about lucky. Close to your artery, close to your eye. The damn guy almost nicked your ear."

Smokey snorted. "Hah! That would have been bad, your ears were always the best part of you."

Jared laughed aloud, the sound filled the tent. "Well, you obviously have never seen his feet. Six toes! Count 'em, six!" Jared and Smokey guffawed. Tony laughed as well. Even Shane's body rocked with laughter, though he tried hard to keep his face unchanged; it felt as if half of it would fall off if he laughed. There was an element of hysteria in their laughter, which receded somewhat as they came to grips with the fact that their primary threat was still sitting across the tent, smiling grimly and holding a shotgun.

With the worst of the bleeding stopped, they strapped heavy bandages across Shane's face. Finally, they sat him up. "Do you want some water?" Smokey asked.

"No, well, maybe, but wait a minute." He ran his hands across his face; the bandages kept him from touching the cut but he could tell it was serious. It hadn't seemed like such a big cut as it happened, just a hand sliding across his face. Must have been a very sharp knife. He still couldn't believe he'd missed the knife when he patted Shrike down.

"Belt buckle," Trey said.

"What?" *What the hell is he talking about?* Shane wondered.

"Belt buckle. That's where the knife was. He pulled it just as he was hauling you in. Speaking of which, you're going to hurt yourself with that thing, Smokey. Trying to hide it like that. Why don't you toss it over here?"

Smokey did so, a look of amazement on his face.

Shane continued. "But how did he get loose? I know what I'm doing with knots."

"Yeah, but you were probably concerned about circulation or some shit."

"Well, I didn't want him to get gangrene."

"I rest my case."

At least the son of a bitch is not lecturing me, Shane thought. *He could easily be reminding me that I should have done what he told me all along. Killed Shrike in the air. Checked him more carefully. Tied him tighter. Now I've got a six-inch scar across my face and I wouldn't be alive at all if he hadn't saved me.*

"Thanks for getting me out of that."

"My pleasure. That asshole has needed killing for years. He was one bad guy. I'm just glad I was the one to do it. We were all lucky. You picked up on my signal real quick."

"Lots of incentive."

"Yeah."

They took their places, same stools as before, with Trey in the far corner. Shane fiddled with his bandages. Blood was already beginning to seep through. Jared watched him concernedly.

"So..." Shane started, then stopped. He looked carefully at Trey. Trey looked back, said nothing.

"I appreciate what you did."

"You said that."

"I owe you."

"Yes, you do."

"I was thinking... maybe we could make a deal."

Trey chuckled. "Are you really in position to negotiate?"

"I guess that depends on you, and whether you were telling the truth about your plans."

Jared smiled inwardly. This is the classic Shane. Never admit weakness. Never give an inch.

Trey raised his eyebrows. "I'm listening."

"If you will give me your word not to kill any more, I'll promise to never mention your name or anything I know about you."

"Ever."

"Ever."

Trey looked up. His eyes unfocused. He sat quietly for a full minute. "Two things," he said. "First, I can't promise never to kill again. If necessary to protect myself or the people I care about, I will not hesitate. But I will never kill again for money." He hesitated a little longer. "Can you live with that?" Shane nodded. "Good. My hope, my sincere hope, is to live the rest of my life without ever harming another soul.

"Here's the other thing, you have to understand the importance of your promise. I am literally putting my life and the lives of my loved ones into your hands and though I have numerous faults they are absolutely innocent. OK?"

"Yes," Shane said. "I give my word."

"Then so do I," Trey agreed. "Everyone one else still all right with this?"

There was a general chorus of agreement, a general exhale.

Trey set the shotgun down and tossed his pistol to Jared. "In that case, if you guys can find a needle, some thread and alcohol, I can give Shane here enough stitches so that his scar at least won't scare his children."

"Well, all right!" Smokey crowed, and went back to the first aid kit.

Chapter 64

"Two more hours until daylight," Jared observed as he watched Trey finish the stitches on Shane.

"Hang on just a second, Jared," Trey said. "I've got most of a plan figured out but I'm having trouble concentrating with this big baby flailing around here."

"Owww! Goddammit! Shane grimaced. "I know you're having fun practicing your technique but do we really need all these stitches? In case you've forgotten, I don't have any pain killer."

"It's one thing to have a beautiful sword scar on your face," Trey said. "Women find them alluring. It's quite another to have the scar look like it was done with a garden hoe. Now shut up and hold still; only two more to go."

Trey had been working on Shane for an hour while Tony and Smokey slept and Jared watched. He'd forgotten how good Trey was with injured men. The former corpsman kept up a steady banter, a mixture of professional information: about the wound, what to expect and how to care for it, interspersed with what his men used to call 'a raft of shit.' He questioned their manhood, made fun of their clothing, speech, height, weight and whatever he knew of their lifestyles. And they loved it. Even Shane, after a period of initial coolness, had started to laugh at Trey's running commentary. Fifteen minutes into treatment it was like the other Trey had never existed. This one was their friend and savior, an easy-going jokester who kept everyone loose and laughing.

Unbelievable. He was going to kill us all. And yet, he came all the way to save me. Put himself and his future on the line because of what we shared in Vietnam. He believed in me. I was good back then. A good Marine. A good husband. A good man. Trey wasn't the only one who believed in me. They all did. Best fucking platoon in the Marine Corps. God, what I could have done if only... If only. If only the grenade hadn't hit the tree. Taking a hill we'd already taken and given back. If only I'd seen it. If only Misty hadn't worked on Tony in the hospital. If only I hadn't seen them together. If only I'd paid more attention backing up. If only I hadn't stayed at the airport with my parents when their flight was delayed, I would have been home with Misty and Josh when Charley came. The terror they must have felt. And I wasn't there. I started this whole fucking mess; killed a five-year-old boy with a car and then I wasn't there when it came time to pay the piper. I left my wife and child to face it alone. I...

"OK, so gather around folks." Trey stepped away from Shane and tapped the sleeping Tony and Smokey with his foot. "Let's figure out our plan."

Shane's face looked remarkably good; the wound was uncovered, and though still red and swollen, it looked neat and well cared for. Smokey and Tony were sluggish, rubbing their eyes but they were attentive and sharp when they sat down. Jared stayed where he was. Trey grabbed a cup of water, offered some all around.

"So, here are my thoughts. I don't pretend to have all the answers, so let me know what you think. This is only going to succeed if we all agree and work together. OK?" Nods all around.

"There will be a helicopter coming in around daylight, which gives us a little less than two hours to get ready. I've got Shrike's handheld radio here and it's tuned to channel 13, so that part of it was probably true. We'll monitor it but I don't intend to say anything."

"How will you call him in?" Tony asked.

"Well, I suspect Shrike was lying about the guy recognizing his voice, but I don't want to take a chance. I think our best bet is to act like something has gone wrong with our radio and try to wave him in."

Jared nodded. "Yeah. Good idea. That means three of us will have to wear their clothes and stand out in the meadow where they can see us."

"We should check their clothing," Tony said. "I think they are just wearing dark pants and black pullovers that they could take off and leave when they were done with us. I doubt they would have wanted to get off a civilian helo at a civilian airport looking like commandos."

"Right. If they are wearing a full set of civvies under their dark clothing we can wear the same when they come in to get us."

"And then what?" Shane wanted to know.

"What do you mean?" Trey said.

"I mean, what do we do when they land? In fact, do we really want them to land, or should we just disappear and let them wonder?"

Trey considered the question. "The main reason we want them to land is because if we don't control them in some fashion, the word will be back to New York in less than half an hour that the mission was unsuccessful. They will assume their team is dead and they'll send out a new one, a bigger one, as fast as they can put it together, which will be a lot faster than this one came. We might not even have time to get out of the mountains. But you bring up a good point. How do we control them? Here's what I'm thinking. Three of us out in the meadow waving the helo in. I suspect there will just be a pilot and he will have his tail numbers masked. He's not going to want anyone to be able to connect his aircraft with one or more dead bodies the team expected to leave here. He'll plan on landing somewhere outside the wilderness afterwards to clear his tail numbers so he looks legit at his destination."

Smokey rubbed his hands together, obviously concerned. "All of that is great, and I suspect he'll come right in, but won't he recognize us as the wrong people when he gets in close?"

Tony spoke up. "Not if we do things right. First of all, the pilot will fly over and check us out but once he sets up for the approach he's going to focus on the landing zone. Helicopters blow a lot of debris around during landing so he will expect us to hold our hats down and look away from his aircraft. Then, if we come in from the side and rear we should have a gun to his head before he knows anything is wrong."

"Good." Trey said. "That will work. But one very important thing. Getting a gun to his head is nice, and hopefully it will make him freeze.

But if he's a pro, he may yank on the collective and hope you won't kill him in the air, knowing you would die, too. So the man who puts the gun to his head has to be ready to pull the trigger."

They sat silently for a while. They'd thought the rough stuff was over, that they were going to survive. Now that outcome wasn't nearly as certain.

Jared took over. "OK, Trey, you and I will come in from opposite sides, carrying pistols hidden. Once we're in the aircraft, put the pistol where he can see it and if he even looks like he's thinking about pulling pitch, kill him."

"If you have to do that," Tony added. "One of you will have to keep him from falling over onto the cyclic. If he does, the aircraft will roll over and eat itself, even if it's just sitting on the ground."

"Right," Trey said. "Whichever of us doesn't kill him has to catch him and keep him upright. Now, who's going to be the other one out there?"

"It just about has to be me," Shane said. "Shrike was as big as me and one of us has to be taller than the others."

Jared continued, "So then, assuming we've got the pilot in hand, we can just make him fly Trey and me wherever we want to go. Wherever that is?" He phrased it as a question.

"Yes we can," Trey answered, and left it at that. "So, Shane, you, Tony and Smokey can take the horses out…"

"Yep, if we're lucky, no one will ever know we came up here and if someone finds out, it was just a trip to clean up our camp and get ready for the next client. Smokey and I have a stock truck at Whitewater and you left a four-horse trailer there, right, Jared?"

Jared nodded. "Yeah. The keys are on the air filter."

"OK, good. What about you, Tony? Do we need to give you a ride back to town?"

"No, I left a rental car at Whitewater, too."

Trey stepped in again. "Good. Sounds like we've got the transportation handled. The next problem is the bodies. As soon as anyone finds a body all hell will break loose and it will be hard on you local guys."

"I think I've got that figured out," Smokey said. "We can't really bury them in this country; too wet and too many roots. But there's a large rockfall about half a mile north of here," Shane and Jared both nodded in recognition. "We can hide the bodies from the helicopter and then, after you and Jared are gone, we can load them on the pack animals and dump them into one of the deep crevasses in that place. We'll pile a bunch more rocks on top and it will be a long damn time and several earthquakes before anyone finds them."

"Sounds like a plan. OK, let's get out there, drag the bodies under cover and check out the clothing. I'd really rather not put on something bloody, but we'll see. Also, let's make sure anything they brought goes into the rocks with them. We don't want anything of theirs left around this camp, including the parachutes. Any questions? Here we go."

****

Two hours later all five men sat outside the tent on stools they'd removed from the bloody, fear-drenched smell of the tent. Jared, Trey and Shane were wearing jeans and sweaters; a close approximation to the clothing they'd found under the killers' overalls. Each wore the baseball caps they'd found in the kits those men had brought. The bodies of the hit men were hidden in the trees. All their equipment, save the guns, was in bags to be buried in the rocks with them. Jared had appropriated two 9 mm Hechler and Koch silenced submachine guns as well as a .40 caliber Glock. When Shane asked, Jared said, "I'm going to disappear but if I get surprised on the way I don't want to be outgunned." Shane nodded. Jared and Trey were flying out, if everything went well, on a helicopter hired by people who wanted both of them dead. It didn't help develop a sense of complacency.

As light began to seep into the darkness, Shane didn't know how to feel. *He was about to lose his best friend for the rest of his life. The sense of finality overwhelmed anything he'd felt before. He wasn't sure how he would deal with a world that didn't offer at least the prospect of Jared in his life. It's not that he looked up to him so much as...he just assumed he would always be there. He'd known his father would die. That's what fathers did. They grew old and died. But Jared was like a force of nature. He didn't die, and he didn't just disappear off the face of the earth. But this was not about Jared anymore, at least not after the helicopter took off. It was about Lacy and the kids. He had to find a way to make sure he wasn't connected to the scene, or, if he and Smokey did their jobs right, there would be no scene to connect to. He knew the rock slide Smokey had described. There were holes and caves and hiding places galore. It was perfect, and as long as Jared and Trey were able to get on the helicopter, this whole evolution should work out fine. Provided he could figure out a way to explain the slash across his face. There was no way that Lacy could be told the truth on this. No way.*

Smokey. Jesus Christ, the little bottom-dwelling scumbag from the wrong side of town, was now his trusted friend. Not sidekick. No, because Smokey has a head on his shoulders and uses it to think for himself. He could see Smokey as a friend, a companion. He couldn't believe he was thinking like this, but he suspected Lacy and the kids would like him, too. Smokey was ready for more. He could never pass muster for the sheriff's department but he could take on more responsibility in the outfitting business. It may be time to create an assistant manager position for Smokey. Chester would welcome the help. He could just imagine Kowalski's and Cutter's reaction to that promotion. They still hadn't gotten used to the new Smokey and never failed to mention it when he met them on Friday mornings for breakfast.

"We need to get ready," Trey said.

Shane grimaced but nodded and stood. *He wished he could be the one to help Jared. It should be him. But Trey was good. Really good. He was the first professional hit man Shane had ever encountered and he wondered, how in the hell could I ever apprehend someone like him? I'm good with drunks in a bar and with family disturbances, but how could I deal with someone who moved as fast as he did, who shot as well as he did? With lots of help, he decided. That's why we have police forces, not just policemen.*

Trey smiled at him. *Could he know what I'm thinking?* Trey turned away, leaving Shane to wonder.

Smokey caught up the horses; shaking a pail of molasses-soaked oats brought them in a hurry. He snapped lead ropes on their halters and led them to the long line, where he tied them on. He didn't want them loose when the helicopter arrived; even hobbled, they probably wouldn't stop running until they got to the river. Once done, he gave each horse a couple handfuls of grain and took one last walk through the pasture. He checked again where the killers had landed to make sure none of their equipment remained.

Smokey hoped he was right about the bodies staying hidden; If anyone ever put together what happened here, he would be hammered harder than anyone else. A convicted felon involved in murders, regardless of whether he pulled the trigger, would certainly go away for the rest of his life. And that would leave Rand to fend for himself. This had to work. But he was confident it would. The truth was, he felt as confident right now as he ever had in his entire life. It was strange; at this point he'd reached the pinnacle of his ambition. Not his job ambition, so much, though he was proud to be a hunting and fishing guide and a wrangler. It was more his ambition for acceptance. For most of his life he'd hated Jared and Shane. They'd epitomized everything he detested about society. But what he'd wanted more than anything else, he realized now, was their acceptance. Their respect. And up here in the last two days, he'd found it. More accurately, he'd earned it. He'd had good ideas they'd listened to; he'd stood up when things got hairy; he'd watched Shane's back. This feeling of worth, of acceptance, of friendship, was his holy grail. No matter what else happened, he had that. He smiled to himself as he waited for the helicopter.

Tony moved the stools into the tent and checked, for the third time, to make sure nothing untoward would be visible from the air. The bodies were laid out in the woods under a camouflage tarp which was itself staked down. *Dead men. Lives snuffed out with no answers, no explanation. He remembered having come home to family and friends who'd already conducted his funeral. It was months before his mother had recovered enough not to cry every time she saw him. Of course, part of that was his severed arm. But these men's families would never know anything, anything at all about their deaths. He'd like to think that killers like these had no families, no one who would miss them, but that was probably not the case. Even the worst of men often had wives and children who loved them, many of whom had no idea what they did for a living. Like his father, a standout among vicious killers. Tony was glad to be finally and completely separated from his father. Being here, knowing that Sal unleashed people like Shrike and Trey put an exclamation point on their estrangement, made it absolute. He was going back to Oregon, back to the Alsea Valley. He could find work of some kind with one of Dean's relatives. He could help out around Mrs. Taylor's place. And maybe his mother could visit sometime. She and Mrs. Taylor would get along well.*

Tony stopped… an ear to the sky. He could just make out the sound of a two-bladed rotor system. "Inbound," he called, and moved back into the tent. Smokey joined him shortly afterward as the other three men took their places in the meadow.

The helicopter approach and landing took place exactly the way Tony had forecast it. A quick low pass followed by an approach into the wind. The aircraft had just touched down when Trey and Jared threw open the doors and leaped in, putting their pistols to the pilot's head. Trey yanked off the pilot's headset so he couldn't transmit and yelled into his ear, "Cinch down the collective. Now, put your left hand on your knee. Try anything at all and you die. We've got another pilot; we don't need you, so don't fuck up!" He slipped into the left seat and strapped in, keeping his pistol on the man all the while.

Jared threw their bags in the back and moved outside the rotor arc to greet the three men who were staying. Smokey came first; they shook hands warmly.

"You've been a good friend, Smokey. I owe you one."

Smokey smiled. His eyes were moist. "I wish I could have been a good friend earlier."

Jared nodded. "You take care of Shane for me, please."

"I will."

Tony came next. He took Jared's hand. "I don't know what to say, Jared."

"Me either. Maybe we can be friends in our next lives."

"I hope so. I'd like that. Take care."

Shane came in like a linebacker and lifted him in a strong embrace. He was obviously crying. "Goddamn rotor wash," he said, wiping his eyes. "I guess this is really it, huh?"

"I guess."

"You're going with Trey and you're going to hide out for a while, right?"

"Right."

"Maybe someday you can send me a card or make a quick call."

"I'll try to, but you can't count on it. You need to go and take care of your kids. You've taken enough chances for me. No more."

"No. You are on your own, well and truly."

"Right, got to go. See you, SixToes."

Shane laughed. "Asshole."

While Jared climbed into the helicopter, Shane walked around to the co-pilot's seat and shook hands with Trey. "You are quite a piece of work."

"And so are you, my friend."

"Take care of him."

"I'll sure try. Be careful, don't walk into the tail rotor."

Shane moved away from the helo to stand with Tony and Smokey.

Trey put on a headset and motioned for Jared to do the same. He switched off the pilot's access to the radios, leaving him capable only of communication inside the aircraft. "All right, he yelled, "Let's go, take up a heading of 270 and climb to a good VFR altitude."

Chapter 65

Damien Tarker was feeling pretty good. Tired, but good. The blonde guy who'd flown all the way in his left seat had turned out to be personable and friendly. Once he was sure Damien wasn't going to do anything stupid with the aircraft, he relaxed and chatted about flying and families, sports and politics. Damien began to feel a personal connection to him and he was sure the feeling was mutual. The blonde guy had some flying experience; that was clear. He kept them on a westerly heading until they were out of sight and hearing of the camp, then ordered a turn back to the east. He found a place to stop and strip the cover from their tail numbers. Then he handled the radios during the entire flight and did a reasonable job of announcing their approach to airfields. And when Damien told him they needed to file a flight plan, he simply said "Bullshit. Not required for VFR flights. Don't lie to me again. Your chance of living through this depends on it." Damien took him at his word and was helpful the rest of the trip.

The blonde guy helped to pick out uncontrolled airports with fuel available so they didn't have to deal with controlling agencies. Flying this way would make it much harder for the people who'd hired him to track their location, especially since he was using fictitious tail numbers when he called to announce their landings. The fuel chits would show the right aircraft—the gas jockeys filled those out—but it would be days, if not longer, before they could trace those...unless they had contacts with the feds. He wished he could have gotten away long enough to make a phone call—or even run—but they'd been real careful and he'd never had a chance. To make matters worse, he was having to pay for the fuel out of his own account. There was something wrong about being kidnapped and having to pay for your own transportation but it was better than the alternative. Besides, he could absorb the loss. The flying business had been profitable for the last few years and he'd find some way of writing off the cost of an unplanned trip to New York. At least, that's where he assumed they were going. Right into the lion's den for these guys. What were they thinking? That made it even more important to get free and make a call. No telling what they were planning.

The redhead in back was quiet. A few times the blonde guy tried to include him in the conversations, but pretty unsuccessfully. While in the air he either slept or looked out the window. He and the blonde guy talked during the fuel stops, private conversations Damien wasn't invited to, but when he went inside to use the rest room or pay for gas, one of them always accompanied him. They lost a few hours in Ohio waiting for the airport to open and the fuel vendor to arrive, and they caught some shuteye. Then it was back in the air again.

The blonde guy raised his head from the flight publications he'd been reading and said, "Take a heading of 075; we're about an hour from Beckwith."

"Is that our final destination?" Damien asked.

The blonde guy's eyes went icy and he shook his head slightly. "You know better than to ask questions. Way over your pay grade." Then, as if to soften the threat, he asked, "Tell me, how did you end up here?"

Damien told him. It was a story he enjoyed repeating, for the most part. The farm where he grew up in western Nebraska was located next to a small airport. At first it had been a grass strip used only by crop dusters, but as the nearby town grew, so did the airport and soon 13-year-old Damien was doing odd jobs in return for flight time. By the time he was 17 he had his private pilot's license and knew he wanted to fly for a living. He attended Embry Riddle University and received a degree in Aeronautics as well as his Airframes & Powerplants License, then joined the Navy to fly jet fighters. He learned helicopters as well. When he left the Navy he had some other flying jobs until he was able to open his own charter company in Seattle. Now he flew all over the Northwest and

Canada. He took jobs as they came. He didn't know the people he was supposed to pick up on this job. It was just a pick up and drop job back in Grangeville. He shouldn't have agreed to fly into the wilderness, but there was already an airstrip in the Chamberlain Basin grandfathered in from the days before the wilderness existed, so even though he was technically wrong to have flown into the meadow, planes fly into the airstrip only a few miles away all the time.

It was all true, except for some of the details. While in flight training, Damien had done well in primary and when the time came for pipeline selection he was virtually certain to be given his first choice of aircraft. Unfortunately, virtually is not the same as certainty and for the first time in memory, everyone in Damien's class was put in either props or helos. As the top student in his class, Damien was given his choice between those two. "But I want jets! I earned jets! I deserve them!" Damien yelled at his flight leader, a crusty Lieutenant Commander.

"Tough shit. Needs of the service, Ensign. Deal with it. One other thing… if you raise your voice to me again I'll have you up for insubordination."

So Damien had gone through helicopter training. He already had 700 hours of fixed wing time and figured if he couldn't fly jets he might as well learn something new. But he never forgave the Navy for robbing him of his dream and after a tour flying SAR off a carrier, he left the Navy and tried to get on with the airlines. The airlines weren't hiring though, and Damien soon found himself taking bottom-rung flying jobs just to build hours. He flew helicopters to oil rigs off the Louisiana coast, and on his days off flew short commuter flights out of Lake Charles. It was while he was eating breakfast in Lake Charles one day that he was approached by a man who asked if he was interested in some extra work. He needed a pilot who could fly both fixed and rotary wing aircraft and who was rated to work on them as well.

"There aren't that many people like you around," he told Damien. And it was true, ratings in fixed and rotary wing along with the A&P license made Damien highly sought after, at least by small-time operators who wanted to save money. The larger airlines could have cared less; their pilots don't work on the aircraft. But he listened anyway. The job involved making night-time deliveries, he was told. From South America to small, unlit airfields along the Gulf Coast.

"Aaaahh," said Damien. He rose to go. "No thanks. I'd prefer to stay out of jail."

Then the man gave him a figure. For one run. It was more than most airline pilots made in a year. Enough so that after four runs he'd have enough to buy two airplanes and start his own company. Damien sat back down.

He actually made 10 runs and quit. Or tried to. No quitting allowed, he was told. He made a counter offer. He had a little leverage. "Let me get out of the smuggling business and open a charter company. I'll still do your work when you need me but it will be as a legitimate businessman." They'd agreed. He'd set up in Seattle and now had a thriving business, subsidized on an irregular basis by organized crime. The money was good, but the people in charge never thought of reservations; they just called and he had to drop everything. He'd had to cancel two reservations from long-term clients and pre-position a Cessna and the Jet Ranger in Grangeville for this operation.

"You know, I have a wife and daughter," Damien said.

"Really! How old is your daughter?" The blonde guy was genuinely interested, or seemed to be.

"She's four. And I can forget any of this ever happened. I can sit in a motel here for two days without talking to anyone so you can…do whatever you need to do. I'll never say a word."

"Promise?"

"Absolutely! On my daughter's life. I swear."

"On your own life."

"Yes, of course. On my life."

"OK."

Damien almost wet himself he was so relieved. On the way into the landing he was chattering like a schoolgirl. The blonde guy smiled and laughed. They told Damien to arrange to hangar the aircraft for two days. That way it would be out of sight while Damien stayed in the motel room.

"It's important you make no phone calls," the blonde guy told him.

"None. Not to your family or your business. No one."

"None. Thank you."

They had the Jet Ranger wheeled into a small, tin hangar and began to unload, after the airport worker had left. They spent an hour wiping fingerprints.

"What are you going to do when you get back?" the blonde guy asked.

Take my wife and kid to a Mariners game," Damien said. He was as happy as he'd ever been. They were buying it, even the wife and kid bit. He was going to walk out of this. "Maybe go have a good steak. Do something besides fly." They all laughed together.

"I hear that," the blonde guy said.

"How long will it take you to get back to Seattle from Grangeville?" the quiet red head asked. It was a good sign, Damien knew. It was the first direct question the man had asked him. It meant he had decided to let him go, too.

"Oh, maybe three and a half hours, give or take. You're usually bucking the wind going that direction, but I've got to get both aircraft back as soon as I…"

The air became still and cold. The red head's demeanor changed from an interested bystander to a predator.

Damien's knees almost buckled.

"I… we… we've got a crop duster over in Cle Elum and I've got to arrange for…"

The blonde guy turned directly toward him. "You never mentioned a crop duster."

"No, it's not mine…ours. I'm picking it up for another guy."

"You have two Cessna 182s, this Jet Ranger and a seaplane."

"Yes, that's what I own. But I ferry aircraft for people, too."

"It's the 182 that you have to bring back from Grangeville. The 182 you used to drop those guys in on us."

"No! No! I don't know what guys you mean. I had nothing to do with…OK, yes. I dropped them but I don't know them and I still won't say a thing. I can stay in a motel for three days, for a week! You can still trust me. I…" And then the world went black.

Jared put the silenced HK back in his bag. He wrapped a tarp around Damien's shattered head and motioned for Trey to help him lift the body into the helicopter. "You were going to let him go, weren't you?"

"No. I don't know. I liked him. But he put those guys in on us."

"Yes. Guys camo'd up, with machine guns and commando kits. He knew what they were and what they were doing and they wouldn't have given him a job like that unless they trusted him; unless he was connected. He would have given us up as soon as he found a phone."

"I know. I would have taken care of it."

"It's done, now. We'll lock the hangar and they won't think to look in it for a couple of days. That's long enough." Jared finished zipping up his bag, lifted it.

"So, Lieutenant. You're not really coming with me, are you?

"No."

"That bit about hiding out, getting better, going on... was all a lie, to me, to your friends."

"I had to make sure you'd let them live. And besides, you're talking to me about lying? You damn near got my best friend killed! Scarred for life!"

"What do you mean? I didn't have anything to do with that. How could I have..."

"Don't give me your bullshit, Trey! I remember everything that happened. You let that... Shrike move all around, get up, sit down, stretch. You had to know what he was doing. You of all people had to know! And then you basically handed Shane to him! 'You go on outside, Shane, and think about it.' He had to walk right in front of Shrike to get to the door. You knew. Don't tell me you didn't know. Christ! He could have been killed. You set him up for that and then you accuse me of lying!"

"You did lie, Lieutenant. I never lied. You all knew what was at stake. I never misled you. I tried hard not to let anyone know my name, then none of your friends would have been at risk. But who could have anticipated Shrike knowing me and spilling his guts like that? And Shane wasn't buying in to it. He was the key to everything. He was going to turn me in and I was going to kill him. And then I would have had to kill the rest of you, too. That little dance with Shrike was my last-ditch effort to save Shane's life, in spite of himself. All of your lives. It was one in a million, but it worked out. He feels beholden to me and that feeling is what saved him. It seems to me the scar is a small price to pay. To be honest, I didn't expect it to work. I had already resigned myself to killing all of you. It was serendipitous, but it wasn't a lie. I had no choice."

Jared sighed, and nodded. "Yes. OK. I understand. And I appreciate everything you did… and not killing us. But nothing has changed for me, except that Corrarino no longer knows where I am. I just have to find another place to hole up and tell them where to find me. You need to go on."

"We are in eastern Pennsylvania, Jared, ninety miles from New York."

"Yes, I know, but…" Jared's entire demeanor changed. "New York." His chest expanded, his shoulders squared. "New York."

"Yes."

"I can take it to him."

"Theoretically."

"Right to him."

"He will be well guarded."

"I have two silenced machine guns, a pistol and lots of ammo for both."

"Those will help."

"Do you know where?"

"I know where his headquarters has been in the past."

"Great. Tell me, and then you go on your way."

"I might stick with you a little longer."

"You can't help me. You've got family."

"I can't be involved. But I might watch."

Chapter 66

The next afternoon they were in a hotel room across a lightly trafficked street from Panetta's Restaurant. They'd taken separate cabs from the airfield to town and then Trey had walked to a small, used car lot and bought a sad old Chevy Cavalier for cash. "It only has to go 100 miles," he told Jared, as they drove away. He'd driven into New York, parked on a street thirty blocks from their destination, wiped off their prints, left the car unlocked with the keys in it and again taken separate cabs. Jared had checked in to the hotel alone. He'd worried about being recognized, but Trey said sunglasses and a baseball cap were all the disguise most people ever needed, and it had proven true. Trey had given him a credit card to use if he'd needed it, but an offer to pay cash up front with a healthy deposit had worked just fine. They'd been watching through binoculars almost non-stop since their arrival. Panetta's was a small restaurant with few diners. Jared said as much to Trey.

"I heard it was owned by one of Corrarino's shirttail relatives," Trey told him. "They serve great food and have a good reputation, but most of their clientele are locals. They don't need to make a profit because they are underwritten by the mob. Corrarino's office is in the back and he sometimes uses the whole place. A guy I knew told me that Sal will sometimes just close it so he's got a secure place for large meetings. He said they have a basement like a bomb shelter they can wall off like a panic room."

"Well, he can't be too worried at this point, because they are still seating customers," Jared said. "Or maybe he's not there at all."

"I think he's there. There are two knuckle-draggers lounging around the front door. Every couple of hours a different two take their places. I doubt if they'd do that if Sal wasn't around."

"Ahhh. I see."

"I suspect those guys are just the normal, everyday muscle," Trey continued. "Which means Sal hasn't figured things out yet. Right now, he just wants you dead and he's pulling out all the stops to make it happen. It hasn't yet occurred to him that you might be a threat. He knows something went wrong because he hasn't heard from the team, but they haven't found the pilot yet. They will find him today or tomorrow. Once they do, they'll know you are in the area, and I'm sure he'll go to ground. You're going to have to take him today or you probably won't get him at all."

Jared looked out the window in both directions. Small shops and restaurants lined the street. Offices and apartments in the upper floors. Another hotel announced its presence with signs a block away. A few people were walking on both sidewalks, but it wasn't overly crowded. "Well, this is your line of work. What do you recommend?"

Trey considered for a moment. "If it were me, I'd make a phone call to spook him, then shoot him from here when he shows his face."

"Wouldn't he go to the basement, if he's worried?"

"Possibly, but the man has pride. I don't think he'll want his people to see him run and hide from one guy. Especially one who killed several members of his family. That's why he won't take the back door out, either. He's got to show strength and certainty. He'll walk out like a politician, smiling and waving and just go home."

"Maybe I could get to him there."

"Maybe, but I doubt it. He owns the whole building and it's a fortress. He rides in a bulletproof car and drives directly into a secure garage. Not to mention, it's an apartment building. There will be a lot of family members there on different floors and I doubt you want to be involved with them." Jared shook his head; the last thing he wanted was the possibility that another innocent might be hurt. "No, I think your best chance at him is right across the street."

"I don't want to shoot him from here. I want to look him in the eye but...."

Trey shook his head slowly. "I know. You want it to end here. It's just as well, I suppose. None of our weaponry is any good for a long-range shot like that."

"It's funny," Jared mused, as though talking to himself, "A few days ago, all I wanted to do was die in a blaze of gunfire and take a couple of them with me. Now, I've got a whole new goal. I want to stay alive...but just long enough to kill that bastard." He turned to look Trey straight in the eyes. "That's pretty goddamn sad, isn't it?"

Trey put his hand on Jared's shoulder. "Sad isn't even in it, Lieutenant. No one deserves the breaks you've gotten. I came with the idea that maybe I could help make things better for you, but it's obvious now that I can't. I'd love to go in there with you." He smiled broadly. "Two men with silenced H&Ks could do a lot of damage. But if they had even a suspicion I was with you they'd hunt me and my s.... family down. Then there's Tony. If he learns I took part in this attack he'll give me up instantly. No, this has got to be your deal. I'm sorry."

"Don't be. You've already done more than you should. I'll get the restaurant number from the phone book. You go ahead and leave now, Trey."

"You'd better let me make the call. Here's the problem. It will take you several minutes to get down to the street and into position. Corrarino is not a fool. He may see through our little plan and figure the best way to avoid it is to move fast. If he does, he could be in the car and gone before you even make the street."

"Good point. You know what to say?"

"I think so. I'll taunt him a little bit about the four, no five people you killed."

"Five?"

"Yeah, don't forget me. I died up there, too."

"Ahhh. OK."

"I'll try to give him the impression you're still a ways out, but you're coming. If he buys it, he may wait an hour or even two. If he doesn't, He may scoot out the front door right away. If I guess wrong, he might sneak out the back door or hole up in the basement and never give you a chance at him."

Jared put the Glock in his belt and zipped the jacket over it. The HKs went into a backpack, which remained unzipped and was slung over one shoulder. He looked for a long moment at Trey, then said simply, "Thanks."

Trey smiled grimly and said, "Sure. Anytime."

Jared hesitated, then reached into a coat pocket. He withdrew something and handed it to Trey.

"Candy?" Trey asked.

"Not just candy," Jared told him. "Mints. And not just mints, but tone mints. My father told me about them years ago. I didn't need them until recently. Take just one at a time. They'll help…"

"Help?"

"Help make things right. See you."

"Good luck, sir."

Jared grunted and closed the door behind him.

Trey waited a few minutes, then picked up the phone book, found the number and dialed it.

"Panetta's Restaurant, how can I help you?"

"I need to talk with Sal Corrarino."

"I'm sorry. He's not here."

"This is Jared McCauley, the man who killed his son, grandson and daughter-in-law. You should tell him. He'll be pretty mad if you don't."

"Wait a minute."

Trey could feel the malice before a word was spoken. "McCauley."

"Hello, Sal."

"You're still alive."

"How about that? Your boys got into a little fight between themselves. Made it quite a bit easier for me."

"It's the last thing that will be easy for you, cocksucker. Your time is coming. You sound different."

"It's that cool mountain air. Stretches your tonsils. You should have joined us. Would have been good for your health."

"Yeah. Sorry I missed it. I won't miss the next one. Where can I find you?"

"Oh, don't worry. I've decided to find you. Should be there in the next day or so."

A heartbeat of hesitation. "Come ahead. I'll make sure you live to regret it! You hear me?" But he was talking to himself.

****

Sal put the phone down, slowly, quietly. *This was the worst possible situation and he had brought it on himself. He never should have sent in that commando team on top of Alonzo. He hadn't been thinking clearly when he made that decision. More is not better. But when Pauly told him Alonzo had wanted to quit and basically held out for more money, it had pissed him off. They probably killed each other off and let that fucking McCauley just walk out of there. No. Not walk. He waylaid the helicopter, too. That's why there had been no word from the pilot. How far would he have gone in the helo? Salt Lake? Denver? He couldn't fly all the way here to New York in a helicopter. Or could he? Christ, the whole world is looking for him. Could this be a setup? Is he out there right now? No. Not a fucking chance.*

He signaled Carmine and shoved over the picture of Jared McCauley from the newspaper he'd kept on his desk. "Make sure everybody gets this picture and pays attention."

"OK, boss. Is this guy around here?" Carmine was incredulous.

"He may get here. Things didn't go right in Idaho."

"Shit. OK, boss. I'll get it out."

"Oh, and Carmine, have Angelo bring the car around."

"Around back, boss?" Carmine's eyes were wide.

Sal hesitated. "No. Of course not. Just around front."

Sal cleaned up his paperwork and moved slowly toward the front of the restaurant. Greeting people and shaking hands as he went.

It was a good feeling. These people looked up to him. Respected him. With them, he could do anything. Of course, that's the way it was with Charley, too. The kid loved him and wanted to be just like him. But Charley had been a bottom dweller from the beginning. Maria had known it very early. Sal always thought something was wrong with her, so obviously not liking one of her own children. But she'd been the smart one. He should have listened and cut Charley off from the business. Made him go his own way. But the kid who went his own way never wanted anything to do with his father. And good man though he was, Tony had not been man enough to avenge his own son, not to mention his wife and brother. He'd not even attended their funerals.

"Do you blame him?" Maria said, when Sal complained. "His son was dead and buried. His wife and brother betrayed him. His father disowned him. What was there to hang around for?"

Sal grimaced internally, even as he glad-handed one of his favorite waiters. *Once we get this McCauley character sorted out all of this will fade into the background. It might take a year or two, but Tony will come back. He knew it.* Sal moved close to the front windows, looking out at the building across the street as he talked and laughed with the front-room customers. All the hotel room windows were permanently shut; it wouldn't be easy to shoot from there. He wasn't worried about those or the roof, either. The restaurant awning hid people near the restaurant far too well from the upper floors and roof to attempt a shot from such a high angle. The boys outside could stop an attack on the ground and once he got in the car he'd be safe. The main thing was to show no fear. Fear. What the hell was going on here, that he, Sal Corrarino, could possibly be afraid of some two-bit asshole? But McCauley was obviously more competent than he'd been given credit for, and Sal knew from personal experience how accurate the old saying was about the most dangerous man being one with nothing left to lose. This feeling of vulnerability was so unlike anything he'd ever experienced. All his life he'd been the aggressor, the hunter. This was alien, wrong. When he got his hands on McCauley he'd make the son of a bitch pay, make him pray for death.

Here came the car; his two door guards moving to flank it. They seemed much more alert than normal. Carmine must have said something to them. Angelo, his driver, stayed behind the wheel. Sal shook a few more hands and made for the door. He made himself walk slowly, confidently. He was almost to the car door when Al, the guard behind the car to his left, coughed and stumbled. Thunk, thunk, thunk. The car's rear window crazed. Fuck! Gunfire! He jumped for the open car door. He saw movement to his left. A man in jeans and a baseball cap was moving down the sidewalk toward him, firing in three-shot bursts. Suddenly Artie opened up from his right, firing his big .45 as he moved closer to put his body between Sal and the attacker. Sal was ducking into the car when one of Jared's 9 mm slugs creased his butt. Had it been a solid hit, the chances are it would have helped propel him into the car. But it wasn't and it didn't. It made him arch his back involuntarily, almost standing him straight up, straight up into the path of Artie's fourth round. The bullet caught Sal on the bridge of the nose, tearing it loose from his face. The impact tore his left eye from the socket and left it hanging across his cheek. It also destroyed most of the optic nerves on both sides of his face. The crushing blow spun Sal to his left and dropped him face down on the sidewalk, with his left foot still inside the car. The bullet then continued on to hit Jared high up in his left thigh, just nicking the femoral artery.

Artie was so overwhelmed by the sight of Sal's face exploding with his shot that he forgot what he was doing and knelt over Sal. "Omigod, boss. Omigod, I didn't…" He would have apologized more profusely except that Jared's next three round burst spread itself on and around the top of his head. He pitched forward on top of his boss.

Angelo had been trained to stay behind the wheel when there was trouble, but when he saw Sal go down he pulled his own pistol and jumped out firing. Because he'd been ready to pull out, the car was still in gear and the brake was off. When he left the car, it began to pull forward. Sal's left foot, still in the car, became wedged between the seat and floor so he was dragged along, carrying Artie, who was spread-eagled on top of him. They continued on that way for several feet, until Sal's left armpit encountered a bus signpost. The contact slowed the car's forward progress, but Sal's body pivoted around and his foot finally came free just after he and Artie slid partway off the curb and into the gutter. The car continued forward until it softly crunched a Yellow Cab, whose driver had taken shelter in a nearby dry cleaners.

Jared was on his knees now. He knew the hit he'd taken was causing serious blood loss but he had other things to worry about. The driver was exiting the car while Jared was still trying to change magazines. Finally he dropped the HK and pulled the Glock from his belt just as Angelo came charging down the street, screaming and shooting. Angelo's first shot clipped Jared's ear. The second hit him just under the collarbone and exited his back without hitting the shoulder. He began folding over slowly, but pointed the pistol out in front as best he could and started pulling the trigger. His first shot ricocheted off the pavement and shattered Angelo's shin. His second ricocheted into the trunk of Sal's car. By the time he'd pulled the trigger the third time, Angelo had finished falling and the bullet hit him in the throat, severing his spine.

Jared was becoming lethargic and deeply cold but he pushed himself upright. He scooped up the loaded magazine and popped it into the HK, slamming the bolt home. He looked toward the restaurant, expecting more people with guns to come at him. But no one came. He looked back behind him and across the street. He could see the window of his room but nothing behind it. He tried to walk toward Sal but couldn't stay upright, so he crawled, first on his hands and knees, but then on his belly. He could hear sirens, but everything seemed to be far away. He was having trouble focusing on the pile that he knew contained Sal, but he continued to crawl. He needed to be closer to be sure. Now he could see Sal's eye lying on the pavement. There were bubbles coming from his mouth. His right hand was dancing across the pavement, like a baby wren. Jared levered himself off the sidewalk and into the street. Some deep recess of his mind smiled at the thought of Sal in the gutter. He crawled on.

"Drop the gun!" Someone was yelling from far away. "Drop the gun or I'll shoot." It didn't seem to apply to him and besides, Jared was not about to drop his gun for anyone.

Suddenly, someone stepped hard on his wrist and tried to pull the HK out of his hand. Jared responded by pulling the trigger. The hand grabbing the gun let go, just as the boot on his wrist lifted. Jared was able to lower the barrel of the HK down in front of him. He pulled the trigger again and kept it pulled until something exploded in his chest and the concrete speckles turned into stars and expanded to be his entire world.

Sitting at the window in the hotel room across the street, Trey Cannon lowered his chin to his hands and watched the event's aftermath unfold below him. "Jesus, Lieutenant. Jesus. I hope when I grow up I can be like you." Tears streamed down his face. Cops were running in from everywhere. Setting up perimeters. Ambulances and paramedics waited outside for the word it was safe to come in. The cop who had shot Jared twice in the back was sitting on the curb looking stunned.

"You sure could have done a lot better than that, Bubba," Trey said softly. "You could have taken that gun away from him easily. Why did you have to jump away and shoot him? Not that it was a bad thing. You helped him end just the way he wanted."

The last dozen rounds Jared had fired stitched across Sal and his human backpack, even as the cop shot him. Sal had shuddered and flopped as the bullets hit him. He must have been considerably more alive than he'd looked. Trey hoped that was no longer the case.

In a few minutes, the EMTs and paramedics came rushing in. The first bodyguard seemed to be alive, and they wheeled him out quickly. The driver was covered, as was the second bodyguard, when they pulled him off Sal. They worked on Sal for a long time but finally they covered him as well.

Trey nodded. That should do it. All the way around. He stood straight and tall and gave a slow, rigidly perfect salute. Then he slipped from the room and headed toward the back stairway.

Chapter 67

Two years later

Smokey liked high country weddings. They were three-day affairs; one day in, one day for the wedding and one day out. And everyone always came back happy, although there were usually one or two a little saddle sore afterwards. This had been a particularly good one. Lots of revelry and heavy tipping. He said goodbye to all the clients, put away the horses and tack, then headed home to Rand. The tents and other gear could wait until tomorrow to be stored.

He was always glad to come home, but he was certainly not prepared for the Rand that greeted him. "What have you done?" Rand yelled happily as he came forward and kissed Smokey strongly. "How could you have pulled it off?"

Smokey didn't want to take credit for something he hadn't done, but he was not above reaping the rewards first and admitting it later. He kissed Rand back.

"How did you do it? Tell me." Rand held him at arm's length and demanded an answer. Damn. So much for the rewards first idea.

"I actually have no idea what you're talking about. Sorry."

Rand looked directly into his eyes, a quizzical expression on his face. "You didn't talk Dr. Malkin into taking me on next month?"

"What? The guy at the Mayo Clinic? The one who said you weren't an appropriate patient?"

Rand stomped his foot and looked at Smokey like he knew he was lying. "Yes, that guy. And you didn't send two first-class plane tickets and reservations at the Kahler International Hotel?"

The stunned look on Smokey's face finally convinced Rand his partner was as confused as he. They both sat down.

"What could have convinced him to accept me?" Rand asked.

"I don't have a clue."

The doorbell rang. It was the FedEx delivery man with an envelope. Rand brought it to Smokey. "It's for you."

Inside was a single sheet of paper.

Dear Smokey:

I wanted to show my appreciation for your discretion and dependability. Upon further reflection, Dr. Malkin has decided he can help Rand and I've taken the liberty of making an appointment for him two months from now. Although complete recovery may not be possible, Rand should be close. I wish you both the best.   T

Smokey smiled and took a deep breath. "Well, now we know why the doctor changed his mind about you."

Rand was positively quivering. "What was it? Tell me!"

"Money."

"We tried that."

"Lots of money."

"Who would do something like that for us, Smokey?" Who? A friend of yours? Smokey! Tell me!"

Smokey looked at his best friend and lover. He'd never lied to him before. He wouldn't now, either. But he could dance around a bit. "A client. Up in the mountains. Years ago. He got himself into a jam and didn't know what to do about it. I basically just talked with him and helped him figure out a way around it. He thanked me for the help but I think what he appreciates most is the fact I didn't tell anybody about his problem. I can't tell you any more details than that, you see?"

Rand thought for a moment and then nodded. "I guess, but I'd like to thank him, myself."

"He doesn't want that, Rand."

"No, I guess not. But... Smokey... how did he know so much about me, and Dr. Malkin? We'd never heard of Dr. Malkin until six months ago."

Smokey shook his head and smiled. "I don't know, but I think there's not a lot this guy can't find out."

He put his arm around Rand and leaned back on the couch. Rand held the letters and plane tickets tight in his hands and wiggled in closer.

****

Lacy leaned back in the porch swing and looked sideways at her husband. He was absorbed in the birds flittering around the feeder in their back yard. Occasionally he would raise the binoculars to his eyes and nod as he recognized a species. He was trying to delay, putting her off. From this side, she could see almost the entire scar, or what was left of it. Time and two sessions of plastic surgery had drastically reduced the redness and swelling. All that remained now was a light-colored line the doctors said would gradually fade until it was essentially gone. Shane had not really cared about it; he would have just let it heal on its own. She and the kids practically had to beg him to get it fixed.

Lacy still remembered when he'd returned from the mountains with that cut. He'd walked in the door with his face all bandaged up and his eyes full of a sadness she could not comprehend. Luckily, the kids weren't home at the time so he could talk freely, but he didn't tell her much more than she'd already known. Yes, he had seen Jared but Jared had refused his help and he'd left Jared to his own devices. She and the kids were his priority. There was nothing he could do for Jared any more. "And Lacy," he'd said into her hair as he held her.

"Yes?"

"No one but you knows I even went into the mountains, much less saw Jared. You can never tell anyone anything. Ever. OK?"

"Of course. I will never tell anyone. So we're out of it. How about Jared?"

"I think so. I hope so. I think he's found a place to live where he can be safe. I don't think we will ever hear from or about him again."

But a day later Shane had called her from the office. "There's news coming in from New York, babe. It might have to do with Jared. I'm going to stay a while longer."

New York. Jared. Could they have caught him so quickly? And why would he have gone to New York? Lacy turned on the radio but heard nothing. They didn't have a television. At midnight she'd called him at the office.

"Nothing for sure, yet, babe. I'm making a few phone calls but I might not be home for a while."

Lacy had gone to sleep then and gotten up to get the kids off to school in the morning. It was almost noon when Shane came through the door. His shoulders were slumped and his eyes were as red as that suppurating cut across his face.

She hesitated, then ran to him. He gently stopped her with his hands on her shoulders. "Jared is dead," he said. "He attacked the Corrarino headquarters in New York and killed three men, including Sal Corrarino. A fourth man is not expected to live much longer. Jared was hit several times in the gun battle but he was killed by a cop as he was putting a last few rounds into Sal." It was like a prepared speech. She wondered how many times he'd had to give it already. She pushed inside his arms, pulling herself close. "I've been at his folks' house since 8 this morning." He lowered his head to her shoulder and cried.

Now, as she looked at his profile, she wondered at the change in him in the past two years. He was leaner than before, almost gaunt. He'd not been outwardly unhappy; but he certainly had not been as outgoing or friendly as before. She thought for the first several months that his problem had been the loss of Jared, but gradually she began to realize there was something besides that horrible loss. Something internal that was eating away at her husband. She couldn't count the number of times she'd asked him what was wrong. She even asked Smokey one time, but he'd given her a non-answer. The fact Smokey might know something she didn't was indicative of her husband's plight. Smokey Stover, Assistant General Manager of Mountain Outfitters, had become a close friend of Shane's, even a confidant, since that trip into the mountains after Jared.

Gift of the Grenadier

He knew, she was sure, how her husband's face was really cut, and it damn sure wasn't a slip with his knife while cutting down a hanging cache. She'd waited for two years. She'd watched her husband's slow descent into ruin for long enough, and by God, she was going to have an answer tonight. She was going to have a bunch of answers tonight. The letter in her hand said so.

"Well?" she said.

He put down the binoculars. "How much was it?"

"Twenty thousand dollars…each."

He put his head back down on the swing. "It's not a bribe, Lacy. I'm not a dirty cop."

"I know that, Shane. I absolutely know that, but I think this is all tied up with whatever's been eating at you for the past two years and I'm going to know what it is, tonight, period."

Shane leaned forward to put his head in his hands. He rocked back and forth. His head shook slowly from side to side. He ran his fingers through his hair. He took a deep breath.

"Damn it, Shane!" Lacy yelled. "I want to know! I deserve to know." She lowered her voice again. "Let me read this to you again."

Dear Shane:

I wanted to let you know how much I appreciate your honesty and dependability. I'm sorry for the loss of your friend. Moth to a flame, as you know. I've taken the liberty of contributing some money to the educational funds you've set up for Marshal, Craig, Julie and Jessica. I'm sure they will do you and Lacy proud.   T

"Well?" she said again.

Shane stood up and sat back down. He turned to her, obviously distressed. "OK. OK. This guy… T… was an old friend of Jared's. He showed up in the mountains to help him, to take him somewhere safe. Other people came while Smokey and I were up there who wanted to kill him, kill Jared. This guy… T… handled them. And he saved me," he pointed to the scar. "I promised, we all promised, to keep his identity secret."

"But why, why did he want his identity secret? It sounds like he was a hero."

"He's not a hero, babe. Not even close. He just did one good thing."

"And what about the people who tried to kill Jared?"

"They're gone. A long way gone and no one will ever find them or care."

"But...?"

"I didn't kill anyone, Lace. That's what you need to know. I didn't kill anyone. But I gave my word to protect the identity of someone who did and I'm having trouble with it."

"This man saved your life?"

"And everyone else's life, as well."

"But how did he convince you to protect his name?"

Shane laughed bitterly. "He drove a hard bargain."

Lacy began to ask a second question, but he shook his head and she closed her mouth.

"OK," she said. "So, I know what I'm going to know, is that it?"

Shane nodded.

"It's enough, I think. Let me tell you how I feel. This man, this T, he saved your life. That's enough for me, no matter what else he did in his entire life. That's enough for me. And as for you, all torn up inside because of your conflicting oaths, well, bullshit!"

Shane blinked.

"You've said for years that nothing about the law is black and white. You've made fun of deputies who weren't capable of seeing the different shades of human behavior. Have you forgotten how you came to law enforcement? How Kowalscutter hogtied you? Obviously, there were things going on up there that exceeded anything we've seen before, but the principle was the same. You had to make hard choices. You made them. You made a hard choice with your father, too, but it was a good choice. Wasn't it?" She watched her husband's eyes tear up.

"And now this guy, T, has sent a letter thanking you and giving a tremendous gift to your children... probably to ensure your continued adherence to your promise, huh?"

He smiled. Talk about a gift, to have a wife who saw things so clearly.

He felt like he was physically leaning on her and she was carrying half his weight. "Yes. That's part of it. But he's also letting me see that he knows all of your names."

"He could have done that without sending $80,000. Besides the information is not hard to find out, Shane. Anyone could have told him."

"True, but not anyone could have managed to transfer $80,000 into our kids' college accounts without getting the information from us."

"Are you afraid of him, hon?"

Shane thought for a minute. "No, not at all. I believe he is totally honest and dependable—in his own way."

"Well, then we should give thanks that he saved your life and the lives of your friends and that he gave us a wonderful gift, besides. He may be a bad man in many ways, but for me, he is an angel from heaven. And you, my husband, are the finest man I've ever known. You should know that, if you don't already, and you should forgive yourself for the few bad things you've done."

Shane smiled and leaned across, putting his head on her lap. Lacy could feel his muscles loosen. His head felt like it weighed 50 pounds on her leg. She could feel his body melt into a putty-like state she hadn't felt for a long time.

They stayed there without speaking for nearly an hour. Suddenly, his eyes popped open. "I'm hungry," he said with a smile that split his face. "I'm really hungry."

****

Simon McCauley tucked his wife in under the covers and went outside to get the mail. The Hospice lady would arrive soon. Sarah was right up against it now, she rarely responded to anything said to her. She'd been fading fast since shortly after their last visit to Bowie, when their whole world began coming apart. She still smiled though, and last night she'd put her hand to his face. Two years of taking care of her. At first just feeding her and helping her get around. Then gradually, dressing her, helping her go to the bathroom, cleaning her afterwards. She'd cried at first, at her helplessness, at her indignity. But gradually, they had both become used to the idea, to the need, and she would put her arms around his neck as he worked with her. She would smile and whisper in his ear, "Thank you. I love you." He'd thought once or twice about a nursing home, or in-home care, but even if money wasn't an issue, he couldn't bear the thought of Sarah being alone, or of having someone between them. Besides, he was still healthy and strong—for his age. And he didn't need much sleep. He could care for her as long as it took.

He moved slowly down the walk. Maybe he wasn't quite as strong as he thought. It could have been so different if Jared were still alive. Sarah could have been happy in her last days, though he knew she hadn't been truly happy since Jared was wounded in Vietnam. Still, a son, even a badly damaged son, a grandchild, a wonderful daughter-in-law went a long way toward happiness. At least we could see happiness from there, he thought. But not now. Now there's just an empty hole where our hearts used to be.

There was no mail in the box but just as Simon turned back to the house the FedEx Delivery truck came to a hurried stop. "Hello, Mr. McCauley. Got something for you."

"Thanks, Colin. I must be getting pretty important to get overnight mail, huh?"

He opened the letter and read as the truck drove away. A single, typed sheet of paper.

Simon made his way back up the walk, moving quite a bit more spryly now. "Sarah," he called as he climbed the stairs to their bedroom. "Sarah…I got a note from a friend of Jared's." He took her hand. "Let me read it…" He stopped and felt her hand more closely. His head shook silently. He felt up her wrist, to her neck. He bent over and put his ear to her nose. "Oh, Sarah. Please. You have to stay just a little longer. Sarah. Please." He hung his head for several minutes.

"Sarah." Simon's voice was firm. He sat up straight. "You have to listen to this. It's from a friend of Jared's. It's important for you to hear." He read it in a clear voice.

Dear Mr. and Mrs. McCauley:

I am an old friend of Jared's and was with him during some of his most difficult moments. I want to tell you that I have never admired a man as much as I did Jared McCauley. Even now, I hope I can conduct myself with the decency, bravery and dedication he did, right to the end of his life. His impact on the people who served with him is inestimable and although I know it is scant comfort, it is probably the best any of us can hope for.

My name is not important, because I am speaking for the many people who knew and served with your son. You should be very, very proud of him. Semper fi.

"You see, Sarah. As bad as everything got for him, our son left a legacy to be proud of. You can be proud, Sarah. And you can be happy. Thank you. I love you." He closed her eyes and sat holding her hand for a long, long time.

When Carla Jean Lassen pulled up in front of the McCauley place she was having another one of what she described as her 'hospice problems.' Carla Jean loved doing hospice work. She'd been doing it since retiring from teaching 10 years earlier and she always felt like she was doing good, helping people get through their final days with a minimum of pain and helping their families deal with the worst times of their lives.

But it was a lot easier helping people you didn't know and like. "Doing good shouldn't hurt so much," she'd told her husband after the first time she'd helped care for a friend. It was the same with Sarah McCauley. Carla Jean had thought the world of her and Simon back when they'd come to parent-teacher conferences for Jared. And though Sarah had gotten a little dingy in the years after Jared was wounded, she was still the sweetest person in the world. And no one ever had a more devoted husband. Carla Jean just hoped Simon could come out of this process in reasonable shape. As strong as he was, the toll on him of being a full-time caretaker was easy to see.

She walked up the steps to the porch and was about to ring the bell when a loud blast echoed through the house. Carla Jean was so shocked she stumbled away from the door, almost falling backwards down the stairs.

"Oh! Oh, no!" Hand to her mouth, Carla Jean turned to run and began skittering down the stairs. Halfway down she slowed to a walk; by the time she reached the bottom her solid, unflappable nature reasserted itself. She stopped and sat down on the bottom stair. She'd been a teacher. She'd worked with hospice patients for ten years. She looked up and down the tree-lined street. No one else seemed to have heard the shot. There were two possibilities, as she saw it. The first was that there would be a second shot soon. Not likely, in her estimation. The second was that the shooting was over, ending the need for her services. She waited a few more minutes to let the second shot occur if it was going to, but when it did not, Carla Jean walked next door to call Sheriff Larrimer.

****

"Mom, there's a man here to talk with you!" Thirteen-year-old Ravi Malom stood in the doorway, effectively blocking the entrance to a well-dressed, middle-aged man in a coat and tie.

"Yes, are you Mr. Norstrad?" his mother said as she approached from the back of the house. Her arrival triggered her son's rapid departure. He leaped on his bike and was gone.

"Yes ma'm. Chet Norstrad. I am the assistant Dean of Journalism at the University of California Santa Barbara, your late husband's alma mater. As I mentioned on the phone, we've recently received a communication that concerns you and I'd like to talk with you about it."

"Please come in," she said and led the way to the family living area, one wall of which was dominated by a picture of her late husband and several awards for investigative journalism, including one nomination for a Pulitzer Prize.

"I can't tell you how devastated we all were to learn of Philip's death; he was…"

She waved him silent. "Thank you, but it's been six years."

"Yes, of course. Well, you can imagine our surprise when we received notification that an anonymous donor had bequeathed one million dollars to our department in your husband's name."

"Philip's?" the woman was nearly dumbstruck.

"Yes, for establishment of a rotating endowed chair for investigative journalism."

"What does that mean?"

"Well, it means that each year we can bring in one of the top investigative journalists in the country for a sabbatical from their jobs and during that year they will teach their skills to our journalism students."

Rita Malom was an accountant by trade and was not impressed by numbers. "It's a nice endowment but it won't cover the money you'll have to pay people like them for more than 10 years or so."

Nordstrom smiled. "Too true," he said. "But there are several other factors at work here. First, the people we invite will be much like your husband, Pulitzer winners or nominees; their employers often allow paid sabbaticals to employees like those, to teach and write books. Our endowment will be necessary only to supplement their paychecks. In addition, the university is aware of the high-profile nature of this gift and the people it will attract. We've already been assured of the university's willingness to help underwrite this effort. And don't forget, some of these people have book publishing deals, with significant advances. They often look for alluring places in which to write and not many towns offer the allure of Santa Barbara."

Rita nodded. "Sounds great. I'm happy for you, but how does it affect me?"

"Of course, we'd like to have you there to help us announce the gift…"

"No thanks."

"…OK, but then there's this." He withdrew a white envelope from his inside coat pocket. "One of the donor's requirements was that this envelope be delivered to you."

She opened the envelope and began reading the note.

Dear Mrs. Malom:

I was a long-time admirer of your husband's work and was sorrowed by his death. I hope this endowed chair will keep his memory and his courage alive. I don't know what Ravi's plans are for future schooling but I have created a trust in his name at your bank, with you as trustee. You need only visit them to identify yourself and provide a signature. In the event he chooses not to go to college the money will be made available to him for whatever use he wants after he turns 30. I feel sure this is what Philip would have done for Ravi. Again, I am sorry for your loss. I wish there were some way to take back the pain you have suffered.

After Norstrad left, Rita picked up Philip's picture and looked at it for a long time. Then she called Ravi home and told him the news. Afterwards, she went to work doing what she always did to celebrate good news. She cooked. It wasn't until the eggplant parmigiana was almost cooked that it occurred to her to wonder how the anonymous donor had learned the name of her bank.

****

John Crowley, the principal of Waldport High School, was just leaving the True Value Hardware when he saw a one-armed man coming through the door. "Excuse me," he said, "but are you Tony Corrarino?"

An easy smile, an extended hand. "Yes, I'm Tony. And you are…"

"John Crowley, principal at the high school." He waved his hand toward the school across the street. "And I think I need to thank you."

Tony laughed. "You think? Well, I think you're welcome."

Crowley laughed, too. He liked this young man. "I was actually going to drive down to the Taylors' place to deliver this, but I guess I might as well give it to you now." He handed Tony a sealed letter. "It came in a package that also included funding for a new high school track and a bench with this inscription." He handed Tony a single typed sheet.

"In memory of Dean Taylor, a man whose life and untimely death in the service of his country reflected his courage and dedication to his family, friends and ideals."

"It was completely anonymous but it said the gift was on your behalf."

"My behalf?"

"Yes. Perhaps you should open the envelope."

Tony ripped it open.

Dear Tony:
I wanted to express my appreciation for your continued honesty and dependability. The renovation of the track where he ran and a dedicated bench will honor your friend Dean. I trust his mother will appreciate it as well. I've also taken the liberty of establishing a scholarship in the name of

Dean Taylor of $2,000 per year for one student from the Alsea Valley to the college of their choice in the study of their choice. You, Mrs. Taylor and Brian Taylor have been named administrators. The paperwork will be delivered by a lawyer in the next few days.

As you have learned, our friend left me and proceeded on his own shortly after we departed from your camp. I'm sorry for your subsequent loss. Both you and he have endured more pain than anyone should bear. But I am glad to learn that you are doing well. It seems that with your vision and input the various Taylor family enterprises are gaining new traction and vibrancy. I know our mutual friend would have been happy to learn of your new direction and success.

Best,

T

P.S. Raven recently sent her husband packing for a variety of excellent reasons. Thought you might like to know.

Tony read the letter three times and stood there looking at it for several minutes more.

"Um," Crowley murmured. Tony looked up. "We'll name the new track the Dean Taylor Memorial Track, obviously."

"Sure." *He knows everything about me.*

"We'll have the work done over the summer and have the dedication next fall."

"OK." *I wonder where the hell he is.*

"I watched all the Taylor kids come through this school system. They were all good kids."

"Yep. Good kids." *A new track. I bet Dean would tell me he could have beaten Prefontaine on a new track.*

"For sure. Dean's sister was the last of them. The teachers were all sorry when the Taylor pipeline stopped. Of course, now we have the next generation coming through. Brian has two kids in the system already."

"And more to come." *A scholarship. In Dean's name. Perfect. And hilarious. We should have the awarding ceremony in the bar where Dean fell off the table.*

"Yes, you can never have too many Taylors." They both laughed.

Principal Crowley went on his way. Tony got in the pickup.

Raven. Is that true? How did Trey find out? It couldn't have happened long ago. But it wouldn't be right for me to call.

He backed out of the parking lot and headed east on Highway 34 toward the Taylor place.

Mrs. Taylor will be glad to hear about the track, bench and scholarship. Very glad. She might even want to call down to Raven's family and tell them about it.

Chapter 68

Trip Cannon drove up the long driveway slowly, soaking up the view of the vineyard and beautiful stone home on top of the hill. God only knew how much Trey had spent on renovating the house, replanting unproductive grapes, starting up a small olive orchard. They also had a nice vegetable garden. Trey wanted to make their home as self-sufficient as possible. They had two full-time employees, a husband and wife, who'd grown up in the Languedoc region and were pleased beyond imagining to have found full-time work so near their home town. They lived in a small house in the back. They owned their own home in a nearby village, but the one the patron provided was so much nicer they stayed there. Rudolfo was the gardener in name, but he also did light maintenance, painting and worked with Monsieur Tomas in the vineyard. Anita was the cook, but also took care of housekeeping, washing and general supervision of everyone in the household, including the patron and Mademoiselle Tina.

Trip ran up the stairs to the house, assuming her name of Tina, and was swept into her brother's arms. As was his habit, he steered her out of the house and into the garden before he opened the conversation.

"How was the trip?" he asked.

"Great. Tri and Hal are doing wonderfully. The book shop is going great guns. They've got the coffee shop going and they are talking about buying a building next door and making it into a theater, to show avant-garde, alternative movies."

"Great! I guess." Trey laughed.

"I'm sure it will work. They are excited about it anyway, and they seem to be making money in everything they touch. She is seven months along and showing out to here! They want to know if you can come back for the baby's birth."

"They know better. Another few years before I'll feel comfortable."

"OK, but still, it's been two years and not a hint that anything is wrong."

"The last mistake a lot of people make is thinking they will have a hint."

"Fine. I love it here. But I get out occasionally. You never get to leave."

"I never want to leave. Were you able to do all the things I asked?"

"Of course. I sent all the letters from different places in the states. No fingerprints. I arranged the scholarship, doctor and lawyer anonymously. I had to work a bit to get money into the kids' accounts but managed it just fine.

"The scholarship at UCSB actually went much more easily than I expected. The university folks didn't really care that the gift was anonymous, so the endowment is in place and operating."

Trey sighed deeply and looked toward the sky. "And Mrs. Malom?"

"Mrs. Malom was very appreciative, Trey. She is moving on with her life and now she doesn't have to worry about her son's education. Trey? Are you OK?"

Trey smiled wanly. "I'm fine, Sis. I'm OK."

"All right. Moving right along, I kept the surveillance in place, though that is one of our biggest expenses. How long do you expect to continue watching all three of them?"

"At least three more years. We'll arrange another nice gift for each of them in three years and then drop out of their lives forever."

"And then you'll be able to travel again."

"Then I'll be able to travel again, though I'm not sure I want to. As long as I can go to Cinque Terra occasionally, I think I'll be perfectly happy." He saw the disappointment in her face. "Oh, I'll go back to the states to see Tri and her family, of course. Don't worry; I'm not going to become a hermit. Now, what did you find out about our other problem?"

"Best news yet. The FBI has put the case of the kidnapping and killing of the helicopter pilot way back on the back burner, as closed as those cases ever get. You guys must have done a great job on that trip because they couldn't find one witness who could describe either one of you. They're not even sure if there were one or two people with him. They've got absolutely nothing to go on. That was the last remaining legal issue. Even better, the Corrarino Family is completely and utterly dissolved. You already know part of this. Sal never did have an effective line of succession in place so internal battling started within hours of his death. Even before the funeral, one of his top two lieutenants killed the other and tried to take over. He didn't last a week. There were no credible aspirants after them. The various segments of his empire continued on, individually, but without a larger organization to protect them they were gobbled up, one after another and absorbed into other families and gangs. Seems like the bloodshed has just about ended now. There's no one left to chase you, even if they knew you existed. That part of the threat, at least, seems to have disappeared. Congratulations!"

Trey reached out to hug her and kissed the top of her head. "Thanks," he said. "It does seem to be coming together. You'd better get washed up and changed. Your favorite tour guide has been asking after you and I'm sure he'll show up this evening to take you to dinner."

He smiled at Trip's obvious joy. She was reveling in her first normal relationship and though she was still working through the emotional wreckage of her kidnapped years, she seemed to have made a healthy break from that experience. She would occasionally come and talk with Trey about the 'bad time,' and once had asked him if he thought she should consult a psychiatrist. "Not here," he'd told her. Too much chance of unwanted connections. "You could go back to California, if you want."

A small smile. "I'm not leaving you. I'll be fine." And fine she seemed to be, now. He never heard her crying in her room anymore and her life seemed happy and fulfilling, especially now that the tour guide had entered the picture.

"Oh, and one other thing." Trip dug in the duffel bag she called a purse and extracted a small cardboard box. "Here is your candy. I can't believe you eat so many of those things."

"I really don't, you know. I only eat them one at a time."

Trip cocked her head and looked at him carefully. "Ah, yes, of course. One at a time. Wouldn't work if there were two tone mints, would it?"

Trey chuckled. "I see you haven't lost the touch. Did you and Tri practice on each other's minds, too?"

Trip laughed aloud. "Yes, we did, as a matter of fact. It's hard on poor Tri because she can't read her husband at all. At least I have you. Of course, I don't need any practice to read your thoughts. Run, Spot, Run would be harder." She leaned over and kissed his forehead. "Those candies might be good for your soul, but they're still bad for your teeth."

Trey sat watching the vineyard for a long time after Trip left. He needed to get out there and trim the shoots, but the need didn't quite overcome his languor. He felt almost lightheaded after his meeting with Trip. Intellectually, he'd known the possibility of pursuit was infinitesimal, but until now he hadn't been completely sure the killing of Sal Corrarino had been put to rest by law enforcement agencies. Someone in the Corrarino Family had blabbed about Jared's phone calls goading Sal to Dry Meadow in the Frank Church Wilderness but by the time the feds investigated, Shane's boys had removed their camp and the country surrounding Dry Meadow was covered by four feet of snow. They never expanded their investigation to Grangeville so Shane's business never came up.

They'd traced the movement of the helicopter back from the airfield in Pennsylvania where the pilot died and made the connection between his death and the disappearance of a team of three hired killers, though they were never able to find them. A careful assessment of his business uncovered the pilot's mob connections. They also learned that a second man might have accompanied Jared McCauley across country to Pennsylvania but if so, every trace of his presence disappeared there. The only prints in the helicopter were the pilot's and the gun used to kill the pilot had been found in Jared's dead hands. It seemed obvious that no one else had taken part in the assault on Sal Corrarino and his people. Since the only suspect in six murders and one kidnapping in three states was dead and no other crime seemed to have been committed, both the New York Police and FBI stopped worrying about a second man and closed their cases, although it took the FBI almost two years to do so.

Trey levered himself out of the chair and looked over his fields. The farm was still two years away from being really productive, but after that, based on the average yield and prices for olives and pinot grapes, Trey anticipated being able to cover all the maintenance and associated costs of the house and farm with the harvest, including Rudolfo and Anita. It's pretty nice, he thought, when you don't have a mortgage to bleed you. Thanks again, Carlo.

Trey wandered into the garden. He had time before dinner to do a little weeding. Big part of his day: weeding. He smiled at the thought but could not bring himself to feel embarrassed or useless. All the work he did in the garden and fields made good things happen. And he did them daily. Good things. He smiled, slipped a mint onto his tongue and reached down to pull a clump of grass from between his tomato plants.

CPSIA information can be obtained
at www.ICGtesting.com
Printed in the USA
FFOW04n1412251117
43702242-42562FF